Con...

Sunset Thunder

Shannyn
Leah

SHANNYN LEAH

Sunset Thunder

The Caliendo Resort

Book One, Violet Caliendo

By The Lake Series

Shannyn Leah

Shannyn Leah

www.ShannynLeah.com

To the sweetest little gal in my life, my niece.

I will dance around the world with you! Love you with all my heart!

SHANNYN LEAH

Chapter One

VIOLET CALIENDO OBSERVED countless couples, as head wedding coordinator at the Caliendo Resort. Couples so deeply in love and were so involved in the wedding planning, they knew the extras available before Violet offered them. Couples who needed their parent's approval for each decision they made and couples who sometimes didn't make it down the aisle at all.

Today's couple however, was a first for Violet.

She had no joy as the sun beamed through her bedroom window, whispering a tranquil good day, while the reminder of her morning appointment brought back the dark and dreary feelings of regret from the previous night.

But Violet had dragged her heavy feet from the solitude of her bed, and the comfort provided by the bamboo-cotton duvet, to slog across the plush carpet. She'd pulled the elegantly embroidered cream and chocolate silk curtains open and soaked up the sun, allowing the warmth to remind her, it wasn't *that* bad. It wasn't *that* good either, but she'd made an agreement with the couple and there was no altering that decision now.

Violet was a professional. Working at her family's resort, she was left with no alternative but to provide the amenities of the resorts five-star rating.

Situated on the outskirts of the little tourist town, Willow Valley, The Caliendo Resort sat alongside the lake with a beautiful beach, where guests sprinkled across the sand like seashells, all summer long.

Violet's grandparents had transformed the little stone inn into an all-inclusive get-away. Ten stories of elegant rooms stretched across a wide, ranch-style, U-shaped structure and centered around a maze of outdoor connecting pools and flower gardens that were shaded by trees guaranteed to help guests unwind and enjoy all the resort had to offer. Guests could easily find themselves taking advantage of the tennis courts, horseshoes, games area and golf course, while the winter months offered the best ski hill around. Chefs and staff prepped three kitchens in classy, on-site restaurants, and offered an outdoor, all-day buffet under a gazebo. But it was the ballrooms that fascinated Violet the most while growing up at the resort.

On warm July days, like today, most brides and grooms couldn't contain their smiles of bliss, listening with eagerness to the exquisite services Violet offered to integrate into their special day. A day which they believed would be the grandest, most wonderful day, as they began their lives together united as one, and continued until the day they grew old, sitting on rockers and watching their great-grandchildren play about the yard.

She shook her head. *What a crock.*

Violet had been escorting couples into the illusion of "happily ever after" since she'd graduated University.

Wedding co-ordinating? Wedding co-ordinating! How did someone with a Master's Degree end up pursuing a career in wedding planning?

The answer was easy. Being the daughter of the down-to-earth Eliza Caliendo, whose guidance in life decisions for her six children lacked education as an incentive, substituting it with the encouragement to follow their hearts instead. That rationale landed Violet in an occupation in wedding planning.

Darned if Violet had known the dream of uniting couples into their happily ever after would come back and bite her on the ass...like today.

Violet had never encountered a groom-to-be who blurted out everything that popped into his small, sluggish head, without filtering his sentences in regards to the people around him. Lacking consideration for feelings...commitment...*vows*.

Joel Bensen was that exceptional groom, sending spikes of irritancy in Violet's direction. And none of the nonsense they were forced to endure from his shark jaws had a single thing to do with his wedding.

Violet, on the other hand, had been raised to recognize the filter in her head and trained to run every single one of her thoughts through it before a word ever left her lips. The action saved her from embarrassment and looking like a fool, both of which Joel was unaware he was undertaking right now.

"Hey Ryder. I've been calling you all morning. What is taking you so long? Are you still tumbling around in bed?" Joel said into his cell phone, and then paused while listening to the reply.

Violet was grateful it wasn't on speakerphone. This gave his audience a moment of silence to absorb the meaning behind his question. Not everyone would understand, but Violet knew Joel was referring to Ryder's sexual engagements.

Vulgar.

Violet was attentive to the implication, having been Joel's wife, for a *long* nine years. Thankfully that had ended two years ago.

Yes, Violet Caliendo was in fact, planning her ex-husband and his bride-to-be's wedding...their *happily ever after*...the day that would be the beginning of the rest of their lives together.

What a crock.

Joel's words came out now loud and inappropriate, ricocheting off the blend of neutral colored marble walls, and trailing around Violet and the entire Bensen wedding party, standing smack-dab in center of the high-class lobby. Joel should have lowered his voice, to no more than a whisper, while crossing the marble floors and Persian rugs. He should have actually taken the tasteless conversation outside. Instead, Violet watched him draw the interest of the three receptionists, stationed behind the front desk. Each time Joel's voice echoed in their direction, their curious eyes bounced up and down from assisting guests to Joel...occasionally landing on Violet. Her eye contact with them snapped their full attention back to their jobs and to the guests they were paid to treat like royalty.

Violet didn't allow the truth, that some of the staff's curiosity was about her planning her ex-husband's second wedding was. There was no room for shame.

Violet's breathing remained steady and calm, even if she had the urge to suck in a deep, restless lungful of air and slap the phone right out of Joel's hand with her perfectly french-manicured fingers. Her smile and eyes remained incomprehensible and professional, even soft, fighting the urge to roll them so far back in her head, for the sole purpose of making this whole image disappear.

Could you possibly attract any more attention to yourself, Joel?

"Dude, are you still with that chick?" Joel asked with a piercing laugh.

Violet cringed.

That chick?

How disrespectful. How was it possible that she had been married to this man for nine years? She wished it was the same reason she'd taken a career as wedding coordinator: following her heart. However, that wasn't accurate. Violet had no say in her marriage to Joel, besides the obvious *I do* at the altar...which had been forced, expected and congratulated.

If only her *I do* had been overflowing with the same magical feeling that tickled her stomach and enchanted her youthful mind, as she pursued her career path. As a child, the summer months at the resort had been her favorite time of the year, as the outdoor pools opened, the golf course kicked-off its season and the lake warmed enough to swim.

But, it wasn't any of those reasons that her little heart fluttered with eagerness, it was the bustle of the resort being booked solid with weddings. Weddings in one of the elegant ballrooms, or under the white tents beside the beach. Formal attire would sprinkle the grounds with laughter and music. It was magical. It was amazing. It was Violet's dream to be a part of that remarkable enchantment, in both respects: as a bride and a wedding coordinator.

Unfortunately, Violet's career path went against her father's expectations of where a Caliendo should reside on the occupational scale and Robert Caliendo had punished her. He disregarded Violet's presence in an even colder manner than normal, as he developed a deeper bond with the next eldest sibling, Anya. In a state of rebellion, Violet had laid her own path of punishment far worse than she'd ever imagined, ending up in a marriage that was nowhere near happily ever after.

Violet and Joel's vows may have united them in marriage, but it was loveless union.

Violet tried to shake off the memories flooding her mind. Being single the last two years, she'd let go of her past...or so she thought. Now, standing here preparing Joel for his second wedding, was the constant reminder of her wedding.

Violet had been left with no other alternative but to marry Joel. The eve of her wedding two men had treaded so hard on her full-spirited heart that it left Violet empty inside. Her desire to find *the* man, that one Prince Charming, as juvenile as the phrase sounded, to pave a future with her, one with everlasting love, devotion, adoration...and so much more, had been ripped out of her and left suspicion, doubt, and distrust instead that eventually consumed the remnants of her heart.

Happily ever after. What a crock.

"No, no. The blonde one." Joel laughed loudly, in an approving bad manner. *Ignorant.*

Yes, it was very well possible for Joel to attract even more negative attention to himself. The Caliendo guests did not pay good money to listen to how Joel's best friend "scored". Or how many times. Or what color the woman's hair happened to be. Or how many women there were. *Ugh!*

Well done. Joel you are officially the most mortifying client I've come across in...forever.

Joel laughed at whatever comment playboy Ryder Carlex offered from the other end of the phone. No doubt, just as obnoxious a remark as Joel.

Violet envisioned Ryder Carlex, standing on the bow of his daddy's boat with the sun glistening off the hard muscles of his bare chest, and his hair, silkier than her own, blowing in the wind, looking so proud for doing...nothing. Because he was a playboy who sailed around on his daddy's fortune, picking up women and wasting money like he had an unlimited supply...which he very well possibly did.

Violet had never been *really* acquainted with Ryder. Even through the years she'd been married to Joel and the two men had maintained a relationship, she'd kept her distance. After Ryder had stood by Joel's side as best man at Violet's wedding, she had seen enough of him to last her a lifetime. He basically pounced on every woman at the reception...single or married...and probably scored a rendezvous in the bathroom on more than one occasion. Like every woman at her wedding, Violet wasn't blind to Ryder's beauty. Lord, he was a gorgeous man...on the outside. On the inside, he was cold, heartless...loveless.

If Violet hadn't known Joel's true intentions, she would blame Ryder's womanizing ways for misguiding her husband away from her and their two children, eleven-year-old Sophia, and seven-year-old Parker, and into the arms of Missy Daniels. However, she was quite aware Joel got exactly what he came into this marriage for...money.

Violet's eyes trailed casually and professionally at Missy Daniels the bride-to-be. There was no uncertainty in the look Violet cast, because her father educated her to master the art of expression, or there-lack-of. The look was not that of a jealous ex-wife, but that of a professional.

Missy was a dedicated maid employed at the Caliendo Resort for many years, questionably shacking up with Joel while he was still married to Violet...*happily ever after...eternity...forever...what a crock.*

Why Violet had ever believed in happily ever after was beyond her now. As an adult, looking back at the foolish, young girl with her head in the clouds, she couldn't believe they were two in the same person. If her younger self had paused from her dreams about love, she would have acknowledged that her parents weren't ever in love and possibly even noticed that Eliza had been cheating on her father with Violet's Uncle Carl, her dad's brother, most of their marriage. After Robert passed away just a year ago, Carl and Eliza made their relationship public, as well as presenting the truth about Violet's oldest brother Marc and youngest sister Izzy's paternity. It turned out Carl was their biological father...it had been a shock to all of them...*but should it?*

Missy was watching Violet and smiled shyly when Violet's gaze fell upon her. Missy was weak and very few people would respect her. She allowed her feelings to write a tale across her face.

For instance, when Missy and her fiancée had initially walked through the door this morning, Missy carried a look of fear at the possibility of a reconnection between Violet and Joel. That had been quickly extinguished. There would never be a reconnection between that selfish, careless, two-timing jerk and Violet. She was too strong to fall for love again. Love was a foolish game that tipped the game pieces of those involved in the direction of lust, desire and whatever else formed, only to knock them over and scream *game over. No, thank you.*

Violet maintained a professional smile in return, but inside her stomach was knotting.

Why had she agreed to this? It was crazy. She was crazy!

When she had agreed, she'd thought it would gain respect from the people at the resort but, even if that was true, it was still the worst idea ever. It was so beyond what normal people did that Violet was wishing she had listened to every single one of her family members who advised her against it. Violet thought she was strong enough and professional enough to soar through the meetings, but right now, listening to nonsense banter and Missy staring at her with suspicion that transferred to her bridesmaids, who were eyeing her up like *she* was the enemy...*her*...it felt like Violet's insides were about to burst. And that was the last thing she'd ever want, but Lord how she needed a break from all this craziness.

Violet casually glanced back at the iPad in her hands, feigning busy, but really scoping the time on the clock.

One fifteen. One fifteen! It had only been fifteen minutes? This was torture. *You are in fact putting yourself through torture!*

"Ryder, I don't want to start without you man. Bring the blonde with you."

Violet was pretty sure she just vomited in her mouth. If anyone was worse than her sneaky cheating husband it was Ryder Carlex.

I need a break from these obnoxious people.

Forcing herself not to roll her eyes, but unable to squander another second looking at any of them, Violet's eyes shifted to the second floor where a thick, ornate wrought iron railing scooped out in a half moon shape above the lobby desk. It was an informal, relaxing area for guests to lounge in overstuffed upholstered chairs and read under skylights. Violet's eyes stopped at the rustle beside a six-foot emerald tree planted in a bed of rocks at the edge of the railing. Attempting to stay out of sight, were her sister Emma and her mother...spying on Violet.

Unbelievable. They didn't think she could do it. They didn't think she could do it! If they didn't think Violet could do it, what did everyone else think...like the receptionists?

This was such a bad idea.

Her mother's vivid, pink dress edged with a leopard print collar and cuffs was a harsh contrast against the green foliage and Emma was even more obvious in her neon orange yoga outfit.

Busted, they both attempted to turn around and out of Violet's vision, which was a waste of time after making eye contact with each of them. Violet watched in horror, as they collided into each other, smacking their heads and hitting their knees. Emma tripped backwards, falling over the chair, her legs flailing in the air like a bad television show then flipping onto the floor. Her mother, unbalanced, sent one hand grabbing her head as the other reached for the railing. Somehow she unhinged one side of the hanging flower box and it tipped sideways.

Violet winced.

Please don't make a scene. Please don't make a scene!

As Eliza's hands flailed to catch the box and straighten it, the dirt and live flowers went tumbling out, landing with a loud thud on the lobby desk...in front of Marc.

The staff and guests, including the Bensen wedding party gasped in horror, heads turning in every direction, questions and voices growing louder.

Violet cast her unimpressed stare at her guilty-faced brother. *When did he sneak behind the desk?* She knew exactly what he was doing behind that desk, even if he held a handful of papers like he was hard at work. He wasn't working. They were only missing Izzy and Uncle Carl.

At the thought, Violet heard Izzy's laughter from the hall to her right that led to the lobby elevators and further down, Violet's office. They were all spying on her. They didn't think she could handle herself.

Violet inwardly cringed at the realization.

They were all going to get a piece of her mind about their childlike behavior when they were privately situated in her office.

Besides being infuriated, Violet was almost glad for the distraction and watched amused as Marc straightened his designer charcoal suit, setting the papers down on the counter to address the situation. "Is everyone alright?" he asked, going from each guest and staff until he was confirmed they were fine. "I will call maintenance to have this cleaned up. Sorry about the disruption. The staff will give you discounts for your next stay." Marc didn't circle around the desk and disappear down the hall like he should have. Instead he feigned work...at the lobby desk, with one watchful eye glancing in her direction.

Joel slipped the phone into the breast pocket of his polo shirt and turned to Violet. His round, plump face danced with amusement against his thick crows-feet and laugh lines stretching from his gloomy hazel eyes. She didn't know if it was from whatever he and Ryder had discussed, or his delight with the notion that her whole family was present for their meeting.

This wasn't the first meeting with the Bensen wedding party, Caliendo's, she silently scolded.

Joel feigned a look of compassion in Violet's direction for the current awkward situation, but even the smallest hint of concern was really non-existent. How could a man who spent nine years with her be so cold toward her? *Probably the same reason you are cold toward him: A loveless marriage full of deception and lies.*

"Ryder's twenty minutes away. I'm going to step out and when he gets here we can meet back. In twenty?" Joel threw the number around, looking from Missy, who nodded, to Violet.

Oh, she was charging them extra for this.

Violet smiled, her professional charming, *no problem, but inside I want to slap you upside the head and kick your feet from under you,* smile. "Alright. Why don't we make it thirty minutes and give him some leeway."

Heaven knew the man was probably wrapped around a skank or two, shacking up in his daddy's mansion on the lake, or tangled in two sets of legs on his daddy's boat.

A sting of reality clicked in. *Who was she to judge Ryder because he was born into money? Or to assume because he was born into money it was the very reason for behaving like the playboy douche he was?*

Violet and all her siblings had been born into money and they didn't act like Ryder Carlex. Playing all day and sleeping with a different person...or two...each night.

Joel's arm was around his fiancée's and they were heading out the front door with her posse of bridesmaids at their heels...cheap non-designer heels at that.

Ugh!

That thought wasn't even like her. She wasn't quick to judge ignorantly, but today she didn't feel like herself at all.

It was hard to believe she had created two brilliant children with that man. A man who had the gall to ask her to plan his second wedding at his first wife's resort. *What kind of man did that?*

17

Violet turned her attention to her disruptive family. The more pressing question was, *What possessed her family to behave like inexperienced spies?*

Violet sent every single one of them a, *in my office now*, look before starting down the hallway, bumping into Izzy, who was peering around the corner with a cheeky smile.

Izzy latched onto Violet's arm and laughed, throwing her head of long blonde, beach-wave hair back to tumble across the bare back of her summer halter top. "Leave it to Momma and Emma to mess up operation Catclaw," she said.

Catclaw? Violet was afraid to ask.

Kate McAdams, Marc's wife, met them down the hall, holding hands with Marc and Kate's seven-year-old daughter Rosemary. Identical wide smiles on their tanned faces illuminated their deep mocha colored eyes and they each wore summer dresses over bathing suits. From their dry hair, Violet assumed that they were likely heading down to the beach.

"Hi Aunt Violet. Hi Aunt Izzy," Rosemary said, waving her hand, holding a sand bucket full of shovels and molds. Almost tipping the bucket over, Rosemary lost interest in her aunts to steady it.

Kate looked like a beachy summer day in a strapless white dress and her dark chocolate locks pulled to a side ponytail that spilled wild curls over her bare shoulder. Before she could say anything, the elevator doors opened and Eliza and Emma stepped out.

Guilty. Guilty. Guilty.

Kate's smile dropped as her eyes moved from each accountable Caliendo to the next, including Marc, who stepped beside Kate, kissing her cheek and scooping Rosemary into his arms.

"Oh, you four didn't," Kate said.

No one replied and her eyes fell on Violet, who silently told her *they did*.

"Oh, you did." Kate sent Marc the hardest disapproving look.

Marc ignored her. "Are you ready to go the beach?" he asked Rosemary.

"Are you coming Daddy?" Rosemary squealed, her arms going around his neck in a tight hug.

He glanced up at Violet's fatal stare. "I am now," he said.

"I told all of you to stay away from Violet's appointment," Kate said, then glanced at the screen of her cell phone like she'd realized something. "Didn't your appointment just start?" she asked Violet, obviously wondering how it was already finished. Kate's eyes widened and her head whipped around at the guilty party. "What did you all do?" she accused, sounding horrified.

It surprised Violet that Kate was so shocked her family had intervene into her business. Kate's siblings were the masters of intervention into each other's lives on a regular basis. There was always a McAdams sister popping in and out of the Caliendo Resort.

At that note, the elevator opened and Kent McAdams, Kate's father, stepped out. He was and had been head of maintenance at the resort for over forty years. A tall, thin man who wore a pleasant smile across a face aged much older than he was.

"Grandpa!" Rosemary cried, immediately holding her arms out to be held.

Izzy was quick to fill Kate and Kent in on the reason Kent was needed at the front. "Momma and Emma knocked over a flower box from the balcony, and it landed on the lobby desk," she explained. "Technically, it was only the dirt and plants. The planter is still attached to the wall. Hardly. Dangling sideways."

Eliza made a hushed motion with her hands. "It was loose," she defended.

"Did you throw the dirt at the Bensen party?" Kate asked Violet, only half joking with a smirk and wink.

Of course she did not throw dirt at the Bensen party. That thought hadn't even crossed her mind...but it was an entertaining one.

"Joel is waiting for Ryder Carlex," Violet explained.

"Ryder Carlex," Emma snickered. "He tried to get up my dress at your wedding." She laughed at the memory, and sobered as everyone's questioning look fell upon her. "I said he *tried*. I didn't sleep with him. He was a mess," she said as if it was the worst thing to happen at Violet's wedding. Violet had a list over ten pages long of worse things at her wedding than having sex with Ryder.

Eliza shared a look with Violet that only she understood, but Violet showed no emotion for that night so long ago in her past. Nor did she acknowledge the worry in her mother's eyes. Violet was fine. If anything, that night had taught her to be the strong woman she'd become. The woman who was able to handle this meeting with the wedding party involved.

Eliza, on the other hand, wasn't convinced. She shook her head. "That poor boy. He was having a rough time. It was unfortunate Kathleen and Donald hadn't been able to attend the wedding. I'm sure his behavior would have been much different. Ryder adored his parents."

Ryder's mother had passed years ago, but his father was still alive and it seemed after his wife's death, he dove deeper into work than he had before. They hadn't seen him at one of Eliza's galas in years.

"Why? So he would have put his perfect son's illusion mask back on and acted like the ideal son they thought he was, instead of the playboy he actually is?" Violet hadn't realized she'd spoken her thoughts until everyone turned their shocked expressions in her direction.

I said that out loud? I said that out loud!

Eliza looked the most uncomfortable. "I don't think Ryder is a...playboy."

Oh, I did say it out loud. Could this day get any worse?

Emma touched their mother's shoulder. "Ryder Carlex, *is* a playboy," she told Eliza, breaking their mother's image of Ryder.

See, Violet wasn't the only one who thought so.

"What is a playboy?" Rosemary asked.

Kate groaned. "And I thought it was my family I had to fear teaching her slang..."

"A playboy is a boy who really likes to play with girls," Izzy said to Rosemary. "A lot of girls." Izzy chuckled to herself.

Kate groaned again.

Violet checked down the long hall for guests. It was clear. She turned her attention to her family.

"In a half hour I will be resuming my meeting with the Bensen party. I expect none of you to be present." She looked at Emma. "Not even you." Sometimes her sister helped her with weddings and she always welcomed the extra pair of hands and opinion...but not today. "If I were you, I would be more worried about making sure that flower pot never comes unhinged again and not worrying about the Bensen party."

Eliza touched Violet's arm. "Sweetheart, we're not worried about the Bensen party. We are worried about you."

Violet was more worried about what the Bensen party was thinking about her ability to handle their wedding with her family spying on them. But her families concern didn't go unnoticed.

Violet stepped forward and hugged her mom. "I'm fine," she whispered in the side of her silver straight hair, styled in an angled bob that grazed her bony shoulders.

Eliza patted her back before letting go. "Alright, we will withdraw."

"Operation Catclaw terminated," Izzy said in a pout.

Kate chuckled her low surprise and murmured, "You named it. Didn't you?"

"Yeah, well, what else am I supposed to do now that your sister has abandoned me to live in Oakston?" Kate's youngest sister, Abby was Izzy's childhood best friend to this day. A team of only two, they were wild, obnoxious, smart and blunt...both of them were lacking the filter Violet perfected.

"To work in Oakston," Marc pointed out. "Abby runs their newest store location, regardless that Riley has enough money to take them both on a permanent vacation in Hawaii." Marc added the jab. It was his way to try and convince Izzy to stop flaunting around the resort, taking advantage of the amenities and work.

Izzy gasped and her big eyes flew around the crowd, mostly questioning Kate and Kent. "Do you think Abby and Riley would go on vacation without me? To Hawaii?"

A round of groans echoed through the hall, as Izzy missed Marc's point.

"I am texting—no I am calling her," Izzy announced, her hand already pulling her cell out. "If she thinks just because her *boyfriend* is a money bag, that she's ditching me on the next vacay, she is sorely mistaken."

"Abby wouldn't just pick up and go on vacation without telling you," Eliza said. "You two have been friends forever."

Marc mumbled under his breath only loud enough Violet and Kate heard him, "Nevertheless, Izzy doesn't need a vacation. She needs a job."

They grinned at him.

"Yes, she would. She went and fell in love with Riley and didn't tell me. Gave me no warning," Izzy pointed out.

"There isn't exactly a warning when it comes to falling in love," Kate said.

Violet wouldn't know. She'd never been in love before.

Izzy waved her off. "Please, you and Marc had years of warning. Mom and Carl had even more years of warning. And Abby...Abby...she knew years ago, she just didn't bother to tell me." Izzy still didn't call their Uncle Carl "Dad" even though he was her biological father and she'd known longer than any of them. She had dropped the Uncle, so hopefully she was on her way to a deeper relationship with Carl. She was just taking it in sweet, slow Izzy style. Funny, when all the other aspects of her life were buzzing busy.

"Catclaw Operation re-opened and I am going to pull the cat claws out on Abby instead of Joel." Izzy made a hissing sound and slashed her nails through the air.

Rosemary laughed. "You don't have claws Aunt Izzy," she said. "You're not a cat. You have fingers."

Rosemary distracted Izzy from her Abby melt-down and she tickled her niece. Rosemary's laughter filled the hallway. The comforting sound mixed with her family's concern made Violet wonder why she had allowed today's meeting to aggravate her in the first place. It was just another meeting. The same as every other couple who believed in their happily ever after. Violet would help them plan for it, when deep down she knew happily ever after didn't exist, but she would convince every couple that walked through the front doors of the resort otherwise.

Now, if she could only convince herself not to roll her eyes when Ryder Carlex walked his playboy-self through the front doors bragging over the phone about his sexual affairs. *What were they? Still in high school?*

Violet would bet that Ryder still hadn't grown up enough to call himself a man. Her bet was of no value since she did not plan on talking to Ryder long enough to evaluate his maturity.

Get this Bensen party in and right back out.

Chapter Two

RYDER CARLEX SLID his cell phone into the pocket of his white cargo shorts. He shook his head at the belittling phone conversation between him and long-time friend, Joel Bensen.

Putting the conversation out of his mind, he stared down at his dad.

Donald Carlex sat hunched over the end of his fishing pole, still attempting to bait his hook. At this rate, they were going to be here until the sun set in a beautiful arrays of rich pinks, oranges and purples in the distance as it disappeared behind the lake.

That didn't sound like that bad of a day to Ryder, but his had promised Joel he'd attend the wedding meeting. Sitting at the edge of the dock, basking under the hot summer sun, with a man who barely left the comfort of his house anymore, was nice...calming...easy−not anything like the meeting was bound to be. Considering Ryder only saw his dad once a month, he wanted to enjoy every second of their time together. Donald was the only immediate family that Ryder had left in this world and more days than not Donald didn't even know Ryder anymore.

From an outsider's perspective, one would assume his father had let himself go. His once tall, broad shoulders were now thin and hunched, lacking the muscle they once carried. The dark blonde hair he'd kept maintained, cut and styled to perfection during his executive and presidential days in the Carlex family business, Carlex Grocers, was now overgrown with more grey than blonde and his chin was often peppered with corresponding grey scruff.

"Dad, I'm late for Joel's wedding planning," Ryder said, sitting down beside him and dangling his feet over the edge of the dock.

Early mornings, like today, the sun rose in the east and the tree's lining the edge of the property shaded the dock and the rippling water at their feet.

The damp wood cooled the back of Ryder's legs, reminding him of this very chapter in his young life. Days spent fishing with his dad during the summers his family stayed at this lake house outside of Willow Valley. Just like now, when he was young it was rare to spend time with his dad. Donald was always working. Often he would leave Ryder and his mother at the lake house for a week or two to return to the office and manage the two-hundred store locations they owned.

Now, their roles had reversed and Donald stayed at the lake house all year round, while Ryder took his position as president of Carlex Grocers. A position Ryder had never wanted, a position he honestly didn't think he was very good at...and now he was leaving his dad to go wedding planning.

Wedding planning? Wedding planning!

Ryder wasn't even sure why Joel asked him to attend the wedding planning in the first place. Wasn't that something the women did? And wasn't it generally done sooner than a month before the wedding?

Ryder couldn't be positive of either of those statements, since he didn't remember much of anything from Joel's first wedding. The planning and the wedding had taken place during one of the hardest times in Ryder's life and he didn't recall what had transpired before, during or after Joel and Violet's wedding.

Ryder had shown up, but he'd already dipped into the alcohol. He threw back more shots and by the time he left, his memory was hazy at best. It wasn't the most notable time in Ryder's life, actually it was rather depressing. At the time, the actions that led up to those days felt like Ryder's world had been kicked out from under him and his whole world was falling.

But now, after the death of his mother and the fall of his father, Ryder was conscious he'd acted a bit dramatic back then over the circumstances.

Speaking of weddings, didn't Joel find it the least bit uncomfortable...unconventional...that his ex-wife was planning his second wedding?

Ice queen. That was Joel's nickname for snobbish, arrogant, and heartless, Violet Caliendo. And now she was planning her ex-husbands wedding, in her families resort, the very one she had married Joel in. She must have one iced-up heart to perform that duty...but seriously, why the hell had Joel or Missy thought sharing their vows in the same resort as Joel's first ceremony was a good idea?

It was damn well odd and didn't make sense to Ryder whatsoever.

As odd as it was, it wasn't Ryder's problem. He had enough of his own struggles redesigning the entire grocery chain, updating the look and product to re-introduce modernized stores.

Besides, Joel had always done whatever he wanted. That was how he'd ended up bankrupt after his parents passed away. He had ignored everyone's advice with his careless smirk and wave while hastily squandering away his inheritance...and it was a helluva lot of money. Of course, he landed himself broke, bankrupt and crawling to Ryder for help.

Ryder would have said no, he'd warned the poor fool, but Ryder's mother insisted on allowing Joel to stay at the lake house until he could pick himself up. That had been almost a decade ago.

"Ryder, I can finish up here," Susan offered from her lawn chair at the lake's edge. Susan Burke was Susan was one of his dad's two live-in workers. Most times, Susan stuck around even when Ryder was spending the day with Donald, just in case he had an episode.

Ryder paid for the finest private care and the two women he hired didn't disappoint. It wasn't anyone else's damn business what was going on with his father and the people Ryder hired had signed confidentially contracts to ensure their silence.

Ryder looked down at his dad, still struggling away. If he was all there in the head still, Donald would have said, *Son, it's Joel's second marriage and he can manage without you. Come on boy, bait your line and let's catch us some dinner.* His voice would have been strong, thick and yet wrapped with love. They would have spent the day fishing and the night cooking their catches.

Ryder missed his dad more than words could express. It felt like a part of Ryder had slipped away with the dementia that was taking all the parts of his dad away, leaving him often confused with a child-like mind. He wouldn't even know who Joel was now.

Ryder didn't want to leave. It was a good day when his dad left the house. Even if Ryder spent the whole day watching his dad try to wiggle that worm onto the hook, the tranquility of it was worth it.

Susan knew when to step back, giving them father/son space and when to step in and take charge. It eased the stress in Ryder's life. It eased his longing for the wonderful man, the wonderful father, lost deep in the depths of his own brain.

Ryder needed to go. If he didn't, Joel would phone him back and start right into extracurricular activities that Ryder had dropped after university...when he had grown up. He wasn't sure if Joel had ever grown up, or if he ever would for that matter.

27

"Thanks Susan." Ryder stood. "You're alright to get back to the house?" He knew she was, but he asked anyway.

The short, slim brunette stood from the chaise, where she'd been reading a book, giving them space. She lay the blue, chenille knitted blanket that had been covering her body against the morning chill, over the edge and settled down on the other side of his father, folding her legs under her.

Susan wore a permanent, kind smile on her oval-shaped face and never did she send Ryder any seductive looks, like most women did. She didn't wink her brown eyes at him, or throw fake laughter his way. She didn't touch him like he was contraband she couldn't resist or make him sexual offers she thought *he* couldn't resist. On top of everything Susan did, Ryder truly appreciated the respect she had for him.

Most women saw Ryder as dollar signs they wanted to tuck into their wallets. Every event Ryder attended single women would flaunt their beautiful bodies at him, using them as a tool to attract his attention. Trying to sort through the ones who were genuinely interested in him from the ones who were solely attracted to his bank account edged near impossible. After Courtney, he lost hope in finding a woman who was what she appeared, who let her true self out, who didn't smile at him with money ringing in her head. After the lies and deceit of Courtney's unfaithfulness, Ryder gave up trying to distinguish women. He was nice to the women who thought they were going to woo him, but he kept them all at a distance from his emotions, from whatever, if any parts of his heart remained after Courtney.

"We're fine, Ryder. Don't worry about us. Right Donald?" She asked the older man in a softer, sweeter tone than she spoke to Ryder. "We will likely hang out here for a while longer if that's okay." Susan knew she didn't have to ask, but flashed him a smile anyway.

The lake house property flanked Crystal River, a winding river giving access to the boats docked along the luxury cottages along the lake.

It was Ryder's favorite property. It had also been his dad's favorite property, which was why he'd planned to spend the rest of his days here. But the main house was too big for his dad to live in with all the confusion already in his head.

Before Donald's dementia had worsened, they'd decided together that he would move into the servant's quarters. A luxurious, three-bedroom house built at the back edge of the property. Now, it housed twenty-four hour, seven days a week, and three-hundred-and-sixty-five days a year care Donald.

"It's never a problem Susan. Thanks again." Ryder knelt down beside his dad, whose focus had been so consumed with his task, that he hadn't heard a word pass between them. Ryder gave his dad's shoulder a squeeze, hating the feel of fragile bones beneath his fingers. "I'll see you later Pops. Love you." Ryder kissed the side of his dad's head, before dragging himself away and toward the house.

Eleven-year-old Sabin, a chocolate brown Great Dane, stood alert at Ryder's movement. His head darted between Donald and Ryder, debating whether to walk his old composed and collected self by Ryder's side to the house or...Sabin chose to curl down beside Donald, his owner.

Ryder ruffled his head. "Good boy," he said, before turning to leave. He wasn't surprised when Tank, the newest member of the family, a light colored Bullmastiff who was just over six months old, clumsily jumped up from the bone he'd been chewing on and ran circles around Ryder all the way to the house. They pup carried the oversized bone up the winding staircase to Ryder's bedroom.

29

Ryder hadn't been able to take his parents master bedroom, but there were five large bedrooms on the upper floor to choose from. Ryder chose the grand "Sailor's Room," as his mother had once called it. The landscaped sea oil paintings hanging on the beige walls added a nautical feel to the room, but his mother hadn't named the room because of the decor. Positioned in the middle of the house, the glass doors that led to the balcony, overlooked the backyard of flower gardens, and large maple trees which lined the edge of the river, and from this room only, you could see right through the break in the trees to the dock where his dad's boat was tied.

Ryder paused at the window, taking in the beauty and wishing he had someone to share it with...like his parents had found in each other.

Tank found his usual spot on the rug at his feet. As the afternoon came around, it would cast a beam of sun through the window warming his fur. He continued to gnaw at the bone as Ryder jumped in the shower.

It wasn't even a fifteen minute drive to the resort, but after a morning spent in the chilly air, Ryder needed a shower and a change of clothes.

As the warm water from the faucet pelted against Ryder's back, he couldn't help the smirk that tugged at his mouth. At the very least, watching the Ice Queen in action was going to be entertaining, and Ryder could use a little entertainment in his life. Day after day passed and he found he was working more behind the security of his office walls in the city, or hiding behind the walls of his house, away from people and their questions...away from life.

Violet Caliendo did not like Ryder. He would go as far to say that she detested him, which again made him smirk. How many women did Ryder know that detested him? Zero. All women liked him, whether it was his money or that Donald had passed his wide, broad body down on him and his mother had passed her good looks. Either way, no woman detested Ryder Carlex.

Ryder would be the first to admit that he'd been a jerk at her wedding, but he'd also attempted to make it up to her after he got his life sorted and was left with the guilt of his behavior. She'd declined dinner invites, or gala events and the few times in the last two years when he'd attended Eliza's social events, Violet had made it abundantly clear she was avoiding him. It only proved the nickname Joel had assigned her was accurate: *Ice Queen.* Joel's description of Violet: a heartless, cold, and rigid lover.

Amusement was what Ryder was going to be awarded with out of today's events, not the pleasure of wedding planning, but the satisfaction of watching the Ice Queen with her faultless posture and vigilant eyes in an absurd situation. Excitement was already stirring in Ryder...and it felt good.

Chapter Three

HOW COULD TWENTY-five minutes pass by so swiftly, while one was staring at the arms on the clock as they ticked by? Wasn't the saying something like, *watch a clock and time ticks by slower...what a crock.*

Violet's heels tapped an anxious beat against the floor under her desk, drumming a matching tune to the rising reaction inside of her due to consenting to this crazy situation. Finally, not wanting to be late, she stood and put a stop to it.

Pull yourself together.

Twenty-five minutes ago she'd convinced herself this would be the easiest meeting of her life. Now...*now...*

She stopped at the full-length mirror hanging on the back of her office door to evaluate herself. Not that it made any difference now, she couldn't change her outfit and give the Bensen party the implication that she was nervous, uncomfortable, and regretting her decision to coordinate their wedding.

Why did Missy have to get wind that there was a cancellation in the gold room on her wedding date?

Now, it was the big decision: silver room or gold room? That's all this meeting was about and yet almost every member of the wedding party was attending...including Ryder Carlex. *Why did he irk her so?* Oh, she knew why, because he's a playboy, that was why.

Violet smoothed the sides of her perfectly twirled updo and straightened the deep purple blazer over her straight, narrow cut skirt. Maybe she should have added a black blouse instead of the stark white one she wore, to suit the dark feelings in her gut.

"This won't be hard," she said to herself in the mirror, her neutral matte lipstick talking back to her. "It's a quick debate and settlement of one room. That's all."

In January, Violet and the happy couple had privately tackled all the details of their wedding day. She had managed that without the panic intensifying inside her today. The bridesmaid posse also hadn't been watching every move Violet made, analysing her, judging her, and hating her. And the date of the ceremony hadn't been just around the corner either. It was all becoming increasingly overwhelming.

Violet felt the panic arsing again. "Two more meetings," she promised herself in the mirror, holding up two fingers as if her eyes needed convincing. "Maybe more, if Missy has a bridezilla attack..."

Her head dropped, dreading more meetings. Then she lifted it back up, breathing reassurance into her lungs. "Pick a room today. Go over the final details next week and home run."

Until the day you watch Missy walk down the aisle. Oh, I'm not watching. Did I just have a double-sided conversation with my reflection? Was it in my head or out loud? Does it matter?

Violet shook off the panic and left her office, carrying the confidence she was accustomed to.

Simple and quick, pick a room and done.

As her long legs took her down the hallway, every step felt like a tunnel was caving in on her. She stared at the end, where she could see the cheerful, engaged couple waiting for her by the lobby desk. Missy was tucked comfortably into Joel's side, with his arm wrapped around her like they were made for one another. Violet had never fit in the nook of Joel's body like that...and Joel had never wanted her to. Joel had never loved Violet like he loved Missy. He had never even *tried* to love Violet. And Violet knew Missy came from an average family and that she wasn't Joel's ticket to more money...like Violet had been. The settlement Joel had sealed with Violet's father left Joel with enough money to live more than comfortably for the rest of his life...and now he was inviting Missy into his life of luxury.

Suddenly, the assurance of a quick meeting vanished and all the craziness of this ridiculous plan that she'd been battling all morning came rushing back, in an overpowering spin from the inside, coursing all the way out and around her body.

Her feet stopped. The speed of her heartbeat increased and amplified so loudly that she could hear it banging in her ears. Her breathing declined and she couldn't catch a breath. No air would enter and none would leave.

I am having a panic attack. Or a heart attack. Or I am about to lose it in front of everyone. What if I pass out? I think I am going to pass out.

Dizziness overtook her body, a feeling Violet was not accustomed to and she flew through the closest door beside her. Slamming it shut, the weight of her body crashed against the solid wood for support, while her shaking fingers had enough intelligence to lock the handle. Trying to force her breathing into a regular, steady pace, she closed her eyes and inhaled deeply.

This was crazy. This was absolutely insane!

Violet had to distract herself from these horrible rushing emotions, which were throwing her *way* off her game. Her dad would be so disappointed...and it was his fault she was in this predicament in the first place.

Don't play the blame game, it will get you nowhere. Focus on the now...focus on a solution...a distraction.

One hand was pressed against her panting chest, while the other was clenching the door handle like it was her lifeline. She forced her tightly squeezed eyes open, to take in her surroundings: the lobby washroom.

A sparkling marble floor was beneath her black stilettos. Mirrored walls reflected her distraught state and the chandeliers hanging over each sink twinkled light, giving the room a romantic feel.

A romantic feel? Why? Why today, did she have to notice the romantic feel of the washroom?

From her position, Violet could see there was no one was in the stalls lining the left side of the room. *Thank goodness.* She didn't need guests to witness her having a meltdown. *Violet Caliendo having a meltdown.* It was absurd.

But she wasn't the only one in the washroom. Standing across the room, unnoticed by her entrance, was a man standing six-foot-five, with his back toward her. He stood with a familiar confidence of a man who had everything and in a nonchalance stance, one hand tucked casually into his slacks, of a man who knew he was women's eye candy. He was the one and only: Ryder Carlex.

He was drop dead gorgeous.

What? Where did that come from?

Ryder was talking on his cell phone. "Susan, hey. I was thinking about stopping by tonight. We got interrupted this morning for Joel's thing, and we really didn't spend enough time together. Can you let me know if Kelly is going to be there tonight too."

Susan? Kelly? Blonde and brunette from this morning's conversation between Ryder and Joel. *Interrupted? Bed tumbling. Sexual encounter...*

"I'm going to bring some supper with me."

How thoughtful. *Feed his skanks.*

"Text me when you get this message. I'm not sure which of you are spending the night and, if I don't get a text, I will bring enough food for all of us."

Spending the night? Two of them?

He was ruthless. He was a playboy...*a player*...just like Joel had always told her he was.

Two women? Two women! Ryder Carlex had absolutely no morals. He was a selfish, sex-crazed male specimen that made others look bad.

But his body was remarkable, there was no denying it. Even wearing clothes, she could still see his upper torso spanning through his white button-up dress shirt that was tucked into the black dress slacks hugging his trim waist. He was hot. It stirred heat between her legs.

Stirred heat between her legs? Stirred heat between her legs! There was no heat stirring between her legs.

Violet crossed her legs.

"See you tonight." He slid his cell phone into his back pocket, and Violet couldn't help but notice how firm his ass was.

Firm ass? Did you really just think that?

Ryder turned and looked at her.

How was it possible that he was even sexier then only seconds ago?

When his smouldering, blue as lake water, eyes registered who was standing before him, an amused dance played across his flawless tanned
face and he flashed his pearly white teeth in her direction.

Violet's legs uncrossed. *Cross them back. Cross them back!*

That look across his striking face, was the exact look he flashed every woman and had them uncrossing their legs. He liked women. He had sex with all women, any woman who batted an eye of interest in his direction...and any woman who didn't.

Susan...Kelly...Hello Violet.

Violet had already made up her mind *not* to let the idea that was rousing in her head go anywhere in the same vicinity as her filter. If she did, her filter would have knocked the idea that had her blood boiling, right out of her head and on its ass. Violet's filter hadn't been helping her all morning anyway, and right now she needed a distraction.

Violet hands pushed her away from the door.

What are you doing? Where are you going? Oh, you know.

Women threw themselves at Ryder Carlex all the time. He was rich, he was handsome, he loved women and he took them. Right now, Violet wanted to be taken. She wanted to be distracted from the situation she'd put herself into and she needed a release.

Ryder Carlex was the perfect man to give her a distraction, a release, and he would walk away from her without any expectations.

***

RYDER STOOD LESS than fifteen feet away from the ice queen as she started toward him, and he didn't see a single shred of ice in those deep blue eyes. He saw a bottomless, malicious fire as she sauntered her seductive hips toward him and it was causing a sudden burning bulge in the front of his pants.

Seductive hips? Seductive hips! Damn right this woman had seductive hips, and they were heading in his direction.

Why, in all the time that he'd known Violet Caliendo, had he never noticed she had a stunning body? It was like a revelation slapped him across the face and time froze, so he could fully take in her exterior in a whole new, much more, exciting perspective.

Violet was tall, equal to his height when she was wearing those sexy black heels. She was slim, with a delicate frame posed under the thin, but crisp material of her blazer, continuing down her silky throat to the ivory skin across her collarbone. Her white, silk blouse was tucked perfectly in the high-waist skirt hugging her lower body and showing off captivating curves in all the right places...and long legs. Violet Caliendo had long, lean legs that disappeared under the skirt just above her knees.

His fingers suddenly had a mind of their own, wanting to inch up that skirt, and follow her thighs to the warm area that...

Whoa! What? No. Back up!

What are you doing allowing your thoughts in that direction...a lusting direction...for Joel's ex-wife?

Wasn't there some sort of bro code he had to follow? *Follow?* It wasn't like Violet was heading toward him to have sex with him, demanding that he dip into the bro code. *Was she? No, that was ridiculous.*

Ryder had seen Violet at least half a dozen times since her divorce from Joel, and she hadn't given Ryder a second glance. He wasn't sure that she'd given him a first glance, so there was no way she was heading his way for *sex*. But she *was* heading Ryder's way and he was allowed to *look*...appreciate how attractive she was....*wasn't he?*

Violet Caliendo was definitely not the grab-a-man-in-the-bathroom-for-sex type of woman...although at the moment, he wished she was.

No, you don't. Yes, I do. Do you know who you are talking about? Ice Queen. Ring any bells?

Oh, Violet was ringing bells alright, but they weren't warning Ryder of who she was, but rather what she could offer.

Why the hell was she *sauntering* right toward him? And why did her eyes look ready to dive into him? And why was the thought that maybe she would dive into him the most exciting feeling he'd had in years?

As he noticed the full, round mounds of her breasts pushing through the white button-up...*move your eyes back to hers*...he wondered why he hadn't ever taken her beauty in. *First, she was your best friend's wife and then she was the ice queen...that was precisely the reason why he'd never recognized her body was a temple he wanted access to.*

Donald Carlex didn't raise a son to steal a woman out from under someone and he definitely taught Ryder to stay away from the loveless ones. That's exactly what Joel told him Violet was. *A cold-hearted, loveless woman. An ice queen.*

But this ice queen could saunter. This ice queen could hold a solid stare and move in a solid sway and walk a steady pace in those spike heels that only added more to her sex appeal.

Violet walked all the way to him. Not inches away, not even centimeters away from his suddenly, very horny self. Her warm, not cold, body came in direct contact with his and he could feel her heat penetrate through his clothing. At the same time her fingers tightly wrapped around the front of his shirt.

And did she just pull him at her in a possessively, super hot, rough way?

As Violet's lips crashed against Ryder's lips, hard, hot and so far away from lovingly, he got his answer. She sure as hell *had* sauntered over to him with sex on her mind. At the very least, a make-out session that was starting off naughtily, exciting, and stirring something alive in him that had been absent for some time.

The instant Violet touched him, her kiss, her fingers, and her body erased the stress of redesigning the stores and the sadness of his dad's decline. Ryder's lips merely reacted to this incredible woman that was arousing every part of him. It had been years since his mind was this clear. Clear of the piling plateful that was his life.

In reality, Ryder should have paused to make sure the door was closed before he shoved the blazer off her shoulders to feel her tantalizing body through the thin material of her blouse. He should have pulled away from her plunging tongue that wasn't shy on dipping into his

39

mouth in search of his, and made sure *this* was what Violet wanted to do. But, as her hands yanked his shirt from where it had been neatly tucked, sliding sizzling hot fingers up his stomach and across his bare chest, he was taking that as his answer and there were no need for words.

Ryder cupped her face.

Violet unbuttoned his belt.

Hard, forceful kisses enveloped him away from his surroundings. He forgot he was at the Caliendo Resort. He forgot the reason he was there and the insanity of the circumstances. Everything, except this woman, was suddenly foreign to him.

All he could do was taste the wine in her warm mouth and feel her tongue flavoring every area possible inside his welcoming mouth.

Ryder hiked her skirt up and his fingers did exactly what they craved, moving up her thigh and damn the bare silkiness sent scorching pleasure through him.

Violet moaned in his mouth. *Moaned! Violet Caliendo. Ice queen.* This was no ice queen.

Ryder's pants dropped around his ankles and he'd had nothing to do with it. It was all this fiery woman, but damn if he didn't kick them off and pick her up all at the same time. Her arms snaked around his neck and she arched her full breasts against him as he carried her to the counter. He wanted to feel those breasts in his hands. They were still wearing too much clothing.

Their lips separated as he set her little rump down, only long enough for her to unbutton his shirt and him to unbutton hers. This woman was sizzling. Ryder was sizzling.

With her arms resting on his shoulders, Violet stopped to look at him. Her glazed, dazzling eyes held his. His hands stopped at the back of her bra, where they'd been ready to figure out if the clasp was there or in the front. Her eyes might be blue as ice, but he found no shards reflecting back at him. Their fixated look pulled him into a silent world that he found, surprisingly, enjoyable. A quiet, tranquil place with a woman that he didn't know all that well and yet, here...there was something. Something he'd never felt and didn't recognize.

His peripheral vision caught the deep panting breaths escaping her lips as her full chest was now exposed in her lace bra, heaving up and down to the pulse of his own breaths. He wondered if that was the moment she was going to change her mind. If she was going to send a pile of crashing icicles down on them.

Then her eyes fell to his lips and he watched her tongue slid across her lower lip before she sucked that full cushioning lower lip between her teeth. He wanted those lips.

But what if she was done? What if the reality hit her? What if—

Violet's grabbed Ryder's hardness and his eyes flew back up to hers. She was smirking at him in a devilish way before she claimed his mouth telling him they weren't finished yet.

***

AS VIOLET CAME down from her high, panting, hot, and never remembering a sexual encounter that had ever been that good, the stark reality hit her: *she just had sex with Ryder Carlex.*

In a bathroom, at the resort, and down the hall from her ex-husband...who was waiting for both of them. Not to mention Violet's entire family was on the premises and...and the list of reasons why this was a bad decision went on and on inside her head.

Oh crap!

For some unexplainable reason, even though her brain told her to pull away from Ryder and without delay, put

41

distance between them, Violet didn't want to leave the warmth of his skin. She could feel every single area of her skin that was flesh-on-flesh with his, like jolts of scorching electricity forming at each spot.

Violet's elbows rested on his brawny, thick shoulders, as her arms wrapped up around his head, clasping above his hair and forcing his face to tuck deep against her shoulder. The roughness of his five o'clock shadow rubbed against her skin and the coarse touch ignited a want to kiss him again. Her naked middle touched his solid muscle wall and because he'd managed to unfasten the snap on the front her bra, her breasts were pushed so hard against him it felt like they'd molded into one.

Oh crap!

She was late. They were both late. Not to mention, their outfits were going to be wrinkled, looking like they just had...

She almost gasped out loud at the thought of everyone knowing what had occurred within these four walls, but she knew the sound would pull Ryder away from her and right now she wanted to feel his hair against her cheek, his hands around her back, and his body flanked between her legs.

Would they look like they'd just had sex? Game face. *You just need to get your game face on and no one will know what you just did.*

Violet would know. Violet had the awakening feeling that she was never going to forget the rendezvous in *this* bathroom. From this day forward, each time she walked down this hall, between the lobby and her office, and passed this door, she would see Ryder's naked chest, feel his pounding heart against hers, and remember the feel of his mind-blowing kisses.

Oh crap!

Ryder's breathing was just as heavy as hers and with every breath she took, the wonderful smell of his designer cologne wafted into her nose.

Pull away.

"That was an incredible surprise." His low, deep voice sent another rumble of desire through her with the inclination to start again from the beginning.

Oh no, no, no! Violet, stop it this instant. Pull away.

"This is going to be on the higher scale of awkward for the rest of the afternoon." He was so beyond right, this was going to be *sooo* awkward.

What had she been thinking?

She hadn't, that was the problem. Everything about today had been carelessly not thought out. She needed a reassessment.

His arms weren't loosening their grip either, and she tried to fight how much she liked that he was as content as she was. She could actually feel one of his fingers swirling a design against her back...*and oh it felt good.*

How had this happened? How had this happened! Why was she not nearly as concerned, worried, or panicked as she should be? Why did she feel like she could spend the rest of the day, right here, wrapped up in his arms?

"I think I should leave first." His whisper was daunting.

How was he planning their escape when she couldn't even register the entirety of what had just occurred, still reeling in how wonderful it felt, and how much she wanted to do it again.

"Since you're in the guys washroom."

The guy's washroom? She was?

"I can go down there first, distract them and text you when the coast is clear," Ryder continued his plan. "I would need your cell phone number first."

He was being so sweet, trying to save her reputation...a reputation she had worked her life to uphold to perfection and this one run-in with Ryder could squash it in a heartbeat. She knew all of this, and didn't need the reminder from Ryder, yet, she still didn't move. *Didn't want to move.*

Ryder's finger stopped and she felt his hands move to her front. When she thought he was going to cup her breasts again...and heaven knew, she wouldn't stop him...he snapped her bra back together. In a quick motion, he lifted her like she was weightless, pulling the hem of her skirt from under her bum and down to her knees.

Suddenly, like the sound of a balloon popping and leaving you stunned for a second, Violet remembered exactly who she'd just had sex with. And how many times he'd likely been in this exact situation: naked from the waist down with woman on a counter top.

Ryder wasn't taken aback like Violet was, or unwinding from the naughty game they'd just played and considering how to plan another round. Violet craved to start the next round, while he was making escape plans and snapping her bra into place because this casual sex was a customary part of his life.

Violet might have initiated this play time, but he was clearing the air, reminding her it was exactly what she'd walked across the floor thinking...a onetime thing and he would walk away without any attachments.

Wasn't that what she wanted? A manipulating womanizer...even if she had walked to him.

Why did her heart suddenly plummet?

Her heart? Her heart!

There was no way in hell her heart just plummeted. For one, she'd given up on her heart a long time ago when Joel crushed it and the better reason there was no way her heart was playing plummeting games, this was Ryder Carlex. *Ryder Carlex!*

Violet pulled away and shoved his chest back at the same time, startling him a bit in the process, but he managed to keep his balance and send her a questioning look.

"Oh please, don't look all shocked." She wasn't about to let him treat her like the nobody. Screw him. She used him. *He* was the nobody. "Get dressed and get out."

She reached across the counter for her blouse and stared at it appalled. *Wrinkled. Ugh.* At least it was under her blazer. She could tightly tuck it in and no one would ever know.

You will know, her body teased, ready for another round with Ryder, while her head needed to put distance between them.

Ryder's pants were up, buckled and he was buttoning up his shirt as he reached down and picked her blazer off the floor, handing it to her.

His spectacular eyes didn't waver from her the entire time, like he was trying to read her. Why couldn't he back off and just worry about himself? She could dress herself. She did it every single morning.

Violet snatched the blazer away. "Can you hurry up so we can get out of here?"

His eyebrows arched in what initially appeared to be kindness, but she was sure she misread it as the look shifted to questioning.

Ryder straightened. Damn his body was amazing, like a wall of sparking gold. "Woman, I will leave when I damn well feel like it. If I want to stand here and watch you get dressed, after touching every piece of your hot body, then I will stand here and watch you get dressed." The way he said "hot body," low and sensual, made her swallow hard. Did he say this to all his women? Did they all just sit back, bat their fake eyelashes and allow him to speak to them like a Neanderthal?

Violet slid off the counter, furious. *Who did he think he was talking to her like that?* She shrugged into her blazer and tucked her shirt into the high waist of her skirt.

Violet stepped toward him, erasing every last inch of lust across her expression and substituting it with her flawless emotionless face. There was no way she was letting him see that she would rather have stayed on that counter all afternoon, when he was dismissing her like cheap wine.

"Stay in here then and stare at my ass as it walks away because it's the last time you are touching any part of this *hot body*." That was such a lie. *Touch me now*. She stood a second longer than she should have, just in case he reached for her, then she turned on her heel and scolded herself for thinking he would.

Violet stepped into the hallway, not caring who was on the other side of that door. She needed to get away from Ryder's smoldering eyes before she pulled him back into her arms. She glanced both directions. She really did care.

Standing tall, smoothing her dress, she was about to head down the hall, when her hands felt empty...and not for Ryder. Her iPad was in her office.

Thank the stars. She needed a moment anyway. She turned away from the foyer and right toward her office.

She had officially made this "finalize a room meeting" one hundred times worse.

Chapter Four

RYDER FOUND THE groom-to-be in the elegant lounge, to the left of the lobby, separated by marble columns and extraordinary large cement urns filled with fresh flowers. Inside, grand sparkling crystal chandeliers hung above the sitting areas with lush, thick carpets under grandiose and stylish furniture.

Joel sat cosily on a white sofa beside Missy, holding hands and laughing, deep in conversation with Missy's five friends, who were seated across the wrought iron and glass table...*the bridesmaids.*

Ryder cringed.

This wasn't the first time Ryder had gathered with the wedding party. However, the last few engagements had involved the groomsmen, who were great distractions to assist Ryder in avoiding the looks and offers of these on-the-prowl ladies. They were single...every last one of them and the way they latched onto Ryder, demonstrated that they were on the hunt for a man...only Ryder wasn't looking.

Today, he solely focused on the groom and bride-to-be, hoping that would deter the aggressive women.

Today, Joel was dressed handsomely appropriate. His khaki-colored slacks and dark knitted sweater set off the black mixed in with his brown eyes, giving him a deceiving look, much like his watchful and private personality. Joel might talk a lot of talk, but Ryder often wondered if it was to keep people from asking about Joel's work and his life.

Joel had cornered himself into numerous financial situations, forcing him to impose his downfalls on Ryder's father, pleading for Donald to bail him out. If it wasn't for Ryder's parents and their commitment to stand by Joel after his parent's death, Ryder would have declined the offer to be Joel's best man. Blood was thicker than his feelings toward Joel, so Ryder pressed forward and did what he knew his parents would want.

Missy's light pink summer dress accented her light porcelain skin and green eyes, soft like her persona. The complete opposite of hard-shelled, Violet Caliendo.

Ryder cleared his throat, and the thought of Violet, as he entered the room. All heads turned to him and like rabid dogs, the bridesmaids sunk their vicious teeth into him, with the all too familiar looks screaming, *I'm checking you out* and, *I want you to know it*. And the regular lineup of, *You can have all of me, just make a move, Carlex*. Sure, he could bang every single one of these sexy and cute women, flashing their white smiles, and winking their seductive eyes his way, but that didn't mean he wanted to. This time, Ryder wasn't in the same dark, dreadful place in his life, so he wasn't interested in quick flings or possibilities of a relationship. Besides, none of them could rock his hips the way Violet had.

Did that really happen?

Ryder was still shaking the image of Violet's swaying hips crossing the room toward him in the lobby washroom from his mind. He recounted the way she knew exactly what she wanted and how powerless he had been to object.

He had sex with Violet Caliendo...in the lobby washroom. Holy shit! How was he supposed to act remotely normal with Joel now? *You better try damn hard.*

It was bizarre, seeing that Violet had done precisely what every woman did with Ryder: threw herself at him. Yet, their interaction felt nothing like what Ryder had ever experienced with any other woman and left him craving more. That was a jumble of confusion he didn't have the energy to sort out right now.

"Hey Ryder," Missy greeted first.

Ryder sent Missy a sincere smile. She was the only woman not ogling his body like it was a slab of meat, freshly cut from the butchers and ready to sizzle. Missy was cute, like the girl next door, with innocent eyes and a young smile. This woman had nothing on Violet Caliendo.

Hold up! Stop doing that. Don't compare the two women...because Violet will outrank Missy every time. Really?

Ryder couldn't believe the thoughts going through his head. His mind hadn't been this active, when not regarding work or his dad's medical condition, in such a long time, he almost wasn't used to thinking about anything else. He liked the distraction, he welcomed the distraction...he just wasn't sure he liked that it was Violet that kept distracting him. She was a thunderstorm. Hot, steamy, sensually sucking his lips one moment then screw you cold, get-out-of-my-way ice queen the next.

Thunderstorm.

Damn windy, whirl whipping, pick everything up along the way and slam it down when she was finished.

Or was that a hurricane?

Joel stood and came in for a hand grasping, shoulder patting, man hug. "Ryder," he said.

"Sorry, I'm late man."

I am not going to tell you why, but it was the most thrilling thunderstorm I've ever been in.

Joel shrugged. "No biggie."

Joel stood a foot shorter than Ryder, and he'd never hit the gym which showed by his rounded belly protruding under his sweater.

"Violet's not back either." Joel lowered his voice to a whisper for only Ryder to hear. "Probably tightening her chastity belt," he said, jabbing Ryder's stomach with his elbow as he pulled away.

Joel always had a low stab for Violet, which made Ryder wonder again, what the hell they were all doing at the Caliendo Resort in the first place or why Joel had married her in the first place?

This particular dig at Violet sent direct heat to Ryder's manhood, knowing that he'd unlocked Violet's chastity belt only minutes earlier, and that he would deeply consider traveling through storms and climbing mountains to find that key again.

Distraction...distraction...distraction.

Missy slid in for a hug too, with her small frame. "I'm so glad you could come. Are you still on for fishing next week? I know it's all Joel has been talking about." Missy slipped back into the nook of Joel's side, and his arm automatically wrapped around her.

"Up bright and early and home late, just like when we were kids," Ryder said, remembering the times Joel's parents would stay at the lake house and the boys would head out fishing with their dads.

Both being only children, they'd bonded back then. A bond that had taken them through boarding school and into university, but since then their friendship had struggled and tapered, only seeing each other when Ryder visited Willow Valley. It was more in the last two years with Donald living at the lake house permanently, a truth he was yet to share with Joel, if he ever did. He just hoped Joel kept his financial life out of trouble, because Donald was now powerless to help and Ryder wasn't putting his neck on the line. That would leave Joel on his own if it happened again.

"Ryder, you really have to take me on your boat," one of Missy's friends said. He'd been introduced by name to each of them, but forgot as quickly as he was told. So he would call this one, who latched onto his arm and squeezed her painted red nails into his skin, Bottom Feeder.

Missy laughed. "Marci, get off him. You're going to have to excuse my friends. Apparently, handsome men make them forget their manners." She was reaching for Marci to pull her away, but Marci wiggled back, pulling Ryder a step back with her.

"And rich..." Joel added with a wink at the ladies and another elbow in Ryder's side.

Please, don't bait them.

Missy gave up.

Joel chuckled, liking the show that had Ryder cringing.

All the women swarmed around Ryder, like piranha's closing in on their prey.

He was trying to figure out a diversion to eliminate him from the grasp of Bottom Feeder, as he caught sight of Violet. Suddenly he didn't feel the other woman's touch.

Violet stood between the marble columns, looking like a Goddess of Beauty and she played the part well. This woman indeed knew how to pull herself together after what he would call a helluva occurrence in the lobby washroom. Her shoulders were pulled back, straightly defined, lengthening her height. Not an untouched blonde hair was out of place, or a smudge of lipstick, not a blush of color grazed her cheeks. All of the details he'd enjoyed watching as she dressed, with her flustered reaction. Her hair had been askew, her lipstick half missing, which he'd wiped clean off his lips after she left, and her cheeks flushed from the intimate touching they'd shared. Instant images of her legs still parted, sitting on the counter and her underwear lying on the floor, found their way into his head.

Back to the now.

The calmness of her eyes told the people in this room that she'd been doing anything else except touching, kissing, and scorching Ryder Carlex.

When Violet's eyes found Ryder first, they were expressionless, like she didn't care that Melanie...Maggie...whatever M-named woman, was leeched against Ryder, where Violet had been only minutes ago...and who Ryder would prefer to have touching him.

Violet's eyes didn't miss a beat, departing from Ryder's to travel around the room, sending everyone an equally quick smile.

No special attention for Ryder. No ogling looks...and not a seductive wink, followed by another lobby washroom offer. That was exactly what Ryder wanted from every woman, to be left alone, not ogled, not touched and not be treated like their next hunting trophy. Why did disappointment wash through him when Violet did exactly that?

Had he hoped she would share a shred of knowledge with him? A wink, a smile, a grin...anything?

"I see we are all here, so why don't we go look over the two ballrooms, discuss the amenities of each and decide on the one for your special day," she said so professionally that an outsider would have no idea she'd been married to the groom.

Why don't we start with the men's washroom...it's way more appealing.

Missy clapped her hands and squealed, leading her group of Ryder-sucking leeches toward the ballroom, including Miss M, who let Ryder's arm free.

Missy knew her way around the resort after years of being employed as a maid. The possibility that Joel and Missy had been fooling around before his divorce to Violet had crossed Ryder's mind. If that question taunted him...didn't it taunt them all? Including Violet?

Ryder couldn't decide which was more awkward...him having sex with his friend's ex-wife or the fact Violet was planning her ex-husband's wedding. Either way, both were distracting and entertaining, keeping Ryder's mind occupied.

Heels dug firmly onto the floor and iPad held tightly against her chest, Violet stood at the entrance, nodding and smiling as each person passed. Ryder waited, casually with his hands in his pockets, until he was the last person in the lobby.

He should have been grateful that Violet was acting like nothing had happened between them. Hell, nothing should have happened between them. But, here he was, baiting on her professionalism as she waited for him and did not scamper away, as his feet made it to the exit.

Ryder stopped beside her. The designer perfume that had engaged his senses as he rose into bliss with this magnificent woman in the washroom now tantalized him...and he liked it. He knew he shouldn't. He knew he should keep walking. He knew this woman was a thunderstorm, his friend's ex-wife, and an ice queen, but Ryder didn't listen to any of the warnings. They were mildly nagging the back of his mind, while front and center was the desire to ruffle the feathers of Violet Caliendo. If that meant he was falling down to the level of bottom feeder and her posse...Ryder was good with that.

Ryder lowered his tone to a seductive whisper only for Violet. "I appreciated that skirt more, when it was hiked up around your waist."

Violet breathed deeper. She stared harder. That was all she gave him, but he damn well knew it was more then she wanted to give.

Chapter Five

IT ASTOUNDED VIOLET, that Missy's debate of each ballroom stretched on, as though she'd never stepped a foot either of them. Then afterwards, she expressed the need to take another tour before making her final decision.

It was two ballrooms, pick one or the other.

However, unexpectedly, Violet's short tolerance had nothing to do with Missy, or Joel for that matter...*it was because of Ryder Carlex.*

Exiting the lobby washroom with her blouse wrinkled, her panties twisted, and her mind...well...*blustered*, in a way that she'd never experienced in her entire life, had Violet shifting uneasily inside...but not on the outside for Ryder to glory in.

I appreciated that skirt more, when it was hiked up around your waist...ugh!

But why did the suggestion make her want to hike her skirt up right there in the lobby, and kiss that badgering man's lips?

The fact that the Bensen couple were marrying in less than a month hadn't even negatively passed through Violet's mind. She should appreciate the diversion in her thoughts. After all, the Bensen wedding *was* responsible for her morning fluster.

If only the commotion in her head wasn't caused by the knowledge that Ryder's relaxed, laid-back eyes were waiting to meet hers and send her a look. Not just any look, like that of a casual acquaintance. No, Ryder continued to send her teasing looks, lusting looks, *I know what we did* looks that were childish and maddening.

Violet knew what they did. She couldn't believe what they had done and she certainly didn't need reminders from Ryder.

Ryder Carlex? Ryder Carlex! Violet, what were you thinking? It was clear, thinking hadn't had any part in that regretful decision. Another prime example of the result of her filter avoidance.

What was Ryder doing here anyway? Playboy, take-a-woman-in-the-washroom, Ryder Carlex was offering his input for his best friend's wedding. *A wedding...a ceremony of united love.* That was odd. He was odd.

He was hot.

Violet's unwelcome diversion clouded Missy's voice as she explained the pros and cons of each ballroom to Joel...again.

Violet didn't notice how more involved Joel was with this wedding compared to theirs, like she might have, if her eyes hadn't went against her will to *not look*, and found Ryder.

What is wrong with you?

His outfit didn't even look disheveled. Not his designer slacks or dress shirt or the sexy way he styled the longer locks of his hair upwards in a wave, while the sides were cut shorter. Nor was his presence unsettled, like Violet, even if she knew she wasn't allowing it to show.

If you weren't allowing it to show, you would have never looked at Ryder...again.

As expected, Ryder was watching her.

Why did you look if you knew he was going to be looking at you?

Did he do this with all the women he sacked? It was kind of creepy. She decided Ryder was odd *and* creepy.

Ryder winked at her.

He was so hot.

55

Violet turned away, appalled.

You're not appalled. Did anyone see her break-down and show how bothered Ryder was making her?

Probably one of those bridesmaids shoved so far up his royal rear noticed.

Could this appointment get any worse? Or stretch on any longer?

She even considered going against her word, and texting Emma to finish this meeting. Emma would think Violet was requesting her presence to avoid the happy couple, rather than avoiding the best man, who was making it clear he would love another rendezvous in the washroom. The scary part was, deep down, hidden behind her filter, Violet wanted to take his hand and guide the way. That was crazy. *That was crazy!* If sex with Ryder was always *that* good, no wonder the bridesmaids were rubbing up against him at every opportunity.

Well ladies, I already took him for a joyride today. Not helpful, Violet.

Violet forced her eyes back to Ryder, deciding to face him head on, finished with playing his game. He could send her all the seductive looks he sent to all the women, but it didn't mean that Violet would fold.

Ryder didn't shy away from her stare, and she hadn't expected him to. It was about proving to him that she wasn't a little toy he could toss around, and that his handsome face wasn't luring her, like he was challenging. What Violet hadn't expected was the abrupt change in his look. Like a sudden change in wind direction, the seduction vanished from Ryder's stare, along with the torturous teasing. The gaze he cast her was new, different than any man had ever given Violet. It was almost as though he was looking at her, actually *looking at her*...not her last name or the trailing line of assets that followed. That was crazy...*wasn't it?*

Ryder left his spot, standing between two of the bridesmaids, to walk across the large tiled floor to Violet. *Did he like what he saw? What did he see? What everyone else did?*

He stopped beside her, less than a foot away...too close for comfort. Their arms were so close to touching. Violet could literally feel the heat tugging them together.

Ryder leaned over even closer to whisper, "I would go with the silver ballroom."

So? She didn't care.

Why would you choose the silver ballroom?

The wedding coordinator in her was curious...not herself. Violet had discovered over the years, couples who chose to unite under the tents at the beach, seemed madly in love, seeking a romantic union, while those who chose the ballrooms selected based on financial status. The gold room was grander, more impressive and upheld a respected reputation. Why would Ryder choose the silver ballroom?

Violet didn't dare ask or show interest in his reasoning, but she didn't have to, Ryder continued. "I mean the gold ballroom is obviously premium, with elegant theater-style decorating, larger area, and draping chandeliers."

How did he notice draping chandeliers?

"However, I like the wall of windows at the back of the silver ballroom." That was Violet's favorite feature too. "It would be incredible for a winter wedding especially."

He was right. Words could not describe how breath taking the backdrop of a winter snowfall through the glass, with the trees lightly dusted, creating a winter wonderland, was.

Violet didn't concur out loud, instead she opted to put him in his place.

"Ryder, if ever the day comes for you to share vows with that one lucky lady, I will personally set you up with reservations..." She glanced at him. "...free of charge and make sure you experience exactly what the silver room has to offer." That day would never present itself.

Violet turned her attention back to the wedding party. *Her attention to the wedding party.* That was a joke. Her concentration hadn't been on the Bensen party since they left the lounge, but rather on the man standing beside her.

Ryder chuckled, a low dangerous, somewhat amused chuckle, before speaking to her in an even lower tone. "Why don't we scrap reserving it for my lucky lady and reserve it for the two of us."

Her teeth gritted together.

Hog.

He continued. "I wouldn't mind hiking you onto the head table..." Against her will, the vision he described flashed in her head.

Violet refused to look at Ryder. Her fingers tightened around her iPad and her jaw clenched. She couldn't help it. She couldn't stop it. Yes, she was showing emotion. Yes, she was letting him witness the effects of his words, but damn it a clenched jaw was better than the glare no one would mistake and inevitably question.

Missy and her posse continued to debate the ballroom.

Pick a room. Pick a room!

Joel made his way to Violet and Ryder. He stopped directly in Violet's vision, so his un-tucked sweater was all she could see. Violet didn't miss his rounded middle or his hands touching the small of her back. She realized a long time ago, that his intentions had not been to protect her or love her until death do them part. No, Joel was a selfish man, and he'd only ever thought about himself.

Joel's attention was on Ryder.

Thank goodness.

"Ryder, tell me about what kept you? Don't leave out any details. I want to hear all about the blonde *and* the brunette."

I don't want to hear! Keep your composure. I should text Emma. I should join Missy and the bridesmaids to hurry this along. I should be anywhere, but right here, right now, listening to this conversation.

Violet's fingers didn't retrieve her cell phone and her feet wouldn't move. They were both attached to the part of her that *did* want to hear what Ryder had been up to before he arrived. It was probably one of the better ideas she'd had all day. Violet needed a crucial reminder of the man Ryder Carlex in fact was. An essential dose of reality telling her that Ryder was not looking at her, or even wanting to know her better. Ryder was a playboy. Her gut told her differently. Or else it was hope. *Hope? Hope! Hope for what?* That Ryder wasn't the man Joel said he was. *Why? What difference did it make?*

It didn't make any difference. In order for Violet to move past the reaction that her body was having to Ryder, she needed to listen to this conversation and experience the authentic Ryder Carlex.

***

RYDER WATCHED THE muscles in Violet's jaw tighten, even more than before Joel had arrived. This time, with Joel's presence, Ryder couldn't observe...and take pleasure in the way Violet's full lower lip pursed with the clenched motion.

Joel could never know what had transpired between them. Bro code, or some shit like that. Besides, Ryder didn't want to fuel the bad blood that ran between Joel and his ex-wife.

Now that Ryder had felt Violet under his touch, his outlook on this woman was changing.

Changing? Why? You had sex with her that was it. Unexpected, mind-blowing, can't-get-it-out-of-my-head, sex.

He felt like a teenager who'd tasted his first flavour of a woman, leaving him craving more. Only he'd had women, but never one like Violet.

Ryder shook his head, as he dragged his gaze away from Violet's luscious lip that he wanted to tug between his teeth, and back to the gold ballroom they stood in.

I need a new distraction.

Neutral framed oil paintings lined the walls around them, encased in exquisite moulding contrasting against the dark cherry wood floor, and brass chandeliers above.

If Ryder had forbidden his feet to take him to Violet, which would have been the better decision, and instead stopped to read the signed art, he didn't doubt the marvelous masterpieces would be renowned artist. But there was something intriguing about the way this woman looked at him, like she *wanted* to look at him, and the battle in her eyes made him want to dig deeper into what made Violet Caliendo.

She was wild fire, that was evident, dangerous to touch and she'd left her mark on Ryder. But, maybe she wasn't exactly who Ryder presumed. He would have never foreseen Violet approaching him the way she had, but expected her rough and controlling touch. It was the gentle affection during, the way she moved, arched, and moaned under this touch that was leaving him confused.

Violet guided this group with a confident stride, presenting immense strength, doing a job no one should ever be tasked with, planning her ex-husband's wedding, and Ryder didn't see a touch of frostiness trickling from her body. That said volumes about her, didn't it? Then when she looked at Ryder, and she did, even against her attempts not to, there was desire flaming in those eyes, with a touch of irritation with him, but then there was *that* look he couldn't identify. Whatever it was, Ryder felt it too. It was more than his desire for Violet, he felt drawn to her.

You don't know her. Joel knows her.

Joel talked a lot of trash about a lot of people leaving Ryder only to ever believe half, if that, of what came out of his mouth. Then why had Ryder trusted his portrayal of Violet, the cold and heartless Ice Queen? Because Ryder hadn't cared one way or the other about who the real Violet Caliendo was. And he cared now? *No...yes...maybe...*

Joel punched Ryder's shoulder, dragging his thoughts away from the Violet debate going on in his head and back to the conversation at hand.

What were they talking about?

Joel wanted every detail of Ryder's morning.

I woke up early to my phone ringing wild, as my cousins who have invested into the company and hired on to re-develop our look were demanding decisions. I spent hours on the phone before another call came in from my dad's worker, saying he was in the mood to go fishing. My dad, who has dementia and doesn't know who I am half the time and I spent the morning sitting on the dock at Crystal Lake, with yes a brunette named, Sabin and a blonde named, Tank and they were the closest to a companion I was looking for...until now.

Ryder's eyes darted to Violet, *damn it*, he couldn't help it. *Companion. She was no companion...was she?*

"Well, you know I've always been a sucker for blondes," Ryder said, hating the way Joel brought this out in him.

Joel laughed his tune of approval. "Yeah, you do. So blonde it was. That's my man."

Blonde beauty with a highlight of violet.

Joel held his fist out and Ryder cringed when his fist was forced to meet it. He hated what Violet might be thinking right now. *Hated what she was thinking? Why? It wasn't like they were in a relationship.* Damn, they'd just done what everyone thought he did: had sex in the bathroom.

Still, it bothered him.

"Honestly though, Joel, I didn't initiate it at all. She walked her long, slim, gorgeous legs toward me, grabbed my shirt with her seductive fingers and planted her wanting lips on mine." As Ryder described only partial moments of this morning, the rest replayed in his mind and he found himself wanting to go back in time and lavish in the encounter all over again.

Violet's head turned full throttle in Ryder's direction. Not just a slight tilt of her head, or an eye stealing side-view, but she looked right at him. When their betraying eyes met for the short flash, her appetite burst, telling him she'd travelled back into that room with him.

Did Violet want a replay?

The anticipation that she might, excited Ryder, but bolts of lightning warded his thoughts.

Ice queen. Tornado. What are you thinking?

This woman was no ice queen and he liked the way the ambience of her tornado twisted his insides.

"Do you hear that Violet? What a guy." Did Joel not see what was happening between them? Was anything happening between them or was Ryder creating it?

"I hear him." Violet's gaze didn't waver and her tone wasn't threatening.

Was it an invitation?

Ryder didn't know for certain. But what he did know, was that if they didn't break the contact, Joel would become suspicious.

Ryder turned to the groom-to-be and told him the truth. "It was the best sex I've ever had."

The comment fetched a roar out of Joel and when his eyes rolled into the air with his laughter Ryder sought out Violet's again. She was still watching him closely, hadn't moved. He expected a glare of warning to not say a word, but as many times today, Violet surprised him with a look of confusion and like she was digging into the depth of Ryder for answers to her own questions.

Just ask me, and then maybe I will understand what is going on here.

"Damn Ryder." Joel hit his shoulder, before turning and walking away mumbling, "If only all blondes were that way."

Missy was a brunette. It was a direct hit at Violet and it sent prickles through Ryder's body. Why did Joel always have to be such an ass? Ryder didn't like it. Violet caught the flicker of hurt over her face and masked it quickly, but not before Ryder saw it.

Ryder was learning Violet was the queen of masking her emotions, but he was curious what was behind those emotions and why she kept letting him in today, a little more each time their eyes met. *Who was the real Violet Caliendo?* It seemed that Joel didn't know her as well as he claimed to, or else Joel was full of himself. Wouldn't be the first time he'd exaggerated or flat our lied.

Ryder hated that Violet was masking hurt inflicted by Joel, when she was being nothing but hospitable to the entire group.

When Joel was out of hearing range, Ryder stepped in front of Violet and said, "Joel talks a lot of talk and he has no idea what he's talking about with you. Everything I said about today was true and everything was about you."

Violet's eyebrows arched, and the mystifying desire clouded her eyes, then slipped away into the depths of her facade. She licked her lips, sucking them into her mouth, a movement that caused a stir down below. When she released them she said, "Ryder, I don't need you to pet my ego and tell me I'm good at sex, because my ex jabs that I'm not."

He didn't feel that he *needed* to say it, but he *wanted* her to know.

"There's a reason we're divorced." With that, Violet walked away, taking any contemplation Ryder had created thinking he met a different version of Violet than Joel.

Ryder was left standing alone, facing the exit and feeling like a giant ass for spending this whole appointment trying to figure out a woman who was nothing more than what she portrayed: Ice Queen.

Joel hit the nail straight on with this woman. Ice Queen. That knowledge should be enough to keep Violet out of Ryder's thoughts from here on in.

Chapter Six

A WEEK AFTER Violet's encounter with Ryder, she was glad to say, the man who took her for the ride of her life, wasn't still in her every thought. Well...not her every *waking* thought. The way his hands traced her skin delicately then parted her legs roughly, and the way his lips kissed her, dark and mysterious, like the moon kissed the sky goodnight, overtook her dreams. Every single night, she'd awaken in panting, hot sweats with Ryder's rock hard body and handsome face flashing through her mind.

That was ridiculous...wasn't it?

She was a grown woman, not a teenager lusting over the captain of the football team...or in Willow Valley, it would be the hockey hero, like Marc's sister-in-law, Peyton McAdams...now Patterson. She'd been victim to the teenage lust and swooned all over retired pro-hockey player Colt Patterson, who had knocked her up.

Sure, they were *supposedly* happily married now, with twins, a little girl and little boy, Leighton and Landon, but that wasn't the point. The point was, Violet was a grown woman with two children of her own and needed to start behaving like one.

Then there was the overbearing, wooden lobby washroom door that brought the child out in Violet. She hadn't made eye contact with that door all week, like a terrified kid fearing what was behind it. Only, it was breathtaking recollections that ignited fire in her...and that was the problem.

Ridiculous.

During the day, against her objections, Ryder was playing hopscotch in Violet's head, jumping in whenever he pleased, and taking her mind down a road of contemplation about the man she'd labeled him as and the player everyone had labeled him as, including her family. But, after Ryder's somewhat, sweet remark, to de-buff Joel's vulgar comment, Violet couldn't ignore the *way* he'd said it: sincerely and truthfully. She'd stood there feeling like Ryder was talking to her because he *wanted* to, not because he felt obliged, like everyone else. If only his tone had held arrogance, humor or patronizing, and left her livid with him, then her week would have gone by in a less puzzling manner.

Violet couldn't fit together the pieces of Ryder that she retained from Joel and the pieces of Ryder that she clutched from her own experience of him, to add up to anything more than uncertainty. Violet didn't like uncertainty, it only led vulnerability for others to swoop in and take advantage of you. Violet would not be taken advantage of...not again.

After an early morning spent with Emma, partaking in the spooky decoration hunt for the annual Fright Fest, Halloween in July at the resort, Violet was hot and sticky. Normally, she would jump in the shower and then head back to work. However, today she had the day off. Instead, she slipped into her one-piece, cream colored, crocheted swimsuit and dove into the heated pool. It wasn't only the heat of the day she was trying to escape from, but the heat that rushed through her whenever Ryder popped into her head.

How could sex once with a person she couldn't even stand to look at, much less desire to touch, leave her craving more?

Violet had done what she knew best, to rid Ryder from her thoughts: overworked herself. Including today, when she'd beat Emma to the storage room to dig out the appropriate decorations for the set-up crew to incorporate in the pavilion at the edge of the resorts property on the beach. The reclusive location was chosen in order to allow the crew advanced time to set up. With the numerous weddings in July, other events needed extra time. Violet was only getting today off because it was the middle of the week, there were no weddings, and she'd booked no appointments, which meant tomorrow was booked solid.

She'd planned on spending her day off with Sophia and Parker, but when Joel promised them a day of fishing and their little faces lit up, Violet couldn't say no.

A day off. A day all to herself.

It sounded like every working mother's dream...except she knew the alone time would no doubt center her thoughts around Ryder.

As the water engulfed her body, she wished the indoor pool, centered in the heart of her family's suites, wasn't heated. She needed a fresh, cold wake-up call.

Craving Ryder Carlex left Violet feeling like one of the ogling bridesmaids that had thrown themselves shamelessly at Ryder at every opportunity...much the way Violet had.

Did he sleep with them too? Did it matter?

The positive point to this whole charade was Ryder didn't run in the same circles as Violet. It would be a rare honor if he showed his handsome face at one of her mom's charity events, waving his cheque book around and leaving a nice donation. His generous contributions made Violet consider that maybe he wasn't as much of a jerk as her first notion of him. But, her common sense was on target to eliminate the consideration. To be more specific, it was his father's money he was flashing and with Donald Carlex absent from parties the last couple years, it seemed like Donald was probably the generous one. Ryder was only standing in his place, with some pretty woman on his arm. A woman, who in no way he shared that light of love with. The light that Donald and his late wife had held. Violet remembered seeing Mr. And Mrs. Carlex's love for each other, and then looking at her own parents and wishing they'd shared the same special bond. They hadn't and that was long before Violet realized happily ever after was the delusion of children's dreams.

Violet should have known this face from the strained relationship of her parents. The lack of love was a result of Robert's selfish, money-hungry ways, until his last days, when the cancer took over his body and crushed him down to nothing. Those days had been the only days Violet had seen anything remotely close to compassion, love, or kindness in her father.

Even then, she'd been wary of him.

He wasn't a man to trust. He was a man to fear, to be cautious of and, sure enough, after his passing, it had been brought to their attention just how corrupt Robert had really been. Behind the walls of Robert's old office, located outside of their suites, Eliza had revealed a secret hidden room, where they found thousands of lives that Robert had destroyed, all packaged neatly in manila file folders, like alphabetized summer activity events.

It had been unsettling.

Eliza, being the exact opposite of Robert, was a loving, compassionate and caring person to her deepest soul and was making sure to right all the wrongs Robert had inflicted on families. It would take years. Violet didn't even know where she would begin.

Anya.

Anya, Daddy's girl. She was the closest to their father, as close as one could get to a brick wall without slamming your head off it. But she had left weeks before their dad's death and had returned only for the funeral, then vanished again without a word. That was over a year ago and Violet would bet her disappearance had something to do with Robert. All that aside, Violet wished she knew where Anya was or at the very least that she was alright and safe. If there was a file, wouldn't Eliza have brought it to their attention and ensured Anya's safety.

Then it hit Violet, *a private investigator*. They should hire a PI to find Anya.

The thought had never dawned on Violet and it startled her at how much it sounded like something her father would think of. But it was brilliant. She could guarantee her sister's safety and ease the worry she held every day for Anya. Violet planned on running the idea by Marc. With his combined knowledge of his father's background, he would know which private investigator they could pay for and maintain a secrecy about it.

Violet swam to the far side of the pool, hoping each stroke would leave behind her worry and clear her head.

After this cool down, she had a date with the lounger beside the pool, a book and a bottle of wine.

She broke through the surface of the water and the tropical indoor paradise of palm trees and bushes around the pool offered a relaxing atmosphere, but the calm was soon ripped away as she heard her son screaming holy terror from the doorway of their suite.

Violet grabbed the edge of the pool, lifting herself slightly to find her panicked son.

What happened? What could possibly happen in the two minutes she'd had to herself to walk and dive into the pool? Where was Sophia?

Violet went straight into mother mode. Joel was picking them up this morning, any minute. *Was everyone okay or was it simply another sibling argument?* Parker was growing a bad attitude that needed adjusting. For being the younger of the two, he didn't fear Sophia and generally it was her tattling on Parker.

"What's wrong?" she called to him, already climbing out of the pool.

"Dad's running late," Parker said, still yelling. He rolled his eyes and with a sneer added, "As usual. Can you drive us to meet him?"

That was it? Joel was going to be late and they needed a drive? Thank the stars neither of her children were hurt.

"Yes." Violet grabbed her towel from the lounger that had promised her a relaxing afternoon, and started drying her body.

Parker put the phone back to his ear. "Yeah. She said she can drive us," he snarled into the phone and Violet could imagine how well Joel was handling Parker's attitude.

When it came to children, Joel's tolerance wasn't very high...even with his own. He was the man in the restaurant demanding the crying baby be removed. His standpoint hadn't bothered Violet while they were married, since she was the woman who removed her children at signs of misbehaviour and returned once the situation was resolved anyway.

Violet was making her way around the pool. "When?" she asked.

"Now Mom." Her son was additionally pleasant this morning.

She was glad his sandy hair and cute dimples reminded her of what a sweetheart he could be, when he wasn't trying to be a rebelling teenager in a child's body.

"Alright. Where?" she asked.

"Where?" Parker snapped into the phone and she was glad his anger wasn't solely directed at her. Violet was midway to her son when he yelled, unnecessarily like she was supposed to know, "Ryder's house."

Violet froze.

Ryder's house? Ryder's house! What were the odds? Why? Why? Why!

"Okay. Whatever Dad. Bye." Parker looked at Violet. "Now Mom. We have to go now."

Violet hadn't realized her legs had stopped moving. *Ryder? Really?*

"Dad's on his way, so come on. Now."

Yes, Violet come on and pull yourself together. Now.

"Parker there's no need to holler. I'm right here." She grabbed his shoulders, turning him around and ushering him back into the house. "I'm going to change."

"We don't have time."

"I'm sure we have time," she said, squeezing the water out of her hair with the towel. She looked like a wet dog. There was not a chance she would step out in public like this, let alone drive to Ryder's house. Looking like a wet dog. Absolutely not.

"No Mom. Dad said now and he will leave without us," Parker continued. Violet was glad her son's tone was straight forward and solid, because if he whined all his worries to her, the sound would drive her insides mad.

"He won't leave without you," she told him heading toward the hall to her bedroom. She passed Sophia who was sitting on the couch holding her overnight bag on her lap.

"He might," Sophia said.

He might? He might! Joel Bensen!

The only time in Violet's entire life, she wished that she wasn't such a clean freak and that there was a dress tossed over a chair, or a pair of shorts just sitting on the couch. Just enough to cover anything this bathing suit wasn't.

The sad, disappointed looks across her children's little faces was all Violet needed to climb into the car, drenched and wrapped in a damp towel and drive her kids to Ryder's house. *Ryder's house.* She wouldn't even need to get out of the car. Drive in, drop them off and drive out. *Quick and easy.*

Violet had never been past the metal gates of the Carlex's lake house, one of the gorgeous estates alongside Crystal River. She wasn't qualified to know whether the gates were closed on a regular basis and left open for them, or whether they remained open all day. The winding driveway was long, taking them under large old maple trees as the sprawling old white brick home, that had been in his family for generations, revealed itself. It was beautiful.

Joel's car wasn't in sight.

Parker and Sophia jumped out. "Come on Mom." Parker said.

"Your dad's not here yet." There was no way she was climbing out of this vehicle wearing only a bathing suit, with her hair matted flat against her head and her face bare of makeup. Not a chance.

"He might already be at the boat," Parker objected.

"Parker settle down. His car is not here." Violet reached for her cell phone. There were no pockets in her bathing suit, the cup holder came up empty, and she hadn't grabbed her purse. She forgot her cell phone. Violet could have screamed.

"Missy could have dropped him off," Parker was saying, making more excuses for her to climb out of the vehicle. "Come on Mom, please," he added, sounding like the sweet boy she'd raised.

Violet's head dropped to her soaked towel covering her bathing suit. *Two minutes. Two minutes would have been all it took to change.*

It wasn't just a little jaunt around the house. Once they made it around the wide estate, the backyard was a maze of flower gardens between thick green paths of grass leading all the way to the dock on Crystal Lake. The boat didn't come into sight until they rounded the tree's lining the edge of the property. *Boat?* Again, the word didn't describe the machine. *Yacht. Huge yacht was a better definition.*

Reluctantly, thinking up a dozen excuses her children wouldn't listen to, Violet followed Parker and Sophia onto the dock. Ryder immediately caught her attention, like a sparkling jewel in the midst of tarnished metals. He pulled open the glass doors at the front of the boat, and like she was watching a slow motion movie, he emerged, shirtless. Violet's eyes traveled from his hair blowing in the breeze, down his solid torso, shellacked in lotion. Her imagination dipped even further past the board shorts riding low on his waist.

Drool. Delicious. Yummy. The exact thoughts of her dreams all week. came to mind. *Violet!*

No Joel anywhere.

Violet considered abandoning her kids at the edge of the dock and running back to the safety of her vehicle, but they weren't Ryder's responsibility.

With each stride against the wooden dock, taking her closer to Ryder, Violet contemplated how she'd ended up here, wearing only a bathing suit and hiding behind a damp towel and sunglasses. *Parker and Sophia.* Her children got her every time. Their needs had always come before her own.

Hurry the hell up Joel.

Chapter Seven

RYDER SPOTTED MOVEMENT as he opened the doors of the cockpit and stepped onto the bow. Expecting to see Joel and his kids, he was surprised to find Violet following behind an anxious Parker and Sophia. To add to the surprise, a beige towel was wrapped around Violet and what appeared to be a bathing suit peeking out from underneath. Or a bikini...*keep the mind guessing.*

Ryder's grin widened. *What was she doing here? And why was she dressed like she was boarding with the kids?* He liked that idea, momentarily. Then he scolded himself for letting it pass into his head. He didn't need an ice queen aboard his boat. *No thanks.* He didn't have room in his life to deal with the hot and cold temperatures of this woman.

Ryder walked back through the cockpit and to the rear of the boat. He stopped at the stairs to the swimming platform and called out to Parker and Sophia, as they walked down the dock toward him.

"Is my dad here yet?" Parker barked. Literally barked, like a pissed off teenager, instead of the seven year -old he was. Ryder remembered this kid only last year, looking up at him and Joel like they were kings of the water. This year, Parker just snarled and barked out every word.

Ryder shook his head. "Not yet. I thought you two were coming with him."

Parker didn't wait for an invitation and boarded the swimming platform, climbing the left stairs onto the boat and tossing his bag on the floor. "He called and said he was late and told us to meet him here," Parker said.

Ryder hadn't gotten a call. He touched the pocket of his shorts, but his phone wasn't there.

Where's my phone? Did I miss a message?

Parker pulled an iPad out of his bag and walked past Ryder heading for the lounge. Ryder snatched the iPad and was prepared for the glare Parker sent him.

Tough shit kid. You are on a boat, in the sun, find something else to do.

When Ryder was his age, they didn't even have computers yet.

"You know the rules Parker. No electronics on the boat. Go find a life jacket that fits from underneath and bring it up."

Parker grumbled away.

Violet was lagging behind, making her way down the dock toward the rear of the boat. Ryder regretted not staying at the bow and watching her hips and backside sway underneath the towel as she walked.

Ryder took Sophia's bag as she boarded. "Thanks Uncle Ryder," she said, taking it back once she was on board. Sophia had skipped the attitude stage that Parker was going through. Three years older than her brother with only four years until she hit her teens, Sophia smiled with kindness and laughed with the wind.

"No problem. Go below and–"

"Find a life jacket," Sophia finished Ryder's sentence, already on her way, but with her sweet tone and genuine smile, a smile she didn't get from her thin-lipped mother standing at the edge of the dock. She looked up at him through a pair of large round sunglasses that overtook her face. He wished he could see her eyes.

Why? So you can read them?

More like *try* to read them. This woman didn't give anything away she didn't want to. Almost nothing. She hadn't been able to resist the desire that passed through them last week.

"Is Joel here?" she called up to him.

"Not yet."

Her lips thinned again.

He couldn't resist offering. "But there's a life jacket your size, if you're planning on joining us."

Violet's hand tightened around the top of the towel. "I'm not," she said, shifting her weight onto one foot.

Ryder shrugged. "Did you stop and have a swim on your way over?" He loved teasing her, and he loved her reactions even more.

She crinkled her nose before answering. "Joel rushed us over," she explained.

Joel. Oh yeah.

Ryder had to locate his cell phone. "Do you want to come up and wait?"

Violet shook her head. "No. I'm fine waiting right here."

She was a stubborn woman.

"Okay." Ryder left her. Even after she'd walked away from him at the resort, he didn't want to walk away from her now. *But, where the hell was Joel?*

Below deck, Ryder found Parker and Sophia wearing their life jackets and helping themselves to a bag of chips he'd left out.

Ryder spotted his cell phone on the counter and swiped it. Four missed text messages and three missed calls...all from Joel.

As he scanned the, *I'm late* texts, Parker grumbled, "No electronics."

Ryder looked up. "Where's your dad?" he asked.

Parker shrugged.

"Alight then." Ryder turned and listened to the missed calls. The first one Joel was running late and would be there soon. The second one was an, *I'm not going to make it.*

Damn Joel.

With clenched jaws and kids sitting behind him, Ryder listened to Joel explain he wasn't in the mood to put up with his son's attitude today. Then instead of calling his children or even Violet for that matter, that selfish son of a bitch asked Ryder to tell them he couldn't make it and make something up. *Chicken shit little bastard.* It was such a Joel move to place his responsibility on someone else.

Ryder was furious. There was a line and Joel seemed to always push the limit with him and this time he crossed that limit. There were other pressing issues in Ryder's life that he could attend to instead of crushing this family's hearts. It wasn't Ryder's family and if it was, he sure as hell wouldn't be canceling on them. Ryder learned the bond of a family was important, a top priority

Ryder dropped his cell phone back on the counter, not noticing Parker was watching him until he glanced over his shoulder. "Well? Where is he?" Parker asked.

Ryder was going to be having a long talk with Joel tomorrow.

"He's not going to make it," Ryder said.

"Why not?"

Yeah? Why not Joel? Ryder's jaw clenched as he answered, even though he tried not to let it show. "He had some car trouble." *Liar. You are a liar. Why with Joel are you always a liar?* It was time to put Ryder's foot down.

It was funny, in every other aspect of Ryder's life, his feet were planted solidly on the ground. His respect and duty for his family had compelled Ryder to step-up and take control over his dad's business when Donald was diagnosed with his sickness. Ryder could sit in front of any problem and study it until he found a solution that benefited his employees and customers. But, one phone call with Joel and he was lying to a child's face. Not just any child's face, but the closest thing Ryder had to a nephew. Ryder didn't like it, but he wasn't going to be the one to tell Parker the truth.

Parker tossed the bag of chips on the table, and a disappointed huff came from Sophia. Parker rose to his feet, while unbuckling the life jacket and tugging it off. "Big surprise," he muttered and took the steps two at a time back up onto deck.

It broke Ryder's heart. How did Joel not understand the disappointment that Ryder saw so clearly? Parker wanted to go out with his dad. By missing events and breaking dates, Joel was giving Parker the ammo for his attitude. Donald had never been a man to break a date with his son on purpose, but when work called, he had to leave. Ryder could relate to how Parker was feeling, but at the same time, Donald had never shied away from expressing his feelings, including his love for Ryder.

"Awe man," Sophia said unzipping her life jacket.

Ryder held his hand up to Sophia, on his way to the bottom of the stairs. "Hold that thought Sophia," he said.

Ryder followed Parker's two feet up the stairs, crossing the deck with his long legs and making it to the ladder Parker was heading towards before he did. Ryder grabbed both sides blocking the boy from going down.

Parker made a fussing noise, but didn't ask him to move. When Ryder glanced over his shoulder Parker was sending him a, *what are you doing* glare, with his hands crossed tightly in front of him and lips pinched tightly together. He looked like he might cry.

Damn Joel.

Ryder looked from Parker and found Violet in the identical stance with an equal fine-tuned face, lacking the tears.

Her bare lips tweaked tight together and the natural pucker gave him the urge to climb down the ladder and kiss them. Her legs were parted shoulder-length apart with the towel tied low around her waist, and he could see now a crochet bathing suit covered her body. That might have disappointed his desire to see her naked skin, if the gaps weren't playing peek-a-boo with his senses.

"He cancelled, didn't he?" she asked, not sounding surprised. Ryder got the feeling this was a regular occurrence. He didn't even have a chance to answer and Violet started calling out orders. "Parker, go get your sister. Make sure you two have everything you brought." She glanced around Ryder to find her son. "And remember to say thank you to Ryder for offering."

"Thanks, Ryder," he grumbled so miserable.

"Thanks buddy," Violet said, softening her tone.

She slid her sunglasses up her forehead and sent Parker a smile. It was beautiful and tender, lighting up her eyes and highlighting her cheek bones.

Parker mumbled an, *okay* before going back down below. Did that boy know how hard it was to get a sincere smile from his mother? It was like Ryder had just witnessed a miracle.

"I will take them fishing," Ryder said.

Violet's smile fell, leaving her lips partially open and her nose crinkled like she'd misunderstood. Then she snapped her lips shut and relaxed her face. Back to masked Violet.

"I won't inconvenience you," she said, but he knew her decision had nothing to do with inconveniencing him.

With his hands planted on each side of the ladder, Ryder jumped over the top and climbed down. He stepped off the swimming platform and onto the dock, in front of Violet. He was glad to be wearing his shades, because his eyes couldn't resist lingering on her glowing face and the all natural allure without makeup.

"It's not an inconvenience. I have the fishing gear on the boat. The fridge packed for lunch and supper, plus Joel promised them a night of eating under the stars."

"That wouldn't be until after nine," she pointed out, looking mortified at the hour.

Ryder shrugged.

"I can't leave my children with you for almost..." She paused to do the quick math. "...twelve hours." At the beginning of her sentence, she looked horrified and he wasn't sure if it was that she feared her kids spending the day with him or that she feared him spending the day with her kids. At the end of her sentence, her lips curved up into a grin that lit her eyes. "They would slaughter you."

Ryder laughed and Violet joined him.

Her laughter was unexpectedly soft, but full and wrapped around them, folding them into their own world. He'd thought her laugh would be reserved and snobbish, just like he was always told she was. There it was again, Ryder thinking there was more to Violet than he knew, then she let people know and that she was letting only him know. *Confusing.*

When they finished he said, "Come with us."

Violet sobered quickly, her smile dropping to her well adapted thin line, her eyes narrowing. She didn't like the idea. *Why would she?* She didn't like him. He wasn't even sure he liked her?

Then why hadn't he stopped thinking about her all week? And why was the idea of going boating with Violet more appealing than with Joel?

Violet would need more convincing though. "We don't have to do a whole day. We can go fishing, eat lunch and head back, if that suits you better. At least then Sophia and Parker's day isn't ruined."

"Okay," she said right away. Too quickly and Ryder thought for a second maybe he had heard her wrong. Or quite possibly made up the answer he wanted to hear in his head.

Okay? Okay! The waves of stimulating shocks her answer sent through him was like the first fish catch of the year.

"Okay." He moved aside to let her climb aboard first. She did so with a smile. *A smile!*

This turn of events almost had Ryder texting Joel to say *thank you.* Almost. Joel was still acting like a jackass with his kids who adored him.

Ryder shook those thoughts out of his head, while unknotting the ropes. This was going to be a good day.

Chapter Eight

VIOLET WATCHED HER son dig his fingers into the bucketful of dirt to fetch a live, wiggly worm out. He held it out toward her.

What did he want her to do with it?

There were a lot of things Violet was capable of, but piercing an innocent, squirmy worm onto a hook, just wasn't one of them.

She waved her hand in front of her son, motioning for him to take the worm away. "I'm going to pass on baiting with a worm," she told him.

Parker dropped his hand to his side. "Mom, you can't *pass*. You have to bait your hook. We are *fishing*." He said it like she wasn't well aware of exactly what the four of them were doing on this yacht.

Parker was baiting his hook and trying to convince her to do the same. Sophia was choosing the fishing spot, using the fish finder at the wheel, with Ryder, who was steering the boat...without a shirt on...or a life jacket. His chest was still exposed and his hard, flexing muscles glistened under the sun like he had wiped himself down with tropical oil...and he smelled delicious. When Ryder passed Violet, the smell of a summer day lazing around at the beach lingered, as though he'd already spent the day sitting in the sand, splashing in the water and baking under the sun, meanwhile they'd only been on the boat for no longer than a half hour. A long, torturous, slow half hour that Violet wished would quicken and end. Violet wished her fingers had rubbed Ryder's body with the oil.

Meow.

Violet kept her eyes hidden behind her dark sunglasses, because it was those thoughts that were going to get her in trouble. Especially when she was stealing glances at Ryder or staring. She was definitely staring.

"Here. Stop. This is the perfect location," Sophia squealed and turned to face Violet and her brother. "Parker, check this out. There's like a hundred fish right under us."

As Ryder was idling the boat to stop, Violet sat back enjoying the view. His long, lean arms were in focused action, flexing under each movement. One hand turned the wheel, while the other pulled levers and hit buttons. This man knew his way around buttons.

He knows his way around my buttons.

Violet flushed. She was sure of it. Her face was as hot as the area between her thighs.

"Let me see." Parker dropped the worm back in the styrofoam tub before darting away. Violet uncrossed her legs, and leaned forward, busying herself, snapping the lid back on the container and pushing away the innocent worms that were destined to doom this afternoon.

Her eyes fell on Ryder as he crossed the deck to drop the anchor. Bare-chested. Perfect tan line. Perfect muscles. Perfect playboy. *Perfect playboy. Remember that the next time you heat up.*

Violet tore her eyes away from Ryder's body and back to her children. Parker and Sophia were all smiles, pointing at the screen, excited to drop their lines. They were her everything and she loved watching her son's miserable tense body finally diminishing into an excitement over the cluster of neon fish on the screen.

"This is awesome," Parker said.

His enthusiasm delighted Violet and in that moment she knew why she'd agreed to Ryder's offer. The answer shot out of her mouth so quickly, without a second thought, she wondered if her decision was because she'd had Ryder on the brain all week. Her intelligence had a temporary *mush moment,* letting her emotions override her thoughts, her better judgement...and that was why she thought she'd said yes. *Her emotions and her lust.* In hindsight, now watching her son act like a kid, eliminating the growling bear she was growing accustomed to, Violet knew her quick, yes had been to avoid her son's disappointment. Parker had been keen on this trip.

Joel might have shared custody of their kids, at her insistence, but he didn't go out of his way to take them often, and rarely planned events. Violet loved her children. Although she and Joel had their differences, and his ulterior motive stung, Sophia and Parker were his children too, and they needed their dad.

Violet watched as Ryder was walking on the back swim platform. The sun radiated off his gold aviators, just as it did his perfect tan....*were these same thoughts going to pop in her head every single time she looked at him? They were getting old.*

While Violet was scolding herself, Ryder hopped over the stairs and walked across the deck, lowering his glasses and sending her a wink as her eyes followed. *No self control...for either of them.*

Violet's breath caught in her chest as he slid the sunglasses back up his straight, narrow nose and continued past her.

Busted anyway, Violet proceeded to watch him, like every other Ryder-crazed woman did. He was probably used to it. Accustomed to the winking, and to using his charm and good looks to win women over, even the strong ones.

Violet was strong, but around Ryder, he stole her strength and replaced it with raw desire.

Raw desire? Raw desire!

But that wasn't her only weakness when Ryder was present. She had thought evading him would eliminate the growing curiosity of figuring out who he really was. He was different in so many ways, but only one truly stuck out: the way he looked at her. Violet couldn't decipher what the glimpses he stole were him trying to discover who she was, who she *really* was, or had he mastered the art of making a woman feel special.

Special? Was that how she felt? No. Special was what everyone, excluding her family, treated her like. Real was how Ryder treated her and real was new and intriguing.

Ryder was gathering the fishing poles, in a manner that told Violet he did this all the time.

When Violet's kids, adorned in their life jackets, jumped into her view, excitedly grabbing their poles from Ryder, they reminded Violet that it didn't matter what was behind Ryder's facade because she was a mother.

A mother.

She couldn't go around trying to decipher the meaning behind a man's *look.* What if all he wanted was a fling? What if he wanted more? But how did a man like Ryder want more? And with Violet? It was very unlikely.

The stark reality was, Violet was not young and carefree like Izzy. Violet was a mother of two with responsibilities. There was no way Ryder Carlex would want to get involved with a mother. She was way out of Ryder's league.

Ryder's league? Ryder's league! Maybe he's out of my league.

Either way, Violet wished her *motherly* body was more covered up. The life jacket buckled around her upper torso gave minor coverage, but a nice long dress would be more suitable and comfortable. Violet wasn't embarrassed by her body. In fact, after two children she prided herself on how good her body had bounced back thanks to a healthy diet and hitting the resort gym regularly. However, she wasn't in her early twenties, like the women Joel told her Ryder took on boat trips.

Joel.

That selfish man was the reason Violet was on this boat in the first place, longing for a dress at the same time longing for Ryder's hands to remove every last inch of her bathing suit. Those two thoughts were forcefully contradicting. She hadn't remembered a time in her life when her thoughts were crashing as loudly as the waves hitting the side of the boat.

Parker sent Violet a straight stare as he pushed the closed styrofoam container toward her. "Come on Mom. Bait your hook. Dad always makes us do it ourselves and we are only kids."

Kids are more adventurous. Kids take more risks. Kids *are* little worms that need guidance to keep away from getting snagged on a hook. Violet felt snagged on Ryder's hook.

Parker turned with that and walked through the cockpit to join his sister at the stern of the boat. Violet wasn't an overprotective mom, but she felt more secure with each of her children wearing a life jacket and standing on the other side of the bow rail to fish. The sharp little hooks on the end of their line had Violet holding her breath in anticipation of their casting the line. They both cautiously looked behind them, as they balanced their poles, before whipping the line through the air and letting it land in the water.

Violet wasn't doing it. She knew that sounded childish, but she absolutely wasn't sending an innocent fish flying through the air to its death.

She should have expected Joel to cancel and brought a book with her. Or her phone...anything to keep her mind occupied with something besides Ryder.

Violet lost sight of him now, watching her kids. That was good. Now she could stop following him around and he would stop following her around. Watching each other. Stealing glances. Winking and flushing.

Oh wow...they were acting like horny teenagers.

Violet hadn't been a horny teenager. While attending a private school, then University, she'd been more concerned with her grades then boys. She also felt she'd sometimes missed out on certain aspects of public school life, which had been her reason for enrolling her kids in Willow Valley's public school, against Robert's wishes. But, if this feeling was what she'd been missing in school, maybe she better switch Sophia into private ASAP. It felt like dangerously, naughty fun that Violet could easily be swept into. And Violet Caliendo wasn't *easily* swept into anything.

A can of corn popped into Violet's vision, disrupting the image of Ryder playing in the background.

Violet jumped.

Ryder chuckled. He walked around her, the low waistline of his shorts hugging his slim hips, right at Violet's eyes level.

Seriously? Seriously! Yes, thank you.

He sat beside her. With a can opener, he twisted the lid off the can of corn and then passed her the full tin.

What did he want her to do with this? Cook it? Eat it?

Violet held the can, and sent him a questioning look.

His smile was toe melting and when he slid the sunglasses onto the top of his head, his bright blue eyes looked amused. "It's to bait your hook," he explained.

"Corn?"

"Definitely." He reached to the ground, stretching his body and Violet bit her lower lip.

Why did he have to go stretch and reach and look so hot?

He picked up a fishing pole from the floor, running his hand down the invisible fishing line and stopping at the hook. She remembered the way his hands slid up her thighs and–

Ryder held the hook out to her.

Right, fishing. Bait the hook...with corn. Focus on fishing. Fishing, fishing, fishing...

Violet dipped her fingers into the corn and took out a few kernels. This she could handle, but she was still unsure whether he was pulling her leg or not. She'd never heard of fishing with corn. She wasn't an avid fisherman.

When Violet grasped the hook, planning on taking it from Ryder's hand, he didn't move. He didn't jerk away from her touch, like she wanted to from his sizzling skin. He didn't even flinch.

Violet's entire insides, on the other hand, were flinching and jerking like a dead fish. Ryder held the hook in position while she poked a few kernels on.

"Does this really work?" she asked.

Ryder nodded. "My mom was squirmy like you about fishing with worms. She absolutely refused to hurt a worm. Even though she cooked the fish we caught." Ryder chuckled. "Explain that one. Anyway, my dad's fishing gear *always* included a can of corn for her."

Violet watched a genuine smile form on Ryder's lips while he spoke of his parents. His mother, Kathleen, had passed away years ago. The Carlex's were not locals in Willow Valley. They were among the many summer vacationers. Mrs. Carlex had attended several of the exquisite, over-the-top galas Eliza hosted and that Violet and Emma had planned. The more elaborate the decor, the more enticed the guests were to open their chequebooks and donate for the fun night prepared for them. Like the Fright Fest.

Violet hadn't noticed Ryder's tense shoulders all day, but the more he talked, the thick, hard hills began to relax...*he* began to relax. This was a new side to Ryder, a softer side with traces of affection, real affection. It was something Violet had never witnessed from him.

As he continued to talk, Ryder took the hook from Violet, loading it with corn. "My dad didn't raise the faint of heart. I fish with worms." He shrugged. "I guess I just like to bring a can of corn on board to remind me of my mom."

Violet leaned back against the cushion, enjoying Ryder's stories and the way he changed as he told them.

"When I was young, she never missed a fishing trip with just me and my dad. You remember my mom, she was always dressed over the top, her clothes and her make-up."

Yes, Mrs. Carlex wore fancy, glittering outfits and more makeup then all Violet's sisters combined. But her filled-in eyebrows, red lipstick and waves of black pinned up hair gave her a fifties look, like a sophisticated pin-up girl.

"But when she boarded the boat, all that was stripped away. Those trips were my favorite. When it was just the three of us and my dad didn't bring his work on board and we just fished and laughed."

Ryder was completely lost in his thoughts, and his smile told Violet he was reliving the memories he was sharing in deeper depth.

"I guess having a can of corn is like she's here with me," Ryder added and if Violet hadn't already contemplated there was more to Ryder than she knew, that comment would have easily altered her mind. Now, it convinced her there was more than he let people see and he'd let her in.

Ryder looked at Violet abruptly. As he took her in, she watched the happiness erase and darkness shadow his eyes. His face tightened, like he forgot who he was talking to. *Violet Caliendo. Joel's ex-wife.*

Ryder suddenly shut down from Violet, the way she recognized and had mastered herself. To be honest, it didn't feel nice to be on the other side of this door.

"Anyway, here you go," he finished up and handed her the pole.

When she took it, he made sure their hands did not touch, did not graze and he did not send her a wink, smile or even the slightest grin. His attention had turned back solely to digging a worm out for his own bait.

Violet stood up with her pole, not exactly sure what she was supposed to do with it.

How hard was it to throw the line in the water? Her children could do it...but her children went fishing more than she did.

Violet didn't like the rising wrench in her gut that Ryder didn't want to talk to her. Was he embarrassed? Or was it because of who she was?

"Ryder?" she said, standing in front of him and looking down at his hunched over, tensed shoulders.

Ryder looked up and their eyes locked...for a long moment. The same way they locked in the lobby bathroom at the resort. The same way they locked on the dock only a short hour earlier. It was a simple lock-down of everything in their region. They just stared at each other.

Why? Why did this keep happening to them? Why was she attracted to him? Why was he attracted to her?

It had to be the sex...the sex was good...real good.

But Violet knew differently.

This stare was deeper, she could feel it. The attraction was there and the lust was like lava bubbling into the surface of a volcano between them, but at the very moment, it felt like each of them was ineffectively attempting to figure out the other.

What do you want from me? What do I want from you? Was there really anything possible between them?

Violet had to break the contact. She dropped her eyes to the floor and took a deep breath. Yes, she took a deep breath in front of Ryder. She had to get her boundaries collected. Everything about them screamed no. She was a mother, he was a traveler. She had sworn off falling in love and him...he probably didn't even know what love was. *And you do?*

Violet forced herself to look back at Ryder and found his eyes hadn't strayed like hers. He was, no doubt, trying to determine why hers had moved in the first place. *Because you drive me hot and wild and thinking about love. Love? Love!*

Violet needed distance. *Now.*

"It is very sweet of you Ryder, to bring along a reminder of your mom," she said. "Even if it seems silly, like a can of corn. It shows how much she meant to you. The way you talk about her is beautiful."

Violet smiled.

She wanted to reach out and touch his hand, but thought better of it.

Would he touch her back? Would he rise to his feet and kiss her? Did men actually do things like that? Just rise to their feet and kiss someone because of a look passing between them?

It sounded like horny teenagers again. She wanted him to act like a horny teenager, but knew she couldn't.

Violet walked to her children, ruffling Parker's hair and kissing the top of Sophia's head. They smelled like coconut from a nice coating of the all-natural sun block she'd purchased at the Old Town Soap Store that Kate's sisters had opened last year.

"How are you two doing?" Violet asked.

"Nothing yet," Parker said and his tone lacked disappointment. Then he added. "But with fishing you need patience. You have to wait for the fish to bite. It could take hours, or it could take only minutes. Sometimes when we fish, we don't catch any fish."

Violet held her lure out between her kids. "I have corn," she said, watching both heads turn, laugh and tease their mom. She loved these two.

Violet being the amateur fisherman she was, moved to the rear of the boat.

She passed Ryder, but didn't look at him. If she had a book, she'd sprawl out across one of the loungers and escape to a world written without Ryder Carlex. Sprawling across the lounger and Ryder Carlex in the same thought caused her neck to break out in a sweat.

Violet climbed on the swim platform and balanced the pole behind her. She glanced over her shoulder to make sure the hook wasn't near anything, than aimed in the water, a guideline she was sure she wouldn't get anywhere close, and swung the pole above her head...just like she'd watched Parker and Sophia do.

The baited hook dangled in the air directly in front of her, nowhere near the water.

What had she done wrong?

She did it again and ended up with the same result.

Well, this was ridiculous.

Violet had a broken pole. Sunbathing and reading were looking better by the second. Ryder had given her a broken pole and left her only two options. She could stand here and stare out at the water until lunch or she was going to have to face Ryder again.

Violet turned.

She caught Ryder leaning against the side of the boat behind her. His legs were crossed at his ankles and his arms crossed covering his chest...good because that gave her eyes a reason to find his.

Ryder was smirking at her, obviously entertained by her attempt to fish with a broken pole, that *he'd* given her. Had he known the pole was broken? The grin on his face sure said he did.

Violet mustered up the words to talk to him. "I have a broken pole," she stated and his widened smirk made her wonder exactly what he knew that she didn't.

Chapter Nine

RYDER WAS GOING to bust a gut laughing. He couldn't help it. Watching Violet attempt to cast her line, without pressing the release button, was priceless. *Twice.* Not once, but *twice* and the confusion that danced across her face was precious.

These were the moments in life that his mother had always talked about. The moments when work escaped your thoughts and worry was temporarily pushed away, leaving you with only the now. And right now...was perfect.

Not only was Violet sensitive about harming worms, like his mother, but she fished as badly as his mother too.

When Violet's blazers and makeup, another quality she shared with his mother, were stripped away, there was the foundation of the real Violet. And apparently the real Violet didn't know how to fish. His guess was she'd never done it a day in her life.

Laughter was on the tip of Ryder's tongue. He grasped at every ounce of strength not to laugh, afraid it would send that confused and accusing look across her face into a fit of anger.

"Are you going to get me another pole or stare at me all afternoon with that dim-witted look across your face?"

Her question was an insult, but damned if he found it as attractive as the rest of her. Ryder had to admit, he'd never had a bossy girlfriend before.

Girlfriend? Girlfriend!

Violet was not his girlfriend. Violet wasn't even girlfriend material. And, furthermore, Ryder was not looking for a girlfriend. His life was too full now that his mother was gone, his dad's sanity was gone, and he was reconstructing the Carlex chain of stores. That left no room for a girlfriend. There was no room left in his broken heart for a girlfriend.

Ryder pushed up to his feet, but didn't walk to her. "Am I getting this straight?" he asked, unable to keep from teasing her.

Teasing her was better than the alternative...kissing her, touching her, staring at her like a fool looking for love. He was not looking for love.

"*Thee* Violet Caliendo, has never been fishing?" It was beyond obvious.

Violet didn't say anything. She simply stared.

Stared!

He was finished staring with Violet.

"And now, Violet Caliendo is speechless," he teased further. Teasing was good.

"I am not speechless," she said right away. "I am trying to figure you out."

He wasn't expecting that type of honesty in her. And she wasn't the only one. He was trying his damndest to figure her out too and at the same time himself, while everything else was telling him not to.

"And what is with this *Violet Caliendo*? And the tone when you say my name?" she asked.

It was because her actions, her words, everything about her continued to surprise him...and he was enjoying it.

"It's okay to be speechless," he said instead of saying the truth.

"I didn't say it wasn't okay to be speechless."

Ryder stepped onto the swim platform and took the fishing pole from her. The fishing pole that was in perfect working condition, but this woman had no idea how to use it.

"Don't get your panties in a twist," he told her, leaning the pole against the back of the boat.

"Who says that? *Don't get your panties in a twist?*" She lowered her voice to mimic him and it took everything not to laugh.

"Who doesn't know how to use a fishing pole?" he asked instead.

He unsnapped her life jacket.

"What are you doing?" she demanded, her hands grabbing each edge of her lifejacket and landing directly on top of his.

He was planning on teaching her how to cast a line...without her life jacket.

"What are you doing?" she repeated.

Wasn't it obvious? "Taking off your lifesaver."

"Why? Are you planning on pushing me overboard?" He liked this snappy temper of hers he was bringing out.

The thought of pushing her in the water made him grin. "Do you really think I would?" The idea was playing on his mind.

"No," she said, but it lacked conviction.

There was no way Ryder would ever push Violet Caliendo into the water not wearing a life jacket. He didn't even know if she could swim. But he liked the idea.

Ryder snapped her buckle back together.

Violet's eyes fell down to where her hands still covered his. Her eyebrows drew together and he took the distraction as an opportunity to slip his hand away and remove her sunglasses.

"Hey!" she cried reaching for them, but he put them on the top of his head and she didn't dare reach for them.

Violet glared at him. "What are you doing?" She was an attentive person, and the fact that she suspected he was going to push her off the swim platform and into the water...which was almost accurate...was written across her face...with a pinch of amusement. *Amusement.* It suited her.

"Do you know how to swim?" he asked, snapping the next buckle together.

The fingers of one of her hands that remained on his, tightened. The richest, bluest, fullest eyes stared back at him. "Do *you* know how to swim?" she retorted.

Of course Ryder knew how to swim. His family were avid boaters.

In one quick motion, Ryder pulled her glasses off his head, and his from his eyes, tossing them onto the towel behind them, and then his arms wrapped around Violet and her bulky lifejacket.

Violet surprised him with a laugh.

He lifted her up, for a split second wishing he did know whether she could swim or not, preferring her body pressed against his, and jumped in the water. She screamed his name, following them as they were engulfed by the cool water. He let her go underwater, but her arms wrapped around his neck, they swam to the surface together.

Violet's laughter bounced off the water as they broke the surface and she didn't let go. His arm automatically went around her, under the life jacket, rubbing against the top of her derriere, as they bobbed.

"I can't believe you actually did that," she laughed.

Ryder wouldn't admit it, but he was surprised he'd done it too. The impulsiveness and the fun reminded him of what he was like before his family started to deplete.

When his mother had died, Ryder and Donald had each other, but when Donald began to forget things, Ryder was left alone. He hadn't found anything or anyone worth being impulsive or fun with...until now.

"You don't even have a life jacket on," Violet said. "You could drown."

"That's why I'm holding onto you. I trust you." Ryder meant for it to come out in a teasing tone, however it came out deep, low and in an unmistakable bedroom voice that Violet caught. Her laughter faltered, dragging her smile down, but the glimmer of temptation that washed over her face was superior.

"Ryder..." The whisper of his name was pleading him not to go down this road, but the passion in her eyes was begging him to go for it.

Sophia and Parker's shouts came rushing to the rear of the boat and Violet pushed off Ryder.

"What happened?" Sophia asked.

"Was it a big fish?" Parker inquired, searching the water.

Droplets of water were running down Violet's face. "We fell in," she lied.

We fell in. Ryder laughed before splashing Violet. He swam to the platform, climbing aboard. "We didn't fall in," he corrected, scooping Parker up first. "I threw your mom in."

Parker laughed hysterically as Ryder lifted him high in the air. "Are you ready?" he asked, but it was more a warning.

"Yes!" Parker exclaimed, and Ryder left him barely enough time to get the word out, before Ryder tossed him overboard. Parker's laughter overtook him before he hit the water.

Out of the corner of his eye, Ryder caught Sophia taking off and reached his hand out, lightly grasping her arm. She turned, laughing and tugging her arm free. "Forget it!" she laughed and ran to the edge of platform. She jumped into the water, wrapping her arms around her legs, causing a cannon ball splash.

Once she surfaced, Ryder followed. His splash was much larger and when he emerged, all three of the Caliendos were splashing him.

"Tag team!" Ryder pleaded.

He sliced the water with his hands spraying them all and enjoying their laughter, objections and threats to get him back.

He soon found himself laughing so hard his stomach hurt. A laugh he'd thought was lost with his parents and the losses in his life. Right now, he wasn't living in the regret, sadness, the feelings that were a constant part of his life. Twice in one week, when he hadn't been ready, he found the feelings removed from him leaving room for happiness to develop. And both times it was in the presence of Violet Caliendo.

If anything, he should thank this woman for drawing him out of the shell he'd been living in the last two years and for reminding him how wonderful life felt when it was lived.

***

VIOLET ABANDONED THE soaking wet lifejacket on the bow of the boat, to dry out, after their refreshing dip in the lake.

It was like the water had washed away all her earlier feelings...well, the pessimistic, nervous, and anxious ones anyway. After splashing around in the water with Ryder and her kids, Violet's other feelings for Ryder amplified.

Amplified? That couldn't be good. Could it? It felt good.

Parker and Sophia also shed their lifejackets, promising to stay on deck, and avoid the swim board or the bow. Alternatively, they both decided there was a bag of chips, right before lunch, that were calling their names and they settled under deck.

Violet had the growing suspicion they'd settled with their iPad's. They were too quiet, being too good and that typically meant their heads were tucked behind an electronic device. Normally, she would yank the iPads out of their hands in order for them to appreciate the day, and their surroundings...however, Ryder offered to show her how to fish. She didn't want to be rude and pass that up.

Ryder stood less than half a foot away from her, on the bow of the boat.

"Alright, so there is a magic button on this reel," he explained, as if she was going to be able to concentrate on anything else besides their closeness.

Why were they always so close to each other?

She could literally lean her bare arm across to feel the muscle wall of this man.

And why did she find her face couldn't help but smile? The entire time. At Ryder.

The actions of an adolescent...or a happy person.

Ryder clicked the button back and forth, demonstrating for Violet, in a smart-ass way, like she was supposed to have known that little secret.

She loved the smirk he sent her.

Alright, so, apparently she didn't have a broken fishing pole, she just didn't know how to use it. Beginner's downfall.

"You're sure I'm safe here...with you?" she teased.

Teased. Teased!

Violet could have laughed out loud at finding herself teasing with Ryder Carlex. It must be the effect of heat stroke.

"Maybe I should strap into my lifejacket."

Ryder leaned closer. *Closer. Closer!*

Her teasing caught in her chest, as the delicious smell of him circled around her like a twister.

"I promise not to throw you in," he said in a low whisper. "Besides loving the opportunity to look at you without a lifejacket on..."

Violet swallowed hard.

He was a constant charmer, hitting on her, teasing her, making her insides feel alive like never before. "...besides I like your kids too much to leave them motherless." He chuckled. "Have you met Missy? She's sweet, but she thinks deep fried pickles are eating vegetables."

Was that his indirect way of giving her a compliment that wasn't sexual?

Violet couldn't help but smile. "I like deep fried pickles."

Ryder made a face of dislike.

"Have you tried them?" she asked.

He shook his head.

"Do you like pickles?"

"I do and I can't see why you have to go and ruin a good thing."

Violet laughed. "You can't judge them until you've tried them and tasted the juicy battered coating and thick pickle inside."

"That's called grease."

Violet licked her lips. "It's called deliciousness that you are missing out on. The first one I tried was when I was pregnant with Sophia. One of the food huts at the beach was advertising them and that was the beginning of my love for deep fried pickles. I was hooked."

"I guess, I will have to try them...someday...maybe." He looked skeptical.

"I order them from The Bamboo Lounge, one of the restaurants at the resort," she explained. "On the rare occasion, when the kids aren't feeling like eating their veggies," she added, surprised to find how easy it was to joke with Ryder.

"Is that an offer?" *Yes, it is.* "I'm sure Missy cannot cook like *Violet Caliendo*." The way Ryder said it again, irked her. It was judgement. He had been evaluating her from the moment she stepped on the boat, but until he said her name like that, she didn't sense it. It was quite the opposite.

Her joking and teasing was spurred from the comforting way she felt around him, as though he wasn't analyzing her. But truthfully, he was.

"Why do you do that?" she asked. "Say my full name, as if you think I'm so perfect that I'm faultless. I am human you know. So I don't know how to fish, but can cook a killer lasagna. That's just who I am."

There was the heat stroke again, affecting her own good judgement and stealing away the filter she'd been missing all morning.

Violet didn't have to ask him why, she fully grasped he thought she was a stuck-up snob. And what was wrong with him thinking that? Everyone thought that about her...even her family. Why did she feel the need to prove to Ryder that she wasn't?

Ryder looked up at her again, in that way he was so good at...and again it bounced attraction between them. *Attraction? Attraction!* But, tangled in there was his sincerity.

"You're right. That does sound condescending. I apologize," he unexpectedly agreed. But wasn't that what she was fishing for? "I guess you're just surprising me today, is all."

"Because you think I'm stuck up."

Violet stop talking. What is happening with my mouth? I feel like I'm watching Izzy. That girl has no control over her mouth whatsoever.

"Yes."

Her eyes narrowed at his honesty.

"And you assumed I would have sex with you in the bathroom." He said it with the same accusing tone she'd used to him.

"You *did* have sex with me in the bathroom," she pointed out.

"So you're positive everything you've always thought about me is accurate?" he asked.

No, I've been dying to have this conversation so you can prove me wrong. So I can find out if you do this with all the women, or you want me, or what the hell all the touching, staring and confusion is about.

"I haven't been thinking about you at all." This time she could have slapped herself for avoiding the truth. He was so straightforward with her, it was almost terrifying.

"You're a liar." Terrifying and fresh. No one talked to her with such honesty. "You've been thinking about kissing me since you've boarded this boat."

Oh my goodness, I have. How would he know that? Was he thinking about kissing her?

That moment while they were bobbing in the water, his arms around her lower back and hers wrapped around his neck the thought had crossed her mind...but Parker and Sophia had interrupted. Thankfully.

Did he want to kiss her?

Violet rolled her eyes, mostly to break the vision between them. "Get over yourself," she said.

"And you've been thinking about touching my abs again."

Every time her eyes fell on his bare torso.

"Here. I don't mind." He grabbed her hand and placed her palm on his chest.

It felt so good.

Violet yanked her hand away. "Are you delusional?"

He laughed. "Alright. I will teach you how to fish."

"Do you do this with all the women?" There it was, out in the open, the question she was dying to know the answer.

He grinned more. "So you *do* think I sleep with a lot of women." It wasn't a question.

"Everyone thinks you sleep with a lot of women."

"That's not what I said."

Why had she asked in the first place? She was ready to be done with this conversation. It was going nowhere, and making her feel stupid, when he asked, "Do *you* think I do?"

"I can't answer that, I don't even know you."

Except that you tried to get up my sister's skirt at my wedding.

He changed the smirk, smart-ass way he was talking. "I want you to know me better. I want to know you better." *I want to know you better.* "I don't do this with all the women."

"So with some?"

"You don't trust me."

"I don't trust anyone. Don't take it personally."

He eyed her quietly, assessing her, judging her, driving her senses wild with curiosity at his conclusion.

"You don't like me." It wasn't a question, nor was it a solid statement. Rather, he said it like the revelation amused him.

When did he think she did like him?

Violet couldn't help but ask, "Why are you making that sound like an appealing aspect?"

"Because everyone likes me."

All the women certainly liked him. "Maybe that's your problem." He was so conceited. What had she been thinking? That she was special to Ryder? That he actually liked *her*, saw *her*? What could the outcome of today possibly be? And why was the reality that *nothing* was the answer saddening?

"My charm?" he asked.

"Your arrogance."

Ryder laughed again. "And no one talks to me like you do."

"Yes, I'm just full of surprises." Violet turned to walk away. Charming, teasing, and joking...it was all flirting. They'd been flirting with each other all morning and for what?

"Hey." Ryder touched her gently. His fingers circled her wrist, but not tight enough to hold her. If she'd wanted to walk away, she could have.

Her feet stopped.

Violet stared past the bow of the boat, across the endless sparkling lake, knowing their flirting could never amount to anything more than the small waves she saw.

"That wasn't an insult." The genuineness of his voice inked a path across her barriers. "Please, don't go. The truth is I haven't laughed with a woman in over two years. And when I did, it has never felt the way it does when I laugh with you."

Walk away. It was the smart thing to do.

Violet turned, finding the arrogance and charm splashed away from his serious face and she met the reflections of his honesty.

If she stayed what did it mean?

But she couldn't walk away.

"If you do a good job at teaching me how to fish, I might invite you over and order in some deep fried pickles."

***

UNWRAPPING THE PLASTIC from around the egg salad sandwiches Ryder had prepared earlier that morning, he cut them in four and laid them on the platter around the vegetables he'd pre-cut at home. When he was finished, the whole platter looked exactly like the ones his mother would prepare.

He missed his mother.

Kathleen had passed away in her sleep only five years earlier after years of battling cancer that finally overtook her weak and depleted body. Not a single day went be that Ryder didn't think about her. She had been an amazing person and even the last years of her life, while suffering through treatment without a complaint, her caring ways had shone through. Her heart was big, and her love for Ryder, her only child, even more. Ryder's blue eyes were from his mother, and every day he looked in the mirror, he saw her. Then he envisioned her warm smile and the way it erased the few wrinkles she wore around her lips. He could still hear her words, until the day she died, telling him to open his heart again, and reminding him all women were not like Courtney. She promised him that if he opened his heart, one day he would know that one woman was the one for him.

Violet flashed before his eyes.

It wasn't possible? Was it?

Ryder had always brushed off Kathleen's chitchat about falling in love.

Why was it coming back to him now? And why was it revolving around the woman above deck right now?

Ryder gripped the edge of the counter, and dipped his head down low, squeezing his eyes closed trying to shut out emotions the memories of his mother were bringing back.

He hadn't let this conversation go through his head since Kathleen died. He'd humored her during the last years of her life, promising to be open, promising to let people in, but the minute she died, Ryder closed his heart down for good. Or so he thought.

Today, the recollections of his mother were different from simply remembering her smile, her laughter, her hugs and the long talks they would have in the gardens. Today, he couldn't help but wonder if it was his mother somehow pushing him to open his heart...*to Violet Caliendo.*

And now what? He snickered and pulled four cold bottles of water out of the fridge. He'd reached out to Violet and let her in. Sure it was the smallest attempt, the tiniest crack, and Violet had stepped one foot inside.

Now what? Was he ready for another relationship?

The only thing that was clear to Ryder was that he liked Violet. *A lot.* There was something about the way she threw her sly comments his direction, followed by her lust-filled looks. Then the next second she was laughing hysterically because she'd had no idea there was a switch on the fishing pole. She was, for sure, a thunderstorm, just like he'd originally thought, but not in a bad way. In fact, he wanted to stand in the rain of her thunderstorm and experience all she had to give.

Ryder slammed the waters on the counter with a little more force than he'd expected.

He wanted to stand in the rain of her thunderstorm? Was he insane? Had he lost his mind? This was all happening to soon. She was Joel's ex-wife. *Ex-wife.* She was Violet Caliendo. *Violet Caliendo.*

"Is everything alright?" Violet asked, from the bottom of the stairs. He hadn't heard the door open or her climb down the stairs.

It was a simple question that was easy to answer, but his mind couldn't even focus when her voice sent desire straight through him. Her voice sent his trail of thoughts in a whole other direction and he was trying to sort it all out.

"Do you want some help?" She was right beside him now. "That looks delicious. Did you prepare this or is it store bought?"

He didn't understand how she was talking so casually when only hours ago they'd basically agreed to go on a date. Sort of. Then Parker and Sophia had come up and they hadn't had an alone time since, but they'd spent a great morning together. Everything had been good until he was under deck, by himself, and thinking.

Maybe he was the problem? Why was he so irritable?

"I made it," he finally answered, but it came out gruff.

He was irritable because he didn't know what to do with this woman. He could tease, flirt, and ask her out on a date, but after the date...then what? He didn't know what the next step was and he didn't know whether he was ready to take it or not.

"I'm sorry. I wasn't insinuating that you couldn't make it. I was–"

Ryder wasn't sure what came over him. Maybe it was the way the boat rocked her side against his. Or that her wavy beach hair was sprinkled down across her bare skin. Or the coconut-scented suntan lotion he'd torturously watched her rub onto every inch of skin the sun would touch. He had been so jealous of the sun's rays all day long.

He kissed her.

He turned quickly, catching her face between his hands and pressed his lips against her startled gasp. A startled gasp that didn't last one second, because as hot as he was for her, her lust for him burned jest as hot. Ryder saw it in her, in the way she licked her lips when he was around, and how her body reacted to his presence. The fact they'd agreed to deep fried pickles. Ryder had to make sure there was something more between them, then just that moment in the washroom. He had to make sure the feelings he felt for her were real and he wasn't creating them because he thought his mother was sending him signs.

Violet kissed him back, forcefully. Her hands grabbed the outside of his forearms and she arched her body against him, opening her mouth and inviting him into the deliciousness he'd been craving all week. He was glad she'd left that damn life jacket off so his bare torso could feel the length of her body against him. In a swift movement, just like at the Caliendo Resort, he lifted her legs, spread them and set her on the counter. She welcomed the decision by wrapping her legs tightly around his middle and her hands snaked around his neck, the sun kissed warmth touching his skin.

Ryder moved his hands up her back. One grabbed the base of her neck, pulling her kisses harder against him, while the other began slipping the strap of her swimsuit down her arm. After watching the water droplets bead down after their swim, he'd wanted to kiss her bare shoulders. His lips moved down her neck and she arched back giving him access until his lips touched her shoulder and his tongue licked her collarbone. She was hot, she was delicious...she was exactly what he wanted.

"Ryder..." she breathed. "Wait..." He felt her hands find his face and pull him away from her skin to look at him. "We can't do this. My kids are up there."

Her kids? Her kids!

Ryder stepped back and tried to pull out of her hands, but she held him harder, pulling his forehead against hers. Their panting breaths met between them, as their bodies settled down.

"What is this?" she asked and he knew she was talking about the fact they couldn't keep their hands off each other.

He'd been asking himself the same question and was no closer to an answer. Having her around only made it harder to determine. "I have no idea."

"That makes two of us."

Ryder stepped away this time, holding his hand out to help her slide off the counter.

Violet took the platter he had prepared and he grabbed the waters.

He followed her up the stairs knowing that he had one answer to the questions going off in his head and that was that his mothers signs had nothing to do with how he felt about Violet. There was lust. There was desire, but there was also something deeper. The way she touched him and his reaction was evidence that he wanted to explore whatever was brewing between them.

He wanted to go on a date with her and he damned well planned on her saying yes before they docked the boat.

Chapter Ten

DAY TURNED INTO night so quickly that they ended up spending the entire day on Ryder's boat, even after the kiss under deck.

The wonderfully hot, steamy kiss that Violet couldn't get out of her head.

The desires were prominent now, more than when she'd first boarded the boat. Tasting those delicious lips again, feeling the way his tongue searched her mouth with the same desire she felt. He had an effect on her that was mind boggling.

Ryder Carlex left Violet Caliendo mind boggled...although she would never tell him that, but she suspected he already knew.

"Here." Violet jumped at Ryder's voice. At first she thought it came from her head, but then her eyes focused on the sweater he was holding out to her.

The night air was chilly and the sight of that sweater sent gracious goose bumps across her skin. That or the fact that darkness cloaked them and just the memory of those lips were creating a foggy haze in her mind.

"Thank you." She took the black knit sweater and slipped her chilled arms inside, pulling it tightly around her throat and zipping up the front. Chilled on the outside, and scorching hot on the inside.

When she finished zipping it up, Ryder held his hand out to her. "Shhh. Come on." He nodded his head toward the front of the boat, where she'd envisioned pulling him on top of her only hours earlier. *Very vividly.*

Sophia and Parker were fast asleep, curled up on the day beds.

Violet should have said no instead of slipping her hand into the warmth of Ryder's, as he led her to the front of the boat. It had been a long day and now as dusk had fallen, Violet felt a sense of wickedness overtake her body...and her good sense. They shouldn't be alone together.

He'd pulled short-sleeved, button-up white shirt on, however he'd not bothered buttoning up the front. His chest peeked out as they sat down, and without her sunglasses on, she made it a point not to glance down.

"Since we both seem to be full of surprises today, I have a surprise for you," he said, reaching beside him to grab something.

A surprise? What kind of surprise? She hadn't noticed him carry anything out.

"You've already done so much today." She could never express how his thoughtfulness to still take her children out for the day meant to her.

"Thank you for inviting us. I know Parker and Sophia had a wonderful time."

It eased the hurt that Joel cancelled on them. It certainly didn't replace it. Her kids loved their father and, generally speaking, he was good to his word. Never great and never with effort involved, but he was good.

"And you?" Ryder asked.

Her?

Violet stopped thinking about Joel and her kids and instead thought about Ryder's question.

Did she have fun?

Besides the kiss below deck, which was naughty, hot fun in an entirely different way than he was referring to, she discovered she *had* enjoyed fishing, once she got the hang of it...sort of. She wasn't going to take up the sport. It was rather mundane, sitting around waiting for a fish to bite. She would rather play tennis, a game where you worked to achieve your goal, not base it on luck.

Violet found she liked Ryder's company, and not only on a sexual level...although it played its part plenty today.

"Yes," she answered truthfully. "I had a lot of fun today."

"The fun doesn't have to end." Ryder's husky voice was followed by one of his sexy winks.

Was he going to kiss her again? Kiss me again!

She couldn't dare, she shouldn't...why did every part of her want him to kiss her and pull her down onto the flat surface and remove the sweater she was not wearing and then her bathing suit and touch every inch of her skin. Oh, how she wanted to feel his hands on her skin again.

Ryder didn't make any such move. He held a foil ball in front of them.

"What is that?" she asked, blinking away the vision.

"Dessert. I made enough for the kids, but they fell asleep, so I guess it's just me and you."

Ryder passed her a fork before unwrapping the foil ball. Inside was a sliced apple. The smell of baked apple in cinnamon and butter made Violet's mouth water.

"This smells delicious," she said.

He held it toward her. Automatically her hand went under the foil ball to balance it, as she dug her fork in. The palm of her hand landed on the outside of Ryder's and she forgot what she was doing. Her skin heated, her lips pursed and her head snapped up to Ryder. Instant desire reflected from his deep blue eyes and chiseled features. He was fighting it. She was fighting it. *Fighting what?*

Violet could have kissed him again. Her lips could graze his or press so hard the contact would numb them. Either way she could have done it. She wanted to do it.

Violet moved the fork to her mouth and chomped almost the entire slice of apple to occupy her wanting lips. She pulled her hand away, breaking the contact.

Ryder looked confused at first.

Violet supposed he was expecting her to kiss him, like she wanted, like they both felt. She had self control for crying out loud. She wasn't always the woman who took a guy in the washroom. In fact, she was never that woman.

Ryder grinned. He bit a slice of the apple before setting it down between them. He stretched his long, lean legs out in front of him, resting his flat palms on the surface of the boat.

"You want to kiss me again," he said and there was no mistaking that it wasn't a question.

How did this man so easily talk about things that were making her insides melt?

"It's your turn," he said. "You initiated the first and I complied. Then I initiated the second and you cut me off..."

He looked at her and she hadn't realized she was staring at him. Open mouthed, eye brows creased together in complete shock.

Where was this man's filter?

"Now it's your turn."

Her turn? Her turn! Should she kiss him? She wanted to kiss him. What exactly did a kiss mean? Did he want to have sex with her? On the bow of his yacht?

How tempting it all was.

"Are you always this cocky?" Violet tried to ask in strong, rather cocky tone herself, but instead she heard the breathy plea in her tone. *Darn it!*

"I guess you'll have to invite me over for deep fried pickles and find out. And I will wait all night for your turn."

Violet grinned at him.

Yes, she'd invited him for deep fried pickles. Yes, she wanted him to spend more time with him. Yes, his presence brought out the wild side of her and the real side of her, but he was still Ryder Carlex. Caution bounced around her head, warning her that this man was trouble.

"Don't hold your breath," she teased.

"Hey, I thought I was an amazing fishing instructor."

She laughed. "You would."

"And I can bring a killer dessert."

The idea of a date was so tempting. But could they? *Could she?*

"I do like your dessert." Violet put another piece of the apple from her fork into her mouth, mostly to keep from kissing him. Edible food was not the dessert she was referring to.

"Sweetheart, this is nothing compared to what I can whip up."

Violet laughed again.

She could get used to smiling and laughing again, after the kids went to bed. Her nights and days, without the kids, had become a long endless pile of work that left no room for entertainment.

"Does that work on the ladies? Do they find that pick up line seductive?"

"I've never tried it on anyone else."

She shook her head at him. "*Don't* ever try it on anyone else."

He laughed too. "Thanks for the advice. I guess following that line with suggestions of a can of whipped cream, strawberries and handcuffs are maybe not wise."

Wild, unthinkable thoughts flew through Violet's head and it took all her strength not to reach over and kiss Ryder and beg him for whipped cream, strawberries and complete control of the handcuffs.

"Depends what type of woman you're going after," she said instead.

Ryder's tone dropped all its humor, all its tease and instead held raw seduction. "You."

Violet's smile dropped and her lower lip slipped between her teeth. They needed to get back to shore before this went somewhere it shouldn't...again.

Ryder shifted so his hand could touch the side of her face. "I'm not going to kiss you first, Violet. Don't get me wrong, I want to kiss you. I do. But I want you to want to kiss me."

Violet wanted to kiss him, but there were warning signals she couldn't ignore. "Ryder, I can't."

His hand didn't fall away like she hoped and the massaging sensation of his thumb worked the words out of her.

"If I kiss you, it won't be just a kiss. We both know that."

One kiss under the deck and she'd landed on top of the counter. If Parker and Sophia hadn't been just above them, Violet wouldn't have stopped.

His thumb stroked the side of her jaw. "Do you think I don't have self control?"

"I can't guarantee that I have self control. Not with you," she admitted.

"I'm flattered."

"I'm scared." Letting someone else know her fears would have scared the hell out of her, but she was glad he knew. Glad that he understood she wasn't as prepared for whatever this was between them as she might look.

"And if you start your next sentence with *Violet Caliendo is scared...*"

He smirked. "I was going to say, we don't have to rush into things..."

"I think it's a little late for that."

Was her head moving toward his? Was she going to kiss him?

"I've learned that in life it's never too late." He dropped his hand back beside him and moved back putting distance between them. "We can start with our date. Deep fried pickles at your place and I will bring dessert. Although I would much rather take you out."

He was so full of himself.

"I didn't say I was going on a date with you."

"You didn't say you weren't."

That was true.

He leaned back and gazed at the stars. "I haven't been on a date in years. This should be fun."

Violet could name off six events in the last two years that Ryder had attended with gorgeous beautiful women on his arm. Why was he sitting here telling her it had been years since he dated? *Was he a liar?* Maybe those had all been one night stands and if so, how many women had he been with?

Was this all a mistake? Who was Ryder Carlex?

"Violet? Where did you go?"

Violet hadn't noticed she'd followed his stare into the sky and her thoughts were lost among the thousands of stars. Violet had already fallen into a trap with a man who hadn't loved her and had used her for his own personal gain. Hard lessons in life had presented themselves over ten years ago and she'd vowed to herself that she would never fall down that hole again. Why was she sitting with a man who made her insides come alive under the romantic blanket of stars above them and talking about going on a date?

Because today had been wonderful.

Everything, since Ryder threw her in the water and splashed a dose of happiness back into her mind, appeared different. The life before she boarded the boat seemed so far away, so lonely, and here, life felt incredible, alive, and finally after years of feeling reserved in the presence of other people, she felt vibrant, she felt like herself.

But was that really how Ryder felt?

"How's your dad?" she asked, changing the topic.

Ryder had a life beyond this boat that she knew nothing about. Except that whenever she saw him at events and galas, it always involved gorgeous women on his arm.

Ryder looked away, and she caught the tension build up in his shrug. She'd never seen a man who tensed up as much as Ryder.

"You know. Working. He's hired on my aunt's kids to redesign the stores. So he's been busy with that."

"I haven't seen him in a long time. He usually attends my mother's galas–"

Ryder cut her off. "I've attended on his behalf."

How could Violet forget? It was those very galas and the women he didn't date that were flanking her mind.

"I know. But, he was always a delight to have attend, with his big stories and his loud laughter. Tell him I said hi when you see him."

"I will." Ryder lost the friendliness in his tone and Violet wondered why. Then he changed the topic. "I was sorry to hear about your dad last year."

Violet could have laughed if Ryder's *not dates* weren't in her mind. It felt like the *not dates* he wasn't being honest about wasn't the only thing Ryder was keeping from her.

People said they were sorry to hear about her father's death and it was ironic since all those people were either afraid of him or glad he was gone.

"I'm sure sorry isn't exactly what you think of his death."

Ryder looked at her. "I didn't have any issues with your father."

"You are one in a million. He wasn't a well-liked man."

"He was still your dad, so you have my condolences."

"Thank you."

"So..." He leaned back again. "Where shall we go on our date? The best place in town is owned by the hottest gal I know..."

He glanced at her and winked, referring to the resort...referring to her...and waiting for her thought about his pick-up line.

"Better," she said, but as much as the tingling pleasure from having Ryder telling her she was the hottest gal he knew, her carefulness regarding inviting other people into her life, reminded her, that might not be accurate. He knew a lot of women and maybe her first intuition of him was right. Violet didn't want to believe Ryder was the player she'd once not questioned, but Violet was vigilant.

Give me signs that you are the man my heart wants you to be, not the man my brain keeps giving me warnings that you are.

Chapter Eleven

RYDER WATCHED VIOLET leave him again. Not physically, but mentally. All day she'd been readable, relaxed and her laughter had awaken his own. It had been wonderful. But tonight, sitting under the stars, just the two of them, finally alone, she was distant and he had no idea why.

"Are you okay?" he asked. "You've disappeared into your own world again."

Violet smiled at him, but it didn't reach her eyes. "I'm sorry. I'm tired."

"That's alright. We can head back, if you want." He didn't want to, preferring to remain here with her and wishing it wasn't growing tense between them. "But first you have to agree to a date with me."

She didn't answer right away, and he could tell she was thinking again. What was she thinking about? *Them?* Or what was happening between them? Or was she trying to get out of going on a date with him? Had she said yes to today just for her children?

"I don't normally...I have never..." Violet sighed. "I am not the woman who has random sex with random men," she finally said. "Like I did with you. That's not who I am."

"I'm not exactly random," Ryder pointed out, trying to alleviate the guilt he thought she was feeling. "We've known each other long before you knew Joel. My parents have been attending the Caliendo galas since before I was born."

"I knew your parents. You were never present until Joel started coming around." Violet paused, disappearing into her private world.

When she looked at him, her eyes shot fire of accusation in his direction.

"And you're right, you aren't random. You are Joel's friend, his best friend. His best man."

Again, Ryder wouldn't go so far as to consider Joel his best friend.

Violet was a strong woman, an even hard woman, but today he'd seen more. He'd watched the shield of protection around her open up and let him in, just like right now he watched her build it back up. The suspicion and caution rushed into her eyes, but she quickly masked it. A shield to hide her emotions from him. She was good at that.

"Take us back to shore," she said in a way that told him nothing was conspiring between them.

What happened?

"Violet..."

"No Ryder." A shocked laugh escaped her chest and it sounded painful. "You're Joel's friend. What are we even doing? Is this some distasteful elaborate hoax you and Joel concocted? To what? Make fun of me? Make me look like a fool? It's a little coincidental he didn't show up today after forcing me here and all you've been trying to do is touch me, kiss me...go on a date with me. Why?"

Because Ryder wanted to touch her, kiss her and he sure as hell wouldn't have asked to take her out if he didn't want to. He had been quite content to avoid all dates since Courtney.

Finally working up the courage to ask Violet on a date, just to have her throw it in his face and accusing him of ulterior motives, made him wonder why he'd broken his rule in the first place. It also made him angry.

Violet stood to leave and Ryder rose with her.

"Violet, you came to me in that bathroom and initiated things between us. You locked us in. You walked over to me and *you* kissed *me*."

Damned if she was going to turn this around on him. He would have been none the wiser if she hadn't instigated their rendezvous.

"Yes, I did. But you're Ryder Carlex. You do this all the time."

He did this all the time? Did what? Did she not hear a damn word he'd said to her?

Ryder folded his arms across his chest, growing angrier with her assumptions of him, but listening as she continued. He wasn't about to interrupt a verbal thunderstorm by this woman.

"I have seen the so-called *dates* you haven't gone on at every gala in the last two years. The women you claim not to hit on with your corny remarks. I'm not another one of those women. It just makes me wonder why you're so keen on me."

Wonder or accuse? Because it certainly sounded like accusing to him.

"Take us back please."

Ryder was furious. He might have labeled her as a perfectionist and she may have called him out on it, but damned if Violet hadn't labeled Ryder too. And he wasn't about to call her out on it.

He stole the shield she'd let fall during her explosion and held it in front of himself.

"Shouldn't be longer than fifteen minutes back," he said, walking past her, prepared to turn this damn boat around and back to shore ASAP.

***

RIDING BACK TO the dock was the longest fifteen minutes of Violet's life.

Ryder cranked up the speed across the lake that rushed alongside Violet's mixed feelings. Her body told her one thing, that Ryder wanted more than a fling with her, while her mind told her the opposite, that he was using her.

How could she defy her mind's warning, putting her back in the vulnerable state she'd been with Joel?

Yes, she had initiated the first run-in with Ryder in a heated moment of...stupidity. The ball was in her court, but now there wouldn't be another run-in with Ryder Carlex. Ever. Period.

As Ryder steered the boat into Crystal River, he geared it down. It was a slow, wavy ride back to his dock, where he immediately climbed out to dock and tied the boat down.

Through the darkness she watched his edgy body move. He was mad at her. Or he was acting mad at her because she was spot on about his intentions. Her gut told her she was wrong. The evidence told her she was right.

Violet lifted a sleeping Parker into her arms. He was the younger of the two, and she didn't want to wake him. He was also the crankier one and, right now, battling her desire to apologize to Ryder, left her with little energy to deal with Parker. She wanted to get them in the car, home and tucked into bed so she could soak in a hot bath and sip on a large glass of chardonnay, on the road to forgetting Ryder.

As Violet touched Sophia, Ryder's hand found hers. "Don't wake her. I got her."

The contact of their hands sent flames through her body that her filter, the common sense that had been vacationing all day, blew out. He was Ryder Carlex. *Ryder Carlex!*

Violet looked at his eyes anyway, against her better judgement, against her strict *no*. He was doing what she was trying to do, read what she was really thinking while she tried to read what he was actually thinking.

Why? Did it make a difference? What are you looking for? An answer to why her heart raced so fast when he's around. Why all day she didn't feel like she had to wear a cover in front of him. And why his touch ignited a fire in her belly that she knew only his touch could handle.

Violet didn't get her answers and with the solemn look she gave him, she knew he wouldn't be getting his either. Because all this was a mistake.

Violet slid her hand out from under his, feeling lonely the moment she did, and stepped back.

It has to be this way. He's Joel's best friend.

Ryder picked Sophia up so gently, like a loving father would and Violet's heart sank. Joel wasn't that loving father, mainly because the kids hadn't been part of his plan. Now, Violet stood here with the man who had taught Joel his ways and she was battling emotions, feelings and desires for him.

What was wrong with her?

After the kids were buckled in the back seat, Ryder opened the driver's side for her. A gentleman, even after the way she'd treated him.

Why? Because she was right and he was using her. However her feelings were toward this man or his were toward her, he had gone out of his way to create a day filled with laughter, jokes and smiles for her children. For that, Violet was thankful.

"Thank you for today. Sophia and Parker had a wonderful time." The words came out in a quick slew past her lips as she tried to slide into the driver's seat.

Ryder caught her upper arm and stepped close enough that their bodies touched, an all too familiar way that felt so right.

Violet swallowed past the lump in her throat. *What did he want? Why did his touch ignite her body into a flaming fireball unlike a touch from any other man. Ever.*

"I'm not the only one who boarded this boat with judgement," Ryder said. "At least I can admit that I was wrong." He let her arm go and stepped back toward the house.

It didn't matter what either of them thought about each other. It didn't matter if she was right or wrong because he was Joel's friend. Nothing could ever form between them.

***

WATCHING THE LIGHTS on Violet's Lexus until they disappeared left Ryder disliking the heaviness of his heart.

Heaviness of his heart? Heaviness of his heart!

That was absurd. He should be thanking Joel for unknowingly sticking a wedge in the center of whatever feelings were brewing between him and the beauty that was Violet, instead of wishing he'd clarified that Joel had nothing to do with any of Ryder's feelings and actions toward her.

Maybe Courtney had been right about him. After you stripped away Ryder's money and his good looks, what was left to offer a woman?

The property was lit by sporadic solar lights and Ryder walked the stone path to his father's little cottage. He doubted his father would be awake, but still, Ryder wasn't ready to go into the big, empty and lonely house by himself.

Light filtered through the windows of the living room and Ryder knocked gently on the front door. Susan let him in, without question, without judgement.

"He's sleeping," she said. "Are you thirsty? Do you want a coffee or something?"

Ryder shook his head.

Heading down the hallway, he stopped in front of his dad's closed door and wished behind it was a man who would challenge him. A man that Ryder could confide in.

Donald had always listened to Ryder, but he'd also never answered the questions he'd been searching for. Donald was the devil's advocate, challenging him until the answer was clear to Ryder. Ryder missed that about his dad. Ryder missed everything about him. He found it more difficult each passing day to see his dad then it had been to lose his mother. Wanting to talk to him, laugh and share his life and listen to his dad's life and have him there, but not there, was killing Ryder's soul.

Until today. Until Violet.

She was the first person to get through his sadness. Ryder wasn't a hermit. Sure, he hid behind his office door, but there was always someone popping in and the fundraisers he'd been attending the last two years surrounded Ryder with people, but no one had touched his soul like Violet had. No one else had lit that place deep inside that he'd thought would remain dark forever.

Ryder planned on pushing the door open, but what was the point. There was only a confused, sleeping man waiting on the other side of that door.

Back in the living room, Ryder found Susan curled up on one of the reclining armchairs, reading a book with the music sound surround humming a light tune, so quiet it was almost unrecognizable.

"Inch Away," Ryder said, referring to the band.

Susan looked up from her book and smiled at him. The sharp lines on her face, and clearness of her skin, gave away her youth. She was at least ten years younger than Ryder.

"Yes. Not only is the band local, I went to school with Avery, Sean, Ems and Drew but they're wonderful too. Their music is soothing. Come sit down. I made you a coffee." She pointed at the mug sitting beside the other recliner. Ryder should have suspected she would.

"Thanks." He stretched in the recliner, not bothering with the coffee. "How was Dad today?"

"He was good."

Ryder was glad to hear that. The days when Donald gave the workers a hard time, dug guilt into Ryder.

Susan detailed her day with his dad, sitting at the garden, what they ate and when he fell asleep. When she finished, she asked, "How was your day?"

Day was great. Night sucked. "Good."

"Did Joel get a new car?"

Violet's Lexus. "No. That was Violet Caliendo's car."

"Oh..." It came out confused then the next, *oh* came out hiked in tone like she was assuming he'd invited Violet.

"It's not like that." He wished differently. As far as Violet was concerned, he would have come to the cottage to sleep with Susan...which he did not.

"That's too bad."

Ryder glanced at her. "Why?"

She shrugged her petite shoulders. "It would be good for you to meet someone, go on dates, you know that sort of thing. Ryder, you might be old, but you're not *old*. You should totally go out and meet some ladies."

"What makes you think I don't?"

"Do you?"

Ryder didn't answer. He turned away. It was none of her business anyway. Ryder closed his eyes and fully intended on falling asleep here for the night. It wouldn't be the first time and not the last and Susan was aware.

She excused herself, retiring to her room.

Before she left she said, "Ryder, was Violet at the meeting last week? The morning you were fishing with your dad?"

Why? Ryder didn't ask. "She is the wedding coordinator at the Caliendo Resort."

"So, that's a yes. It explains that glow you came back with."

"I do not have a glow," he grumbled, beyond finished with this conversation.

"Okay. Sure. No glow, my mistake. Goodnight."

Glow. Ryder had no such thing.

Ryder didn't need to date and he certainly didn't need to date someone who didn't trust him. He had a hard enough time trusting women after finding Courtney in bed with another man. In *their* bed. Then, as if the woman he'd chosen to spend the rest of his life with hadn't shattered his heart and soul, to listen to all the reasons why Ryder wasn't good enough. He wasn't prepared to go down that road again. Violet was already putting him down, there was no way in hell he was going to tolerate it.

Chapter Twelve

VIOLET DROVE STRAIGHT home. She didn't let Ryder's warning sink in until she parked the car in front of the resort and turned off the engine. Silence enveloped her while her mind went wild with questions.

What was Ryder saying? That he wasn't a playboy? Or he wasn't using her? Or was he saying neither because he was both and trying to confuse her?

Mission accomplished. Violet was confused. Her mind had never been such a mass of disorder, bouncing around in no solid direction, and leaving her without a clue how to put it in the right order.

A knock on her car window made Violet jump. Marc smiled through the glass with a little wave, still dressed in his charcoal slacks, however his shirt was un-tucked and the three top buttons were undone and his tie was missing. She hadn't seen him come around her vehicle, which wasn't surprising since all her mind was concentrating on was Ryder.

Violet climbed out of the car and asked in a low whisper so she didn't wake the kids, "What are you doing? You scared the devil out of me."

"Sorry, Vi." He looked empathetic, but with a small smirk of entertainment. "No one has heard from you all day. We were worried. I was worried."

That was careless of her. Her family was close-knit and staying away all day and into the night without sending a text was abnormal...and would make them worry. Violet should have asked Ryder to use his cell phone and gave at least one of her family members a heads up on her whereabouts. The forgetfulness was just another thoughtless moment in the presence of Ryder Carlex. *Ryder Carlex.* She had to stop doing that, saying his full name in her head, exactly the condescending way he said her name.

"I'm sorry," she apologized to Marc. "I was rushed out by Parker and left my phone beside the pool."

Along with my wine and the novel I had fully intended on escaping all thoughts of Ryder...not planning on going out with him and making them ten times worse. And they *were* ten times worse.

"Joel was late picking the kids up. He was supposed to drop them off at Ryder's house for a day on the boat and asked if I could take them to Ryder's lake house."

Marc listened, quietly observing. He had been that way from a young age, in a quiet, kind of geeky boy way, watching everything around him with eagle eyes, taking it in, and remembering.

Right now, Violet knew Marc had already noticed she disappeared inside Ryder's big and baggy sweater with only her bare legs peeking out the bottom, on top of the face she'd been sitting in the car for who knew how long *thinking* about Ryder. The knowledge left her feeling rushed to explain where she had been and why she was in a man's sweater.

"Joel didn't show up at Ryder's house and cancelled while the kids were on the boat waiting for him. Ryder was all packed to go, so he kindly extended the invite to take the three of us fishing, regardless of Joel's absence. Parker and Sophia have been looking forward to this all week so we spent the day on Ryder's boat."

And I spent the day trying to figure out my feelings and Ryder's feelings, only to run away when Ryder offered a date...a real date. That was terrifying.

A date made it real. A date made it no longer a fantasy playing in her head and that scared the hell out of Violet. At the moment, worse than that, was having Marc watching her so closely and likely judging her for going out with her ex-husband's best friend, the player...even if the pretense was that it was for the children.

"Did you have fun?" Marc asked.

Not them...not Sophia and Parker, but her.

That wasn't the question Violet had been expecting from her bother.

Why would she agree to go out with Ryder Carlex? That was what she'd been ready to defend, not answer if she'd had fun.

It threw the preparation to defend her decision to get on Ryder's boat for a little loop, leaving her baffled...again. Honest, this bafflement stuff was annoying. How did people go around life not knowing what was around the next corner? It was exhausting. It was scary. It was driving her mind wild.

"Yes," she answered honestly.

Marc smiled. "Good. I will grab Sophia." And just like that and without another word, he moved around to the other side of the vehicle to fetch her daughter.

Once the kids were in their bedrooms, tucked in like sleeping angels...even Parker with his innocent face...Violet shut the doors and slipped into her bedroom.

She peeled the bathing suit off her body, sighing a huge thank you, as the constricting material fell to the floor. Pulling on a pair of yoga pants and matching black t-shirt, she stopped at the edge of her bed where Ryder's sweater lay.

Ryder Carlex? Ryder Carlex.

She hated to admit it, but before she concluded Ryder had tag teamed with Joel to make a fool of Violet, she had met a completely different man than Joel had always referred to during their marriage. Today, she'd met a family man whose mother's death still touched his heart. A generous man, who gave up his whole day to keep the disappointment of Joel's cancellation from her kids. More so, she discovered a man who wanted to touch her, kiss her...go on a date with her. *Her.*

But did he? Or was it a ruse developed between him and Joel?

Violet couldn't chance it, not when her children were involved. She wasn't the young girl rebelling against her father anymore, choosing to date Joel out of pure disobedience. That had backfired badly. If she hadn't been so angry with Robert at the time, if she hadn't been going against every word he spoke, her life could have been so different, uncomplicated, and maybe she would have found her happily ever after.

Walking away from Ryder tonight, felt like she'd walked away from her *happily ever after.*

That was crazy.

She shook her head, pushing the thought away. She headed down the hall, but Ryder's words played in her head, like her happily ever after screaming for her attention that had been lacking for the last ten years.

I wasn't the only one boarding this boat with judgement.

She couldn't deny she had created an image of Ryder on the information Joel had supplied her over the years. Even if she was wrong...and it was a big *if*...how could they go on a date?

It was a useless battle inside her head and all the way to the kitchen where Violet found Marc boiling water in the tea kettle. *Boiling water?* For what appeared to be tea. Marc didn't drink tea.

"What are you doing?" she asked, climbing onto the bar stool at the high island counter and watching her brother skeptically.

She missed the years he had been was away from home. Violet clicked with her brother differently than she did with her other siblings.

Emma and Anya had always been closer and Izzy loved and treated everyone equal, but kept her true feelings to herself, hiding behind several masks of charm, tease, and straight up wildness.

She was also a huge momma's girl, had been her whole life, which was why Izzy still wasn't required to work, having her mother wrapped around her little pinky finger.

The kettle whistled and Marc poured the steaming water into the mugs. He didn't answer until he moved around the counter and sat beside her. As he handed her the mug, she knew it was lemon chamomile even before she inhaled the delicious aroma. It was the only tea flavor in her cupboard.

"Mom always prepares tea when she suspects something's bothering one of us," Marc answered.

The warmth soothed her fingers which she hadn't noticed were shaky.

"Is something bothering you?" Violet asked automatically, flexing one hand and then the other, annoyed with her tremble.

Violet kept her life to a minimum of drama, but Marc on the other hand, was digging around, with Eliza, through their father's hidden room of files. Files that were full of broken hearts and broken families that Robert was responsible for destroying. Lives her family intended to repair.

"No," Marc said.

"I didn't mean with you personally. I was referring to Dad's errors." Violet settled back on the stool, tightly holding the mug and sipping the hot liquid that scorched her throat.

"No."

Hot, hot, hot! She set the mug on the counter.

"But something's bothering you," Marc said.

131

Violets eyes snapped up from bouncing the tea bag up and down in the water and met Marc's supportive eyes, offering to listen to her.

How did he know about her feelings for Ryder? Was she that transparent?

They sat in silence, while Violet weighed her options.

Who else did Violet have to talk to?

Her mother would encourage her go on a date with Ryder, unrealistically living in the fantasy world about love. Violet was leery to take advice from a woman who cheated on her husband on and off with his brother for over thirty years. Violet loved her mother and could even relate to the reasons backing her mother and uncle's connection to one another. They'd bonded while Robert pushed everyone away from him. Still, Violet wasn't sure her mother was the one to talk to about Ryder.

Then there was Emma, and the newly developed news that Ryder had tried to get up her skirt at Violet's wedding. Talking to Emma was out of the picture.

And Izzy...there were so many reasons why she wouldn't talk to Izzy that Violet didn't even have the energy to list them off in her head.

Anya, the middle child was still missing. This was the perfect opportunity to bring up Violet's suggestion to hire a PI to Marc. But that wasn't what Marc had asked about and right now, at the late hour, after a day in the scorching sun, and Ryder dancing around her head, she didn't have energy to drag Anya into the conversation. Decision made, if she was going to talk to anyone about Ryder, it was Marc.

Violet opened her mouth to tell Marc about her day with Ryder...not their morning, strip-off-our-clothes-and-make-love-in-the-lobby-washroom, but all the events at the boat, her feelings, Ryder's feelings, and him asking her on a date. She needed to know if she overreacted. Violet's mouth drew back together when she found herself at a loss for words.

I had sex with Ryder? I like Ryder? I think he likes me, but maybe he's using me?

Every way she steered the events in her head, she was left feeling more idiotic, more confused and more embarrassed by all these emotions.

"I think we should hire a private investigator to find Anya," she said instead, unleashing the worry of her sister's whereabouts onto both of them.

Marc's dark brown eyes shifted at the topic he hadn't expected.

"I don't want to confront her. Clearly, she needs space, but I would like to ensure her safety. I thought maybe you would know who Dad used to discreetly find people that were hiding from him."

The fact people had to hide from her dad was disconcerting.

"I can look into it. I will talk to Carl and see if he suggests anyone before I look into Robert's PI."

Carl, Robert, Dad, Uncle...Marc was so good at keeping them straight, where Violet still automatically considered Robert the father of all her siblings.

It was complicated. They were complicated, which shouldn't surprise her that whatever she had with Ryder was complicated.

For a woman who hated complication and drama, Violet sure seemed to always be in the middle of it.

They sat in silence again.

Violet's thoughts revolving around Ryder. Maybe she had judged him poorly and he wasn't the man Joel portrayed, but how could she know for sure? And if she went on a date with him and he was *that* guy, then she would be left feeling like a fool. But if she went on the date and he was the man Violet had seen today, then that looked like her happily ever after. But happily ever didn't exist and it was funny because after years of the term never passing her mind except in regards to her work, all of a sudden, the term stuck beside Ryder's name.

"Violet?" Marc's low voice gave her a fright and her body jumped.

She smiled at him, embarrassed for getting so lost in her thoughts, she had forgotten he was even there. "Yes?"

"I don't mean to pry. I know you're private and proud when it comes to your life, but I'm your brother and I'm concerned."

Violet didn't say anything. She was afraid if she opened her mouth, her pride would tell him she was fine, when she was so far from okay. And she had no idea what to do, but she didn't want to ask for help.

"Do you need Emma to step in for you with the Bensen wedding?" he asked.

The Bensen wedding? Huh?

"She doesn't mind. I've already talked to her, anticipating this might be too much for you. It's getting close to the wedding date, which could understandably become upsetting to you and—"

Violet held up her hand to stop him.

The Bensen wedding.

She wasn't upset about the Bensen wedding. She'd hardly had time to even think about that wedding while Ryder was enchanting her mind. Besides, she didn't love Joel. She wasn't in love with Joel...she never had been.

"It's not the Bensen wedding," she clarified and her tone convinced him.

He nodded and waited patiently for her answer.

Oh, just tell him. Oh, I don't want to. Oh, spit it out.

"I'm attracted to Ryder Carlex." The words flew out of her mouth before she could double-think it.

Marc's face fell open in surprise, total, complete, and utter shock at the declaration. "What?"

Violet continued. "And he's attracted to me. At least, I think he's attracted to me. By think, I mean he acts like he's interested in going out together. Like a date. He actually asked me on a date, flat out, there was no confusion. But then does he really want to date me? Or is it just him and Joel playing mind games? In case you missed it, Joel has never been discreet on his feelings for me. Especially after the divorce. Anyway..." She twisted her lips. "I don't know. Shouldn't I be able to tell the difference?" She rambled everything so fast that she hadn't noticed the look on Marc's face, trying to keep up with her, until she stopped to look at him, expecting answers.

Marc opened his mouth and then shut it. He squinted his eyes, looked away from Violet for a quick second and when he looked back there was more confusion across his face.

"I did not see that coming," he admitted. It was an answer Violet had also not seen coming.

Violet groaned and covered her face with her hands.

Why did she say anything?

The look on Marc's face told her what her mind had been telling her all day, *she was crazy.*

"I know, it's crazy. I'm crazy. I'm Izzy crazy, right? You can tell me the truth, your opinion, what you think of the situation. I can handle it. I need a snap of harsh reality because look at me."

She dropped her hands and waved over the madness she had become.

"Oh gosh, just listen to me. I'm rambling. *I am rambling.*" It sounded awful.

"Yes, you are rambling," he admitted.

"Rambling over a guy. Over dating a guy." Violet lowered her voice to a whisper, as though someone was within ear's reach. "Not just any guy, Joel's friend. Isn't that worse than Izzy? See what happens when you send a girl to private school...she misses out on feelings of lust and becomes an adolescent fool. In front of her brother."

Hit me over the head and let me sleep this off!

Marc was smirking at her.

"What?" If her children had asked her that word in that tone, she would have knocked them back a week.

"Rambling, with a glimmer of happiness in your eyes. A spark of impulse and drive that has nothing to do with work, but instead life. It's refreshing to see those qualities in you," Marc said.

Violet pressed her lips tightly together, hoping to extinguish the glimmer and spark. *Glimmer and spark. What was wrong with her?*

"However, considering the basis of this topic, I'm not sure I'm suited for the conversation," Marc said.

He was the most suited. "Marc, just tell me I'm crazy and behaving inadequately."

"I don't think you are doing either of those things."

He had no idea what she'd done in the lobby washroom and what her crazy inadequate actions were creating every time she was around Ryder.

"We can't keep our hands off each other," she told him, then realized how immoral that sounded after spending the day with Sophia and Parker and rushed to give him details. "Not in an inappropriate way around the kids. Never around the kids. It's not like that."

"Violet, I don't doubt you're not putting your children first."

"But when we're alone, it's like we have magnets strapped to our bodies. *And the looks*. We have looks. Serious, deep, lustful desire-filled looks."

Marc looked uncomfortable. Good, that was what she was going for. Now he would tell her to snap out of it. Lord knew if their father was alive, he would have been more than ready to tell her to act her age, behave appropriately like a Caliendo.

"Again, not sure I'm suited."

Violet groaned. "Why did you ask then?" she snapped. "And why did you make me tea? And wait up for me? And press me to share!"

"Because I thought you were having Bensen wedding issues," he said in his defense.

"I'm not. Why do you people not listen to me? I don't care about the Bensen wedding."

"I can see that. Apparently you have other thoughts on the mind. Lust and desire-filled thoughts."

Violet hit her smirking brother. "Shut up." She didn't remember feeling so out of control in years.

The last time was when she was pregnant with Parker and her cravings for deep fried pickles were more than she could handle...and now the thought of deep fried pickles just brought her back to Ryder.

Marc brushed off her light hit with a chuckle. "Ryder brings out the good old Violet in you," he said.

Violet grew serious at his statement, not sure if she should take it as praise or insult. "What's wrong with the now Violet?"

Marc touched her arm resting on the counter. "I have been gone for a lot of years," he started, bringing up his six-year absence.

Until their father's sickness, Marc had travelled south working as a manager in other resorts, spiting his father by not proceeding in the profession he had studied. When Robert fell ill, Marc felt obligated to return and now he was back for good.

"There is absolutely nothing wrong with you now, Vi," he said. "But you've shut yourself away from happiness. It didn't start when Joel left you either. It was before your rushed marriage to Joel. Something in you changed and you withdrew a little from all of us."

Violet had no idea Marc felt this way.

Did all her family feel her disconnection from them?

"I don't know what happened Violet, but it was as though you thought maybe you didn't deserve to smile anymore. I am not saying that you don't smile or that you're not happy and wonderful, especially with Parker and Sophia. They are lucky to have a mother who loves them as much as you do and you are amazing with them. I'm saying you lost the extra in your smile, in your laughter, and you pulled away. It's not a bad thing, I pulled away too when my heart was broken...or for you the opportunity of finding love was crushed."

Violet's body stilled and everything inside her went numb. Her rambling, her sharing, and the way her mouth seemed to flow tonight changed.

Marc knew? Marc knew! If Marc knew, who else knew?

"Dad told you didn't he?" She hadn't intended for it to come out as angry as she sounded, but her father's betrayal brought that side out in her.

"Violet..." The way Marc said her name she knew Robert had told him the truth about her marriage to Joel.

Damn it. It was nobody's business. It wasn't a discussion she wanted to have or a road she even wanted to step her pinky toe on.

Violet stood up and walked away from Marc.

If her father wasn't dead, she would strangle him herself. She hadn't wanted to talk about it with Robert when he was alive on his death bed, and she certainly didn't want to talk to Marc about it now.

"Don't lie to me Marc, or try to sugar-coat it. Unless there's a file floating around..." Violet gasped, turning to face him. "Does Dad have a file on me?"

It shouldn't surprise Violet that the selfish bastard had a file on her. He had a file on everyone! And not a normal thumb drive file either. No, he had manila folders with print out after print out of everyone he ever screwed over and right now she wondered if Marc or Eliza had found one about her, or had Robert simply told Marc.

"Did you read it?" she asked.

"No. I haven't seen a file about you. Robert told me on his dying bed. You wouldn't talk to him."

Violet was pacing and stopped at Marc, who had also stood up. "Do you blame me?" Robert was awful and what was the point in dragging up the past. It didn't change what happened.

"No."

"Did he tell you that he forced, *forced...* " she repeated the word so there was no misunderstanding. "...me to marry Joel because I was pregnant with Sophia?"

Marc's defense fell to sympathy. "Yes."

"Then I guess you're lucky Carl's your real dad. He would never force you to do anything."

Marc drew serious. "Robert was my dad as long as he was yours. And he threatened Kate and her family if she didn't leave and abort our baby," he reminded her. "I'm just thankful Kate couldn't go through with it or we wouldn't have Rosemary today."

That was so much worse than her marriage to Joel.

Violet's angry shoulder's dropped. "You're right. You win."

She turned away and collapsed on the couch in the living room. She was overtired, confused and not thinking straight. Having any conversation tonight was going to lead nowhere.

Marc sat beside her. "It's not a contest. And one of our feelings are not more important than the other. Violet, he told me because he wanted you to forgive him, to forgive yourself and open your heart back up to the possibility of finding the happiness he stole from you."

"He didn't deserve forgiveness."

"I don't know what that man deserved. If he was alive today, I would drill my fist into his face for taking Kate and

Rosemary away from me all those years. But he's not here and we can't change the past. However we can live now. Mend his mistakes. Mend our lives and the repercussions of his actions."

Why was Violet even still mad at her father? It was over ten years ago and after the way she rebelled against him and purposely dragged Joel, who her father disliked, into her family's life, maybe she deserved to suffer a marriage with him for not being more careful.

"Maybe take a step and fall in love." Marc nudged her side. "Real lust, desire, can't-keep-your-hands-off-each-other, love." Marc shuttered and made a face. "Images. Images," he said.

Violet laughed. "Oh, stop it."

"I say listen to your heart Violet and go for it."

Go for it? "But Ryder Carlex?" That was the question of the week.

"What's wrong with Ryder Carlex?" Marc asked, as if he hadn't been present when Emma mentioned the dress incident.

"Plenty. He's Joel's friend and his best man...again," Violet pointed out.

"And he tried to get up Emma's dress at your wedding." Violet heard the teasing in his tone.

"Not helpful."

"I'm just giving you the pros and the cons. But Violet, listen to your heart. When Kate came back, after everything she'd done to me, I told myself to stay the hell away from her. She had crushed my heart and I knew that she had the power to do it again. But even after all my years of hating her for disappearing without a word, when I saw her...my heart told me she was the one. It didn't matter what my head said, because my heart knew better."

"My heart's never had good practice. What if my heart is wrong? What if Ryder's using me? What if he and Joel are coming up with this elaborate plan to humiliate me?"

"First of all, elaborate and Joel do not exactly go together."

Violet would have laughed if exhaustion hadn't claimed her body. Her body wasn't going to make it to her bedroom. The couch was feeling comfortable and satisfying.

"Secondly, take a pause from your reasoning and listen to your heart. It will tell you."

Listen to her heart. She was too tired to even dip into that tonight, fearing she wouldn't be able to separate the feelings in her heart from her desire. She would deal with this in the morning.

Chapter Thirteen

THE BENSEN WEDDING was creeping up fast. *Too fast.* In less than two weeks, only twelve days away, a gorgeous Saturday morning...yes Violet had checked the weather...Joel and Missy would be wed in the gold ballroom.

Monday evening, two days after spending the day on Ryder's yacht, Violet had an appointment with the Bensen bride and groom. They needed their last sit-down to summarize the final decisions and make necessary changes, if any.

It was perfect with Parker and Sophia at Kate and Marc's suite, playing with Rosemary and knowing Ryder wouldn't be present. After a week of I-can't-get-my-mind-off-of-Ryder Carlex, Violet wasn't ready to face him. Her so called *trusted heart*, as Marc had told her to follow, flip-flopped all over, depending on her mood.

What did Ryder want from her?

Violet couldn't answer that question, and she knew the only way to know what his true intentions were, was to ask Ryder himself.

Did he still want to go on a date with her, after she'd called him a womanizer and accused him of using her? Or had she been accurate and he was only interested in one night stands? Or was he using her as a pawn in a game that Joel created?

Wasn't that a bit of a stretch? But was it?

After Violet had witnessed what her father was capable of, the fact Ryder could be using her wasn't that much of a stretch. The larger stretch was if he wasn't planning on using her...if he liked her as much as she liked him.

Did Ryder want a relationship with her?

All those questions needed to be answered, but before she asked Ryder a single one, there was a pressing question in which Violet had to determine the answer. It was the only question Ryder couldn't answer for her.

Was Violet ready for a relationship?

Just the thought of a relationship and all it entailed terrified her. Dating again and opening herself up to another person, giving them the power to hurt her was a whole new round of frightening emotions. The decision wasn't easy, and trying to decide whether to let someone...not just someone, Ryder...into her life, into her heart, into her soul wasn't a question she could answer in only two days.

Violet felt a headache coming on.

The sides of her hair were pulled into a tight bun, urging on her throbbing temples. She pulled her hair loose and her wispy bangs fell, framing her oval face.

The throbbing continued. She settled her face in her hands, elbows on her desk, and wished she hadn't made any appointments this evening so she could go home early to the slumber of her bed.

She was a mess.

Violet clenched her jaw in disgust. A mess which included the bun she'd just ripped out, a meeting with Joel and Missy in a short time, and Ryder popping into her thoughts like bubbles bursting with alarm all through her at the same time. The rush was incredible.

Violet abandoned her desk, stood in front of the mirror on the back of her office door and started gathering up her hair. *No excitement. No alarm. No Ryder.* She had a job to do today and−

Violet's office door opened swiftly, before she had a chance to secure her hair, and slammed into her lifted elbow.

Ouch!

Violet dropped her locks and rubbed her funny bone, which wasn't funny at all, shooting horrible, painful, tingling pain instead through her elbow and up her arm.

Izzy peered her head around the door, a mop of blonde hair pulled into a messy bun right on top of her head. Her manicured fingers gripped the side of the door and she sent Violet a quizzical look across her flawless face, that made her look even years younger than her early twenties. It didn't matter that it was almost eight in the evening, Izzy's face was always painted with a fresh coat of makeup and bright, ready to take on the day, eyes.

"What are you doing?" Izzy asked, innocently.

Why was she asking what Violet was doing? She was the one not bothering to knock.

"What are *you* doing?" Violet asked.

Izzy ignored her question. "Is Emma here yet?"

Emma? Here yet? Why?

Violet had an appointment in...she glanced at the clock...twelve minutes, she didn't have time for sister chat.

"No." Violet didn't even ask why.

Izzy stepped into her office, not bothering to close the door. Izzy's fingers followed the trail of her dramatic, dark eyes, lined with thick liquid black liner and dug her fingers right through Violet's hair, ruffling the sides and digging her nails into her scalp to fluff the top.

Violet pulled away, swatting her sister's hands away. *Boundaries, Izzy, geez.*

"Why are you wearing your hair down?" Izzy's voice was laced with suspicion.

Why would she be suspicious? Marc was the only Caliendo aware of Violet's feelings for Ryder and he'd had a difficult enough time talking with her about it, he certainly wouldn't have talked to the rest of the family...especially not Izzy.

"I'm putting it up," Violet informed her, pulling the elastic from her wrist, preparing for Izzy to move away from the mirror, so she could see what she was doing.

"You never wear your hair down."

Why were they still talking about her hair? "I'm not wearing it down."

"I like it down. All wavy and sexy..."

Hair down is sexy? Get it wrapped back up.

"It softens that hard-ass look you're always wearing."

Hard-ass look? Violet would give Izzy a hard-ass look for wasting the precious moments she needed to tie her hair back up.

"Like that one right there." Izzy touched her nose. "And this is cute." Izzy pulled on the edge of Violet's dress. "Nice change from the old lady blazers and—" Izzy gasped. "Ryder's coming here today isn't he?"

Ryder? Ryder! Why...how...what?

Violet maintained an unfazed look, finding it the most difficult time in her life with the steam of questions bursting to come out. And darn it, another explosion of excitement bubbles went off through her body at the mention of Ryder's name.

Why was Izzy bringing up Ryder? How had she even related Ryder to her? And why was she giving her that annoying I-know-something-you don't-know look? Ugh!

If Izzy, in fact, knew what Ryder and Violet had done, this conversation would be going in a completely different direction...a naughty and exciting direction.

"Do you have a Bensen appointment today?"

Violet didn't have the chance to point out her sister that Ryder would not be attending. Izzy rolled her eyes, the distasteful action reminding Violet why she didn't perform such gestures.

"I still think agreeing to their request is bullshit. I swear he's getting married here just to get a rouse out of you. Like honestly what a douchebag."

Violet would never use that term, but it summed Joel up to perfection.

"I know you're not letting your hair down and dressing sexy for Joel..."

Sexy? Did she look sexy?

Violet caught a glimpse of herself in the mirror again. Above the knees, clingy, soft color, dipping neckline, armless, sexy dress...*oh crap.*

Where was her jacket?

Violet moved through her office searching out a jacket, a great distraction to get away from Izzy's watchful eyes. She had less than ten minutes and she should have been in the foyer early.

"So this all must be for Ryder Carlex," Izzy summarized.

Violet was glad her back was facing Izzy, as she searched around her desk for anything to throw over her shoulders. At the mention of Ryder, Violet's lips parted and her lungs sucked in the air Izzy's declaration had extinguished out of her.

How had Izzy figured it out? She couldn't have. Why was she bringing it up? Where was Emma?!

Violet regained her composure, gave up her hunt for a jacket and turned to face her sister. She disliked the playful glimmer behind Izzy's eyes or the way her lips curved mischievously, teasing like the off-the-shoulder lace top that was grazing her skin, just above the low rise ripped denim that hugged her curvy hips.

"Izzy I'm not sure where you're going with this, but I do have an appointment with Joel and Missy in less than five minutes. I do very much doubt Ryder would attend and even if he did, I don't understand, nor do I really want to understand, why you would assume I would let my hair down and wear a sexy dress for him. I can hardly stand him."

Hardly stand him? Why did you add that? Don't feed the fire. Say less listen more.

"That's not what Parker and Sophia told me," Izzy continued.

Her children were little traders.

"I had a delicious supper tonight, which thank goodness you missed out on, or else I wouldn't have been so informed about your extracirrcular activities."

Traders!

Izzy continued. "Parker and Sophia were full of enthusiasm as they told the whole family all about how much fun you three had on Ryder's boat." Violet did not have time for this right now.

"Parker and Sophia did have fun."

Clarity: Parker and Sophia, not us, not me, not Ryder. Take the hint Izzy, drop the subject.

"I was surprised you even went on his boat."

Clarity not taken. Let me spell it out for you Izzy, so we can drop this topic and I can continue to figure out what I am going to do with Ryder...if anything.

"I dropped the kids off at Ryder's house because he and Joel were taking *them* fishing. When I arrived, Joel canceled and I had a sad couple of kids who had been looking forward to fishing. Ryder offered to take them but I certainly wasn't going to leave them alone with him, which is how I ended up on the boat."

Izzy's grin widened, like Violet's explanation was testament to whatever she was conjuring up in her head. "Mmhmm."

"Don't *mmhmm* me." Violet's eyes caught the clock. She was late. "I have to go."

She grabbed her iPad off her desk and started toward the door.

Ryder wouldn't show up. Would he? Was that why she had dressed...more casual than normal? Because she thought he might show up?

Izzy stepped in front of her and before Violet even realized what was happening, her sister had swiped lip gloss along her matte pink lips.

"Izzy!" She pulled her head away and glared.

Izzy smiled. "There. That'll get him. You always wear matte let's change it up. Glossy, shimmering...sexy hot."

Was she for real?

"I like Ryder and if he is responsible for this new you that you've been trying to hide, than I like him even more." Izzy paused and bit her lower lip like she was concerned, even though her eyes still sparked mischief. "Even though he did try to have sex with Emma. I mean that was a long time ago and I'm sure he's changed. People change. Besides, Mom said he was probably going through something and she would know."

Was her family always going to remember Ryder as the one who tried to get up Emma's dress at her wedding? This was mortifying and added another brick to the layers she had to evaluate before she saw Ryder again.

Violet sent her sister a no-nonsense look, having had her fair share of this conversation. "Step away from the door before I take Marc's side on his determination to make you work."

Izzy's smile dropped, but her attitude remained. "I was being helpful. You're just being plain mean."

Izzy stepped out of the way and Violet swung the door open, while looking over her shoulder at Izzy. "Not another word about Ryder Carlex," she warned and caught the biggest smile cross her sister's lips.

What was she thinking now?

When Violet turned back, her mind didn't have time to react to the body standing on the other side of the doorway. She bounced right off the solid chest and she would have went flying backwards if his arm didn't wrap around her waist, drawing her firmly against him. So firmly she couldn't have squeezed away if she tried.

The beach smell drifted into her nostrils and before she opened her clenched eyes, she knew exactly who was holding her: Ryder Carlex.

Are you kidding me?

Izzy's amused giggle dug deeper into her embarrassment.

"Are you okay?" Ryder's sincere question and the warm, caring tone threw her off her game.

She should have straightened her body, stepped back with posture and grace, and she would have if it had been anyone else that caught her. Being Ryder, she wanted to wrap her hands around his neck, kiss his lips and ask him what time he was picking her up. The idea caused the biggest bubble burst in the middle of her belly.

Wasn't that her decision right there? She wanted to go on a date with Ryder.

Her deep and startled breaths, mixed with the anger, embarrassment, and defeat of the way her entire body was reacting to his touch. At the same height, his face was so close she could feel his breath graze her lips and his eyes captured all her attention, with its lust-filled stare.

Don't stare at me like that here. Not now. Izzy's watching. If you're so worried about Izzy, take a step back.

She didn't.

"Yes," she managed.

Managed! You are Violet Caliendo, you do not manage anything you succeed, you triumph, you RULE.

She attempted to step back. He didn't let go.

"Did I hurt you?"

My ego. You have killed my ego, so please pick it up and carry us both to the desk for the quickie I'm terrified is the only thing you want.

"No."

"I wanted to talk to you about the other night," Ryder started and Violet could imagine what was going through her sister's already wild, naughty, and dirty little mind. "Joel is late again and I thought maybe we could talk privately in your office."

Ryder's eyes moved past Violet and looked at Izzy. As if only noticing her for the first time, Ryder let Violet go and stepped back.

The quick action made him look like he'd done something wrong. Like *they'd* done something wrong. The wheels in Izzy's head would be turning and she would be creating a whole lot of *something wrongs* that the two of them could have done. Violet was skipping the family breakfast for the next year.

Violet turned to Izzy. "Was there anything else you needed?"

Izzy's lips were pressed together like she was holding in words. It was unlike her but for the best.

Izzy shook her head, walking past them both. "Ryder. It's nice seeing you again," she said. "I think the last time was Violet's wedding and as I recall I think I spotted you talking to Emma, or trying to get up her dress."

It was becoming increasingly clear to Violet that she could never go on a date with Ryder.

"You look good," Izzy said, not in a seductive way, but rather an observant way.

"It's always a pleasure Izzy. And I think the *last* time we saw each other was at the Christmas Gala Eliza threw last year and I'm pretty sure you had your share of drinks, possibly responsible for your lack of memory."

Izzy smiled largely, not at all insulted as another person may have been. "Touché." Izzy looked at Violet. "He's a keeper Violet. I like him."

"You like everybody," Violet pointed out.

"I like him more."

"I'm right here," Ryder reminded them.

"Oh, don't you worry, you're not forgettable," Izzy said.

Ryder slid a look to Violet. "Is that what Violet told you?"

Violet would never. "I didn't tell her any such thing."

"But she's been *Violet-twisted* all week and now I see why." Violet was ready to deny her sister, but Izzy said, "And I didn't like Joel." Izzy turned to Ryder. "No offense, but he was a douchebag. He is a douchebag and he will always be a douchebag."

"You are entitled to your opinion," Ryder said.

"My opinion is you better apologize to Violet for the whole Emma thing, and grovel, because my sister is all about image. If we aren't the only ones that remember that incident, then it's less likely she will continue to date you..."

"We're not dating," Violet said, but it went unheard as Ryder and Izzy continued their conversation without her.

"That sounds more like advice," Ryder said.

"Take it. And if she gets all little Miss Snooty, nose-in-the-air, attitude too difficult to deal with, just touch her. Apparently your touch shuts her right up."

Violet was going to shrink into the plush carpet under her heels and hide between the fibers.

"I will keep that in mind," Ryder said.

Violet was going to keep that in mind too and that was the last time Ryder's touch was having any sort of effect on her.

"Alright, this has been fun," Izzy said. Violet had other words to describe the last ten minutes: *Unbearable. Distasteful. Mortifying.*

Izzy left, shutting the door behind her and letting her loud giggle waft through the wood.

Ryder turned his attention to Violet. Now he turned his attention to her, after everything that had conspired. Violet wasn't ready for his attention. She wasn't ready before Izzy had dug her vicious claws into him and she certainly wasn't ready after adding more cons to her list...trying to have sex with her sister was a big one.

"Violet-twisted? Unforgettable?" he teased.

That was the perfect description of how Violet had been acting. And Ryder Carlex was hauntingly unforgettable. "Get over yourself," she said and dismissed the conversation by flipping open her iPad.

"I wonder what Violet-twisted entails," Ryder continued.

Violet looked up. "What did you want to talk about? I have a meeting."

He grinned.

She melted.

Ryder stepped toward her slowly, mimicking the low and seductive tone of his voice as he spoke. "Besides, our obviously heated departure two nights ago...and not heated in the way I would have liked...I had an amazing time on the boat with you. It was the most fun I've had in years."

In years? Who was he trying to kid? Or was it the truth?

Violet watched Ryder's hand moving toward her and fought wanting him to touch her and knowing the effect if he did. She could feel the warmth and sizzle his delicate stroke begin to fizz inside her. Izzy was right, if he touched her, she would be lost and right now, Violet didn't have her feelings for Ryder sorted out.

"If you touch me, I'm going to break every last one of your fingers," she warned.

Ryder stopped...and grinned...and she almost reached out and grabbed his hand and kissed his lips. "You're not very convincing."

Violet folded her arms across her chest. The action was one she used to give the appearance that she had everything under control, even times when she didn't. Right now, she hid her hands so they wouldn't disobey her and reach for him.

"Oh really, then why did you stop?"

Ryder folded his arms across his chest, mimicking her, and his stance dominated hers. They might be the same height, but Ryder's broad shoulders were twice the size of hers and his flexing, bare arms pulled from under his blue and white button-up shirt pressed out from his thick torso. The solid way he stood, like he was in complete control, was so damn sexy, her mouth watered.

"I don't continue when a woman says no."

Continue, continue!

"So it was Emma who said no? Or did you actually make it up her dress?"

Violet was in a hostile mood. Being angry with Ryder was only accountable for a part of her struggle. It was her own uncertainty that had her feeling weak. Anger masked weakness and she didn't want Ryder to see weakness...*him*. If all the signs against them had been with any other person, they would have turned Violet in the other direction. But Ryder...he was her weakness.

"I think you know the answer to that." Everyone knew the answer. Emma had said no.

Why did that knowledge sting?

"That's the reason I came today," Ryder said.

"To tell me you tried to sleep with my sister, but she said no?"

Ryder took a deep breath. "You're not going to make this easy for me, are you? You are a fighter."

She was a protector, of letting people see her weaknesses.

"I like that about you. That you challenge me instead of bowing down to my every word."

"Is that what women do? Bow down to you? To your every word?" Violet felt it difficult not to bow down to this man, while at the same time a sickening feeling was emerging of every woman that had bowed down to him before her.

Ryder grew serious and the blue in his eyes deepened to a threatening color like clouds before a thunderstorm.

"What I don't like is that you don't trust me. You have misconceptions about me. I don't mind a challenge, but I want all the cards on the table, so we both know what we are fighting for."

Was he fighting for her?

"I thought we could do this over dinner, but I get the feeling dinner isn't even an option, unless I start talking." His darkened stare sent her a mischievous look that had her fingers tightening their grasp on her arm. "And I really want to try deep fried pickles...with you."

Deep fried pickles? Yes. Let's abandon the meeting and go to the beach for the day.

"For starters, let's clear up the Emma situation and I guess I should start with groveling..."

Yes, please! Grovel at me feet.

"Please don't."

Please do.

"Your wedding to Joel was a long time ago. And, honestly, I hate to admit it, but I don't remember making a move on your sister. I don't remember a lot of that night, or the nights that led up to your wedding." He paused and she watched him swallow the pain of talking about this part of his life. Then he took liability for some of the distrust Violet had against him and said, "Which is probably partially responsible for your mistrust in me. I didn't sleep with Emma. For what it's worth, that was one of the darkest times of my life. It felt like my life was over and there was no light around me."

Just like Eliza had thought. Ryder had been going through a complicated part in his life. *What?* What could make the man who stood with immense confidence and flashed her parts of his past that demonstrated family loyalty and love, turn into the monster with one hand wrapped around a whisky bottle and the other on the closest woman's ass? *What?*

The haunted look in Ryder's eyes pulled the strings in her heart. For the first time, as she watched the suffering tug his gorgeous features into sadness, Violet wasn't mad at Ryder for the way he'd behaved at her wedding.

"It was like when I woke up and the pain took over, the only way I could escape it was by reaching for the closest bottle of alcohol." He shook his head and looked disgusted at his past behavior. "There were a lot of people in my life that I hurt. My parents, my friends..." Ryder's eyes found her again and said, "You."

Violet had been furious at Ryder, each drunken day that led up to her wedding. But, on the very day itself, she saw the regrets of that day weren't Ryder's fault and he'd simply been an outlet to unleash her resentment. He couldn't deny that he'd been an ass, but Violet was mad at herself for being forced to marry Joel.

Ryder might not remember, but Violet had found him the evening of her wedding, when the guests were dancing, laughing, and enjoying the elaborate Caliendo celebration in the gold ballroom.

Violet remembered that night when she'd merged into a loveless marriage, on her way out the door, her dad had stopped her. She'd hoped Robert had changed his mind after seeing the pain the union was causing Violet. Instead, he'd told her to stop sulking and acting like a foolish girl. *Girl.* The way he said it sent the disappointment a child felt straight through Violet.

All alone, she headed down the hall alone and away from all the lies they were telling people. The silver ballroom had welcomed her gloom into the pitch black room with the only light streaming in from the moon beyond the large window. It was unnerving how Ryder had no memory of a night Violet had never been able to forget.

Violet was lost back in that night, listening to Ryder slur sentences she couldn't comprehend as he greedily drank himself foolish and slapping his hand away each time he offered her some. She only wished she could do the same, but she never would carrying her baby.

Ryder continued talking in the present and she had to force herself to give him the attention she didn't that night, when her problems felt like they outweighed his.

"When I look back now, after losing my mom and other hard times I've had since, I feel embarrassed. I overreacted."

"What happened?" Violet was surprised she asked, but she had always wondered.

Ryder looked more shocked that she'd inquired, but he left no room for her to retract and dove right into an explanation.

"I was heartbroken," he said and sucked in his lips, making a hissing noise like he was embarrassed. He continued through his emotions. "Courtney Brenden, was her name. My whole life, women have thrown themselves at me. I'm not saying that to be cocky or smart, it's simply the truth. I have money and with that, comes this title that ladies presume perfection, when the truth is, I am just like everyone else, except that I was born into money."

Violet could relate to Ryder. Only people shied away from Violet because of her status...or was it the hardness she portrayed to keep people out of her life, fearing the outcome of friendships or love?

"Courtney was different. She wasn't interested in me and that only made me more interested in her. When I thought I found the only woman who saw the real me, I fell in love. Hard. At the time, I thought I was in love with Courtney, but looking back I think I loved that I could be myself around her. When I thought we were making a future together, she was planning a wedding and marriage to my money."

Just like Joel.

"Violet, I may have bedded a lot of ladies in my time and that might be a deal breaker here. I hope it's not. I have a past, we all do. I can't change it. I can only apologize and honestly tell you that I am not proud of the events that transpired at your wedding. I promise you that I am not the same person that I was back then. I'm not looking for a quick fling with you."

Ryder stepped closer and touched the side of her face, sending confirmation that she longed to feel his touch. Without giving her body permission, she bent into the solid promise and strength of his hand.

He continued, "When I'm not with you, you're still invading my thoughts."

Her feelings were mutual.

"You, Violet Caliendo, are so much more than I ever knew, wanted to know or would let myself see, because of who you were, Joel's wife...who you are, Joel's ex-wife."

He was questioning the same things she was.

"Now that you've weaseled your way into my thoughts and more importantly, my feelings, I can't get rid myself of you and I don't want to. I haven't laughed, or smiled, or felt the way I do when I'm with you, in a long time. I didn't even know I could feel like this again."

Violet found herself feeling the exact same way whenever she was with Ryder. He brought out a part of her that was missing.

"I would never use someone for another's expense. Especially not you. When I'm with you, Joel is the furthest thing from my mind." *Joel who?* "It took a long time to figure out that you're not the ice queen Joel said you were."

Like a sharp sword, his sentence sliced through the emotional fog she was in.

Violet pulled away from Ryder's touch and asked, "Joel called me an ice queen? Those exact words?"

Ryder retracted his hand to his side and stuffed both in the pockets of his slacks, looking like a guilty boy caught with his hand in the cookie jar.

"I shouldn't have said that."

Whatever was happening between them was gone, vanished.

"But it's the truth?" she pried.

"Those are his words, Violet. Not mine. Your touch is nothing like he said."

Nothing like he said? Nothing like Joel said?

"Wait a minute? Nothing like *he said*?"

Violet felt sick to her stomach. Not only had Joel called her an ice queen, he had talked about their intimacy with Ryder. And by the sounds of it, her fingers were like ice.

"Joel talked about our love making? With you?"

"Violet..."

"He did." She scoffed and took several steps back, until her legs bumped against her desk and the truth settled into her head. Her fingers gripped onto the edge and the horror of difficult intimate times she'd spent with Joel caused her upper torso to drop forward.

She took in deep breaths, clenching her eyes shut, unable to not compare the two. With Joel, everything had been forced, her desire, her lust, and her pleasure caused by the man's deception. Maybe it hadn't been good. Alright, it was awful, but Joel was telling people...*telling Ryder.*

Violet swallowed the bile threatening to come up her throat. Joel's touch was so different than Ryder's and even how Ryder looked at her melted her into a whole different level of sexual desire, safety and wholeness she'd never felt.

Ice Queen.

Violet couldn't do this right now.

Why was everything so complicated with Ryder?

There were so many barriers between them and every time she felt like they passed one, another popped up to mock her. It was exhausting.

Violet felt Ryder's hand press against her upper back and lightly rub. She wanted to slap him away, but at the same time she wanted to reach for him. When Ryder was brave enough to wrap his arms around her, Violet commended him for caring when she was hot and cold like the weather, Violet let him.

He lifted her from the desk and her weight fell against the solidness of his body. Violet didn't cry. She let the strength of his hold soothe away the hurt she felt.

"I'm not Joel," Ryder whispered against the side of her head. "I would never talk about the times we've spent together. Not with him, not with anyone." Ryder wasn't Joel. Nothing about Ryder had ever been like Joel.

Violet moved to look at Ryder. "And I'm not Courtney."

Ryder smiled. He pushed hair away from her face. "No, you are not."

"So now what?"

He shrugged. "Is that a yes to deep fried pickles?"

Violet grinned at him. "You want to take me out for pickles?"

"I've never taken a woman out for pickles before."

Violet chuckled. "This conversation sounds like something Parker and Sophia would have."

Ryder chuckled too. "What do you have planned after this meeting?"

Tonight? Tonight! "Nothing."

"That's perfect. We can go on a deep fried pickle date after your meeting."

"Okay. But, can we keep this between us? I don't want to explain this to anyone...to Joel...when I don't know what this is."

"It's called dating."

159

"We're not dating."

"There you go, challenging me again. My parents used to challenge me instead of directly answering my questions. I loved the way I always knew what I wanted when we were done talking. Just like each time you challenge me, it becomes clearer all I want is you."

All he wanted was her. He was definitely charming, like everyone said.

"My lips are sealed." Ryder didn't let her go.

"The meeting started fifteen minutes ago," Violet reminded him.

Ryder didn't move. His eyes traveled from hers, down her face, landing on her lips, and then back up to her eyes. He wanted to kiss her, but he was trying to restrain himself. It was adorable.

Violet closed in the distance between them for a small, *get-us-through-the-meeting* kiss. But, it was never a small kiss between them.

Chapter Fourteen

DAMN JOEL.

Ryder remained behind the closed doors of Violet's office, waiting for her text to meet her, Joel and Missy in the gold ballroom.

Before her departure, while adding her number to Ryder's contacts, Violet disclosed their plan in her listen-closely-I'm-not-going-to-repeat-it-tone and speed. Ryder had listened, but that didn't stop him from kissing her senseless when she finished.

Violet's instructions were clear. Ryder was pretending after his early arrival that he'd wandered around the resort and lost track of time. Instead of the truth...making out with Violet in her office.

Ryder still tasted the flavor of Violet's lips.

That one little lie, on top of the omission that Ryder planned on taking Joel's ex-wife out on a date, was nothing in comparison to the fake smile Ryder put on as he walked through the double doors and joined Joel and Missy at the round table with Violet.

Ryder was downright down pissed off at Joel.

Looking at his smug face, carefree attitude and clueless of the results his actions had, was sickening. *Didn't Joel realize the hurt he put in people's lives from the bullshit that came out of his mouth?*

When Ryder was battling whether to spare Violet the truth of Joel's admission about their intimate times, but not wanting to add another lie between him and Violet, she concluded the truth. Ryder's heart ached at the effect Joel's ignorance had on her. Strong, independent Violet Caliendo, bent over like she was having a panic attack and all because Joel couldn't keep his bedroom stories to himself.

And there wasn't a damn thing Ryder could do to demonstrate to Joel how ticked off he was without putting Violet in the middle of it. She'd asked him to keep it between them and Ryder didn't go back on his word.

Ryder forced a painful smile, a fake hug, and laughter that his body was having difficulty creating, as he recited Violet's plan.

"Lots of hot guests on the ground, isn't there?" Joel asked.

Ryder fisted her hands and jammed them in his pockets before one made contact with his face.

How was he supposed to stand up beside a man, at his wedding, when he was having growing hatred for him?

"Especially in the pools. Did you make it out to the pools?" Joel whistled.

Missy slapped him. "Stop it."

Joel squeezed Missy's shoulder. "You have nothing to worry about, babe. You haven't had kids, you're still smoking hot."

A direct jab at Violet.

Ryder's blood boiled.

He was sick and tired of these jabs and games Joel was playing. He was a selfish, heartless bastard. Joel was beginning to look more like the Ice King than his former wife was the Ice Queen.

Ryder's hands came out of his pockets and his feet began to move. He was going to pulverize Joel. The short distance that separated him from Joel was blocked as Violet stepped between them and faced Ryder.

He sent her a, *get out of my way look,* which she ignored...of course.

Violet mastered professionalism. "You've made perfect timing to catch the last few questions and then it's off to whatever plans you have this evening," she said to him in the tone of a woman who couldn't stand him. But, her eyes promised him an entirely different story...if he didn't mess it up.

Fine. He would back off. For now. But if Joel didn't get his shit together, he was going to be waiting at the end of the aisle with a black eye.

"Should we sit back down?" Violet asked, turning to everyone. Missy and Joel moved back toward the table.

Violet sent Ryder a warning.

"He's being an ass," Ryder snarled.

"You're acting like a Neanderthal." Violet didn't give him a chance to respond and walked to the table, sitting beside Missy. Joel was on the other side and he pulled out a chair for Ryder to sit in. Ryder shook his head and continued his pace around the table. He couldn't sit down. He couldn't even think straight. All he wanted to do was make Joel apologize and promise to never let an ignorant remark about Violet leave his lips again. This was the woman of his children, didn't that mean anything to Joel?

Three questions. That was it. *One. Two. Three.* Then Ryder would get to spend the rest of his night with Violet. And for no other reason than because they both wanted to.

"That about sums it up," Violet was saying. Ryder wondered why they needed a meeting if it was so quick. Or had Violet moved the meeting along quickly, for their date. *Date.* He loved the sound of that. Finally, they were past some of the road blocks between them and able to move forward. He hoped they stayed on track.

"It's your day to be a queen," Violet was saying.

Ryder hadn't been listening closely until *queen* came out of her mouth.

Ryder stopped pacing and turned to the backs sitting around the table.

"Why not surround yourself with sparkle..." Violet continued.

Ryder grinned. What was she up to?

"...with ice." Ryder found his anger diminishing as he listened to Violet fight Joel in her own way. Ryder made his way to the opposite side of the table to enjoy the reactions of the happy couple. Mostly Joel's reaction.

"Ice?" Missy glanced at Joel, who shared the unsure look. "I'm having a summer wedding," Missy pointed out.

Violet smiled wide, fake smile she'd never sent his direction. "I know but there's this amazing company that makes beautiful ice sculptures that would accent your decor. Look..." Violet began flipping through her screen. "We could arrange ice flower bouquets or swans..."

"I don't like swans," Missy said.

"Alright. We could do a king and queen sculpture at the head table." There was no mistaking the pure pleasure across Violet's face.

Oh shit. Was she going to say something?

Ryder's feet nearly gave out on him as her next words left Violet's mouth. "An ice queen..."

Ryder gripped the back of the wooden chair in front of him.

Violet continued. "...doesn't that sound amazing?"

Missy shook her head.

Joel shot a glance at Ryder, but Ryder shrugged it off innocently. If Violet wanted to come right out and mention the on/off and up/down craziness between Ryder and Violet, Ryder would stand by her side and hopefully he would get to throw a punch or two in Joel's direction. But Ryder had no idea where Violet was going with this, so he remained quiet.

"Doesn't ice at a wedding seem...cold-hearted?" Missy exchanged a look with Joel that confirmed Joel had mentioned Violet's nickname to his fiancé.

Violet didn't miss it.

Ryder wanted to clarify that Joel was a lying bastard and Violet was anything but an Ice Queen. Ryder was one hundred percent positive about that. No matter how thick she built the barrier around her, every inch Violet let Ryder in, he saw more of who she really was.

But, Ryder was stuck. He couldn't say a damn word. He wanted to take Violet out of this whole ludicrous situation, but it wasn't his place.

However, a little helping hand wouldn't hurt.

Ryder moved behind Violet for full view of the ice sculptures across her iPad. He could have stood between Missy and Violet, but much preferred taking in the womanly smell of Violet and feeling her shoulders tense as his grazed her.

"I like the idea of ice sculptures. Let me see what the options are." With one hand on the back of Violet's chair, Ryder used the other to scroll her iPad, purposely rubbing his body against hers with each movement.

Violet didn't move. She didn't take her machine or ask him politely to remove his hand, she simply watched.

Ryder stopped at two lovers entangled...naked. "Oooh, that's interesting."

Violet let a giggle escape and the sound was soothing music to Ryder's ears. He wanted to make this cautious woman let loose everyday of their lives.

"They're naked," Missy observed, appalled, as if she'd never seen a naked person.

It was art. Actually, it was amazing. "It's two lovers entwined in the beautiful art of lovemaking and that, Missy, is magnificence."

"That is porn," Joel said.

Another laugh bubbled in Violet and she cleared her throat. "Let's move on."

Her finger touched the screen and Ryder swatted it away. "I'm not finished."

"Yes, but it's not your wedding." Violet slapped his hand away.

Ryder caught her hand. "That's right, because if it was my wedding, we would all be in the silver ballroom." The silver ballroom where images of Violet sprawled beneath him on the head table were so enchantingly real it was like they'd already been there together.

Violet glared at him and the way her little nose squished together was adorable. He almost reached down and kissed her.

"Yes, we all know you would choose the silver ballroom and have a winter wedding with snow falling in the background. I'm sure a naked ice sculpture of two lovers entwined would fit perfectly in your decor. I will make a note of that for your future wedding." Violet stopped suddenly.

With her head still turned at him, Ryder watched as the awareness of everything she'd just shared in front of Joel and Missy, crossed her face. Her eyes pleaded an escape she would never find.

"Yes, let's make notes now. I think I want three ice sculptures at my wedding. This love making couple..." Ryder clicked the add button on the screen and Violet forgot her fears, distracted by taking his order off.

"Would you get your hands off my iPad."

Ryder didn't listen. "And the ice king and queen..." Ryder stretched the last word as he began flipping the pages on the screen. "You never know what lies under the chillness of an ice queen..." he muttered under his breath, for Violet only.

"Ryder Carlex," Violet scolded reaching for his hand again.

"Violet Caliendo," he mocked her.

Violet laughed, a wonderful mixture of frustration and humor, and he knew she'd forgotten they weren't alone.

She grasped his hand and pushed him away. At the same time, she turned her whole body for leverage.

"You are worse than Parker, I swear. Next time we are on the boat, I'm taking the electronics away from you." She poked his chest with the last word. "And we will see how you like it."

Next time? Next time! He would like that plenty.

As Ryder tripped backwards, he laughed at her empty threat and pulled Violet to her feet with him. Suddenly, he was lost with her, forgetting that they weren't alone, or that there were truths between them still unresolved. Violet stumbled against him laughing.

"Maybe I will skip the life jacket next time we are on the swim deck."

Violet's eyes flared. "You don't even know if I can swim."

"Then don't tempt me."

She laughed again only this time it was interrupted by Joel clearing his voice, then he asked, "You two went on the boat together?"

Violet stiffened, and then surprised him, when she sent Ryder a look that said, *that's not all we did,* and he loved that it was laced with humor too.

Ryder knew right there that they could get through whatever Violet was scared of. Whether it be his past, or her future, Ryder didn't want to spend another day without her smile, her laughter and that naughty side of her that excited him.

"I like the window in the silver ballroom," Missy said, oblivious to the tension in the room. "Violet, is that room still available?"

Chapter Fifteen

ESCAPING THE PITS of hell, better known as the painful meeting with Joel and Missy, which Ryder had derailed into a childish laughing fit between the two of them, had been quick, short and fun.

Violet found that Ryder was always challenging her. Whether it be after their encounter in the washroom followed by the taunting and teasing looks he sent, to today and jumping in with the ice sculptures, and there were so many things in-between. Each for instance, made Violet smile inside.

She loved that he didn't treat her like she was a scary monster or on a pedestal. Ryder was open and honest with her. He always had been and that made all the admissions in her office even more believable.

Standing in the foyer of the resort, Violet excused herself, feigning work obligations, but alternatively trying to hurry Joel and Missy on their way. Joel had stopped for a quick chat with the girls at the receptionist desk. Violet didn't even want to think what background they had together. And she didn't have a chance because Joel's absence gave Ryder the opportunity to send her a sly wink. Fireworks went off in her stomach, like the long weekend.

Regrettably, Joel had other plans.

"Missy, I will meet you in the car, I just want to talk to Violet for a minute about the kids," Joel said.

Missy tiptoed up to kiss Joel, before leaving with Ryder at her side.

I wish I was at Ryder's side. Only a few short minutes away. Just get rid of Joel first. ASAP.

Violet prepared herself for whatever issues Joel had with the kids.

Parker was too bossy. Sophia wouldn't eat her broccoli again. Make the girl carrots. She was ten, if she said no to broccoli, buy carrots. Really it wasn't that hard. Or deep fried pickles... Violet would never think about deep fried pickles the same way again.

"Can we talk in your office?"

Her office? Why? It was all the way down the hall, and then all the way back to the foyer. They were wasting precious minutes. Just spit it out and let's part ways. We talked less when we were married.

"Of course." Violet handed her iPad to Mandy, the receptionist behind the counter. "Can you get this to Melissa and ask her to process the Bensen changes before tomorrow and leave it on my desk in my office please." From the gold to silver room...Missy was as flip-floppy about the room as Violet was about her feelings for Ryder.

Mandy flashed a wide smile that showed a dimple on her right side, almost hidden by the freckles across her face. "Certainly." Her green eyes popped under sweeping, thick eyelashes.

Once they were in Violet's office and Joel shut the door behind them, he asked, "What's going on between you and Ryder?"

More than ever went on between us. And I've only been out with him twice.

That was unusual, wasn't it? To feel closer, safer and more desired by a man she'd known not even two weeks than the man she'd been married to for years?

"I don't know what you're referring to," she said instead.

169

"You went fishing on his boat." It sounded like an accusation, but not in the context he was saying. Violet wasn't quite sure what he was accusing her of, but knew it was spurred from the closeness she and Ryder allowed to show for that brief moment...the best moment of the entire meeting.

Violet was sick and tired of tiptoeing around Joel. After watching Ryder almost punch Joel in the face, she needed to step in and stand up for herself. Enough was enough. Yes, he was their children's father, but his disrespect toward her was finished...today.

"Yes, I did go fishing on Ryder's boat, with *our* children. The fishing trip *you* planned with them and *cancelled* at the last second. Not only did you leave Parker and Sophia disappointed by your lack of commitment, but you selfishly put your friend in an awkward predicament. Don't you go around accusing me of anything, when you were the one who cancelled. Why did you cancel, Joel? What was so important you couldn't make it for a day out with your children...again?"

Joel didn't miss a beat. "My car broke down." It lacked condolence for the children Violet would give her life for.

Violet couldn't guarantee that she didn't roll her eyes at his attempted, poorly attempted, and pathetic excuse.

"Ryder was definitely the bigger man that day, offering to take *our* children and his best friend's ex-wife on a boating trip that he'd planned with *you*. So you should turn yourself around and go thank Ryder and apologize to your kids." Violet stepped toward him. "Don't you ever accuse me of anything again and remember that my business is no longer any of yours. And while you are at it, stop making sad excuses that the kids see right through and spend some time with them instead."

There was something about the way Joel was staring at her, still accusing, that only infuriated her more.

Why was he so angry with her? Why did it seem deeper than a boat ride?

Violet had spent a great deal of her life married to this man and after discovering his ulterior motives to his proposal of marriage, Violet had been able to seek out the moments in his dark eyes that were hiding something. Right now, there was something about this topic that he was keeping from her.

"You're lying," Joel said.

The nerve of this man. Violet had never wanted to slap a man across the face like she did at that very moment. "Excuse me?"

"I was married to you for years. I lived with you. I know you and right now you're lying to me. You're keeping something from me."

That made two of them.

"Is what we had what you call a marriage and living with someone? Spending your nights at the bar and your early mornings on the couch?"

"You slept with him, didn't you?"

Venom was rising through Violet's veins at the nerve of Joel asking her about her sex life, when it was clear to everyone that he'd been cheating on her during their marriage...and not only with Missy.

"Who I sleep with is none of your damn business." The words hardly made it past the growing lump of anger in Violet's throat. This was the punishment of letting a man into her life, his accusations and threatening stares. Joel could accuse and threaten all he wanted, he had nothing over Violet, not anymore.

"So that's a yes."

"Joel, if you have nothing to discuss about our kids, then get the hell out of my office. Emma can take over your wedding. I'm not doing this bullshit anymore." Violet did not have to tolerate his crap...not anymore...not ever.

Joel stepped toward her and the smell of men's spruce body wash stung her nostrils. "You think you are a master at hiding your emotions..."

He was so close that Violet felt his breath across her skin, causing her stomach to rotate. She would not bow down to this man. She was not scared of him, nor did she care what he had to say or what he thought. All she wanted was for him to leave and take his assumptions with him.

"...you think your feelings aren't written across your face, but Violet, I know you. I knew when you were faking during sex. I knew you didn't want me, that you felt obligated. I knew you dug into my finances and assumed exactly what I did." He paused dramatically before saying what they both knew. "That I married you for your money."

Violet felt her legs shake beneath her and her strength diminish. Never in her life had she felt so weak, and it was all because of Joel, his words, his truths.

"To be honest, at the beginning it was rather a turn on. Seducing you after a shower, and taking you in our bed, when I knew you didn't want me. Feeling your body tense beneath my touch, my kiss. But, then it got boring and I was left with a cold bitch."

Slap him! Step away! You don't have to listen to this. Where was Ryder?

For the first time in Violet's life, she wanted another person to step in and save her. At the same time, letting Ryder in would be giving him the same knowledge about her that Joel had. That was terrifying. Look where it had gotten her.

Violet didn't move or say anything.

"Do you think Ryder doesn't know what a cold, heartless lay you are?"

Hearing him say these things and calling her a heartless lay stung worse than she'd ever imagined. It made her past so real and her future so clear.

"I hardly know the guy. But, I do know he is drop-dead gorgeous and from what you've told me, you better hurry up back to your car before he gets frisky with your fiancé." Violet drew all the remaining strength she had and moved even closer to Joel. "Apparently women have no self-control around Ryder Carlex." Violet was among one of them, but she would never admit it to Joel.

Joel stared her down on his way out. It wasn't until the door shut that Violet's legs gave out and she found the closest chair to collapse in.

Boring. A cold bitch. A heartless lay.

Violet felt sick.

She could say the same about him. He'd been a selfish and heartless lover. But, what did it matter? She would never try to hurt a person the way Joel did to her. That was exactly what happened when you let someone into your life, they used your weaknesses against you.

Now Violet was left trembling and in the end...alone. It wasn't worth it. This feeling of violation at the hands of someone else.

This was the last time.

***

RYDER STAYED BEHIND as Joel and Missy drove away. He thought about texting Violet that the coast was clear, but after the crappy way Joel treated her, he thought picking her up was more appropriate. Joel was an ass. Violet deserved to be treated like the queen she was...and not the ice queen that Joel called her.

Ryder knocked on Violet's office door and entered with her permission.

Violet was standing from a chair and when she looked up at him, Ryder knew something was wrong. The smile was swiped away from her lips, leaving a thin line. He thought he caught her chin tremble.

Violet turned her unreadable eyes away from Ryder. "I thought you were Melissa bringing me back my iPad," she said.

"What happened?" Ryder knew he should tread on this water carefully, but something had her upset and he could swear he saw fear play across her face.

Violet ignored him, walking around her desk and not turning back to him until the massive antique was between them. Didn't she know that piece of wood wouldn't keep him away.

"Ryder, this isn't going to work between us," she started, but the way her voice trailed away with her eyes told him it wasn't what she wanted.

Joel had been grouchy when he'd arrived back from her office. Slamming his car door, ignoring Ryder and snapping at Missy when she didn't get in the car quickly enough.

What had they talked about? Or more like what had Joel said to her? Did Violet mention their date to him?

"Violet, what happened?"

"Nothing happened," she snarled. "I'm not ready for a relationship."

It was a date, not an invitation to a wedding.

"What did Joel say to you?" Damn it, he should have clocked him when he'd had the opportunity.

"This isn't about Joel." Her temper was flaring which only added fuel to Ryder's fire.

"Damned it isn't. Ten minutes ago, you were flashing me seductive glances and now you're not ready for a date? *A date?*"

"Or is it an attempt to get into my pants?"

Ryder shook his head and moved to the edge of the desk, as close as he could get without moving to the other side. His hands landed on the edge and he leaned forward.

"Don't do that. We've moved passed that. Don't bring it up when it's obvious something else is going on here and it has to do with Joel. If you don't tell me, I will go ask Joel myself. Only I won't leave without an answer."

Violet's jaws clenched together and she glared at Ryder, long and hard. He thought maybe she was preparing to be honest with him and put their lies to rest. He was wrong.

"The man I *thought* you were was the man I needed that day in the washroom to make me forget how hard it is to watch Joel wed someone else. The man you're trying to prove that you are, isn't who I need right now." Her words stung, but she wasn't fooling him. He wasn't blind to her true feelings for him. Lord knew the two of them were terrible at hiding feelings from each other. It wasn't just about lust and desire and she knew it. This change of heart had something to do with Joel.

"Don't give me that bullshit."

"We're done here," she said. "Shut the door on your way out." Violet sat down and started moving papers around on her desk.

Ryder was far from done. He walked around the desk and swung her chair around, then bent down on one knee, so he met her in height. Her hands pulled away when he reached for her, so he grasped both sides of her head and brought her face to his. Her hands tried to pull him off, but he was stronger.

When he started to speak, she stopped struggling. "Don't shut me out," he said. "I am not the bad guy, Violet. I promise. Be honest with me, please. We can go so much further if you are just upfront with me. What did Joel say to you? Why are you pushing me away? Why are you scared?"

Violet struggled emotionally, as her eyes went through several phases and when she finished, he thought she was going to talk to him.

Instead she asked, "Who are Susan and Kelly?"

Susan and Kelly? Susan and Kelly! What the hell did they have to do with anything? How did she even know about them? It wasn't Joel, because even he didn't know about his dad or their workers.

"Speechless," she said.

He hated what she was thinking. Was it Joel planting more lies into her mind. "Where—"

Violet cut him off, finishing his question for him. "Did I hear their names? In the bathroom. Remember when you were trying to decide which one, or both, were going to be waiting for you at home? Susan and Kelly? Or have you forgotten about them already?"

He wasn't ready to tell her about his dad. If they had gone forward in a positive direction, he would have been more open to the inevitable. But, right now, he didn't know what she was thinking and giving her that kind of information, when his father hadn't wanted anyone to know, wasn't happening.

"Violet, that wasn't what it sounded like. What you're making it sound like."

"I'm not making it sound like anything. It sounded like you were having a threesome."

Did this woman hear anything he said earlier?

"Exactly. It's not what it sounded like."

"Well, what was it, Ryder? Please enlighten me."

Ryder remained quiet and his eyes fell to her lap. He wanted to tell her. He didn't want lies between them, but this was different. This was loyalty to his dad and he couldn't go back on his word, not right now, not like this.

"I can't," he finally said. He looked up and saw that even if he told her, it was a losing battle. She was finished with him, just like an ice queen. "Not right now Violet. I'm sorry."

"That's not enough for me."

"It's not enough or it's an excuse to walk away from us because you're scared? Because Joel has hurt you so badly that you can't even imagine what it feels like to not be scared of trusting a man. Is it so hard to believe that the incredible feelings soaring through you are real and that you deserve them? You deserve them Violet."

Violet pulled away from him and Ryder let her go. He didn't want to, but he also didn't want her to have a reason not to trust him.

Violet rolled back on the chair, but stayed seated, sending an ice cold stare.

"Don't act like you know me just because we spent one day on your boat together. You don't know me, Ryder Carlex. You don't know my past. You know nothing."

Ryder stood, accepting that he was done here. Violet wasn't ready to let him into her life. Ryder might not know all the things that conspired between her and Joel, but he knew he couldn't help her figure them out. Violet needed to do this on her own.

"I know you better than Joel ever did." He didn't doubt it and wished he'd gotten her first, before Joel had put all the fear and doubt in her.

Ryder had thought his trust in people had diminished, but it was nothing compared to how this woman held tightly to her emotions. Since the day Courtney hurt him, Ryder had used his distrust to push people away, much like the woman in front of him. Only he knew...he *felt*...that he could trust Violet. He was ready to take the step, but she wasn't.

"Say hi to Susan and Kelly."

Her final dismissing jab did not faze Ryder like she hoped. He remained calm, but he spoke forceful. "When you're finished acting like a lost child, hiding in the dark shadows, feeding your fear the lies that what you feel for me isn't real, you come find me. Because Violet Caliendo, I don't care if we've spent one day together or one-hundred, I'm not afraid to admit that I like you."

Ryder's mother had always told him that the day he found his soul mate, his heart would be clear. His heart couldn't be any clearer that it was this woman and only this woman.

Chapter Sixteen

AFTER ANOTHER SLEEPLESS night, in which Violet had been pretending was the result of her underlying urge to return Ryder's sweater and be done with him forever, she awoke and just allowed everything sink in.

Letting her guard down, opening her mind and heart to other possibilities was like touching a prickly rose stem. Violet wanted to pull away, but she pushed passed each thorn.

Finally, succumbing to facing her past with Joel, her time spent with Ryder and what a future with Ryder would be like, was a huge and complex step for Violet. She had stopped thinking about her future long ago and focused, instead, on her children and what was best for them. Now, envisioning a future with a man who challenged her, made her smile and lit her insides on fire with only a look, had Violet craving that wonderful potential future.

Maybe if that knitted piece of material hadn't been acting as a constant reminder of Ryder's closing argument, before he walked out of her office, all calm and collected unlike Violet's trembling body and whirlwind mind, she might have been able to ignore the poignant feeling of her heart. But, that sweater was sitting on her bed, when she slipped under the sheets at night, and wrapped up around her when she awoke in the morning. It smelled like a warm summer breeze, with a masculine hint of Ryder. It was tantalizing.

Now, Ryder's scent was all over her sheets and her pillows. She'd awakened two mornings in a row to the majestic smell that made her pulse race with excitement and at the same time sent an unfamiliar contentment through her. Only to open her eyes and find she was alone and it was Ryder's sweater beside her and not the man himself.

If that wasn't bad enough, and it did indeed feel like torture, she was waking up to Ryder's voice in her head calling her a scared child while claiming to like her...a lot.

A lot? A lot! Did he even know what the definition of that word meant?

Not to mention, who did he think he was spouting off that she was a lost child hiding in the dark?

Oh, please. I'm not lost and I do not hide. They why are you skipping breakfast with the rest of the family and preparing a private breakfast with Parker and Sophia?

Violet whisked the eggs more vigorously, anticipating how this conversation would go.

She glanced down the hallway and wondered if her kids would ever climb out of bed. *What time was it?* More importantly, what would she say to her kids? How much would she tell them? All the while she was scared how they would take it.

Scared. There is that fear again.

Pouring the eggs into the fry pan, she inhaled the buttery aroma and pushed forward. She decided today was the last day she would hide in the darkness.

Waking up this morning, sweater tightly tucked at her side, she stopped thinking and arguing. She would instead listen to what she wanted. What *she* wanted.

It had been a long time since Violet listened to what she wanted and not what others expected of her. Whether it was the haunting voice of her father demanding perfection for the Caliendo name or that of the filter she'd created in her head to obey her dad's expectations, she persistently stepped out of the light whenever things got complicated, whenever fear arose, and into the darkness.

This morning, lying in bed with the hushed ambience of the early morning, she only listened to what she wanted and Violet found her answer came easily: Violet wanted Ryder.

There was no uncertainty in her conclusion, not from her heart. She stepped out of the darkness and stood up to the reasons that kept her from going after what she wanted.

Ryder had been right, he *did* know Violet and unlike any other person.

How was that even possible after spending such a short time with him?

Ryder knew Violet was damaged, even before she did, mistaking what she thought was strength only to find fear.

Realizing the truth, suddenly Violet had accepted her filter wasn't always empowering her, but instead holding her back. It was humiliating to admit, but thinking her marriage to Joel had made her stronger, thicker, and ready to fight the work, had in turn made her weak and scared, cowering from the rest of the world.

Instead of courageously moving forward and accepting a date with Ryder, the fear she'd allowed had caused her to pull away. What she'd mistaken for strength, was truthfully her fear trying every tactic to make him leave, to hate her, anything so she could...hide. But, Ryder had seen right through her and looked deep into the parts of her soul that she'd thought were solid rocks. Instead, the pieces of her life she'd thought were secure were a tumbling rockslide.

Why had it taken Ryder to make her see that?

It didn't matter. She was finished hiding in the dark.

But she wasn't ready to stand outside of the shadows without first talking to her kids. Ryder would not only affect her life, but her children's too and they were still her top priority.

Violet heard the loud trudges that belonged to her son, then listened as he banged on Sophia's door, before making his way into the kitchen.

Parker stopped in the hallway and stared at Violet, confused. "What are you doing?" he asked.

During the summer months, when Violet's schedule was almost booked solid with appointments and weddings, they had breakfast at the buffet, where one of Violet's family members would take Sophia and Parker for the day and meet back for lunch. Violet had pushed back her morning appointment, because as soon as they were finished breakfast, she was heading over to Ryder's, depending on how Sophia and Parker reacted to her inquiries.

"I'm making breakfast."

He rubbed his eyes, and then stretched his arms high above him and murmured, "Why?" just as Sophia stepped up beside him and sent the same look as her brother.

Violet dished the eggs onto a platter. "Come on guys, sit down." Violet grabbed the plate of toast with the other hand and walked behind her pokey kids to the dining room table, where she'd already set the table and a tray of bacon.

"Do you have a day off?" Sophia asked, pouring a glass of juice for herself, then offering to pour Parker's.

"No. I missed having breakfast with just the three of us." *Liar*.

Each of them filled their plates with eggs, bacon and toast, then silently ate. She watched as each of her kids began to slowly wake up. Parker was first to start his regular continuous banter. Violet found Parker was in a better mood in the mornings, before whatever was bothering Parker set in for the day.

Sophia wasn't far behind waking up and detailed her plans for the day at her friend's house in town, which consequently brought up fishing. Violet relaxed as Parker and Sophia began recalling the fun they had on Ryder's boat.

"So, you guys like Ryder?" Violet causally asked, sipping her coffee and watching their reactions. Neither flinched as they said, *yes* and continued with the exciting conversation of the fish finder.

"I was thinking of inviting Ryder over tonight. For supper. A thank you for taking us on the boat after your dad's car broke down."

"Dad's car didn't break down," Sophia said. "We're not babies Mom, seriously. He didn't want to come."

Violet was about to object, even though she suspected as much, and she hated that her children saw Joel's selfishness, but Parker cut her off. "Yeah. Dad doesn't like us."

Violet's heart broke. It crumbled into a thousand pieces and pooled around them. Violet forgot about her reason for sitting down with her kids and was thankful she had made time for the three of them, because there were broken little hearts at this table, and probably the reason for Parker's moods lately.

"Parker, Sophia, your dad loves you."

Parker grunted.

Sophia stabbed her plate with the fork.

Selfish Joel.

"I know that our divorce has been hard on you both, but I am so proud of the way you two have handled it." Violet reached over and touched Sophia's hand to stop the sharp sound of her fork repeatedly hitting the plate. "Your dad is under a lot of stress with the wedding—"

"You have weddings all the time and aren't stressed out," Parker grumbled.

"Yes, but that's different. It's my profession. I plan other people's weddings and try to make it easier for them."

"And you're planning Dad's," Sophia added in a snarky tone that indicated she didn't like that arrangement.

Violet looked at her daughter's solemn face, staring at the remaining bits of egg on her plate. "Is that a problem?" *Why had Violet never considered that her planning Joel's wedding would bother them?*

Sophia glared her ten-year-old eyes full of attitude at Violet. "Mom, it's embarrassing."

Embarrassing? How had Violet missed that? "I'm sorry, Sweetheart. I didn't know you felt that way."

"Well, I do," she scowled.

"Your dad and I still care about you, about each other. When he asked me I didn't think it would be negative on you or Parker. If you feel this way I will ask Emma to take over−"

Sophia cut her off. "It's too late." Sophia tossed her fork and it went skidding across the table with a loud clang that made Parker and Violet jump. "Why are you defending him?" Sophia accused, standing abruptly and sending the chair falling backwards.

"Sophia!" Violet stood.

"What? He left us all for *her*. And now he's marrying Missy and you're helping him!"

Violet wasn't going to have a heart left after this conversation. Sophia knew and by the questioning look Parker sent Violet, she assumed he'd heard the rumors of the affair also. Violet didn't know what to say. She couldn't confirm or deny whether there had been an affair, because she didn't know.

Parker stepped in front of Sophia and told her to shut up. "It's not Mom's fault," he snapped.

Violet shook her head at the direction this conversation was going. If anything, she would have suspected Parker, who had been grumbling around for weeks, to be furious at Violet. Instead, her son was defending her.

"And now you want to date Ryder," Sophia accused.

"So what," Parker said. "I like Ryder and if you haven't noticed, he likes us."

"He likes *Mom*," Sophia corrected. "He's only being nice to us because he likes Mom."

"That's not true. Ryder's always nice to us."

Sophia snarled at Parker. "Because he was Dad's friend and now he's Mom's *special friend*." Sophia made air quotes. "Why would Ryder like us if Dad doesn't even like us? He could be just like Dad." *Just like Dad? What did that mean?* Violet didn't have a chance to ask.

"Ryder *likes us*," Parker snarled back, sending up his own air quotes that Sophia slapped away. That sent Parker into defensive fighting mode and he threw his arms in the air at Sophia.

"Whoa!" Violet yanked Parker off Sophia and instructed her daughter to take a seat on the couch. "We do not hit in this family," she told Parker and pointed at the empty spot on the couch beside his sister.

Parker grumbled unhappily to the couch after yanking free of Violet and sending her a killer stare. *He was on my side.*

Violet sat across from her kids, little bundles of anger and resentment. She had thought they'd moved past this after Joel had left. They'd sat down, the four of them, as a family and discussed Joel's moving out, the divorce, everything. Where were all these newly developed feelings coming from and how did Violet miss them?

Violet took a deep breath. She didn't even know where to begin.

"First of all, I would like to clarify that your father loves you. Both of you." Violet took the time to look between her children's glaring snickers. "People are not the same. We all show our emotions differently. We behave differently, but that doesn't mean your dad doesn't love you."

"He barely comes over anymore." Parker's voice had settled and now tears underlined his voice.

"He's been busy with the wedding. But, if you feel that way, I will call him and we will sit down and talk to him."

Parker pouted. "I don't want him to know."

Violet moved from the couch and sat on the edge of the coffee table so she could reach out and touch Parker's knee. "Sweetheart, your dad is just as confused as you are. He probably wonders why every time you visit him, you are snarky and mean. And if we don't talk to him, he won't know why and we won't be able to move past this. Alright?"

Parker nodded.

Violet turned to Sophia, whose arms were folded tightly across the chest of her printed shirt, as she stared away from them, tight lipped like she was on the edge of crying too.

The moment of silence she allowed for herself to take in Sophia's anger, spread guilt through Violet. Violet's own fears to put her trust in people had washed off on her daughter. A week ago, Violet would have thought, *Good, Sophia will be strong.* Now, the fear she saw in her daughter's eyes chased away Violet's own reservations. Ryder was right. Now Violet had to be strong for her daughter.

"Sophia, we can't hide from people because someone has hurt us."

"Someone? Everyone lies Mom. Dad lied to all of us. Grandma and Uncle Carl lied to Marc and Izzy about who their real dad was. Kate lied to Marc about Rosemary. Everybody lies."

When it was said so plain, so simple, it was no wonder Violet didn't trust.

"I can't defend why any of them kept those secrets and told those lies. I know some of them were done out of love, to keep our family together."

"Not Dad."

"Your dad didn't want to hurt either of you. We grew apart and that's not either of our fault or your own." Violet took a deep breath. "We can't hide from life or from people. Life is wonderful and there are a lot of amazing people out there. Some might hurt you, but others will love you and that love is worth putting yourself out there."

"Like Ryder?"

"I know it's scary Sophia. I'm scared too. I don't know that Ryder's not like your dad and that he won't hurt me. But I trust in my heart that he's good and kind and thoughtful. He didn't invite me to go fishing, he invited you two. I just tagged along because I was scared Parker might rip him to shreds."

Sophia grinned.

Parker smirked.

Violet's heart lightened.

"If I thought for one second that Ryder would hurt us, I would never invite him in. I promise."

Violet sank onto the beige leather sofa beside her kids and pulled Sophia into a firm embrace. Her children came first.

Parker crawled over top of Violet and settled himself awkwardly in the middle of them, to stretch his short arms around both the girls.

"Are you still inviting Ryder over?" Parker's muffled voice asked.

"I don't know if we are ready for Ryder to come over," Violet admitted. They had trust issues that ran deeper than Violet knew.

"I'm ready," Parker's muffled voice said.

"You're heavy and annoying," Sophia said, pushing at Parker. Parker caught the humor in her voice and fell against his sister, rolling onto the floor. "Dork." Sophia rolled her eyes.

Parker ignored her and ran down the hall toward his bedroom yelling he was getting his swimsuit on because Eliza promised to take them swimming after breakfast.

Sophia didn't follow. She curled her legs against her and wrapped her arms around them, staring at Violet with eyes that had more to say. Violet didn't pressure her. She leaned into the sofa and sat quietly with her daughter. When she was ready to talk, Violet was here to listen.

"I'm going to ask Emma to finish your dad's wedding," Violet said. "If you had told me that my planning his wedding was embarrassing, I would have handed it over to Emma right away."

"Mom, it's embarrassing that he's getting married here at all. *Everyone* in the resort is talking about it."

"People are always going to talk."

Sophia dropped her head. When she slowly looked away from her fidgeting fingers she said, "They talk about Dad having an affair with Missy. Like when you two were still married. Is it true?"

Violet had no other answer but the truth. "I don't know, Sophia. I've heard the rumors."

"Don't they bother you?"

"They did, of course. But, your dad and I weren't in love with each other anymore. It doesn't mean we don't still care about each other. If you need to know the answer to that question, then I guess you should ask him. Either way, it won't change the past and it won't control my future. It won't scare me away from letting people into my life."

Thanks to Ryder.

If he hadn't opened her eyes, she would still be cowering with the illusion it was her strength.

"You don't think I should ask, do you?"

"You do what you need to do. Don't hold back on the account of others...of me. Whatever the truth is, it won't change me."

Sophia sighed loudly, a trait she didn't get from Violet and curled up beside her mother. "I like Ryder," she said, as if it was being forced out of her. "And he smiles more when you're around and you smile more when he's around. So, if you like him, I guess I like him too."

"You guess?"

"I like Tank and Sabin more."

Violet laughed. Oh, her daughter was going to be just fine.

Chapter Seventeen

WEDNESDAY ROLLED AROUND and Violet still hadn't tried to make any contact with Ryder.

Damn, she was one stubborn woman.

Ryder had stared at her number in his phone contacts and thought about sending her a little, *have you stepped out of the dark yet? Or are you ready to get some deep fried pickles?* He thought better of it, giving her the space she needed.

So he'd tried his hardest to not think about her, but it seemed the blonde beauty was unforgettable. The abundance of exhausting Skype meetings with his cousins, the Kendricks, back in Oakston had distracted him momentarily. They demanded the final decisions, *his* final word, for the redesign of the store, which in turn required his full attention.

But the moment his feet hit the wooden dock, the bow of the boat reminded him of the apple they shared together under stars that had cast a luminous glow across her smooth face, which only heated his desire to kiss her again. And the swim platform brought back the exact moment a weight, Ryder hadn't realized he was carrying, lifted, reminding him that it felt good to smile, laugh and tease. It was all because of Violet.

He wanted to be angry at himself for being foolish enough to let another woman past his guard and provide her with the weapons to hurt him, but Violet had given him a gift she would never know, his desire to live life again. The down side was that he wanted to live his life with Violet. He wanted to board the boat with her at his side, open a silly can of corn for her fishing bait, and *he* wanted to massage the sun block across her entire body, before wrapping his arms around her and kissing those saucy lips.

Ryder needed a break from his head...from Violet. He decided spending the day with his dad would keep him busy.

Susan took the opportunity to run into town and complete some errands, which gave Ryder one-on-one time with his dad. Sadly, Donald was having a bad day. The two of them heading to the dock with their fishing gear was now out of the question. Donald didn't even want to go to the gardens, and that was his favorite place.

Ryder and Donald spent the morning watching old movies on television instead. Old black and white Westerns, with poor effects and comical conversations were minimally distracting.

Ryder felt like he was glancing at his phone every five minutes, to see if he'd missed a text from Violet. The volume was hiked to the max so there was no way he could have missed it, but he looked anyway.

Ryder opened his eyes, not realizing he'd fallen asleep. His exhausted body begged him to return to sleep. Ryder stretched his body out in the recliner and glanced over at the matching beige chair, expecting to see his dad. Donald wasn't there.

Ryder sat up, pulling the lever on the side of the chair and standing, all in one motion. "Dad?" he called. "Dad?" Besides the noise of Tank scrambling to his feet, silence answered Ryder.

Where was his dad?

Panic thundered through his body as Ryder checked every room in the house, even where Susan and Kelly slept. Nothing.

Ryder dialed Susan's number as he stepped out onto the small wooden porch to scan the property.

She picked up on the first ring.

"I fell asleep," Ryder said right away.

There was no time to play games. His dad was not stable enough to roam the grounds by himself and with the river... Ryder almost screamed. He didn't even know if his dad could swim anymore. In his prime years, Donald had been an avid swimmer, but now, now he was deteriorating and Ryder didn't know what he was capable of these days.

"I didn't mean to. And when I woke up Dad was gone. I can't find him. He's not in the house."

"Alright. Ryder, calm down," Susan said in a tone he'd often heard her use with his father to ease his alarm.

Was that even a possibility?

"Check the gardens first. Your dad will sit in the gardens all day."

"Okay."

"I'm on my way. I shouldn't be more than fifteen minutes. Check by the river and on the boat."

Ryder was running to the garden, then changed direction toward the river.

Where did he check first?

Some of the paths led to the dock, so he would take those paths straight to the water.

He stopped suddenly. "What if he's not there?"

What if Ryder couldn't find him? What if he fell in the water? What if he got lost in the bush across the road?

There were so many what it's clambering in his head that he almost missed Susan's promise that they would fine him.

"I will call Kelly and we will both help you find Donald."

"Okay." Ryder hung up and ran until he hit the gardens. They were his grandmother Carlex's gardens, which was why Ryder figured his dad loved to sit for hours staring at the bright bursts of color.

The estate was huge.

Why had he fallen asleep?

He had one thing to do today, watch his dad, and his distraction for Violet had clouded him into a deep sleep. His feelings for Violet, a woman who was fighting against them, were the reason Donald was missing, possibly hurt, possibly...

Ryder swallowed the fear of losing his father, as he rounded the edge of the property and found no sign of his dad. He knew the day would come when this disease took over his father's body, but Ryder wasn't ready to lose Donald yet. He wasn't ready to be alone.

***

VIOLET TURNED ONTO Crystal Cliff Road. Her eyes darted from the luxury estates, hidden behind wrought iron-gated properties along one side, to the trees lining the woods on the other side. The leg not pushing the pedal bounded at a rapid pace.

What if she chickened out? You're not five years old, you're an adult. Adults don't chicken out.

Violet pushed a hand on her left leg, as she spotted movement in the long grass on her right. A man walked away from the six-foot grass blowing in the breeze and toward the road. Violet wouldn't have pressed on the breaks had she not recognized the man wearing only brown slacks and no shirt.

Mr. Carlex. *Ryder's dad.* Only, he was half the size he used to be and his burly figure was now frail bones.

Violet pulled over and climbed out, leaving her worry about Ryder behind her.

The closer she walked toward Mr. Carlex, the worse he looked. His once knowledgeable, smiling eyes were sunken and confused, darting around like he was lost.

What was he doing walking around in a bush wearing no shirt, and still a quarter mile from the Carlex estate?

Donald turned away from Violet and started back toward the grass that led to the bush. A bush one could easily get lost in, and from the confused look across the older man's face, it didn't appear as though Donald was aware of where he was headed.

Violet panicked. She was still over twenty feet away from Donald and would have to climb down the steep ditch. *What if she lost sight of him once he went back through the long grass?*

"Mr Carlex!" Violet called, stopping short at the edge of the road, the tips of her heels kicking up pebbles and dust.

Donald didn't look back at her, he didn't even acknowledge her voice. He disappeared into the green shrubbery and Violet was forced to climb, slide and trip down the sharp ditch scattered with two-foot high grass and hard soil beneath her heels. She wished she'd worn shorts or pants, instead of the cotton, navy, t-shirt dress she'd chosen, so she could slip into her office after talking Ryder.

She made it half way down on her feet and then fell the rest of the way on her rear. Only the thin material of her panties separated her from the rough grass, rocks and dirt. Violet didn't have time to pay attention to the damage on the back of her stinging legs. She dusted her derriere and without reservation, she ran through the high grass, struggling to follow the flattened path of Mr. Carlex.

"Mr. Carlex! Mr. Carlex!" She continued shouting his name until she broke through the grass and stopped abruptly, almost falling forward.

Violet sighed a breath of relief when her eyes fell on Mr. Carlex; he had stopped too.

He stared at the ground, where she'd emerged, making no eye contact with her. Sabin stood at his feet, obedient to his owned, but wagged his tail when Violet called out to him.

Trying to catch her breath, Violet sucked in a deep lungful of air, before she turned her full attention to Ryder's dad.

This man neither looked nor acted like the Mr. Carlex that had gracefully made speeches at her mother's events, with his poised, confident smile, that encouraged others to open their chequebooks for every wonderful event Eliza had thrown. Violet was sure, if anywhere else, she might not have recognized him at all. He looked like he'd ages twenty years in the last two years since she'd seen him last.

"Mr. Carlex, what are you doing out here?" Violet asked, but she prepared herself for him not to answer.

He didn't answer right away, more interested in staring intently at the ground around them. Violet was more concerned about how she was going to get him back up the ditch.

When Donald finally answered, it came out slow at first, as if he was struggling to remember what he was thinking and sounded like a child answering her.

"I want to go home."

The bush was not the way to his house.

"Do you need a ride?" she offered, omitting the part where she was heading to his house, planning on confessing her stubborn feelings to his annoyingly handsome, pushy and sweet son. She had a sinking feeling Mr. Carlex wouldn't have heard her if she had.

Donald still avoided eye contact with her and repeated, "I want to go home."

"I will take you home."

"I want to go home." He said it louder, shouting at the end. "I want to go home." And louder again. He was acting...*child-like.*

Violet had seen symptoms like this before and they were an awful lot like Alzheimer's or dementia.

Dementia? Mr. Carlex had dementia? How did Violet not know this? How did nobody know this? It finally struck her...*Because Ryder was hiding it.*

After great effort, including using soft tones to Donald like she did with her grouchy son, and mentioning every name she could in hopes of sparking a memory, Violet finally got him in the car and drove to the Carlex estate, but not before Mr. Carlex had planted an elbow across her jaw. She didn't blame him, he was confused.

Her jaw pounded with pain. When she touched the area, it swelled against her fingers. She was going to need some ice.

Her concern for herself diminished when she parked in front of the Carlex estate, and absorbed the pain and worry Ryder conveyed from where he stood beside the grand circular stairs.

He stood with two women. Both looked to be in their early twenties. Ryder's hands were flaring in every direction, while the shorted blonde-haired woman, who wore mask of concern, tried to calm him by touching his arm. Ryder jerked away only to start the action with the tall brunette, whose soft blue dress matched her tender approach.

When they became aware of Violet's vehicle, their eyes relaxed when they realized Mr. Carlex sat in the passenger's seat. Relief danced across all three of their faces.

Who were these women? Had Ryder moved on so quickly? Was she the fool who thought she was falling in love and he was the player everyone said? No. Stop it, Violet.

These were her terrified thoughts. The very ones that would have her simply depositing Donald and excusing herself so she didn't have to face the reality. Good or bad, she wasn't running away from this.

Both women rushed to the passenger's side of her car, pulling the door open. Their soft voices soothed the man who had screamed a fit not even a minute earlier, scaring the daylights out of Violet. Donald was quick tempered but quick to settle down.

When Donald emerged from the car, Ryder's arms went around his father for a long embrace.

Violet stood back and watched. There was no recollection in Donald's eyes for his son, who was filled with fear and relief at his dad's return.

Violet felt the tears for Ryder form along the rim of her eyes. She held her breath, hoping...praying...that Donald wouldn't pull away from Ryder in another fit. She watched how much Ryder needed his dad...or what was left of him...and her heart was breaking with each long, aching second that went by. Ryder hadn't only lost his mother, he'd lost his dad and nobody had known it.

"Hi, I'm Susan." The shorter of the two women stopped beside Violet and squeezed her hand.

Susan? Susan!

"And this is Kelly." As Violet's eyes moved to the young...so very young woman...who gave a little wave, Violet's heart stopped.

Susan and Kelly? Susan and Kelly? What was Violet thinking coming here? Trying to win Ryder back, when he'd already moved on and was here with Susan and Kelly?

"Hello. Nice to meet you both. I'm Violet Caliendo." Professionalism was her best trait...even when she was dying inside.

"Yes, I recognize you."

Who didn't?

"Kelly and I are Donald's workers and I can't tell you enough how grateful we are for you bringing him back safe. We will still call the doctor in to confirm his condition, but thank you."

Donald's workers? Donald's workers!

Of course. It all made sense now. Ryder was hiding his dad's condition from the outside world and when she asked about Susan and Kelly, he hadn't been ready to tell her.

Why not? Because you were acting like a child hiding in the shadows.

Before Violet could express a welcome, Susan hugged her. Susan was a good foot-and-a-half shorter than Violet and her head rubbed against Violet's arm. Violet patted her back, feeling out of place.

When Susan pulled away, she wore a huge smile. "If Ryder's mood lately has anything to do with you, which I know for a fact it does, then I'm sure we will be seeing a lot of each other in the future."

Ryder's mood? Was it good? Or bad? Was it both?

Violet wanted to ask, but knew now was not the time. This was the secret Ryder couldn't tell her. These women that he couldn't explain but had nothing to do with shacking up with.

Violet felt like a heel.

"I found him down the road. He was wandering through the grass and heading to the bush. I would have called Ryder's cell, but he wasn't that uncooperative. We managed." Skinned legs, a sore jaw later and she was pretty sure this dress was unsalvageable.

Kelly touched her arm. "Thank you for bringing him back."

Ryder let go of Mr. Carlex, only to grip his shoulders and run his eyes across his dad, for what she assumed were signs of injury. When he came up empty-handed, besides a handful of minor scrapes across his bare torso, Ryder looked relieved...a little.

Ryder cupped the sides of his dad face and pulled him against his forehead. "Dad, you scared me. I'm so sorry."

His coarse whisper travelled all the way to Violet. The pain that laced his words, as Ryder talked to a man who didn't acknowledge them, brought tears to Violet's eyes.

Donald yanked away, lost in his own world of confusion, stumbling out of Ryder's grasp.

The horror of his reaction showed an exhausted tale of years dealing with his father's memory loss across Ryder's face, along with grief and a look of agonizing acceptance.

Violet wiped away the tears that slid down her cheeks.

The two women rushed over, escorting Donald away and leaving Ryder to stand alone. The color of his face was stripped away, like he'd seen a ghost. With Donald unrecognizing his own son, wasn't it like Ryder *was* staring at a ghost?

Kelly squeezed Ryder's arm, before leaving, in a caring, *platonic* manner. It stabbed guilt into Violet's heart. She had battled every stage of their connection, not knowing the complex life Ryder was hiding, or the grief he was living with.

Sabin followed behind the trio, moving slowly and exhausted like his owner. Tank was nowhere to be seen, leaving only Ryder and Violet.

Violet wanted to close the distance between them and embrace Ryder as hard and long as he'd done with his father, but his tense shoulders and pacing kept her grounded.

His face was tear-stained and puffy, with clouds of a storm rolling through his eyes. The agony transformed his sea blue eyes, to an unsettling navy blue. His leather, thong sandals slammed against the ground, thudding anger, frustration and misery that looked to be intensifying with each step. Ryder looked like he was ready to explode. Violet wasn't sure what to do.

Violet couldn't be certain Ryder even acknowledged her presence. He hadn't looked at her, not once. His attention was consumed by the safety of his father.

What had happened? Why was he out wondering on his own?

Violet didn't dare to ask.

"Ryder?" she said softly, but loud enough that he would hear her.

Nothing. His pace continued, drilling his eyes to the ground.

Violet stepped to his side, as he passed and touched his arm. "Ryder?"

Ryder yanked away, his feet keeping him along his path.

On his way back, Violet took a deep breath and stepped in front of him, hoping he didn't push her to the ground. His strapping, powerfully built body, just like his father's had once been, would take Violet's tall, tiny body down the ground.

Ryder stopped.

Her body thanked him silently.

The breath she'd been holding, blew out and was lost by the deep breaths coming from Ryder, breaths of a man trying to hold back the tears that threatened.

Violet only stood still long enough to look at him and give him the time to recognize her. Once those blue eyes softened and his lips pinched together, Violet's arms went around his neck. She pulled him against her.

He had no one.

Cancer had taken his mother and dementia was taking his father. Nothing in the world could prepare someone to deal with this change, this loss. And Ryder, an only child, was taking care of his father alone. Violet couldn't even begin to comprehend the ache, the sorrow or the isolation Ryder must feel keeping this secret.

Violet hadn't known what Ryder would do after she watched him yank away from Susan and Kelly, but even a strong-willed man like Ryder had to stop and let someone in...sometime.

Ryder hugged her back.

His thick, strong arms squeezed around her so tightly around her ribcage that it hurt. But Violet didn't move, wince or object. Right now, he needed her strength and she gave it to him.

Ryder buried his face into her shoulder and the tears she'd known were at the surface fell with great sobs against her shoulder. This was why *he* was redesigning the company. This disease was the reason no one had seen Mr. Carlex in two years.

This was the best kept secret in Willow Valley.

Violet was sure they'd stood there for a half hour or longer, listening to the wind rustle the trees around them. It felt like forever and every second that passed she felt more of his pain creating a stronger connection between them.

When Ryder finally pulled away, it was as though he took part of her with him. He didn't go far, about a foot away, and then he grasped the sides of her face, much like he'd done with his dad, only Ryder kissed her.

The taste of his salty kiss was only a reminder of his pain. The force of his lips, were not motivated by lust or desire he had for her. No, Ryder was hiding from his pain. *Hiding with his secrets.* Apparently Violet hadn't been the only one hiding...the question was, why was Ryder hiding his father's condition from everyone?

Violet wanted to kiss him forever, but he needed someone to talk to right now and not distract himself again with someone else.

She gently covered his hands with hers and pulled her lips away from his. "Ryder," Violet breathed against his lips, a plea for him to stop. A plea for him to talk to her.

Ryder didn't take it well. He pulled away, turned and started up the stairs.

"Ryder?" Violet called after him. Her feet didn't move, her mind froze and she wasn't sure what to do.

Do I leave him? Do I follow him? What is he doing?

Ryder turned and was back down the stairs in an instant, standing so close she could reach out to him. The glare he sent her, didn't allow her fingers to move.

"What?" His snarl made her swallow, unable to answer. *What was she supposed to say?*

Ryder ran his hands through his hair. She'd never seen him look so dishevelled. An expensive designer suit didn't emphasize his brawny build like the white t-shirt he was wearing now.

"What are you doing here?" he said and the coolness from his tone ran across his face. It wasn't the greeting Violet had been hoping for, but he was only lashing out because of the situation.

It wasn't the right time to tell him her true feelings. "Ryder, no one knows about your dad," she said.

Ryder's demeanor turned as cold as ice, as Joel had claimed she was and asked, "Did you want something?"

Violet didn't know if she should answer, but she'd come all this way and feared if she didn't tell him now, she might not be able to work up the courage again. "I wanted to tell you that I am finished hiding in the shadows."

***

SHE WAS FINISHED hiding in the shadows? Now, she was finished hiding in the shadows? What was he even supposed to do with that now?

This woman had more dementia than his father. A father he'd put in danger. *His father.* The only person in this whole damn world he had left, probably not for long, and he'd put his life in danger. *Over a woman. Over Violet.* Because Ryder's head was consumed by this female thunderstorm in front of him and she had no damn direction where she wanted to go.

The guilt was eating Ryder up inside. The lack of sleep, because he couldn't get Violet out of his head, anticipating that she might show up like this very moment, confessing her feelings, was the cause of him falling asleep when he should have been watching his father.

"Now's not a good time," he snarled.

Would there ever be a good time?

Ryder had more important things to do than go back and forth with this lady. Only she wasn't just some lady.

Let it go, Ryder. Let her go.

He needed to get a better alarm system set up in the cottage that included door buzzers that went off each time any door opened and shut.

Why didn't they have door buzzers? Or did they? Had he been in such a deep sleep that he'd slept through them?

Ryder pushed away the desire to walk into Violet's embrace again, and let everything he was holding in, go. It had felt so good. But Violet was like a batch of threatening clouds rolling in, unable to decide whether to rain or pass by. Her indecision had allowed Ryder to put his own father in harm's way. Ryder didn't deserve her embrace.

Even if he took it, how long before she decided to tell him it was all for sex? How long would it be before she ran away again and cowered in the dark?

"Right..um...okay. I'm going to go." Violet took a few steps away and Ryder ignored the constricting in his chest, telling him to call her back. She turned toward him again, he felt the tightening release.

Damn it Ryder, get some control.

"Ryder, are you okay?" she asked.

If he wasn't so mad at himself, Ryder would love that every single look across her face was raw. For the first time, Violet wasn't holding back anything. He saw her pain, her worry and her sadness, and it was all for him. Only he didn't deserve it. Violet didn't understand. *He* was the reason his dad had been lost. *He* was the reason he was put in danger. He didn't deserve consoling.

"I'm fine," he growled, but he was anything but fine. More tears were threatening and his body was trembling. His dad could have been seriously hurt...or killed...and it was all Ryder's careless fault.

Violet took a few steps back to him. "I can see you're not fine. That was the wrong question. Do you need anything? Do you want to talk or—"

He wanted her to leave so he could be angry at himself in peace. He didn't want another person to tell him that losing his father today wasn't his fault. Kelly and Susan had done plenty of reassuring that he hadn't welcomed. He damn well knew it was his fault.

"Violet, this is not your damn business and no I don't want to talk about it. Just keep it to yourself." His rage came out worse through his words and his heart dropped even more watching her take a step back at his aggressive tone.

Good, back off.

"And I know you're good at keeping things to yourself."

"Of course, Ryder. I would never tell anyone about your...situation. It's not my business I was only offering as a—"

"Friend?" he snapped. "You've made it clear that I'm only good for a quickie." Ryder watched her face drop in horror as her words thrown back wounded her. They weren't true and she hadn't meant it. He knew that. But right now, he needed her gone and she was a pro at using insults as tools to avoid confrontation.

Take the hint and go.

Ryder didn't wait for her to leave. If he stood there any longer, he might cave into the desire to hold her. He turned and took the stairs two at a time into the house. He slammed the door and his body fell against it, sliding until he was sitting on the floor.

The floor of his empty house.

His head fell into his hands as the sobs returned.

He wanted his dad, his mom...he wanted Violet.

Every part of him wanted Violet, just as he had the last two days, hell the entire week, but he didn't deserve her. He couldn't take care of her. He couldn't even take care of his dad. Maybe everyone's image of him was right: useless playboy.

Chapter Eighteen

WATER SPLASHED AND laughter echoed as Violet's family gathered around the pool for another one of Marc's burnt hamburger barbecues.

Before Marc returned home, Uncle Carl would guard the barbeque and he knew how to cook a delicious, juicy hamburger. Her brother, on the other hand, was the go-to-guy if you liked hard patties between the buns. No one dared tell him.

"Are we almost ready?" Violet asked, leaning over his shoulder. He was tall, like Ryder, so, bare-footed she had to tip-toe to see the grill. The burgers were on fire. "You better turn your heat down," she said with a laugh and stepped beside him, reaching to turn the knobs with her free hand.

The other hand steadied her half-full glass of wine. Drinking wine at meals was standard with her family, however, the three glasses she gulped down in the privacy of her own kitchen had been to kill the edge, after leaving Ryder...alone.

But, what was she supposed to do? Chase him in the house?

It was clear he wanted...or needed...to be alone and Violet could relate. It didn't take away her concern for him, but hopefully another glass of wine would help.

Marc pinched at her fingers with the tongs. "Get out of here, or you get none." It wasn't a threat like he was intending. "You better go make the salad," he said.

"Are we ready for that? Or should I get a jug of water? A fire extinguisher? Possibly a take-out menu?" she teased, but seriously it was an easy phone call away to one of the on-site restaurants.

Marc sent her a playful glare. "Is Ryder responsible for this light-hearted side of you?"

Violet's smile fell.

"I guess not."

Violet was not about to go into this morning's events with Marc. Where would she even start, without mentioning Donald's condition? "It's a long story."

"Sorry Vi."

Violet bit her lower lip, raised her eyebrows and scrunched her nose together, preparing for his reaction as she said, "I take half the blame, since I told him I used him only for the sex."

She knew that had nothing to do with why Ryder wasn't standing at her side. But the reaction Marc gave was exactly what she needed to distract herself this evening. Heaven only knew, once she was behind closed doors, she would wrap up in Ryder's sweater and worry about him all night long.

Marc dropped the tongs on the grill and asked, "You slept with him?"

He reached again for the tongs, but instead of paying attention, he was looking at Violet for the answer and missed the tongs, burning his hand on the grill. Their eyes broke contact as he cursed, which was very unlike Marc who rarely lost control of a situation. He jumped away from the grill, knocking the tongs to the ground and sending a few burgers following.

"Dammit!"

"Are you alright?" Violet reached for him, but he shrugged her off. She stepped back, unable to suppress the grin.

"Do you need some help?" Carl called from where he and Eliza sat, tucked together on one lounger. Eliza lifted her head from the resting spot on Carl's chest to see what all the commotion was.

"Let your dad cook the burgers!" Kate called from the tables, where she and Emma were spreading out the place settings. "You are wonderful on a stove, but sweetheart, let your dad man the barbecue."

"I'm fine!" Marc barked at them, before bending down to reach the tongs that had fallen under the pot burner on the side of the barbecue. When he stood up, he hit the back of his head and snarled loudly, "Son of a–"

"Children!" Violet cried.

Marc growled the rest under his breath as he attempted to regain his composure. He dropped the tongs on the counter and began tucking his deep purple dress shirt back into his slacks, while sending Violet an unhappy stare.

"Maybe you should have thought of the children before spouting off about your hanky-panky." Marc lowered his voice at the end of his sentence and Violet couldn't hold it in any longer. She laughed out loud, so hard her stomach hurt.

Hanky-panky? Who says that?

"Don't you have a salad to go make?"

Violet laughed again. "Do you want to know a secret?" she asked her brother.

"Not likely."

Violet was a lock and key at keeping secrets. Nothing got past her, however today, she felt like standing far outside the box she kept herself locked up inside. "I know what actually happened in the sauna the week Kate came back for her grandmother's funeral..."

Marc scowled. "I'm going to pretend you didn't say that."

"And the cabin..." Violet enjoyed the way Marc shifted uncomfortably. "...Kind of think that's where this whole idea you pitched about horse-drawn buggies and building little cabins in the woods originated. A little romantic winter escape for the two of you when one's not rented. A little...*hanky-panky*..."

Marc groaned and turned away from his smiling sister. Marc didn't kiss and tell. The McAdams siblings, on the other hand, aired their dirty little secrets that should remain behind closed doors. Private, who-did-who-where seemed to be a luncheon conversation staple in that family. Violet learned from experience when a brunch with Kate and her sisters had left her fully filled in on Marc and Kate's little shenanigans in the sauna. AND the rendezvous they'd had at a cabin up north, during one of his so-called business trips. Apparently, he hadn't gotten very much work done that weekend.

"I'm just saying you aren't a saint, so don't judge me," she said.

Marc turned back to her. "I didn't say I was a saint and I'm not judging you—"

Violet cut him off. She couldn't take anymore lies after her dad's room of deceptions. This family needed to be truthful with each other. "Yes you are." He couldn't fool her. His brotherly, protective wheels would be spinning so fast, that the burgers wouldn't stand a chance of coming out unscathed.

"Just be upfront with me about it Marc. Don't lie to me. Don't you think there have been enough lies in this family?"

"Yes, there have been plenty. But I'm not judging you. I'm your brother, I'm concerned about you. It's not like you to go..." Marc looked around the room and his eyes fell on Kate. "Tap people, at all."

Tap. Hanky-panky. It was called sex people. What was wrong with the actual word? And, at all...what did that mean?

"You're making me sound like a dried up old lady, who sits on her rocker and knits all day with her legs tightly crossed, warding off men," she said defensively. She was younger than Marc for crying out loud! She wasn't even in her thirties yet and he was heading toward mid-thirties.

"I'm not saying you're old. I'm saying you're cautious. I didn't know you had already gone that far with Ryder. And, I don't want to know more details, thank you." He sighed. "Violet, this is so uncomfortable. Why are you not uncomfortable? Why are you even telling me? Wouldn't Mom or Emma be better suited to listen and give you advice? If that's what you're after? Go ask Kate. Trust me, she is used of all this...stuff."

"No."

Violet looked at her mom staring up at Carl with the love she'd seen Ryder's parents share. Then her eyes fell on Emma, who in the last year had silently sworn off men without an explanation.

"I honestly don't know if there's anything going on between me and Ryder at this point. But, I am happy to announce that I have come to a decision that I no longer care what other people think about me and my choices."

"You have?" Marc said it like she couldn't do it. Didn't he know she was as competitive as they came?

Violet sipped her wine. Life was too short and Violet was too exhausted hiding behind her last name.

"Yes."

"Mom!" Parker called. He was standing on the diving board above the deep end of the pool, wearing only his cartoon character board shorts. With a pool in their backyard, almost literally, and the lake at the edge of the property, Sophia and Parker had both been taking swimming lessons since they were born.

"Yes?"

"Did you invite Ryder over like you said you were gonna?" Parker yelled.

Every Caliendo eye turned to Violet. Eliza and Carl both sat straight up. Emma and Kate were in mid-laughter and stopped to turn around. Izzy, who was lounging on the far end of the pool, even glanced up from her cell phone screen. She shared her big, bold I-bet-that's-not-all-you-did grin.

All of them had questioning looks, looks full of judgement. She felt Marc's eyes burning into her side, silently asking, *You have?*

"He was busy," Violet said.

"Did you go to his house?" Marc asked.

What was with all the questions?

"Remember when Ryder picked you up and threw you off the boat?!" he called.

"I remember him throwing *you* in the water," Violet said to Parker.

The curdling feeling in the pit of her stomach told her it would take some time before she truly didn't care what other people thought, but she had her whole life to work on it. No longer would her name keep her from doing what made her happy.

"He's so strong. He lifted me in the air this high." Parker held his hands above his head. "And then he cannon-balled into the water like this!" Parker did a cannon ball off the diving board with a loud splash, as his body sank into the middle of a wave pool.

"It's a good thing that you're finished caring what other people think because I'm sure suppers going to be full of Ryder questions," Marc teased.

"Shut up." Violet punched him in the shoulder. "I have a salad to prepare."

"Maybe you could start with how you got that shiner on your chin..."

Violet touched the purple bruise under her chin that she'd tried to conceal with the disguise of makeup. It had only masked the color, the swelling remained, but she'd let her hair down and kept her head tilted in hopes people wouldn't notice. Apparently she was only fooling herself.

"Or the scratches down the back of your legs." Marc wasn't teasing anymore. His concern about her bumps and bruises were digging for the truth.

"Salad," she said. Violet slugged the rest of her wine back and headed to her suite, where there was a full bottle waiting for her.

Inside, she pulled out two heads of lettuce, tomato, cucumber and avocado, arranging it along the counter. She stopped at her reflection off the chrome fridge and caught a glimpse of her chin. She was going to have to soak this bruise with witch hazel tonight and really reduce the color.

Violet turned her attention back to chopping the lettuce and wondered how Mr. Carlex was doing...how Ryder was doing.

Ryder was a lot like his father had been before his sickness. In appearance, they were both over six feet tall. While Mr. Carlex had been a little burlier than his son, it was clear by Ryder's physique that he spent a good deal of time at the gym. It wasn't their looks that connected them, but the way they both spoke, with smooth confidence, and a genuine smile that you wouldn't forget. After Mrs. Carlex died and Mr. Carlex attended the galas alone, Violet had noticed a part of him had died with his wife. There was a glimmer missing, the extra push of his smile was gone. This morning, watching Ryder suffer, she'd seen the same thing in him.

Let it go Violet. Worrying about Ryder won't change anything, expect give you an ulcer.

That was easier said than done.

She welcomed the distraction that the knock on Violet's front door presented.

Please be Joel.

Violet had left several messages on his voicemail about Parker and Sophia. She needed to talk to Joel alone first, and demand to know exactly what his plans were with the children. Joel loved his kids, but he had a hard time with commitment. Parker and Sophia needed stability and assurance from him right now. No matter how hurt Violet was after his appalling insults, she had to let it go and move forward for their kids. It didn't matter what either adult thought of the other, the truth was, their only connection was Parker and Sophia...and possibly Ryder.

Ryder. Was he alright? She wished he would text, phone, anything.

Drying her hands, she opened the door while tossing the towel over the foyer table.

It wasn't Joel.

"I thought maybe this could be our thing. Chasing each other back and forth with an apology," Ryder said, with a smile that didn't reach his eyes, although some of his sparkle was back.

He was so handsome.

Violet loved his teasing, but she loved that he was on her doorstep more. Her worry eased at the sight of him, but after witnessing his distress this morning, she was aware he was masking his pain. She knew the love and worry for his father was overwhelming his thoughts like her concerns for Ryder had been just a few moments earlier.

"You don't have anything to apologize for," she said. If anything, she should apologize for dropping her feelings on him after the horrific scare involving his dad. That had been tasteless. *How was his dad?* She wanted to ask, but didn't dare...not yet anyway.

As if reading her thoughts, he said, "My dad is a touchy subject that I don't discuss with anyone." Ryder looked away, and Violet saw the raw, hard pain he was trying to hide.

Don't hide it from me.

That wasn't fair to ask, when they hardly knew each other, yet knew each other so well.

213

When he looked back at her, it came with a sharp inhale that he didn't conceal. This was difficult for him, but had he come to her house to share...or just apologize? Maybe he didn't want anything more from her, except to say he was sorry.

"My dad has dementia. As I'm sure you already suspected. He's in the moderate stages, moving rapidly into the last stages. He's getting worse, faster. I pay Susan and Kelly substantially for my privacy. Their silence."

An apology and a request to keep her silence. Violet's heart felt like it was rupturing with each word he spoke. Her heart cracked for the pain he felt, and shattered for the yearning she felt for him. But, right now, he wasn't offering her anything more.

Violet reached out and touched his bulky arm. He was trembling. "You have you my word, Ryder. I won't tell anyone."

He nodded his thanks, and then said, "That's not why I'm here."

Why are you here?

"I told you to stop hiding yourself from me, from the world, and face your fears. I waited days for you to figure it out on your own and when you finally showed up, I pulled away and did exactly the opposite of what I preached. My dad is the only person I have left and he's not even there. I lost him this morning. We were watching television, and I was responsible for him, but I fell asleep and when I awoke, he was gone." Violet watched the guilt of his blame touch every last area on his face before he continued. "If he had died..."

Violet abandoned her restraint and reached for him. "Ryder, he didn't die." He was two steps down, making her a little taller as she hugged him.

He buried himself right into her shoulder again, just as he had at his house, with the same strength and force that stole her breath away. No man had ever needed her like this before or relied on her strength.

"He's going to die," Ryder whispered into her hair, sounding like a lost child.

She wished she could assure him that wasn't the case, only it was. Inevitably, this disease would claim the life of his father. So she said all she could think of, "I'm so sorry, Ryder."

He pulled away and said, "No, I'm the one who is sorry. I should have never spoken to you the way I did this morning. Ever. I'm so sorry, Violet."

"I should have never taken you in the bathroom the way I did." The words were out of her mouth before she had a chance to run them through her filter. If she had, the sentence wouldn't have been passed along.

Violet gasped, horrified. How inappropriate and uncalled for.

The strained look on Ryder's face softened and he laughed.

"I shouldn't have said that." Violet straightened herself away from Ryder. "I don't know why I said that." *Why did you say that?*

"Just do not follow it with an apology, because it was the best bathroom sex I've ever had." He lowered his tone and his humor. "It was the best sex I've ever had."

Violet didn't know what to say. It was the best sex she'd ever had too. Was he here for more than an apology and a friendly, supportive hug? "I'm speechless," she said.

He chuckled.

"It's not funny. You always make me speechless. I don't know why you're here. Are you here just to apologize? Or did you mean what you said in my office? Or did I lose my chance with you? Please don't tell me I lost my chance with you. I know I can be difficult and stubborn."

"You are definitely both of those things."

"Well, you just say whatever pops into that cute little head of yours and sometimes it just leaves me speechless." It was frustrating and exciting at the same time and she wanted more of it.

Ryder's eyes sparkled. "You think I'm cute?"

Violet's face lightened. "Don't you fish for a compliment. You know cute is not how women see you."

Ryder stepped up, putting them at eye level. He rested his arms on either side of the door frame, enclosing them in their own space of solitude. "I'm not interested in how other women see me. I'm only interested in you. Can we stop saying sorry, chasing each other back and forth and spread our true feelings out? So neither of us are confused. I will go first."

That was good because right now her breath was caught in her throat and all she could think about was kissing him.

"I like you Violet Caliendo, said without condescension. I can't guarantee I won't be scared of whatever is going on between us. I've never felt for a woman what I feel for you and that honestly scares the shit out of me." This was exactly what she wanted to hear. "And, yes I want to kiss you right now, but I promised the next time was your turn."

Her turn? Her turn!

Violet's fingertips touched his forearms then slid around the strong muscles as she pressed her lips against Ryder's waiting mouth, for the kiss she'd been dreaming about. It was nothing like any of their other kisses, which were wickedly rough, wild and so out of control neither of them knew what the hell they were doing. This kiss was soft and gentle, just like this side of Ryder. When he went to move away, Violet deepened the kiss, needing to feel his tongue against hers. After spending nights craving this kiss, she never wanted it to end. His kiss took her to a place she'd never been with anyone else.

When they parted, only centimeters away, she grinned at him. "Your turn next," she teased, expecting one of his deep chuckles that tickled her insides. Instead, his hands dropped from the doorframe and cupped the back of her head, lifting her lips against his, while stepping into the house. Missing her shoes, she was inches shorter than Ryder, but he bent down as they moved backwards and into the hallway of her suite. He'd tossed away his gentle touch, and Violet was finding she enjoyed the raw passionate side of Ryder Carlex.

Violet slipped her hands under Ryder's shirt, feeling his muscles flex beneath her touch. She wanted him to know that she wanted more than just his kiss. He groaned in understanding and she smiled against his lips. He caught her upper lip in his teeth and pulled, while his hands were moving down her back. His fingers inched the fabric of her dress upwards.

Violet was fully aware that all the curtains in her suite were drawn back to let the skylights above the pool cast the warm sunshine into her suite. They had to get out of the open space, before her whole family saw her butt.

"The hallway." Was all she needed to say and Ryder picked her up, taking her out of the possibility of family view, Violet wrapped her legs around his middle, plunging her tongue further into his mouth and loving the feel of his warm arms wrapped under her bare legs.

"Which door?" he moaned against her.

Violet bit his upper lip, tugged on it and, in a husky tone, breathed, "Last door."

Ryder slammed the door shut with his foot and crossed the room to her queen-sized mahogany bed. He laid her on the soft bedding and remembered his sweater hidden underneath. Finally, Violet had the man himself. She'd dreamed of this moment for weeks, thinking it was a delusional fantasy that would never transpire. But here Ryder was, kissing her, carrying her, touching her and it felt so right. She cursed herself for waiting so long to accept what was happing between them. Violet was falling in love with him.

Falling in love...like her happily ever after.

The thought almost scared her enough to push Ryder away, but his touch kept her grounded and stripped away her alarm.

Violet pulled him down with her. At first, his knees climbed onto the bed with her, and his warm hands pushed the hair away from her face to give him access to kiss her lips, her cheeks, and her throat...then he stopped.

Violet compressed the disappointed moan about to escape her and looked up, expecting to find him smirking and teasing her. He was a charming tease, just like everyone said. Only he was *her* charming tease.

Ryder's back curved overtop of her. His hands found resting spots on either side of her, instead of stroking her skin. The passion was missing from his face and he wore hesitance that she wasn't accustomed to seeing.

Violet touched his hands, wondering what had happened in the last ten feet. "What's the matter?" she asked.

She watched his eyes dart around her bedroom. His eyebrows burrowed together as his moved from her, to the headboard, beside them to where pictures of her children sat on her dresser, across the room where her double closet doors were closed and stopped at the bathroom, staring at the double sink and mirror, then fell on her.

"This is Joel's room," he finally said.

Joel's room? Violet hadn't envisioned this room as Joel's for a long time, or ever. He'd invaded her space with his presence and she'd resented it, that he'd tricked her for money. A lot of nights, more often than not, Joel had fallen asleep on the couch or the spare room, but how would Ryder know that.

"Joel's house...Joel's bed...Joel's..." Ryder didn't finish, but the way he said it she knew what he was thinking. *Joel's ex-wife.* Ryder pulled out of her grasp and stood up.

"Ryder, wait..."

When he turned, Violet wasn't met with the anger she'd thought he was feeling, but instead misery. Her heart ached for him. "I don't want a quickie with you," he said.

"That's not what this is." Violet slid off the bed and grasped his hands. "That's not what this is," she promised. Sliding her hand up his arm, she touched the stubble across the side of his face. "I'm sor—"

She stopped as the word started to leave her mouth. He didn't want any more apologies. *Alright.* How about promises.

"I like you too, Ryder. A lot. You were right, this is fast and we have been playing a game of back and forth, between our feelings and our titles. I am a Caliendo, just like you labeled me. My whole life I've felt like I had this responsibility to do what is appropriate, no matter the damage that might do to my feelings, or my life. We have an image to uphold and you...you are my ex-husband's friend. The first thing in my head is, 'How will this look to people? What will they say? How will it affect my family?'"

Violet let her hand fall away from his face to find his other hand.

"But, you got to me in a way no one ever has. I don't know why or how, since I had it my head that I didn't like you very much." Her honesty lifted his lips into the smallest smirk, but it was a start. "Ryder, when you touch me, my heart skips a beat over top of who I thought I had to be. And *thought* is the correct term. I don't care what anyone *thinks*. Not the staff, not the town, not Joel. I only care about what you think. I don't want a quickie with you."

"I am without a doubt falling in love with you," he said.

He continued like he was reading her thoughts. "My mother always told me I would know when I found the right woman. The one who I couldn't get off my mind, out of my thoughts, that my body craved and that woman is you, Violet Caliendo."

Her? How was that possible? And at the same time she knew she was going down the same path as him.

Violet smiled at him. "If anyone knows the true term of falling in love, it would be your parents," she said.

Falling in love? This is what it felt like? No wonder she couldn't get Ryder out of her thoughts. It wasn't just a onetime fling in the bathroom, they were falling in love with each other and he was worried she wanted another fling.

"Ryder, will you be my date to my family barbeque?"

"Your date?"

She nodded. "Yes. You're very slow at asking a girl out," she teased, with a half smile. She loved how easy it was to tease this man and how much she looked forward to the smile that broke his lips.

Ryder hugged her.

Chapter Nineteen

RYDER WAS NERVOUS. He wasn't sure the last time he remembered feeling nervous, but he sure as hell didn't like how weak it made him. His legs felt like rubber, ready to collapse with each step, or turn him around and make him run out the door.

What is your problem?

Stepping out the french doors of Violet's suite led to the incredible indoor pool that Ryder had only heard of through Joel. Palm trees, the brick walls, street lights, that wouldn't brighten nearly the way the skylights above did, it was as though Ryder had stepped outside. It was the Caliendo's private tropical getaway.

The ambience should have relaxed him. However, Violet's family were taking their seats around two tables and would soon be sending him their *what is he doing here* looks.

This atmosphere didn't help his nerves.

Ryder stuffed his hand in the pockets of his denim pants to keep from reaching out and grabbing the support of Violet's hands. After the many embraces they'd shared while dealing with his dark times, he knew her touch would calm him. But, they had to take extra cautious steps in their relationship because of her kids.

He was their father's friend. Would they accept him?

Sophia and Parker liked Ryder, but that was when he was their dad's friend. How would they feel about him dating their mom? Eventually they would move in together.

Would they be okay with that? Or would they grow to hate Ryder and resent him?

Maybe they were moving too fast. Maybe supper with her family was a too quickly decided mistake and he should retreat.

He felt like he was running and hiding, just as he'd told Violet not to do. Only this was much different.

But was it?

Violet would also carry all his worry; she was their mother after all. Violet loved her children and from the protective stare she cast, he knew all his worries and more would have already crossed her mind too.

As though she sensed Ryder's apprehension, Violet touched his back. A motion he would much rather do to her, but he was surprised at how much her touch reassured him.

Violet was not a pushover, and her family would be aware this woman did not make decisions lightly. Therefore, she would not have invited him, had she not thought Sophia and Parker were ready.

"They don't bite," she said. "Out of all these Caliendos, I'm the scariest. You've already won me over, with your cute smile. They'll be a snap." She dropped her hand away, but not before sliding it over his rear in a slow, seductive way, and sending him a wink before she stepped in front of him.

He grinned. He couldn't help it.

This woman was full of surprises and he was ready to discover every last one of them.

Her teasing, that was usually his department, took away some of his uneasiness and made him wonder why he stopped kissing her inside...what a stupid move that had been. Now, all through supper he was going to be back in that bedroom with her kiss and her rear-touching hand would run through his head, through his blood.

"Look who I invited for supper," Violet called out casually in her strong, solid voice, like she hadn't just seductively touched him. Her voice didn't hold an inch of fear about who she was bringing into the Caliendos reclusive area. Then again, she was good at hiding what she didn't want others to know. She could be as freaked out as he was and would never show it. His gut told him she wasn't.

All eyes turned to Ryder. Surprise laced each face and Ryder did his best to send a round of smiles personally to each family member. All, except Marc, who half-smiled, but sent him a face laced with doubt, suspicion and accusation.

Ryder's apprehension returned, slamming full force into every step he took.

"Ryder!" Parker waved as they approached. His light hair was drenched, pooling dark marks on the lime green t-shirt he was wearing. "Have you caught any big fish lately?"

Parker's voice eased him...a bit.

"Not lately. Haven't been on the boat."

I've been working, losing my dad and thinking about your mother...haven't had time to even think about the boat.

"I could go with you next time."

Sophia elbowed her brother, sliding down beside him. "Cause you were such a big help last time. You didn't even catch anything. Remember?"

Parker shoved her with his body, but she hardly moved reaching across the table for the ketchup. "I *have* caught fish, Sophia," he said then looked at Ryder. "I have caught big fish."

Ryder couldn't help the grin that took over his face. He'd never had siblings, but he'd been around the Kendricks growing up and the banter between siblings was very much like this.

This isn't so bad. Yeah, but they don't know your intentions with their mother yet.

"I believe you buddy. And yeah, you're welcome on my boat anytime." That got a huge smile from Parker.

Ryder glanced at Sophia and caught her eyeing him up. She turned away quickly, focusing her attention on her plate.

She suspects my intentions. She hates me.

"Don't make promises I might take you up on when he gets in a bad mood," Violet teased.

While Ryder would have preferred to sit in one of the two empty chairs across from Parker and Sophia at the far end of the table, Marc and Kate moved to the opposite side of Rosemary, leaving two empty chairs right in the middle of everyone.

You got this. How many galas and events have you been to your entire life easily interacting with hundreds, even thousands, of people?

Those people weren't the close-knit family of Violet. Ryder had interacted easily with these Caliendos, but not while he was dating Violet, a daughter, a niece, a sister, and a mother to this close-knit family.

Dating. He liked the sound of that.

Ryder pulled Violet's chair out for her before sitting down directly across from Eliza Caliendo.

Where Ryder's mother had a dark, dramatic look with her deep auburn hair often colored to keep the grey away that coordinated with her red lipstick, Eliza accepted the silver that had taken over her once blonde locks. Against her porcelain skin and bright blue eyes, like Violet's, she had a softer look about her.

Today, her pursed lips looked like she was pleased but at the same time she was holding in her words. She and Violet not only resembled each other physically, they also dressed similarly in a chic, sophisticated manner.

"Where's the salad?" Marc asked Violet. There was something in the way he spoke that matched the way he looked at Ryder...full of suspicion.

"Salad?" Violet asked.

"The salad you've been preparing for the last fifteen minutes," Marc said. There was definitely no salad involved with what they'd been doing the last fifteen minutes.

"Oh," Violet said, as if recalling what she was likely doing before he knocked on the door and distracted her. "The lettuce was bad. Can you believe that?"

"Did you buy it at the Carlex grocers?" Izzy snickered under her breath. Ryder knew better than to take this woman's snickering to heart. She was, and always had been, the wild, loud, inappropriate sibling of this bunch and Ryder knew her type.

"So Marc, I hear we are short staffed a server," Violet said. "Maybe Izzy should step in until we find a replacement." Her head slowly turned to Izzy with a smirk. "Could be a week. Could be a year..."

Carl chuckled. He was sitting beside Eliza, sending Ryder a wide friendly, even welcoming, smile. Ryder had been gone for a year, but he'd heard from Joel, that Marc and Izzy weren't Robert's biological children. The truth had only come out the last year or so. It turned out the older couple now rubbing arms together had been having an affair and Carl was Marc and Izzy's dad.

Emma sat to their right with Parker and Sophia on the other side, watching Ryder with skeptical blue eyes. The blue eyes these women got from their mother were like staring into the blue water on a sunny day.

"Alright," Eliza said, breaking up the sibling banter. "Ryder, how are you?" she asked.

"I'm good. Thank you."

"And Donald? How is he? I haven't seen him in..." Eliza paused and looked at Carl. "It must be coming into two years now," she said and Carl nodded in agreement.

No one had seen Donald in twenty-two and a half months.

"He's good," Ryder said, and, before he could stop himself, he went straight into the rehearsed story he told everyone about redesigning the company. Ryder didn't come right out and lie, stating that it was his father who was doing the work and most people wouldn't catch it. However, Violet would catch the omission and guilt built up in him for lying to her family, forcing her to partake in his lie. But what was he supposed to do? He'd promised his dad. Ryder didn't like it, but he didn't see another alternative.

"How so?" Marc asked and Ryder sensed his mood change as work-talk was brought around the table.

Ryder could handle work-talk and these people could relate with accurate interest, because they owned and operated their own businesses.

Ryder went straight into describing the changing look of the stores, taking them from the industrial, chrome appearance back to an old country look, with a personal feel. They were neutralizing the atmosphere with a homey feel, while ditching the commercial look. They were adding wood baskets in the produce area and changing the shelves from stark white to honey-colored.

The family listened closely and as he answered questions from each of them, he felt his nerves begin to relax.

What did he think these people were going to do? String him up to a tree and throw rocks at him? No, but he hadn't expected them to be so welcoming either.

"It sounds like you are very involved with the process," Carl observed with an approving nod.

"I am. We hired the Kendricks, my dad's sister's family. They are contractors and helping to redesign the new look. I've been there every step."

"Good for you," Carl said. "It's nice when the business can stay in the family."

"My father agrees. He is a huge believer in family sticking together and has instilled his beliefs in me. There is no other place I would rather be, then working with the family chain. It's been a long line of Carlexs that have built it into the corporation it is today."

In the olden days, the Carlex Grocer had been a small store on the main street of town. Now they had large box stores across the country.

"With Joel's wedding, I have been unfortunately forced to communicate back and forth through email, phones and texting. It's not the same, but we are getting close to finalizing the construction that will take place."

Ryder hadn't noticed the mood shift until he finished. The Caliendos all seemed to look away from him. They were looking at their plates, at the kids and at Violet. At first he didn't know what he said to make every face drop their support and draw their eyebrows uneasily together.

Then it hit him.

Joel. Joel's wedding. Idiot.

"Awkward," Izzy muttered from the end of the table. "Not as awkward as Emma's dress..."

"Izzy," almost every Caliendo scolded.

"Ryder?" Rosemary called and Violet bent back so he could look around at the young girl, whose chestnut curls were a dark contrast to the rest of the Caliendo family, obviously getting them from her mother.

"Yes?"

Rosemary squished her nose up and asked, "What do you like to play?"

"Play?" he asked.

"He likes to boat," Parker said.

227

"No," Rosemary said. "I like to play hockey and my Uncle Colt is coaching my team. But I play with girls and boys. So I am a hockey player," she explained and Ryder grinned, nodding his head but not quite following the girl. "So Aunt Violet called you a playboy..." Ryder slanted an amused look at Violet, while the young girl continued.

Violet couldn't hide her wide eyes, and her short intake of breath at being exposed by her niece.

"And Aunt Izzy said you only like to play with girls. I was just wondering what you play with the girls?"

A playboy who liked to play with girls.

Ryder might have been insulted, had it not come out of the adorable innocence of Rosemary and her awaiting brown eyes.

Kate gasped and Marc choked.

Izzy couldn't contain her laughter, but the sound was lost to the rest of the gasps around the table.

Kate began to hush Rosemary.

"That's alright," Ryder told Kate, trying his hardest to keep a straight face. It was apparent Violet wasn't the only one in this family that thought he fancied the *girls.*

Violet moved to block Ryder's path, her eyes apologizing. He gently pulled her shoulders back to catch Rosemary's eyes. "Rosemary, I guess my favorite thing to *play*..." He couldn't help but glance at Violet who looked mortified. "...is fishing."

"Fishing?" Rosemary asked.

"I like fishing too," Parker said. "And I fished with Sophia and she's a girl."

Sophia jabbed his side. "A playboy isn't someone who plays with girls, you dork," she told her brother. "A playboy is a rich man who has se−"

The whole table roared to life, covering the end of Sophia's proper definition in front of Rosemary and Parker.

"What?" Sophia asked.

"That word is not age appropriate for some of the people around this table," Violet told Sophia.

"I want to know," Parker whined.

"I will tell you if you give me your dessert," Violet offered him.

Parker looked mortified. "No."

"Alright, moving along." As Violet turned to once again apologize to Ryder, he caught sight of a mark on her lower bottom chin. A dark, large, round bruise. The size of a hand. The swelling looked fresh.

How had he not noticed the mark before?

"She had that when she came back from your place this morning." Ryder looked up to see Marc staring at the bruise, no doubt in horror at the black, purple and green painting her porcelain skin.

Violet's hand went straight to her chin and her head whipped in Marc's direction. Ryder couldn't see, but by the quick snap of her head, he assumed she had a warning look on her face.

Marc continued, despite whatever look Violet had sent him. "We were all wondering where it came from too..."

"Marcus," Violet hissed.

What was he saying? That Ryder hit Violet?

He would never lay a hand on her, or any other woman for that matter. Violet was only at his house a short time. Long enough to console him after driving his dad home.

His dad.

Ryder had witnessed Donald's fits. His father wasn't deliberately violent, but when his symptoms overtook him, they caused the older man great distress. Donald might not be as strong as he was before his illness, however Ryder had taken a knock or two from him when he was agitated. And he could become forceful...forceful enough to make that mark on Violet's face.

"Did my dad do that?" he whispered. Not for the sake of her family or keeping his father a secret, but for the sake of Violet's children.

If Violet's forced smile hadn't given him his answer, when she looked at her kids and said, "Parker, Sophia. Today is your lucky day. Once in a lifetime opportunity here. Today, and today only, if you go right away, I will let you eat in the cave." Violet didn't have to repeat that sentence. Both her kids jumped up and grabbed their plates as Rosemary begged her parents to go too.

"Of course," Kate said, helping Rosemary off the chair while Marc handed Rosemary her plate.

The three kids all but ran to the rocks where the water slide to the pool weaved in and out of the rocks. At the midpoint of the slide was a small fenced-in area facing them. They could eat in the caves as they loved but Violet could still see them.

Her family glanced around at each other, but Ryder had no interest in them. He repeated his question to Violet, regardless of what anyone thought about his dad...or were about to discover. There was no way Ryder would sit though dinner now knowing what had caused that mark on her face.

Violet turned to him with softness in her face that contrasted the ugliness of the bruise, from which he now couldn't peel his eyes.

He was so angry that he'd missed sight of her chin when he'd arrived. Spending the rest of the day twisted with remorse at the way he'd treated Violet was already eating him up inside. He'd spent the afternoon in the garden with his father and Ryder had decided his dad wouldn't want him to punish himself or run away from the only love he'd ever known. Confessing his feelings on Violet's front step, then their kissing, Ryder simply hadn't noticed the bruise.

"We don't have to talk about this right now," Violet said.

That was his answer. Donald was responsible for the bruise on her face.

The rest of her family wasn't as quick to let the topic pass. "Donald did that to your face?" Eliza asked, sounding like a worried mother, in shock. She had every right to be.

"Momma, I'm fine," Violet assured her.

Eliza didn't look convinced, but she said no more. The rest of the table looked mortified, with a thousand questions in their eyes. Curiosity that Violet would never be able to fill if she kept the truth hidden from her family. Ryder couldn't ask that of her. Neither would he find trust in them if he didn't explain, especially with the whole Emma situation still in their heads.

Ryder silently apologized to his father and hoped the day they met again on a level of equal communication he would understand why he couldn't keep this secret any longer.

"My dad was diagnosed with dementia a couple years ago," Ryder said. "Shortly after my mom died."

He watched their faces all shift from accusing to confusion and at last to sympathy. The very thing his father did not want.

Violet touched his leg and whispered, "Ryder, you don't have to do this."

He squeezed her hand, loving the comfort and strength her support gave him. "He stayed in the spotlight as long as he could before the symptoms became too obvious. Then he stepped away and asked me to not to tell people of his condition. Which until now, I haven't."

"Ryder, I'm so sorry," Eliza said immediately. "Donald is an amazing person, with a good heart. I am just so sorry."

"No, I'm sorry." He turned to Violet. "I didn't notice it today. You should have told me." He tilted her head with his finger to get a better look. "I can't believe he did this to you. I'm so sorry."

Violet caught his hand. "It's alright. It was an accident. He didn't mean to. He was confused and upset and his elbow accidentally hit my chin." She smiled, but it did nothing to reassure Ryder. "I'm okay."

Her face didn't look okay.

"I'm okay," she repeated. She turned to her family. "I drove over to Ryder's house this morning, to invite him over for supper." Talk about laying it all out there for her family. She was going to shock their systems...if Donald's marks across her face hadn't already. "I saw Mr. Carlex walking along the ditch, so I gave him a drive home. He was disoriented and upset, but he is fine now."

Ryder had been such an ass to Violet this morning, after she had gone out of her way to bring home his dad and was hurt along the way. Now Ryder felt like even more of an ass.

"Is that where you got the scratches on your legs too?" Izzy asked.

Scratches? Scratches!

He felt Violet squeeze his hand before she said, "Well, I'm not outdoorsy, alright," she said, turning the incident in to a joke on her. This was nothing to joke about. "I was in my heels, wearing a dress that ended up in the garbage, I slid down the ditch, and scraped the back of my legs on the way."

She did all that today?

Izzy laughed. The rest of her family only found slight humor in her story.

Ryder didn't find the humor at all, but maybe that was because it was his dad who had caused all these marks on her body.

"Can't you just picture Violet in her tight blazer, running through a ditch, trying not to rip her pantyhose?"

Izzy said between fits of laughter. Ryder had never even seen this woman in pantyhose.

The table gave a half-hearted round of laughter. Good, at least his wasn't the only one not finding the humor.

"Sweetheart I'm just glad you found Donald," Eliza said in a serious tone. "That would have been very scary having to search the woods for him."

What? How was Eliza thinking about his father when he'd hurt her daughter?

"How's your father now?" Eliza asked Ryder. "That must have been very dramatic for him."

Ryder didn't answer right away, not sure he'd heard the question right. But the waiting eyes assured him she was referring to Donald. "He's fine. He also has some scratches, but no big bruises." Ryder turned to Violet again, wishing they were alone so he could pull her into his arms and hold her.

Susan and Kelly were trained in dealing with the symptoms of his father's condition, but Violet was not. He was never leaving her alone with Donald again.

"I'm just glad it wasn't you causing the bruise or I was going to have to have a word with you," Marc said. By the half-serious, half-joking tone, he realized Marc meant he'd planned on leaving a bruise on his face in retaliation.

The rest of the table caught on and all chuckled, then started speaking at the same time, taking all the attention away from Ryder.

"You? Stand up to Ryder? You would lose!" Izzy said from the end of the table in a fit of laughter.

"Kate would have a better chance of getting in a punch," Emma teased.

"Stop picking on your brother," Eliza said. "Some men are fighters and others are lovers. My baby is a sweet little boy."

"That's not helping his case Momma," Izzy cracked before another burst of laughter.

Ryder would have normally grinned at the banter, but he couldn't get past the bruises and scratches on Violet. Violet had been there for Ryder when he had no one. She'd held him when he needed support. He'd greedily taken it and then yelled at her when he was finished. The whole thing caused Ryder to feel claustrophobic.

"Would you excuse me? I'm just going to use the men's room." Ryder slid his chair back.

"I can show you where it is." Violet slid her chair back, but he stopped her. He needed a moment to himself.

"I saw it earlier. I'm okay."

His stride couldn't carry him away fast enough. Once inside Violet's suite, he headed straight to the bathroom he'd seen in her bedroom. There was a bathroom in the hall, but he didn't even register it. Ignoring the bed where Joel made love to Violet, and *their* kid's photos on the dresser, Ryder shut the door and let out the breath that had been suffocating him. He sucked in fresh air and the smell of Violet filled his lungs.

Ryder splashed his face with cold water and let it air dry as he hung his head over the sink. One of the double sinks. *One Joel's. One Violet's.*

Ryder looked up at the marble backsplash, the white makeup bag on the counter, toothbrush sitting on a charger and a basket of jewelry, Ryder realized he was using Joel's sink.

He pushed away.

Was he jealous? Of Joel?

If Violet was still in love with Joel, then yes, he was jealous. He'd left the table needing a break to settle his constricting chest, and now the compression was growing worse. The bathroom was closing in on him more with each new realization.

Ryder could try to blame his new discovery on his lack of sleep, or the stress of losing his dad, or the sudden confession of Violet's feelings, but the evidence was clear.

The very first moment of his interaction with Violet, was because of Joel. She'd initiated sex with Ryder, which had been incredible, minutes before a meeting with Joel and his fiancée. What other reason could Violet have, than the obvious...she was still in love with Joel.

Why hadn't he seen this before coming here?

Ryder closed his eyes.

What was he doing here?

Joel and Violet had children together. Two. They'd had a life. In this suite. In this resort. And Joel was so damn flip-floppy, that he could decide on a whim to get Violet back. Ryder had nothing in comparison to offer Violet. Joel was the father of her children.

The more Ryder tried to convince himself differently, the more points Joel gained. This would never work. He needed to get the hell out of here.

Chapter Twenty

"SOMEONE'S IN TROUBLE," Izzy said, when the suite of Violet's door closed behind Ryder. The sassy blonde tossed a chip down the table at Marc, as though she hadn't sent Ryder her own bundle of attitude.

Violet's intense stare must have given away her intentions as soon as Ryder was out of listening range. She wasn't about to scope them out one-by-one, and she knew Marc was worried about her, but still she hadn't invited Ryder here to be insulted and accused.

She turned to her family. "Let's get this over with. Ask me all your questions quickly before Ryder gets back and then you all can stop digging into what's happening between us and just get to know him. Or, tell me if you don't approve and I will take that into consideration, as well." Her family's opinion *did* matter, especially Emma, who might feel uncomfortable.

No one said anything.

"No one?" Violet asked, taking her time to look at each of them sitting around the table with discomforted looks across their faces. How did they think Ryder felt?

Violet purposely left Emma until last. "Emma?"

Emma made a face. "Why are you asking me?" *As if she didn't know.*

"Because he tried to bone you at Violet's wedding." Izzy rolled her eyes at having to state the obvious and a chip went flying across the table in Emma's direction.

"Marc, maybe we should consider hiring Izzy to clean the pool room," Violet snapped.

"Maybe we should hire Ryder as the pool boy," Izzy retorted.

"You couldn't afford him," Violet snapped. "Especially with your lack of income."

"Are you kidding me? In case you missed it, Carl's my dad and not only did I get Robert's portion, but I get half of Carl's too. I can afford a playboy pool boy."

"I don't plan on dying anytime soon. So I won't be parting with my portions anytime soon. Thank you," Carl said.

Player? Player! "You could afford a lesson in—"

Izzy cut her off. "A new filter," she said, and grinned. It irritated Violet that sometimes Izzy didn't take things seriously. She'd not only insulted Ryder in this conversation, she'd insulted Violet and Carl, and seemed dense to all of the above.

Emma waved a hand. "Ryder was so drunk that night, he didn't even know who I was, and it wasn't a big deal. He wasn't crude or ignorant. He was drunk and sad. It was kind of sad. Anyway, that was a long time ago and I'm not worried about it. If you like Ryder, then you definitely don't have to be worried about that incident putting any label on Ryder." Emma chuckled. "Does Ryder even remember?"

"No." Violet ignored the questioning faces on how she was so sure. "Next question."

Silence.

"Now you all are quiet?"

Eliza spoke first. "Do you like him?" she asked.

"Yes," she answered honestly, and prepared herself for the eruption of her family.

Nothing.

A smile Violet recognized crossed her mother's lips. It was her proud mother moment smile. Violet had the same smile for her kids. When Violet had decided to pursue her career in wedding planning, she'd received that exact smile. The day Marc announced he was marrying Kate, this was the very smile Eliza sent them both, standing in front of Mrs. Calvert's bakery, freezing their bottoms off.

"I don't really see what else we need to ask you or know about Ryder," Eliza said. "Sweetheart, if you're happy, then we are happy for you. And I'm thrilled." Eliza stood, almost knocking down her chair and rushed around the table to pull Violet into a hug. "I thought you gave up on love and now look at you." Eliza pulled away and searched Violet's eyes. "You're falling in love..."

Violet wanted to melt into liquid and merge into the pool water.

Falling in love? How could she possibly see that?

Eliza pulled her into a longer hug and Violet caught Izzy snickering to herself, Emma rolled her eyes. Eliza whispered in Violet's ear, so low no one else would possibly be able to hear, "Love is not easy Violet, and I wasn't sure you would find it after Joel. But I was giving you some time and space and I hoped love would find you. I am proud that you were brave enough to open yourself to another person." Not just any person, Ryder. Her heart only opened to him, because he challenged her in a way that no one else did.

"Did you have sex with him?" Izzy asked.

All heads flew in Violet's direction, with curious eyes. Violet purposely avoided the route to Marc, who knew the answer.

Did they all think she was going to reply to that?

Eliza lightly scolded her daughter.

As Violet took her seat, she said, "I'm not answering that."

Izzy shrugged. "I was just curious who was better. Joel or Ryder? I assume Ryder. Actually, I would put money on it."

"Please don't," Violet begged.

"He's all muscle and sexy and strong..." Izzy continued.

This was not happening. Is this karma for mentioning it to Marc, only to get a rise out of him? Now Izzy was bringing it up to get a rise out of her.

"And Joel's all weak, dull and boring. I mean it would be like an elephant to a lion." Izzy roared, literally like a lion, and the family groaned in disgust.

"Sometimes you are too much, child," Eliza scolded.

Izzy laughed, loving the attention. "You all were thinking it. I just asked."

"I wasn't thinking it," Marc and Carl said at the same time and Violet couldn't help but grin at the strain in Marc's tone.

"I can't believe the Caliendos are having this conversation," Kate said with amusement. "I feel like I'm sitting with my sisters."

"That's because Izzy is besties with your sister," Emma pointed out.

"Besties. But I never see Abby anymore."

"Oh here we go," Marc said.

"Why don't you go to Oakston and visit Abby and Riley?" Eliza suggested, again.

It went unheard to Izzy, who was lost in her own world of sulking. "Maybe I will go to Hawaii. By myself. I can charter a fancy plane like Riley...doesn't Abby remember?"

"Or you could just drive to Oakston," Carl said.

This was going nowhere. "I'm going to start dating Ryder," Violet said. "The kids and I have already discussed it and they're on board. We aren't going to flaunt it, and I would like to move slowly for the children's sake. He *is* Joel's friend, so it's going to be weird for them. But I don't want you all to be weird around him or in front of Sophia and Parker. No more accusing him of hitting me." Violet turned to Marc meeting his guilty frown and he nodded, agreeing. Violet turned to Izzy next. "No more mention of Emma and Ryder, because the kids won't understand."

Izzy held her hands in the air in question. "Why are you directing that at me?"

A handful of support moved around the table, as her family told Izzy, in no better way, that she had a big mouth. Violet would tell her it was her lack of filter, but by the time everyone around the table made rounds, there was no need.

Where was Ryder?

Violet figured his absence had to do with his dad. Not only had he admitted a handful of secrets to Violet, he'd admitted his father's sickness to her entire family. Violet was learning that Ryder was a loyal family man, and if it was his dad who asked him to keep his sickness tucked away from others, Ryder would be racking up the guilt of exposing the truth.

Violet excused herself. "We will be back if you all didn't scare him away."

Inside her suite, Violet found the hallway bathroom door wide open and no Ryder. She made her way into her bedroom and found that door shut with light coming from under the door.

She knocked. "Ryder?"

Silence.

She knocked again.

"Ryder?"

The door opened so quickly it startled her into taking a couple steps back. Ryder looked down at her as he never had. She saw hurt and accusation that drew his lips thin and narrowed his eyes.

"I'm going to go," he said.

Huh? Go? What had happened? Oh no, it was the playboy comment. Was it?

"Why?"

He didn't answer.

Violet took a step toward him. "Maybe we rushed into things, having dinner with my family. They're a little overwhelming, I know. They like you, Ryder. But I understand if it's maybe too much too soon. Why don't we have supper. Just the two of us. Cliff house?" He'd mentioned it on the boat, so it would be the perfect place.

"Did you frequent the Cliff House with Joel?"

Joel? Joel! Why was he bringing up Joel? His accusing tone was a partial answer and put her in immediate defense mode. "Excuse me?" she asked.

"Are we going to repeat everything you and Joel did?"

Violet watched his eyes dart back to the bed and Violet knew she'd walked into a jealous anger.

Where had this come from?

When she didn't answer, Ryder snarled, "I can't even talk in here." He stormed past her and into the hallway. Jealousy was a new side of Ryder she hadn't seen before and she didn't really like it.

Violet followed, but Ryder stopped right in front of the door, so she was forced to stand in the doorway of her bedroom. His back was to her.

"I can't change my past, nor would I want to. Joel gave me the best two things in my life and because of them he will always be in my life." As Violet said the words, a part of her heart came to peace, recognizing the truth of her spoken words. She'd blamed her dad and Joel for the last ten years of the betrayal and misery she felt, but in the same heartbeat she would do it all again, if it promised and protected Parker and Sophia.

The veracity took her resentment and bitterness away, leaving only room in her heart for the love of her children, her family, and the man standing before her.

"Joel is my past, Ryder. I'm not sure what to do here," she admitted, inhaling a deep breath.

241

Violet wasn't ready for another game of back and forth with Ryder so she drew on her inner strength and spoke, "I don't know how to deal with you being jealous over Joel."

He turned. "You think I'm jealous over Joel?" The thought was as ludicrous to her as it sounded coming out of his mouth.

"Aren't you?"

"No." That was a relief. "Well...not like that."

What did that mean? "Not like what?" *Was there a different kind?*

"Are you still in love with him?"

Had Ryder not seen the way that Joel treated her? Did he not see the vile feelings she felt toward Joel? "He's getting married next week," she said.

"That's not what I asked."

"Why are you asking?" *This was absurd.*

"Why aren't you answering?"

"No. I'm not in love with Joel."

"Then why did you search me out in the lobby washroom?"

When he said it that way, it sure seemed like she was still in love with Joel and seeking out a distraction. She had been seeking out a distraction, only it hadn't been because she was jealous or upset that Joel was getting married. For a man who saw so much of her, how had Ryder missed this?

When Violet answered, she was surprised at how out of control the words escaped her mouth, like they were begging to be set free. Her voice sounded astonished, as if Ryder should already know the answer, and pitiful that she didn't set the truth free earlier.

"Because I agreed to plan my ex-husband's wedding to his new bride in *my* resort," she started and rolled her eyes at the absurdity of it...and it felt liberating. "It was crazy. My pride and need to appear flawless edged me to accept the wedding that I wanted nothing to do with. The minute

Joel walked out of my life I was done with him. But I'm a Caliendo, and how would it have looked if I said no to them? Missy has been employed here for years, and she is a resident of Willow Valley, gossip-line Willow Valley. I had no choice. But the resort is my home. The halls were my playground. The restaurants are my kitchens. The pools are my backyard. Each ballroom is a part of me and here I was bringing Joel and Missy into it. Opening up my home to them, for them to marry each other. *Marry each other. In my house!*"

Every last one of her family members had been right, she'd never been okay with the arrangements.

"I didn't go *search you out* because I'm in love with Joel. I didn't search you out at all. I was panicking inside that morning. I was walking down the halls and suddenly it all hit me and everyone was judging me. The staff and the bridesmaids..."

A broken laugh escaped her lips.

"My entire family was spying on me, and...and..." Violet sighed and her agitation plummeted, her voice quieted. When Ryder said nothing, she continued. "I don't know what happened. I saw you and I wanted to forget everything. But when we were done, I didn't want to let go of you. I felt so safe in your arms. You touched me and held me like a protector. Then you devised a plan to spare my humiliation and you were being so nice and I thought, why is this man who doesn't even know me treating me like a person, *a real person?*" She watched as Ryder's eyes slowly came back to her, instead of to his thoughts about her heart belonging to someone else.

He immediately looked embarrassed and she thought he might leave.

He said, "And then I snapped vulgarly at you."

Violet touched Ryder's biceps and they flexed beneath her. "Ryder, I am falling in love with you. There's a connection with you that I've never felt with another person. And, trust me, I don't spill all my feelings to just anyone. Please don't leave."

If he had to, at least she hoped he took her truth and would return. She couldn't leave it like this, with him looking so conflicted.

There is no conflict. It is so easy. Ryder you are the one.

"Joel might have lived here but it was never his home. This is my house, but I understand if you're not comfortable here." Her fingers moved up his arms. When they reached his shoulder, he bent down and kissed her, squeezing her arms between them. It was a short, quick kiss and when he pulled away, guilt laced his eyes.

"I'm sorry I doubted you."

"It's okay. Maybe we didn't put enough of our past out on the table."

He ran his hands over his face, and then rubbed the back of his neck. That was when Violet saw the dark circles under her eyes, and the weight of his eyelids. He was exhausted.

"Let's get out of here," she suggested. He looked like he would fall asleep if his head hit the pillow, but she didn't want to part from him yet.

"Where?"

"Anywhere. Your house. Your boat. Anywhere."

Ryder kissed her. "Let's finish supper with your family."

Her family? How were they even a thought in his head with everything going on between them?

Because he was a family man and family was important to him, whether it be his own or hers. Family, also being important to Violet, fell a little more in love with him at that very moment. She knew the trip to saying, *I love you,* was going to be a short and sweet one.

"No more running. No more jealousy. And by the way, I can handle a hand full of measly Caliendos."

Measly.

Violet laughed.

Fine, they would finish supper, but afterwards she wanted him all to herself.

Chapter Twenty-One

"I DIDN'T EXPECT this is what you meant by somewhere special," Ryder said sending Violet a smirk. "Are you trying to get in my pants?" he teased.

Violet laughed and it echoed through the darkness of the silver ballroom. He loved her laughter.

She sent him a half-serious glare. "No. We are not having sex here."

He couldn't deny the thought had been crossing his mind since the very day he'd suggested hiking her up onto the very table they sat on.

"There is a wedding in here tomorrow," she told him, as if the idea was so appalling.

Silk linen covered the tables, dressed with place settings and tall vases that would surely be filled with fresh flowers in the morning. Violet had moved the place settings carefully, before they had settled on top of the head table.

Ryder sighed like he was disappointed, but sent her a wink before turning away. Leaning back on his hands, he stared out the enormous window that looked out over the woods that touched the lake, which reflected the moonlight above. It was as beautiful as he knew it would be.

"I thought maybe you would want to go somewhere I've never been with Joel," she said and he heard the reservation in her voice at the mention of his name. "Somewhere that's our own."

Ryder grimaced inside. What a childish ass he'd acted like. He wasn't sure what had come over him. It was the stress of his dad no doubt. He knew Violet wasn't in love with Joel. He didn't think he needed to hear it from her lips, until that was what he was demanding. Then in the next sentence, probing her honesty, which deserved a slap across the face, not the soft stroke she pressed against his skin.

Why had he doubted her? Why had he doubted them? He needed a good night's sleep.

Ryder ran his hand across his face, embarrassed about his behavior in her suite.

He conjured up enough courage to slant a look at her. "Listen, Violet, I'm sorry about what I said in your suite, about us repeating your life with him. That was uncalled for. Please don't go out of your way to try to relieve my thoughts about you and Joel."

She covered his hand with hers. "I don't want you to be uncomfortable," she said.

"I'm not." He was never more comfortable with another person.

"But you were."

He groaned and sat up straight, taking his hand away from under hers.

"Hey." Violet moved the wine they'd been sipping and sat on her knees beside him. She touched his face and tilted his head to look at her. "For someone who claims I hide things, you are pretty good at hiding yourself," she accused. "And I am not just talking about Donald. Although I give you credit for Willow Valley's best kept secret."

He chuckled.

Ryder wrapped his arms around her and lifted her onto his lap. She straddled him, her knees against the table, and sent him a mischievous look. "I said we are not having sex on this table," she told him, but it lacked conviction.

He kissed her. "You are such a tease."

She smiled against his lips.

"I guess the thought had crossed my mind, obviously, that you may still be in love Joel. Honestly, I didn't really believe you were. Or at least I couldn't understand how a woman would be with a man who has treated you as disrespectfully as Joel has. And for what? For..." Ryder stopped and Violet gasped.

"You know?" she accused and he didn't have to ask what she was talking about.

"You know?" he asked, more surprised.

Violet frowned. "Of course I know. I'm Violet Caliendo. You don't give me enough credit. First you think I'm still in love with that selfish ass and then you think I didn't know he married me because he was bankrupt?"

"Why did you marry him, if you knew?"

Violet's face fell, along with her eyes. She stared for a long time at her fidgeting hands between them. Fidgeting hands. Violet Caliendo. He didn't like how much this topic upset her.

Ryder covered her hands. "You don't have to answer that," he said.

"I pride myself on being strong." He knew her strength. Violet inhaled deeply. "Says the woman cowering away and wrenching hands." She smiled at him shyly and pressed her flat palms against his chest. He felt them tremble.

Ryder pushed the hair that had fallen across her face behind her ears.

"You don't have to put a disguise on with me and you don't have to tell me things if you're not ready."

"It's embarrassing Ryder. I might never be ready."

He shrugged. "I can think of other things to pass our time." He kissed her, slipping his tongue inside her mouth and searching out her warmth.

Violet pulled away. "Is sex your solution to everything?"'

He shrugged again. "With you, it always seems to go that direction." But Ryder saw that Violet was still battling his question. He pulled her closer against him, but not in a sexual way, even if the pressure warmed his groin. He waited in silence until she was ready to talk.

"I was pregnant with Sophia and my dad wouldn't...he threatened to cut me off and fire me if I didn't marry Joel."

He stroked the side of her cheek with the pad of his thumb. "That's not your fault, Violet. That's nothing you should be embarrassed about."

"It's bigger than that. My dad was punishing me for not moving to one of the new resorts he had bought to manage it. So I rebelled and it was so unlike me." She let out a startled laugh, shaking her head and looking away. "I was always more cool-headed than the rest of my siblings, so when I decided to make my dad angry, it figures I would get pregnant with the man I didn't love...or even really liked. Joel was obnoxious, rude and crude and my dad hated that. *Joel is like his dead father*, my dad would say."

Ryder didn't like speaking ill of the dead, but it was true that Joel was hot-headed like his dad.

"The eve of my wedding, I had finished school and was working as wedding coordinator, my dream job, but I was engaged to a man who didn't love me. I found my dad in his office and begged him to call off the wedding. When he refused, I did the only thing I could and threatened to leave..."

Violet's eyes dropped.

Ryder knew this would be hard for her, trusting him enough with the parts of her life she didn't tell anyone.

He stroked her skin, silently giving her the time she needed to work up her courage to continue. He could wait all night if that's what it took for her to talk to him.

"But it was an empty threat and my dad knew it. He was in charge of my trust fund." She sent him a half smile with a shake of her head. "And the threat only gained a sneer sneer-like snicker and warning of his own, to cut me off if I gave birth to..." Violet bit her lower lip and stared at him for a long second. "...a bastard child," she finally said.

A bastard child? A bastard child!

What kind of father was Robert? Donald would never have spoken so ill-mannered and disrespectfully to Ryder. Never.

"Violet, that breaks my heart," he told her, running his thumb along her jaw.

"I was leaving my dad's office thinking, *Joel is a good guy. We are having a baby together, and he seems excited and he did propose. A life with Joel I can make work and be happy.* But then, as if marrying Joel hadn't been punishment enough, on my way out the door my dad casually mentioned that I hadn't been the only one with shady intentions. Joel had been hiding his true agenda from me. Marrying me for my bank account."

Ryder could relate. He'd been on his way down that path with Courtney. He hated to think what might have happened had he not caught her in bed with another man.

"I can't imagine a father who would treat his own blood like that, his own daughter. I can't imagine a person who would treat *you* like that," he said. It made Ryder want to Robert to the ground. If he wasn't already deceased, the thought may have become a reality.

Her hand covered his and she closed her eyes. "I can't imagine it either, but I lived it." She brought his hand to her lips and kissed the inside of his palm.

Ryder reached up and kissed her lips. "No one will ever treat you like that again. Not while I'm around."

"Thank you. I don't know how Joel got my dad to agree to the divorce, but he must have held something over my dad. Joel was always running around for him, so maybe he got wind of something Dad didn't want out and traded."

"Blackmailed?"

Violet shrugged. "I guess. Although, I can't see my dad taking the bait. I don't know."

"Maybe it had nothing to do with Joel and Robert made the decision because of you. Because you're his daughter and he realized all the wrongs he'd done."

Violet snorted and rolled her eyes. Her hand flew to cover her lips and she laughed. Ryder enjoyed watching the light fill her eyes again. Violet laughed so hard and so long, he thought she might tumble over beside him.

"I snorted," was all she said through her fingers when she could finally speak.

He grinned at her. He hadn't seen this adorable side of her. There was a lot about her he didn't know or hadn't seen, and he was ready for all the shades of Violet. Ryder pulled her hands down. "You did and it was very unladylike."

She laughed again and lightly slapped his chest. "You bring the unladylike out of me."

"I'm okay with that," he teased, then turned serious. "I'm sorry about Robert and Joel."

Violet's legs squeezed around him and her body tensed, while her eyes darkened. "I shouldn't have said any of that. Joel is your friend." She pulled out of his grasp, was lifting her leg over him but Ryder caught her and settled her back down on his lap.

Violet spoke first. "This is so hard. Is it always going to be this hard? I am so good at knowing when to speak and what not to say, but with you, everything just blurts out of my mouth, then I'm snorting and the next minute while insulting your friend."

"Don't hide your truths from me because Joel is my friend. Don't hide them from me no matter who they are about. I don't want a relationship with you where we hide things. I don't want to hide from you and I don't want you to hide from me. Joel's actions are his own. They do not make you a bad person because you lived through them or because you tell me. Which by the way, makes me want to go beat the shit out of him."

Violet gasped. "Don't you dare."

He shrugged. "I can't promise anything."

"Ryder!"

"Should he happen to make one of his snide, inappropriate comments about...anything...just the tiniest remark may set me off and my fist will probably land across his face."

"Stop it. I don't want to be the wedge between you two."

"Did you not live with Joel for years? He makes the wedges all on his own."

Joel had a lot of enemies. Ryder just happened to be the son of the people who had a soft spot for Joel. But Ryder was feeling his loyalty shifting from what his parents expected of him to what this woman in front of him needed. Violet was his now. Just like sharing his father's illness with her family, he knew they would understand his commitment to her, and the wedge it might cause between him and Joel.

Not wanting secrets, Ryder was about to tell Violet the truth about Joel and his weaseling ways into his family, but she presented a much more curious conversation.

"Do you really want to know why I brought you here?"

He grinned as she pressed against his hips. "I am very curious."

"I brought you here to jog your memory of the last time we were here."

"My memory doesn't need any memory jogging." He pulled her against him and kissed her lips. "I remember stealing glances at you when the wedding posse wasn't looking. Wanting to be exactly where we are, right now." He paused. "Only naked. No more lies between us. I was envisioning you naked."

Violet laughed. "Oh were you?"

"Yes. You have way too many articles of clothing on."

In a quick movement, he pulled her dress over her head, leaving her reaching for it as he tossed it on the floor. He took the moment to look over her straddling him, with the moonlight casting a glow over her gorgeous body. Left in only her panties and bra and wiggling against his growing bulge as she moved, he could have devoured all of her right there. He was only teasing. A bathroom was one thing, head table of a wedding was...wrong. It was wrong. But it felt so good.

"Ryder..." His lips caught his name and he pulled her warm body against his, wanting his shirt off too. If she hadn't been worried about his feelings in her suite, they likely would have been making love for the last hour.

Ryder had assumed Violet's hands would push against his chest and she would scoot off him to retrieve her dress. He was ready to play hard to get, pulling her back and kissing her bare throat. But when her hands moved over his shoulders and around his neck, she pressed her body harder against his, moaning in his mouth, and he forgot where they were. Ryder's hands slid up her warm back, unsnapping her bra, before continuing up the nape of her neck. He dug his fingers into her hair and pulled her back, exposing her long throat. He kissed her silky skin, licking, nibbling and loving her moans with every touch. By the time he reached her breasts, she'd already slipped out of the bra. Her fingers grasped the hem of his shirt and he broke the contact with her skin long enough to rip it off.

He wanted to kiss every last inch of her. Violet wanted every last piece of his clothing off and was working at his button and zipper. Her hands slipped inside his pants and it was his turn to moan. Violet's lips crashed against him, as she rose on her knees above him, still rubbing underneath his denim.

Her tongue trailed a path to his ear and she whispered, "Get rid of the rest of your clothes."

Then her body pulled away. Ryder stared in amazement at the beauty of the woman in front of him. Still on her knees, she backed to the edge of the table and climbed off. As she turned away from him, she stripped off the last piece of her clothing and tossed her panties at him. As he caught the material, she glanced over her shoulder and smirked.

Where was she going?

Ryder wasn't waiting around to find out. He slid off the table and shed the remainder of his clothes, following her across the distance to the window. Ryder stopped. Slowly she walked across the distance of the window and her silhouette was captivating. She stopped at the edge of the window and curled her finger at him, beckoning him on.

Ryder didn't waste any time. He crossed the distance and pulled her naked body against his, kissing her thoroughly and taking every last taste of the sweet wine in her mouth. It wasn't until Violet pulled him down, onto an edge, that he realized there was a window seat across the length of the window.

Ryder was resistant. "Violet, people might see us."

She smiled at him, wickedly, and he loved the sinful glimmer the moon reflected in her eyes. "Then we better give them a show worth watching."

Ryder glanced one last time into the darkness outside. It was all bush and didn't appear to have access to the resort's trails. If Violet wasn't worried, he didn't have anything to be worried about. And if she wanted to give a show, he would give a show...but it wasn't going to be for any other woman except her.

Chapter Twenty-Two

"THIS IS WRONG," Violet heard Ryder's voice follow her as she crossed the ballroom and stole the linen tablecloth off the cake table. "No. Not that table," Ryder said.

Violet wrapped the silk material around her hot, warm, and aroused body.

"You did it." Ryder laughed, and she turned, catching him shaking his head in the moonlight.

From this distance, the silhouette of his body warmed the area between Violet's legs all over again. Waiting for her on the window seat, his naked body was stretched out on his side and one arm propped on his elbow, holding his head.

Violet giggled and ran across the room feeling like a caped crusader moving through the darkness, but the only person she was rescuing was herself.

"It was the emptiest table," she defended, stopping in front of him.

He stared up at her, but she didn't notice as her eyes trailed over his taut muscles. Up close, the light displayed each groove of his body and it was amazing. *He* was amazing. They were amazing...together.

"Didn't your mom teach you it isn't nice to gawk?" he teased, reaching under the material wrapped around her and pinching her leg. "Get over here."

Violet snuggled into the crook of Ryder's elbow, as he wrapped the "blanket" around them. Leaning on his side, his legs tangled in hers, he traced his finger along her throat, watching her.

"What are the odds that we are going to get caught?" Ryder asked.

She shrugged, a little tease, at him, but they weren't going to get caught. No one stepped into her ballrooms the night before a wedding, without consulting her first. No one.

"We could go back to your place," Ryder said and Violet felt herself stiffen, even though she tried not to. Ryder must have felt it too, because he said, "I *want* to go back to your place."

Violet didn't believe him and she didn't want to ruin this perfect night. There was so much attraction between them but their differences continued to get in the way, even today. She didn't want anything to get in the way of how she felt right now.

The best solution was a topic change. "You know, I wasn't referring to our last visit to this room,"

"Was there another time?" he asked, then mortification filled his face and she thought maybe for a second he remembered. Then he said, "Please don't tell me this has something to do with my drunkenness at your wedding."

Don't tell me? He didn't remember. *Why did that bother her a bit?*

"I guess in a way, it did. It was the night of my wedding." His blank face stared back at her. "Apparently, I'm unsuccessful at jogging the memory of a heart-broken, drunken fool," she said.

"We were here?" He sounded so surprised, if she hadn't remembered it so clearly, she might wonder herself. "On your wedding day?"

Violet nodded. "Wedding night. Most of the wedding night. While the guests were dancing and celebrating, we were in here, celebrating our pity."

Ryder didn't look happy about that.

"Let's just say, you were attempting to be the source of my hard liquor."

Ryder's face fell and he searched her eyes trying to confirm she wasn't making the story up. When he realized she was telling him the truth, even more mortification crossed his face. "On your wedding night? While you were pregnant?"

Violet touched his cheek, thinking he might pull away from her. "I said attempting. Besides, you didn't know I was pregnant. No one did." She reached up and kissed him. The lips that spun her world were tightly pinched.

"No wonder you've been mad at me all these years. First I ruffled your sister's dress, then I intoxicated you."

Violet laughed. He had intoxicated her, but it wasn't the result of alcohol. "Don't put that blame on yourself. You don't even remember. But I did try to stop you from drinking anymore and when you tried to take your flask back from me, I knocked you off the table."

Ryder stared at her. He was skeptical.

"Yes, that's right. I knocked big, muscle man, Ryder Carlex right on his ass. And it felt incredible. Then I chugged the flask and tried to help you back up."

"Tried?"

"You're all muscle and when you're dead weight, you are heavy as cement. We stayed on the floor. Hung out. You and I spent the beginning of my happily ever after together."

Ryder's eyebrows knitted together. "Happily ever after?" he asked.

Violet covered her face, embarrassed as he said it out loud, like it was the fairy tale everyone thought. "Yes." She uncovered her eyes to find him still staring at her. "It's what I tell couples who are getting married here," she explained. "That their wedding day is the beginning of the rest of their lives together. That day is their 'happily ever after'." She sobered. "I know, it sounds silly, but couples gobble it up."

"And you?"

"What about me?"

"Do you believe in happily ever after?"

She shook her head, her eyes falling to where his hand was outlining each of her fingers. She ended in a shrug. "I did and then I didn't. Now, I don't know."

Could she find her happily ever after with Ryder? After all these years, was it possible?

"I was young then and the term is so appropriate with my clients. They smile and love the idea." Violet smiled. "Do you believe in happily ever after?" she asked him.

It was Ryder's turn to shrug. "I guess that depends on the definition of happily ever after. My parents, for example, were madly in love while they were married, but their happily ever after was cut short when my mom died." His tone changed as he said it. "My dad loved her every single day she was gone, until the day he couldn't remember. Is that his happily ever after?"

Violet had never thought about it like that.

Ryder sighed and squeezed her hand. "Anyway, we should go." He sat up and Violet pulled him back down, this time to settle on top of her.

"I don't want to go."

He kissed her. "I don't want to get caught."

She kissed him. "We won't."

"Violet..."

"There's only two ways to get in here. One through the main french doors and the other through the corridor that leads to the kitchen. For both you need a key card to get in."

"If it's so impossible, then how did I get in here on your wedding?"

"Well, because of the amount of guests my parents had invited not only was the gold ballroom kitchen packed with staff preparing meals and cleaning up afterwards, but so was the silver ballroom. From the platter of food you had in here when I found you, I assume you came in through the kitchen."

He chuckled and she was glad to hear the blame he held for himself was gone. "And, did we sneak back out that way?"

Violet pressed her lips together. The kitchen staff had been long gone by the time her mother had wandered in, finding Violet and Ryder passed out on the window seat...exactly where they were right now. "My mom found us. Sleeping."

"No." Shock coursed through his chuckle.

"Yes. She brought me out to wish farewells to the guests. We left you here and I honestly don't know what my mom did about you. I was sent to my bedroom like a child after the last speech and the party went on without me." Violet searched his eyes. "Do you really not remember?"

He shook his head.

Violet left their conversation at that. If she told him the truth, she knew his guilt would pull him away. They were better together, then apart.

"Let's make some new memories in this room," she suggested, moving her legs up and around his waist.

"I think we've made plenty," he said, but his lips found her throat and his soft touch arched her body harder against him.

"I don't think we've made enough," she whispered hoarsely into his hair.

Chapter Twenty-Three

THE NEXT WEEK went by so quickly. Violet could hardly believe that tomorrow Joel and Missy would be tying the knot...and she hadn't given either of them another thought in the meantime.

Violet was more excited about the Fright Fest party that evening. Ryder was taking her. It was officially their first date and Violet felt as eager as a teenager on prom night...only it was just past lunch and there were still hours to wait.

She had even talked Emma, Izzy and Kate into hitting the costume shop in town, as if their extensive accumulation of Halloween costumes over the years hadn't been enough to choose from. Violet had wanted something new, something for just her and Ryder. Plus, convincing the girls hadn't been hard and they'd made a fun afternoon of it, meeting up with Kate's sisters Sydney and Peyton. Aside from one Izzy-round of, *your sister sucks*, referring to Abby and directed at the McAdams, Izzy had behaved. And Violet got something extra special for the evening. Sophia and Parker were spending the night at Eliza and Carl's and there would be no sneaking around.

After finally talking to Joel, and thanks to her good fortune, they were on the same page in regards to the kids. Violet and Joel had sat down with Parker and Sophia and together worked through some of the underlying feelings the kids were having. The smiles it left on their heavy hearts was a relief to Violet.

When Joel spontaneously decided to take them for the weekend, Violet was secretly excited at the opening to go on her first date with Ryder. The kids hadn't been so excited. Violet's weekend had been booked solid with weddings in each ballroom, Friday, Saturday and Sunday. Plus, there had been two tent weddings at the beach. The mass amount of demands required Emma to step in and help, which alternatively gave Violet the opportunity to ask her to fill in on the Bensen wedding. Emma did so gladly.

"I didn't mean to just drop by," Ryder said, when Sophia and Parker disappeared down the hall. After having lunch together, the four of them, in Violet's suite, the kids took their dessert to the toy room. Violet would have been more concerned and strict had she not been eager to curl up on the couch with Ryder.

"You mentioned they were going to the Fright Fest events this morning, and since you had the day off...I didn't think they were home. I should have called," Ryder said.

Violet was glad he dropped by. They were being cautious around the kids. They might have jumped into their relationship fast and it felt amazing, but this was new to Parker and Sophia.

As much as Violet wanted Ryder over every second she wasn't at work, it wasn't realistic...not yet. She was glad he understood, but she wasn't surprised. Ryder's thoughts automatically revolved around family. Sophia and Parker were Violet's family, and they were always included in Ryder's thoughts. Just like his current apology.

"Ryder, if you never come over when they're home or awake..." Violet grinned at him and watched his shoulders drop from their tense position. "They will never get used to having you around," she told him.

Even though Ryder had been avoiding spending his days and early evenings with Violet, when the kids were tucked in bed for the night, Violet let Ryder in through the poolroom. With the curtains drawn in the living room, and neither kids bedrooms being on that side of the house, they easily snuck right in through the french doors of her bedroom. Ryder wasn't tip-toeing around her suite, with access to a bathroom, he stayed all night and when the sun still hadn't risen, he snuck out the way he came and the kids were oblivious.

"I know. I just don't want to overstep my boundaries." *Overstep?* This was the first time, since the supper the evening they spent in the silver ballroom that he'd seen the kids.

"You are not overstepping. I'm so glad you came over today." She kissed his lips gently and he stiffened until she moved back.

Violet grinned at his caution. Ryder didn't notice her grin as he glanced over his shoulder toward the hallway to make sure they were alone. He was nervous and it was adorable. She was glad his stress was due to the children catching them together instead of being about Joel. When she'd thought he would never step foot in her suite again, regardless of his promise that she not worry about him, she'd been relieved to find out, he wasn't only talk, and had made the effort. Now she couldn't imagine spending one night in her bedroom without him.

"The kids really do enjoy your company." Maybe not as much as her, but they were being wonderfully supportive about Ryder being part of their lives.

Ryder stretched his arm across the back of the couch, and Violet took the opening to scoot in against him, bringing her plate of dessert with her. Although he tensed at the closeness, he reached down and kissed the top of her head. "Thank you. I don't want to rush them."

Violet scooped a forkful of apple pie and ice cream saying, "I don't think you coming over once a week is rushing it, and maybe you should start coming over a few times a week."

Violet bit the deliciousness that Kate had dropped off the night before. It was another treat from Mrs. Calvert's bakery. If Violet was as close friends with the older lady as Kate was, she'd have a whole extra behind for Ryder to grab. The thought wasn't that appealing.

"We've only been seeing each other officially for a week," Ryder pointed out. "I don't want them thinking I am honing in on their territory or trying to steal their mother, or..." He lowered his voice and glanced over his shoulder whispering, "Trying to take Joel's place."

Violet feigned worry, pushing off his chest and twisting to look at him. "Are you using the children as pawns, because you are having second thoughts about dating me? It's my snoring isn't it? I know. I'm a loud snorer," she teased and shrugged. "I don't know where I get it from."

Ryder smiled shaking his head.

Violet wasn't a loud snorer, but she liked it when he looked at her like she was being ridiculously cute.

"It's the snoring," he agreed. "I haven't gotten a good night's sleep since I started spending the night here."

Violet set her bowl on the coffee table, legs folded underneath her she leaned toward Ryder whispering in her bedroom voice, "It's not my snoring that's keeping you awake."

Ryder's body stiffened. She loved that she knew what was coming next and she was going to push him to his limit anyway.

He whispered, "Your kids are down the hall." There it was.

Violet touched the top of his thigh and felt his muscles tense beneath her.

"Violet..." The low moan of his voice was intoxicating. If the kids weren't down the hall, she would certainly drag him down there. Unfortunately, they were and that left them with not much else they could do.

"One kiss," she begged and teased at the same time.

As her hand moved up toward the bulge in his jeans he caught it. "You're torture."

"Sweet torture." Violet licked his chin to his bottom lip and took the wonderful thick padding between her teeth, sucking and tugging. When she couldn't handle her own sweet torture, she kissed him. Her body moved without permission, lifting her onto her knees so her body was above him, pressing her hand onto his thigh, hard with all her weight.

He wasn't as much of an objector as he liked to believe. His head moved up with hers and his free hand gripped her neck, pulling her mouth down harder against his. The kiss couldn't last long or extend to anything more.

Violet wanted to give into her body, pleading her to press the thin material of her dress against him and straddle him so her arms could snake around his neck and she could push her wet panties against his bulge. The whole notion had her wishing maybe she hadn't initiated this kiss. This wonderful, intoxicating–

"No! Parker! Mom!"

Violet jumped away from Ryder so fast her neck cracked and pain flared up her back. She ignored it, searching for sight of her kids, only to find Ryder's horrified face doing the same. There were no children.

Violet let out a breath as she realized the voice came from the toy room. How the joke was on her.

Sophia screamed for Violet again in a sound of anger and horror, but not pain. They weren't hurt...except Violet's neck.

Violet smiled at Ryder.

He did not smile back and that made her give into a fit of hysterical laughter.

"It's not funny," he growled, standing up and pulling the tightness in his pants. When he caught her watching, he murmured a string of curses.

Violet's heart was only beginning to settle down. "I don't think I can handle that again," she said putting her hand over her pounding heart.

That made him smirk...a little. "Oh it's not so funny now, is it?"

"Mom!" Sophia snapped from right behind Ryder.

Ryder's glower returned, not daring to turn around and meet Sophia.

Violet tried to shake away her grin as she moved around Ryder and his distracting bulge, to peer at her daughter's flustered face. Only the horror that greeted her extinguished Violet's grin faster than she'd jumped away from Ryder.

Violet's eyes didn't make it past the center of Sophia's purple chiffon flower girl dress soaked in a circle of rainbow ice cream.

Violets smile dropped. "What did you do? Why do you have that on? *What did you do!*"

The wedding was one day away. *One day away!* And the dress...the dress!

Take a breath. Pull yourself together.

What did you do! Screamed on repeat in her head and Violet wished her kids had walked in on her kissing Ryder. It would have been so much easier to fix. These dresses were custom made, months in advance. Violet knew, she'd taken Sophia to plenty of fittings to make this dress perfect for Missy's vision.

A sickening bunch of bile was pushing its way up Violet's throat. She was going to have a panic attack. Her chest constricted tightly, and her breath was lost to her.

One day. One day!

"Parker did it," Sophia said, as her guilty-faced son walked into the living room objecting with a, "She started it."

Who cared who started what. This was a disaster.

"You go take that off," Violet instructed Sophia, as her voice came back to her and her mind went into overload.

265

She turned to her son. "And you, go get the ice cream bowls, rinse them and put them in the dishwasher. I want you both to meet me in the foyer immediately."

They took off like little puffs of smoke at their mothers tone.

Oh no. Oh no. Oh no!

While Ryder helped Parker with the dishes and ice cream, Violet Googled *ice cream and silk stains,* and a half hour later after trying everything, the stain looked worse. *A lot worse.*

Sophia needed a new dress. ASAP.

"I have to go to Secret Wishes Weddings in town and get a new dress for Sophia," Violet told Ryder. Would Lana Morris, owner of the shop, be there on a Thursday right after lunch? Would she be reachable if she wasn't? And would she be able to either fix the stain or make her a new dress?

"I can drive," Ryder offered.

That sounded wonderful. Violet's trembling hands thanked him.

Fifteen minutes later the four of them walked into Secret Wishes Weddings. It was a cute little boutique on the main street of Willow Valley.

Violet was relieved when she caught sight of Lana's stark black hair behind the counter. As Violet approached, Lana greeted her with a smile. Her jade colored eyes pulled shades of green out of the blouse she wore under her striped black blazer.

"Good evening Violet," she greeted with a smile that dropped when Violet laid the dress on the counter, stain facing up. Horror widened her eyes and her painted pink lips fell open. "What happened?"

"Ice cream and kids." Violet was as disgusted as Lana. "I need a new one."

"In two days?" Lana had dressed the entire wedding party, unfortunately she had the date off by one day.

Violet shook her head, slowly, feeling awful for the job she was about to require. "Tomorrow."

"Violet," she breathed as if it was impossible. It almost was impossible, but with the right amount of money, she would make it possible. She couldn't imagine the look on Joel's face if he saw what she'd allowed to happen to the dress.

The vision was horrifying.

"I will pay you greatly for your service," Violet whispered.

"I don't doubt it," Lana said, but she still didn't look convinced she could pull it off. "Let me get Sophia measured up for a quick recap."

Lana rushed around the counter, ushering Sophia toward the change rooms in the back. Parker followed behind, explaining how the ice cream on her dress wasn't really his fault. Her darling children...she could string them in the air by their ankles.

Violet rested her back on the counter and closed her eyes. She rubbed the back of her neck, which was growing tenser with each movement. She needed a muscle ointment. She wondered if Kate's soap shop had an all-natural one for sale.

When she opened her eyes, she found Ryder leaning against the flat side of a belt rack, arms crossed and sending her his cocky look. She knew immediately he wasn't thinking about the dress at all, and rather the thrill of being caught in her living room.

"Stop it," she said.

"That was a close call." He inched closer.

"That was the last close call. I've learned my lesson. I think I have whip flash like an old mother hen."

He inched closer, each step slower with purposefully seductive movements. "Want me to give your neck a rubdown?"

"No. I want you to keep your distance so I am not jumping out of my skin."

"You know what I've learned?"

Violet shook her head at his question, afraid to ask.

"I've learned what a thrill it is to almost get caught doing something you're not supposed to be doing."

Violet laughed. "That was not a good thrill."

"That was a magnificent thrill." He lowered his voice as he came up in front of her. He didn't touch her with his hands or his body, but his lips reached over and kissed her.

Violet pulled her lips away, but only her head gave any distance from him. He'd trapped her between the counter and himself.

"Stop," she said, but even she knew it sounded weak.

"You don't sound convincing." He kissed her cheek and the warmth of his lips flushed her skin.

"Ryder..."

"Hmm." He kissed her ear and nibbled on her earlobe.

Violet melted. Her eyes glanced over at the change room area but no one was visible.

"Ryder..."

He took her hands. "They have gone into the women's changing area." Ryder pulled her away from the counter and as he walked backwards, he grabbed a suit off the rack. "I need a new suit for Fright Fest tonight," he said. He gave her a harder tug and she stumbled forward into his arms.

Violet laughed. "What are you planning on being with a suit?"

"A business man," he said, as though that were a real costume. She couldn't wait for his reaction when he saw the outfit she chose. "We should go try this on." He kissed her lips, wrapping his arms around her waist and pulling her against him as he continued toward the change room door.

Violet giggled against his lips. "Oh, this is so not how a mother behaves," she said, but damn how it felt so good.

"This is how someone behaves when they love someone," Ryder whispered.

Violet stopped. Loved someone? He'd mentioned that he was falling in love with her, but falling in love and loving someone were two entirely different things...unless Ryder didn't mean them differently. Unless, he was just mixing up his words and he was still only falling in love with her. What did he mean?

"You heard me," he said, but she still wasn't sure exactly what she had heard.

"I'm not sure I heard you right."

"You just want me to say it again," he teased.

"I want you to clarify what you meant."

Ryder kissed her. "My mom always told me about what it felt like to find the right woman. And the day you threw yourself into my life you opened a part of me that I hid from the world and gave me a reason to want to live again. I only wish my parents were here, physically and mentally to meet you. They would love you as much as I do. They would love your strength, your stubbornness. They would love that you made me fight for you."

With each admission, tears gathered in Violet's eyes and he continued as though her tears weren't enough. "And they would see the tender side of you that you don't show many people. Worse than not telling your kids, is getting caught and confusing them. So if you are ready to tell them, then I'm ready. I'm not in this for a one time fling. Violet I'm in this for life. I want to be *your* happily ever after."

Her happily ever after? Her happily ever after! "I gave up on that."

"I know you did. And I want to spend every day of our lives together showing you that you're mine."

That was so romantic and tacky all at the same time, Violet didn't know whether to laugh or gasp. The only thing her brain could form was an, "I am?"

"Do you have to ask?" The deep love that she saw in his eyes told her as tacky as it might be, Ryder was serious.

"I always thought it was the wedding that made the happily ever after. The perfect day. The vows. The promise in front of all your friends and family. But right now, for the first time in my life, I realize it's everything that happens before the vows. I was so scared to let you in. I was terrified of the feelings you brought out in me, but deep down under my cloak of caution, over my heart, was love, for you. A love stronger than anything I've ever known or felt and that was you, my happily ever after. I love you. I'm ready to tell the kids. I'm ready to tell everyone.

Ryder kissed her. "Let's try this suit on first."

"No." Her objection was weak. She pushed her hands against his chest, which only tightened his grip around her waist. "Ryder..." His lips lavished her neck, his gruff tickling it and she forgot why she was fighting him. Violet giggled like a schoolgirl, loving the feel of every part of this man. She didn't hear the bell above the door chime when it opened, or the loud footsteps of the person who entered.

"What the hell is going on?" If the question had come from anyone else, with Violet lost in her blissful state, she would have giggled and hid her head in Ryder's shoulder, hoping he would move them into the back change rooms and out of plain sight. But it wasn't just anyone else. *It was Joel.*

The sound of Joel's voice sent hot flashes of panic through Violet. His insults, his warnings, the entire conversation they'd had in her office, when Joel had all but threatened her, flickered before her. *Seducing you after a shower, and taking you in our bed, when I knew you didn't want me. Do you think Ryder doesn't know what a cold, heartless lay you are?*

When they'd met last week to talk about the kids, they'd both put aside the conversation from her office and had been civil. But now...kissing Ryder...Joel knew...

He witnessed the kiss they shared, and it hadn't just been a kiss...Ryder had been all over her. There was not hiding from this, even if her first instinct was to do exactly that.

Violet had ignored the voice in her head, knowing that one day she would have to face Joel about her relationship with Ryder. But being caught like this, with his sharp words still cutting her insides, she wasn't ready.

Violet pulled away from Ryder, like Joel was the principal who had just walked into an empty classroom during prom. Ryder let her, but caught her hand and made the next moment theirs...not Joel's.

Violet's back faced Joel. Staring down at Ryder's tight grasp, she felt him squeeze her a promise, that he would step out of the shadows with her. *How could he know she was scared?* Her eyes found Ryder's watching her with the same promise but lacking the fear consuming her.

You don't know what he said. Why didn't I tell him?

With Ryder's support, Violet turned to face Joel. His pale skin was now piping red and his narrowed gaze was transfixed on her.

This is Ryder's friend. How is this Ryder's friend. As suddenly as they'd been caught, Violet had answered her previous question. She hadn't told Ryder what Joel said because she was scared of what the outcome would be. She was terrified Ryder would leave...for Joel's friendship. Ryder was a man of loyalty and they'd been friends since childhood. Even holding his hand, she didn't know where Ryder's loyalty stood and that was scarier than telling Joel the truth about them.

Ryder pulled her firmly against his side, widening his body like a protective shield around her. She wished that eased her worry.

What did Joel have to be angry about? Joel left Violet. He married her for the money he was able to walk away with. Joel had found the love of his life and was marrying Missy in two days. He had no right to be mad. Except that Ryder was his friend and Violet could understand the tension that might bring to their friendship...or the destruction it might cause to their relationship.

The tight grip Ryder had on Violet's hand almost reassured her that she came first, but without getting past this conversation, she didn't know for certain.

Violet opened her mouth to ask Joel what he was doing here, avoiding the obvious, but Ryder jumped right in. He ripped the bandage off and Violet felt blood drain from her face.

"Joel, we didn't want you to find out like this. Violet and I have been seeing each other. I was going to talk to you—"

"Seeing each other? Or screwing each other?"

Ryder tensed.

Violet tensed too and swallowed past the growing lump in her throat.

"This ends now." The stern, cold tone that came from Ryder had even Violet turning to look at him. He paid no attention to her. His stern glare was solely focused on Joel. "That mouth you can't seem to control has chewed off its last ignorant remarks regarding Violet."

There was her answer. *Was Ryder going to punch Joel?*

Violet almost cried. Tears she couldn't control pooled in her eyes and she pushed them away, but didn't take her eyes off of Ryder.

He chose me. He chose me! Why had she ever doubted him? After everything they'd been through together, of course he chose her.

Joel tugged for her attention with his snarky remarks. "Talk to me? What for? To ask me or tell me? Because by the looks of you two, this has been going on for a while."

Ryder answered again and still his voice lacked the sympathy it had carried at the beginning of this confrontation. "To talk and to tell you," Ryder clarified and if that wasn't enough he continued, "I certainly wasn't going to *ask* your permission to date Violet. Our dating has nothing to do with you."

"Except that you're dating. Do you do this with all your friends ex's? Sleep with them? Make them think you've gotten a little feeling for them, something special?" Joel looked at Violet. "You're just another one of his tramps."

Violet inhaled sharply, and narrowed her eyes on Joel.

Who the hell did he think he was talking to her like that? Tramp? Tramp! Did he forget who he was marrying in two days?

Violet summed up the courage to tell Joel exactly where he could stuff it, but Ryder took the first step. Literally, he released Violet's hand and closed in the distance between him and Joel.

Violet held her breath.

Ryder hovered over Joel, not only in height, but in width and the hostile way he moved would send any person quivering. Joel didn't even take a step back and tried his hardest to dictate Ryder's domineering posture.

"Joel, I will only tell you this one more time, so you better listen closely. You will *never* disrespect Violet again. If I even catch wind that you've uttered a tiny ignorance in her direction, it will be my fist you have to deal with."

Violet opened her mouth to end the threats, but then snapped it shut even quicker. This son of a bitch deserved to be threatened. If Ryder even caught wind of what Joel had said in her office, there wouldn't have been words exchanged but rather fists.

Ryder continued without lessening his tone. "I do not want this to come between us, but if you're going to make me choose." Ryder glanced over his shoulder at Violet and his smile lightened as he sent her a wink. He turned back to

Joel. "Don't make me choose. You won't like the outcome."

He said it. Ryder chose her. Ryder chose Violet. Violet felt like a waterfall, as her eyes filled for the second time. Her restraint to keep from jumping and throwing her arms around Ryder and dragging him into the change room to say thank you, was proving difficult.

There was a long awkward silence between them as Joel and Ryder stared each other down. Finally, Joel's shoulders lightened and he glanced around. "I came here after Parker texted me and told me Sophia ruined her dress."

Parker.

Violet stepped forward to stand directly at Ryder's side and his hand curled around hers. Violet caught Joel's eyes drop to their connection quickly.

"She did, but Lana is measuring her and will have a new dress by tomorrow. They're in the change room if you'd like to go see them."

Joel glanced toward the back fitting room, considering, and then he shook his head. "I have things to do still." He eyed them both over. Ryder longer than Violet, but when Joel's eyes met Violet she felt a knowing threat arise. One Ryder would not understand.

Joel grumbled a goodbye as he left, giving the door a little slam.

"I think he took it well," Violet said. She was still excited Ryder chose her over Joel, but she didn't want to throw the sensitive decision in Ryder's face.

When Violet glanced up at his grim face, her smile faltered. "What?" she asked.

Ryder shifted on his feet, his eyebrows drawn together. He was trying to read her.

Violet shifted her weight to one foot and tilted her head at him. "You have something you want to say?"

"Are you going to tell me if I don't ask?"

Huh-oh, he suspected. Why was she surprised? Joel's ignorance had been the reason she insulted Ryder in her office and demanded he leave. "Tell you what?"

Violet was ready to deflect him. There were some things that were better just left alone. Ryder surprised her, when he hugged her. Her legs stumbled at his force, but his strength kept her standing.

"You are a stubborn woman, Violet Caliendo," he breathed against her head. "I meant what I said, if Joel makes me choose, it's you." She loved hearing him say it. "And if I find out he's responsible for that terror I saw in your eyes, and I suspect he is, you're going to have promise to bail me out of prison."

"Ryder, let it go."

He pulled away and cupped her face. "I will let it go this time, because I know you are strong and I know you can handle yourself. But from here on in, we are a team. If anything inappropriate is passed between you and Joel. *Anything.* I want to know. Agreed?"

Violet had never had someone love her so much that he was willing to step away from the loyalty he held for a friend.

Violet nodded. "Agreed."

Ryder relaxed. "Are you sure you don't want to tell me what happened in your office?"

Violet shook her head. "I handled it. And, from your threats, I imagine Joel will think twice next time he talks to me." Violet reached up and kissed him.

"You know what I really want to do?" Ryder asked, wrapping his arms around her waist and pulling her tightly against him, telling her exactly what he wanted to do.

"I can imagine."

"I..." His kissed her chin and she licked her lips wanting more, as the warmth that always found her when she was in Ryder's arms consumed her now. "Am..." He licked her chin and her legs trembled. "Hungry."

Violet's shocked expression found him grinning at her.

"I hear there's a little hut on the beach that has killer deep fried pickles," he said.

Deep fried pickles. Deep fried pickles!

Violet laughed and pushed him off her, just as Parker came running from the change room announcing they were done.

"Hey sport, you want to go get some lunch at the beach?" Ryder asked him.

"Yeah! And ice cream," he negotiated with Ryder.

"Deal."

"Alright." Parker high-fived Ryder then tugged his arm. "Let's go now and the girls can catch up."

Ryder glanced at Violet for confirmation and when he got it, the two most important guys in her life laughed and joked their way out of the shop.

Now if Lana could finish the dress by tomorrow, everything would be perfect.

Chapter Twenty-Four

RYDER WAS LATE arriving at the pavilion for the Fright Fest.

Originally, he'd intended on picking Violet up early at her suite and meeting Emma for a last minute check list before the party began. But after he'd showered and changed into his suit, he was attending as the very businessman he alleged, his cell phone rang. Sitting in his home office, his time quickly disintegrated on speakerphone with the Kendrick's, discussing hold-ups and solutions for the re-design.

Although Ryder hadn't picked Violet up, like the mandatory rules of a date required, when he stepped under the cobweb and bones archway of the pavilion's front doors and spotted Violet, he knew, for both their sakes, it was good he hadn't picked her up.

She was beautiful.

There was no way he would have been able to keep his hands off her if they'd been alone in her suite, with her bedroom only down the hall and a perfectly good couch only feet away. He would love to have started where they left off earlier that day.

The pavilion was half-full when he arrived, but the blonde beauty was the only individual that Ryder catalogued. Her beauty radiated across the dark room, like a light at the end of a tunnel. Her hair was loosely braided and draped across one shoulder. It ran down over her magnificent dress, which shimmered against the disco ball and sporadic spotlights.

Ryder tucked his hands in his slack's pockets and slowed his pace across the room, giving him time to take in the magnificence of the woman he loved. *The woman he loved.* He could get used to that.

The phrase didn't scare him away, but instead excited him. He could see his future with Violet, doing all the things he'd given up the last couple of years. Summer vacations, birthday celebrations...Christmas.

Christmas had been the most difficult holiday spent alone. Of course. his extended family always welcomed Ryder to their homes, but he'd declined. Wherever he spent his holidays lacked the lavish decorations Kathleen would have used and the love he'd grown up with. But now, he'd found the love of his life and he was ready to celebrate every holiday, to sweep this woman off her feet and whisk her away on his boat for summer vacations. Everything. He wanted everything with her.

Right now, he just wanted to look at her. The thin material slipped off Violet's neckline, secured around her shoulders and tapered into sheer sleeves. The blue dress hugged her waist, showed off her round derriere and spilled around the floor, with a sheer cape attached to the back. *Beautiful.*

Ryder walked straight to her, ignoring everyone around him. The music captivated her exquisiteness and, as he approached, he was glad when the guest she'd been talking to excused herself.

Ryder stopped behind her.

If he wasn't trying his damnest to give Violet the proper date he'd promised her, he'd scoop her up and find them some privacy.

Ryder caressed the shoulder with her side braid. Her bare skin was silk beneath his fingers and the desire to wrap this silk around him was powerful. He bent down and ran his lips across her exposed shoulder, drinking in her delicious flavor.

Violet leaned into him. "Hey." The new soft, loving tone of her voice created more desire in him to scoop her into his arms and carry her to the suite. He contained himself.

"Hey." He kissed her ear before moving in front of her. "You are stunning."

She smiled at him. The dim lights caught the shimmering white makeup around her eyes and added even more blue to their depth. "Thank you." She watched him for a moment, then grinned. "You have no idea who I am, do you?"

"Not a clue."

She laughed. "Rosemary would be very disappointed in you."

"You better fill me in then."

Violet did a little courtesy and said, "Blue dress, snowflakes in my hair, glistening around my eyes..." He was clueless. "I'm a snow queen."

Ryder's smile fell. "You mean ice queen?" He wished he'd never slipped that nickname out. She was anything but an ice queen.

Violet kissed his frown away and not just a little peck on the lips. Her mouth covered his and he felt her tongue lick his lips. He was taken aback by her quick exposure of them and before he had a chance to kiss her back, she'd pulled away...and smiled at him.

After all their battles and struggles to be together, he'd honestly thought his tiny kiss on her shoulder might possibly cause her to withdraw from him in public. But she'd leaned into him and now, in front of a room full of her family, employees, guests and friends, she'd kissed him.

"Trust me, this ice queen is a well loved movie character to whom every little girl dreams of being."

Violet kissed him again and this time her tongue slipped between his lips for a taste. Ryder was ready for her and the warmth of her eagerness, giving all she had to offer. He held her a second longer after her body tried to step away. When their lips parted, he kept one arm wrapped around her waist, and held her close.

The loving look her sapphire eyes sent him captured him. Desire and lust were mild emotions when love wasn't blended into the equation. "I missed you too," she said softly.

"I wanted to pick you up..."

"I wanted you to pick me up."

"I don't think we would have made it out of your suite.'

"You wouldn't have got a complaint from me."

Ryder's moan made Violet grin wider and her teeth caught her lower lip in her mouth. He wanted to catch that lip.

Ryder let her go and stepped back, over a good foot away from her.

Violet cleared her throat as her eyes roamed the guests, proving she'd been lost in that haze with him and unaware of their surroundings.

When she was straightened out, she took a deep breath and ran her eyes over his body. "Let me guess...you're a..." Violet clamped her lips together and smirked at him.

"What?"

She shook her head.

"Violet..."

"You're wearing a designer suit with leather loafers. You're rich and handsome as hell, with an edge of danger and charm that has all the girls swooning...should I continue?"

She was all but calling him the player she'd assumed he was. "I'm a businessman," he said.

Violet's bottom lip pushed out in a pout and Ryder laughed to keep from latching onto it. "I was really hoping to get charmed out of my dress tonight," she teased.

This woman was relentless. He was having a hard enough time staying here in the first place and she was already talking about sex.

"For you, I will be whoever you want. The charming player you once thought I was or the amateur businessman that I was going for."

"Amateur?" Violet laughed, then she sobered and he watched a spark of fire light her eyes. She took one step and the side of her body rubbed against his. He had to swallow hard to not dip inappropriately into her mouth.

"Caliendo, I swear..." he breathed. His hands were unable to resist sliding down her side.

She laughed again, only this time it held a blaze of desire. "Mr. Amateur Businessman, I've been in this industry for a long time." Her fingers wrapped around the knot of his tie, pulling him even closer. The curves and arches of her lips were painted glossy pink and turned upwards. She slowly slid her fingers downwards, pressing firmly against his shirt. "Maybe I can teach you a thing or two about what happens behind closed doors..." Her lips met his ears, and she whispered, "I have an extra special outfit for the after party."

He moaned.

"My thoughts exactly," she said.

Ryder was going to lose it. He grabbed her hand and led her to the darkened dance floor, to distract his body from guiding her to the front door. It also gave him an excellent excuse to pull her body firmly against his, touch, move and rub without causing an unsuitable scene on their first date.

"If you keep up like that, we are going back to your suite," he gruffly whispered in her ear.

"I'm okay with that," she whispered back. He felt her tongue slide across his earlobe.

He moaned again.

"Do you like that?" she teased.

"You know I do." His hoarse voice only prompted another one of her sweet giggles.

"Then let's get out of here. My mom has the kids for the night and we have the entire suite to ourselves."

Ryder tipped her head to look at him. "As tempting as that is and trust me, it's tempting as hell and if you keep teasing me with your lips, your touch and your seductive bedroom voice, everyone here is going to see how much I want you."

Ryder glanced down at the front of his pants, and Violet blushed, acknowledging his words.

Who's the amateur now?

"We have all night to lie in each other's arms. Right now, we are on a date."

She pouted at him and he continued. "I want to dine and dance with you. I want to stand at your side as we visit your family and friends." He lowered his voice to the bedroom voice she was so persistent on tormenting him with. "I want *you* to want *me* so badly, that at the end of the night, when you get me, it's going to be the hottest lovemaking you have *ever* experienced."

Violet stopped dancing and pulled him away from the dance floor saying, "Let's get started then. The quicker we make rounds, the faster we can get to this hot lovemaking. This snow queen needs a reset."

Ryder chuckled as she waved for a couple drinks from one of the servers, dressed in a pink, soda shop fifties outfit.

He sipped the wine, thinking about the last time he'd enjoyed a party of this size. It had been the last Carlex Grocers Christmas party in Oakston.

Ryder remembered it so clearly. He'd known it was the last event his dad planned on attending and Ryder had done his best to observe his behavior with the employees and their families for future reference as he planned on taking over. Donald, being the family man he was, didn't hold evening parties for only the parents. Instead he had parties for the entire family. That year, they'd rented a private sitting at the De'laine Theater in Oakston, and entertained the children with a carnival show on the stage and small fair games to follow.

As Violet moved Ryder around the room, doing rounds with the socialite regulars, then to her family, Ryder found that even though he hadn't been looking forward to the crowd tonight, he was smiling, laughing and enjoying himself.

His event presence over the last couple of years had generally been quick, go in, open the bank book and out again. Avoiding the questions regarding his dad had made life easier. Remembering those nights, made him remember his first night on the boat with Violet and her accusations about his dates at galas.

When they had a moment alone, he pulled her to the side for privacy. "Violet?"

"Ryder?" Her teasing relaxed him, even if his next words were hard to say. He might not be a player, but he had slept with other women.

"Remember the night we were on my boat. Sharing the apple dessert?" She nodded. "You asked...or accused me of sleeping with all the women on my arms at the galas."

Violet's teasing smile fell. "Ryder, you don't have to tell me."

"I don't want secrets between us."

Violet took a deep breath and when she blew it out she smiled at him. "Being a player and being single are two different things. What you did when you were single doesn't interest me. I only want what you're offering now."

He wrapped his arms around her and pulled her tight against him. "I'm offering you all of me."

"I greedily accept. Let's get out of here."

They were pulled into another conversation with a vacationing couple. Ryder's attention was elsewhere. He couldn't believe he found a woman who was so good to him. She was the one. Violet Caliendo was the one woman, the one love that his mother had told him about. He smiled and sent a private *thank you* to his mother.

When Violet stiffened under his hand pressed on the small of her back, he followed her scrutiny. It was the deceiving pirate that stole her attention.

Ryder's blood went cold.

Watching the light in her eyes struggle, zeroing in on Joel, irked him.

What had he done to her? Or what had he said? Why did she have to be so damn stubborn that she wouldn't tell him?

Ryder excused them from the couple, guiding Violet back to the dance floor.

"Take me home," she pleaded, wrapping her arms around his neck.

He didn't like that Joel was the reason for the sadness in her tone.

"One dance," he promised, pulling her closer. He wanted tonight to be about them. When she thought back to their first date, he didn't want her to remember rushing away because Joel showed up. "Tell me more about this after party you promise."

When Violet's smile didn't quite reach her eyes, he wished they'd left sooner. He wanted her full attention, not her lost attention.

"Did you talk to Joel today?" she asked instead. So much for keeping Joel out of their night.

He shook his head. "I will see him tomorrow. Tonight, you're the only person on my mind. You and that after party outfit."

Her shoulders relaxed.

He lowered his voice. "I don't think we will have time for you to change into your special outfit, I want to peel this dress from your body and touch every last inch of you."

"Then why are we still here?" Violet kissed him. It wasn't soft and appropriate, as the rest of their kisses and touches had been all evening.

As the night had gone on, the open bar had flooded with guests who were now lost in their own haze of alcohol within their own groups. Ryder bet no one even noticed as Violet's fingers dug into his scalp and her body pressed against his. He was sure no one cared that his mouth hungrily covered hers, pried open her lips and greedily tasted every area his tongue could reach. He'd been dying to feel the pressure of these lips since the change room. He was confident if Joel hadn't walked into the store, Ryder could have convinced her that a quick dressing room rumble could be amazing.

When Ryder finally pulled away, deciding it was time to leave, they were both breathing heavy.

"Let's go." He gripped her hand hard and started weaving her through the couples on the dance floor. Violet hugged his arm tightly and he wasn't letting her go until they were behind closed doors. That's what he thought, anyway. When the barrier of people broke through, so did Missy and Joel.

"Can I borrow Violet for a quick second," Joel asked touching Violet's arm. Ryder sent a protective look intently at Joel. "It's about Parker." Joel held his stare and said, "In private."

Ryder didn't like it.

Violet touched Ryder's face, but his rigid jaw didn't relax. "I'll be right back," she promised.

If the roles were reversed, Ryder knew Joel would flaunt Violet, his catch, in front of Ryder. Ryder wanted nothing more than to lead Violet away.

Violet reassuringly squeezed his hand. "Then the after party," she promised.

Ryder tensed as he watched Violet follow Joel out of the pavilion. It should be him guiding her out the door and back to her suite. Ryder had a bad feeling about this...about Joel and his intentions. He was a selfish prick and everything he did was to solely benefit himself.

If that ass sent more confusion in Violet's direction, it was going to be Ryder he had to deal with and Ryder was finished playing nice.

Chapter Twenty-Five

JOEL LED VIOLET away from the pavilion, along the sandy beach, in a quick stride. The music rode across the waves, crashing beside them and into the silence around them.

As they climbed onto the wooden boardwalk leading to the pools, she yanked her arm out of his death hold grip and stopped. This man's touch sent trickles of anguish through her blood. Maybe he always would. No doubt, this talk about Parker was in regards to their son's behavior at Joel's wedding. Violet wasn't going to be in attendance, leaving Joel the guardian parent. There was nothing she could do if Parker decided to lash his little attitude out.

It irritated her that Joel was interrupting her first date night with Ryder...and from the way Ryder looked at her with his steamy, dark eyes, she knew it was going to be one of the best nights of her life.

The resort's background was a paradise of pools, wooden loungers, gazebos surrounded by flowers and foliage bestowing a tranquil ambience that contracted against the hard features across Joel's face. His heated, angry stare took away the dreamy glow the outside lights fashioned. She wished she was holding Ryder's hands, leaning against his side on their way to her suite. Instead, Joel was stealing her precious time.

"What is so important?" she asked, wanting to get to the point, get it over with and get back to Ryder.

Joel's menacing steps toward Violet sent her the first warning. In her heels, Violet was taller than him, but that didn't seem to deter his intimidating tone when he spoke. "You listen about as well now, as when we were married."

Ryder. This was about Ryder.

"Joel, I'm not yours to control. I never have been. If the reason you dragged me out here, was tell me not to date Ryder, it's a waste of your breath. And both of our time. I'm on a date and your fiancé is waiting for you."

Violet turned.

They were a good distance from the pavilion, but Violet could still make out the couples lingering around the building and along the shoreline. She searched for Ryder, hoping he'd followed them out, and they could retreat to her suite together. She'd had her fair share of enough of tonight. But Ryder was nowhere to be seen.

In private. She should have guessed it wasn't about Parker at all.

Joel caught Violet's upper arm. He yanked her back so hard she stumbled. Violet began to object. She tried to pull away and yelled for him to release her, but Joel ignored her, forcing his phone in front of her face, demanding she watch a video that was playing across the display.

Video? Why? What was he doing?

"This is who you want?" he demanded.

At first, Violet couldn't focus on the screen he was waving in front of her, but she caught sight of two people making love. *What was this?* Her arms attempted to free themselves, but Joel held her with a force that she didn't know he had. *Where was Ryder?*

"Do you see who that is?" he demanded.

Violet didn't care who it was, but she had a sickening feeling deep in her gut that it had to do with Ryder...that it was Ryder. Standing by her decision that Ryder's past was his to bear, not hers, she didn't want to watch the video. But the questions still ran through her mind. *Why did Joel even have this? Where did he get this? When had this sexual encounter taken place? Who was on the screen?*

Maybe it was Joel's persistence that fixated her eyes on the screen, or maybe it was the deep desire to know the truth. Either way, she recognized Ryder right away. How could she not? Even from the distance of the video being recorded in the darkened room, the moonlight streaming through the window revealed the length of his hard, taut body. But that wasn't what stopped her from fighting Joel's grasp.

In that instant, the timeframe and the surrounding twisted her whole world.

The silver ballroom. The night of her wedding.

At first, she thought the woman was Emma. Against her want to know, her need to know demanded her eyes observe the white dress abandoned at their feet...a wedding dress...*her* wedding dress. The naked couple entangled in their intimate moment on the window seat, were so engrossed in each other, they were clueless another person was lurking in the shadows, watching, observing...taping. An intimate moment that shouldn't be on anyone's phone. But here it was.

How did Joel have this? Joel knew?

"Daddy's not here to save you this time," Joel whispered so close to her ear, she felt his lips graze her skin and her stomach lurched.

When had her father ever saved her from anything?

The darkness enclosed around her as she accepted who the woman was. Who Ryder was making love to: *Herself.*

She couldn't drag her eyes from the night of her wedding. The night she'd found Ryder alone in the silver ballroom, drunk like a naive adolescent dipping into the intoxicating liquid for the first time. So drunk that he didn't remember their encounter the next morning when the wedding party met for brunch. A night Violet thought only she knew of. *The first night she'd made love to Ryder.*

It wasn't their lovemaking that had her eyes glued to the screen, it was her need for time, to figure out why Joel had this, what her father had to do with it and why he was showing her...now.

Joel had this for ten years? Did he? Or had someone given it to him? Who was recording this intimacy? Her intimacy. Did Ryder know?

"Alright, that's enough." Joel snatched the phone out of her hand and slid his phone into his back pocket.

Violet turned to face him.

Disbelief seized her questions. In the back pocket of Joel's pants was a video of a private moment shared between Violet and Ryder.

She felt violated like never before and it brought stinging bile up her throat. She had to swallow down the suffocating tightness and wasn't sure she had the ability to speak to him right now.

"Shocking isn't it?" Joel said. "Violet Caliendo had her very own sex tape. Could you image the publicity this would bring to the resort?"

Violet's jaw clamped shut in disgust.

"Splashed worldwide across social media in relation to one of the owners of the Caliendo Resort franchise?" He was blackmailing her. She didn't have to ask what about, she knew it was Ryder.

Violet was surprised to find the business her family built and reputation hadn't even crossed her mind, as it would certainly have two weeks ago. "You would dare put a video on the internet that would destroy your children?"

Joel shook his head. "I didn't want it to come to this. I was using the video as leverage against Robert. You know, that egotistical bastard you called, Dad. The man was ruthless. Not that blackmailing him worked, until it was his terms. Then he demanded—because your father never asked for anything—that I give him the video in exchange for allowing us to have the divorce we both wanted from day one."

Why would her dad do that? So many years later?

Robert's actions were self-satisfying, and concealed with hidden agendas.

At first, Violet considered what Robert's ulterior motives could be to offer Joel an out, but then she recalled her conversation with Marc and his admission that during Robert's sickness Violet hadn't given him the heart-to-heart he'd wanted.

Could it be that the last year of Robert's life, he'd gained a conscious? That the guilt of his years of betrayal and hurt upon others had caught up to him?

Violet had believed he was up to something...but maybe Robert was actually sorry.

Joel continued and Violet had to let go of her wandering thoughts to listen. "I was more interested in ending our marriage the *night* of day one. After witnessing my newlywed wife screwing my best friend." His words were harsh, laced with resentment and betrayal.

Joel knew? From day one? Was Violet any better than her own father?

Her intentions hadn't been to hurt Joel but her actions had been selfish and it was apparent Joel had been affected directly by her decision.

"But of course, as you were there for all the years of marriage, I had as much choice in our matrimony as you did." Why did Joel look so wounded by her betrayal if he'd been using her for her money?

"Joel, I don't understand."

Joel shook his head. "It's simple Violet. Stop seeing Ryder."

That wasn't what she meant, but the anger darkening his eyes told her their past wasn't open for discussion.

"This is your revenge for that night?" she asked.

"*Revenge?*" He looked appalled. "I'm not your father."

"You're sure acting like him," she snapped, regretting it the second it passed her lips.

Joel's face drew together and his warning eyes returned. "Listen to me. He is my friend. You are my ex-wife and I don't want the two of you sitting around talking about me."

"Talking about you?" Violet felt the anger rising up her chest. "After all the untruthful stories you told me about Ryder and the lies that you told him about me, you have the nerve to accuse *us* of talking about *you*. You're a piece of work."

"See, it's already started..."

"Because you are a liar."

"Enough!" Joel yelled. "It's not up for debate. End it, or I post this online and Violet Caliendo's sex tape goes viral. This will destroy your name, your image. And Ryder, it will only bring out exactly who he is."

"You don't know him at all." For two people who grew up together, they were so distant in the other's lives that it was shocking. "I don't care about my name or image!"

"No. But what will our kids think? They won't blame me anymore for cheating on you and destroying our family, because clearly you started the down that trail way before I met Missy."

"You wouldn't dare."

He stepped toward her. The smell of him made her sick. "I won't have to, because you won't chance devastating our children or damaging their future."

Joel was right. Violet would end it. Her heart nearly exploded knowing what she would have to do.

Shadows glazed Joel's eyes again, exposing a sadness he'd never bared to Violet before. If he wasn't blackmailing her, she would have felt compassion for him. What was breaking him inside?

"You might be incapable of loving a man..." His eyes darkened. "...of loving me, but you've always loved your children. You're a good mom, so I'm not worried what your decision will be."

Joel had tried? Or had been willing to try before he found her with Ryder? Violet had been prepared, with no other alternative, to try before her father told her of Joel's true intentions. *Was Robert lying? Was Joel lying? How would she ever know the truth?*

What Joel didn't understand was that Violet was in love with Ryder. Violet loved Ryder. She'd never known a love so strongly bonded with another person. It wasn't just a fling between her and Ryder.

How could she fix this? How could she make Joel aware of her true feelings for Ryder without enraging more anger and betrayal?

When she spoke, she tried to sound confident and positive, but her voice came out weak and broken, like she was defeated and had already lost a battle today she hadn't even known she was fighting.

"Joel, he won't let me just break it off." *And I don't want to.* "You're right. I've never loved a man..."

Violet took a deep breath.

This would either infuriate him or help him to see it wasn't just a fling between them. Either way, accepting his blackmail or attempting to barter, it was Ryder she could lose, so she had to try. Sending up a prayer, she hoped her honesty would release the grudge Joel held.

"I'm in love with Ryder and he's in love with me."

Joel didn't move a muscle in his face, but he didn't speak either, so she continued.

"He gets me like no one else ever has and it has nothing to do with that tape, I promise. He doesn't even remember that night."

"Bullshit."

"If I tell him it's over, he will know that you had something to do with my decision. I won't be able to convince him otherwise." She felt the tears welling in her eyes. This video could not get out. "Please Joel, let us be."

Joel stepped toward Violet. "I won't let you turn him against me."

"I don't want to. That was never my intention. He is your friend and if anyone is turning him against you, then you're doing it yourself."

"End it. I don't care how."

"I won't." But she knew she would.

"Then this goes viral."

Strain ricocheted between them. She silently begged him to not to release the video, but when he walked away, her inner soul screamed as she grabbed his arm. She hated that she had to beg him. *Hated* that he had this control over her.

"Wait. I will do it."

"Convince Ryder that you don't love him?" he asked.

She nodded.

"I want him out of your life. Permanently. No connections. No friendship. No rides around on his boat because I don't show up. Understood? Nothing."

Violet wanted to cry. Joel knew she loved Ryder.

How would she convince Ryder? He was so in tune with her feelings and emotions that he would see straight through her. "I will try..."

"There's one way that he won't be able to deny." The low mysterious tone of his voice startled her so, that she looked up in time to find Joel moving to her side. He embraced her so quickly and unexpected, that when she retaliated back, they went tripping over the end of a lounger. Violet went flying backwards onto the springing material and Joel fell on top of her. They should have split and parted ways. However, Joel's mouth landed on her unexpected lips and crushed her against the chair. She couldn't move. Both of his hands locked with hers at her side as his tongue dived into her mouth. She tasted dirt. Low life, dirt and her stomach lurched.

What was he doing?

Violet had spent years with this man. He was the father of her children. The last thing she's ever envisioned was him taking advantage of someone. *Of her.*

Suddenly Joel was lifted from Violet and she heard scuffling, shouting and punches contacting with bodies. Then she heard Ryder's voice. *Ryder.* She couldn't be happier to hear him.

Violet scrambled to her feet as Joel slipped behind her, using her as a shield. *Coward.*

He was completely out of breath. "Whoa. Whoa. Whoa!" Joel said waving one hand at Ryder and the other gripping Violet's arm so tight it hurt.

"Get your filthy hands off of her," Ryder snarled.

"She kissed me first," Joel said.

She did not. Disgusting pig. Then it hit her. This was Joel's way of separating her from Ryder.

"She kissed me first," Joel repeated and every word broke her heart. "Tell him Violet. Tell him about your feelings for me."

Violet had no choice. What was she supposed to do? Joel held all the cards. How was it possible that the man she'd used that night to erase her sorrow had turned out to be her happily ever after?

Her heart shattered as the words left her mouth. "I kissed him first."

The fight drained from Ryder's face, but she watched his defenses go up instead. He was going to fight her, just like she thought. He wasn't stupid or foolish. Damn, the man ran an entire chain of supermarkets.

"I kissed Joel first," she said.

Ryder stepped toward her and Violet stepped back, backing right into Joel's now feeble feeling body. She wanted to turn around and slap, punch, and scream at Joel.

The least he could do was back up and give her some damn space.

Ryder stopped. "Violet?"

"I'm sorry Ryder."

"We have a past." *Shut up, Joel.*

"You have a fiancé," Ryder snapped through clench jaws that raised veins in his throat.

"Ryder, this isn't about Missy," Violet said, softly. Her heart wasn't the only one that was about to break.

"Who *is* this about?" Ryder sent an accusing glare at Joel.

"I'm sorry man," Joel said.

"Give us space," Ryder growled at Joel. "Before I make it two black eyes."

Violet glanced over at Joel to catch the shiner shaping reds and pinks that would turn into an array of greens and blues under his eye. Just then, Joel kissed her. Not on the cheek or the side of the head, but right on her lips and she tasted salty filth, as her tears broke the surface.

"End it," he whispered before walking away.

Violet didn't look at Ryder right away. Her eyes fell to the clenching fists he held at his side. *Clenching.* Only ten minutes ago, they were heading to her suite where his hands would have gently touched every part of her. How she longed to go back before Joel walked into the pavilion. She wanted tonight with Ryder, and now that she could never have it, she wanted it more.

"What's going on?" Ryder's tone was softer, but held reserve. She looked up to find his jaw pulled so tight she wasn't sure how he got the question by.

Joel is blackmailing me as punishment for sleeping with you on my wedding. A night you don't even remember. A video with the evidence.

Violet couldn't confide in Ryder. She wanted to tell him, but look what happened just now with Joel. The end result would be her children's lives, and their future.

"Ryder..."

He held his hand up to stop her. "Before you answer that, come here." He held his hand out to her. Violet stared at it. "Don't hide from me," he said.

Violet didn't move. "I have no choice..."

He left his hand out as he said, "You have a choice. Let me in."

"I can't."

"Can't or won't?" His hand retracted and her trembling legs were ready to let his arms hold her steady, calm her sadness, and love her the way he promised.

Violet could feel her strength draining away with each word he spoke. They were accusing and insulting and yet loving and begging. She had to get her control, before her kids paid for her mistakes.

"Ryder, I'm ending this," Violet said, sternly.

"Because you love Joel?" The suspicion in his tone was unmistakable.

I love you. I love my kids. I don't know what do? I don't have another option.

"I kissed him," she finally said. "You were right all along, Ryder. I'm having a hard time dealing with his wedding and losing him permanently. He's my kid's father."

"Do not insult me by using the pathetic excuse *he* created as a way to end this. You want out? That's your decision, but do not lie to me. Give me the respect I deserve and the truth. What did he say?" Ryder stepped forward again and Violet stepped back.

Violet hated herself.

You're doing this for your kids.

If Ryder knew, he would understand, but he wouldn't let it go.

"You're just the guy I found in the washroom."

Just like that Ryder shut down. His eyes glazed over, his stare hardened. Every piece of him that he'd opened to her, closed off.

Good, it was easier this way. Then why did it hurt so damn much?

Chapter Twenty-Six

RYDER SAW RED.

Violet was lying straight to his face. Not only was she lying to him, she wouldn't trust him with whatever line of crap Joel had threatened her with.

Just the guy I found in the washroom.

Bull.

She'd tried this deception already and their feelings for each other had known better, and had developed into love. He loved her. He damn well knew she loved him. But she didn't trust him. *She will never trust you.* The admission stung his soul and every part of him that he'd opened for her.

When Ryder stepped toward Violet, he did it so fast she didn't have the chance to retaliate. He wanted to kiss her. Only he wasn't playing this game with her every time she got scared. Whether it be Joel or herself. If she couldn't trust him, there was nothing left between them except lies.

He gripped one arm and pulled her body against him, so she couldn't look away. Forced to look into his eyes and remember what she was letting go for her pride...and her fear.

"You're throwing away the only person who will ever love you as completely and wholly as I do. I can't pull you out of the shadows if you don't want to leave. Cower here with your pride and your fear if that's what you choose. But *don't* tell me you are still in love with him and sure as hell don't tell me that what we have is nothing more than a bathroom bang."

Ryder watched her shadowed blue eyes register every last word and he thought...he hoped...maybe she would confide in him. Hoping this distrust would be the last, together they could conquer the world, or at the very least their hearts.

But then Violet iced her emotions. "If that's what you have to tell yourself to accept what I'm saying, so be it."

Ryder let Violet go. "You're responsible for destroying your own happily ever after."

Ryder walked away.

He couldn't decide who he was angrier with, Violet or Joel. Joel for bringing up the distrust or Violet for not taking the plunge and stepping forward into their future.

Ryder couldn't force Violet's hand, but he sure as hell was going to put Joel in his place. That selfish son of a bitch was keeping them apart. For what? What reason? Because Violet was once his wife? A wife he never loved and treated worse than an enemy. Bullshit. It wasn't acceptable. How dare Joel have his happily ever after and rip Violet's away from her at the same time.

Ryder found Joel back inside the pavilion with his soon-to-be wife fretting over the red marks on his face that matched the red sheer ladybug wings sweeping across her back. Joel deserved worse. Much, much worse.

When Joel caught sight of Ryder, he smiled like he'd won. *Won what? What are you after?* Ryder sure as hell wasn't going to ask.

As Ryder approached, she turned toward him and the black spots across her nose and under her deeply black lined eyes, crinkled at Ryder's expression. She was oblivious of the details conspiring between her fiancé, Ryder and Violet, but not of the face itself.

Control yourself. Get out of the public.

Ryder didn't want to cause distress to Missy, and more so, he didn't want to interrupt the guests at a party Violet's family was hosting.

He stopped beside Joel and grabbed his arm, pulling his ear close to his head. "This goes one of two ways. I announce your kiss to Violet right here, right now in front of Missy or you man up and walk away with me."

Damn coward.

Ryder honestly wasn't sure what he would do, but the pansy manned up, kissed Missy's cheek and excused them, leaving behind a baffled little ladybug.

They didn't walk the distance back to the resort. Ryder stopped outside the pavilion.

"Listen, Ryder, I'm sorry—"

Ryder's anger flared as he turned to face Joel and his first instinct was for his fist to make contact with his condescending smirk. "Cut the shit," he said instead. "We haven't really got the chance to talk about Violet privately."

"I don't really see that there's anything to talk about. Whatever Violet told you, is likely not true. She paints a picture of her life in the form of what she wants others to perceive. She is more like her father than she knows."

Ryder inhaled the beach air so deeply his lungs hurt.

Don't punch him. Don't punch. Punch him square in the bloody jaw. The little shit deserves it.

"You don't know a damn thing about her."

The leer across Joel's face fell. The frown added more age to his face. "And you do? What you've been sleeping with her a whole of a week? Two weeks? I was married to her for years."

It wasn't Joel's business how long they'd been together and Ryder wasn't satisfying that asshole by correcting him. Even if he wanted to tell Joel that Violet hides herself from the world because of Joel, at the same time, he didn't want to give him the satisfaction of knowing how his actions affected Violet.

"If that's your perspective of Violet, then you only know her skin deep. That woman is so much more than the mask she wears around people she doesn't trust."

Joel's jaw twitched at the insult. "Now, you're an expert on my marriage?"

Ryder shrugged. "If that's what you call a marriage."

Joel's hands fisted at his side.

Ryder narrowed his eyes at Joel.

Hit me. Hit me once.

Ryder would take him down before he lifted either of those fists, and Joel knew it.

Joel freed his fists and exhaled the breath he'd been holding. Then his condescending smirk returned and Ryder had the urge to remove it.

"Blame me if you want. Maybe she realized you're only skin deep." *Only because that's what you told her.*

"What did you say to her?"

"If you know her so well, go ask her yourself."

"I'm asking you."

"Because you don't like her answer. Because she put her mask on and shut you out. Welcome to the world of Violet Caliendo."

The way Joel said her name, mirroring the condescending way Ryder had said it to Violet's face, revealed the source. Joel had been feeding Ryder bullshit about Violet from the day he married her. *Why?* What had he gained by fueling hatred between them?

Ryder was finished playing games with Joel. So many games. He didn't care that guests lingered by the door in the distance. In three steps he had Joel pinned against the pavilion.

Joel's sly laugh droned in Ryder's ear.

"I *will* find out what you're hiding," Ryder said.

Joel laughed.

"If you hurt her, the next time we meet it won't be a friendly tap against a wall."

Joel glared at him. "This one's not on me. It's on you." he said. "Besides the three of us, Robert was the only other one who knew and he took it to his grave."

Knew what? Took what to his grave? What did Ryder, Joel and Violet have in common? Why would it be on Ryder?

"Took what to his grave?"

Joel shook his head. "Not my place to say."

Ryder grinded his teeth together. He got his answer. Joel had said something on Violet, but while he thought it was a threat, he couldn't be so sure. Joel was a constant liar, so maybe everything he was saying wasn't even true. How could this possibly circulate around Ryder? *What the hell was going on?*

Ryder needed to talk to Violet again.

"Like I said, if I find out you hurt her, I'm coming after you."

"Is that a threat?" Joel asked, sounding like a threat of his own. It fell short with Ryder. Beating the shit out of this slime and taking the consequences with the law wasn't an issue with Ryder.

Ryder moved his face so close to Joel the tips of their noses brushed. "Yes," he said through clenched teeth, then shoved Joel hard against the wall and walked away.

"Was it a cold chill between the legs?" Joel called after him.

Son of a bitch.

Ryder turned to find Joel brushing off his outfit and pulling at the front of his shirt. Ryder barely took the whole scene in. There were only four large steps between them and Ryder's fist landed where it had been begging all night.

"Explain that to your fiancé."

Ryder left.

Finding Violet would prove to be unsuccessful, however Ryder knew one person who would know what the hell Joel was talking about: Eliza.

Chapter Twenty-Seven

VIOLET DIDN'T GO back to the party. She didn't knock on the door to her mother's suite either. She breezed right inside finding Eliza and Carl curled up on the couch watching television, smiling at one another with a love that Violet had just walked away from.

The sight slammed sorrow into Violet's chest, so unbearable and making it hard to breathe. Violet wanted to curl up on the couch with Ryder. Violet wanted her happily ever after with only that man and she'd let herself think she could have it. Her heart was wounded by far worse in her life and it was her own damn fault.

Eliza and Carl both glanced up with smiles that quickly dropped.

Eliza rose to her feet. Carl was right beside her as they came to Violet. "What's wrong?" Eliza asked. "Where's Ryder?"

The tears spilled down Violet's cheeks and the sobs shook her body.

"Violet?" Eliza's arms wrapped around Violet, but today her motherly warmth eased no pain.

Violet hadn't expected her mother's touch to resolve the throbbing in her chest, but she needed to be held. She needed to cry. Her heart had never experienced the wrenching that squeezed it so tight she didn't know how she would ever move past today, past this feeling.

The pain of the deceit and lies that Joel and her father had saddled her with, along with Robert's easy discard of

Violet was nominal in comparison to losing Ryder. She pushed him away. And he walked away when he'd promised to stand by her side forever.

When she could no longer produce another tear, she asked, "Where's my file?" *Her file.* The file her dad would have on her and no doubt a file that Eliza had already located and taken out of the hidden room where all Robert's files were. Eliza wouldn't have left them there for her other siblings to find. But she hadn't admitted to having them either.

Eliza stiffened.

"I will go get it," Carl said.

Eliza let go of Violet and reached for Carl, scolding him for giving away the truth that one existed.

"Momma, give me my file," Violet repeated. She needed to know if Joel had been using her or had her father lied to her that night. That hurtful truth had sent her rebelling again and into the arms of Ryder, who ultimately was the man of her dreams. But that one night stood in the way of her happily ever after. *She* stood in the way of her happily ever after.

Carl talked to Eliza with love, but his tone was forceful. "Violet should have the file. It is *her* file. All of the children should be given their files."

"I am protecting them," Eliza said.

"You're not," Violet interrupted. "I gave my heart to Ryder. I love him and now I can't have him." Maybe if she'd had the file first and known about the video then she could have been prepared to fight Joel. Maybe there was something in her file that would help her to fight Joel. *What were his secrets? Where was his file? Why was her dad so manipulative?*

"Violet, what are you talking about?"

Her mom's innocence scraped her trust. Violet had never trusted her father, but she'd always trusted her mother who had, more often than not, been straightforward with her. Violet couldn't handle losing trust with her mother, not now, not when she had no one. "You know what I'm talking about. The video that Joel used to bribe Dad for a divorce. The same one he's now threatened to make viral if I continue seeing Ryder."

Eliza gasped and guilt washed over her face, the guilt of knowing about the video.

"Did you watch it?" Violet asked.

Out of the corner of her eye, she watched Carl move into the office and knew he was retrieving the file...and the video.

Violet stepped toward her mother and repeated, "Did you watch it?"

"I didn't have to. I know what happened, Violet. I found you that night."

"But it's there," she said. "Dad would have watched it. Why didn't Dad fight him? Why would Dad allow Joel to blackmail *him*? I don't understand." The tears she'd thought were gone began to gather again. "It's not like Dad to just bow down to someone else and Joel of all people... Dad must have had worse evidence on Joel. Joel was dishonest and he had enemies, so I don't know why Dad didn't take the tape away and use his own knowledge to set Joel straight."

Violet felt her uncle touch her arm from behind. He stepped beside her, holding the file.

"Violet, he did it for you." He passed it to her shaking hands.

"Did what?" She held the file against her chest, needing the support to calm her shakes.

"Gave Joel the divorce and the money. Sweetheart..." He touched her shoulder and the warmth was comforting, as much as she was breaking inside. "...Joel wasn't a bad person back then. I don't think he's a bad person now."

Carl hadn't been standing on the beach twenty minutes ago.

"He was just as cornered in this marriage as you were. When Joel married you, for whatever his reasons were, and I believe them to be solely that of Sophia, he lost his freedom too. He was bonded to you and your dad in a way that made it impossible for him to leave."

"But he had the tape from our wedding. From day one he could have used it to barter out of this marriage."

"No one bartered with Robert. You know that. When Robert approached Joel and offered him his freedom for the tape, it was because your dad was sick. He was trying to make amends. He was terrible at it and there is a hidden room full of people he didn't have the time or energy to reverse the pain he caused. But he tried with his family. He did it for you. Not for Joel."

"But Joel still has the tape. Joel is using it against me." Violet opened the file as she said, "There has to be something in this file against Joel. There has to be—"

Eliza touched her arm. "Violet, stop. Don't look in the file for answers. Look in your heart—"

Violet yanked away. "No, you stop. You are my mother. You were supposed to protect me. I would never let Joel force Sophia into a marriage she didn't want. I would never stand aside and allow what Daddy did to all of us. Never. You should have stood up for us. There shouldn't be a file about me. There shouldn't be a file about any of us." Violet waved the file at her mother. "This isn't normal. We aren't normal. You and Uncle Carl hiding a relationship behind Dad, is not normal."

Violet threw the file at her mother and the contents spewed across the floor.

"You two let us believe that Corbin was dead. You took our brother out of our lives because you were trying to protect him. Now he doesn't even want to come back. That is not normal."

Violet watched the pain wash across both her mother and uncle's face as she dragged Corbin into the conversation. He was the smart one to stay away from this family. This family was a mine-field waiting for someone to take the wrong step and it would explode.

"Leave Corbin out of this." Tears filled her mother's eyes and pain streaked her voice. Carl wrapped a comforting arm around her shoulder and Violet resented that they got their happily ever after.

"Why? Does it hurt to think about someone you can never have?"

"He will come around."

"Maybe, but Ryder won't. It's done...we're done..." Violet's eyes fell to her life spread out on pages across the carpet. "We're done," she whispered, dropping to her knees. Water blinded her vision as she began gathering up the papers. Eliza and Carl helped and when they were done, the file was in Violet's hands. *What good was it?*

Violet looked at her mother. "You're right. The file doesn't matter, because I am chaos. Even if I found something to use against Joel, it would be useless. I'm a walking catastrophe and the look Ryder gave to me this evening was my indication that he is finished trying to keep up with me. I continue to push him away. We take one step forward together and I take one hundred steps back, because I'm not strong. I'm weak."

Violet held the file out until Carl finally took it.

"I could have confided in him tonight and he would have been standing here with me, and looking through my file for leverage on Joel I know...I knew...was in there, but instead I pushed him away. You can only be pushed away so many times..."

Loud banging stopped the tears that had started again. How were there tears left? How long would these tears remain?

"Eliza?" It was Ryder.

As much as she wanted to answer that door and take her file from Carl to reside alone in her suite with Ryder, her love for him stopped her.

"Don't tell him I'm here. He's a good person and he's not like us. I don't want to drag him into our lives. We might be a close family, but we are broken beyond repair. Please?"

When Eliza finally nodded, Violet started toward the back door and then remembered Sophia and Parker. She wanted to check on them. She *needed* to check on them, so she disappeared down the hall.

***

RYDER POUNDED ON Eliza's door again and finally Carl opened it. The grey-haired man greeted him with a friendly smile within his five o'clock shadow.

Ryder wasn't in a friendly mood. "I want to talk to Eliza," he barked. His first instinct was to push past this man and find Eliza, but he waited a few seconds and Carl stepped aside.

Eliza was standing in the living room, of an identical laid out suite as Violet's, only this one had grey walls and black backsplash instead of Violet's beige and whites.

"Ryder, I wasn't expecting to see you." Eliza didn't ask where Violet was, so it was likely she'd already been to the suite. Her blinking, tear-glazed eyes gave her away.

"What does Joel have on Violet?" Ryder cut straight to the chase. This woman wasn't blind. She was Robert Caliendo's wife and she would know things. No doubt, the man who walked around Ryder, warily watching him, knew as well.

"Ryder, it's not my place."

"I'm not leaving until someone tells me." Eliza or Carl, he didn't care.

Eliza glanced down the hall with tightly pinched lips.

"I'm sorry, Son, we have no answers for you," Carl said.

Ryder crossed his arms across his chest. "Like hell you don't. I refuse to let anyone else hurt Violet. I refuse to stand here and allow the two of you to not stand up and defend her. Don't you both think Robert has put her through enough hell? And not to mention the result of her marriage to Joel. Do either of you have any idea how scared she is?" He turned to Eliza. "Don't you think it's time to make it your place and stand up with Violet? Instead of letting other people walk all over her?" Carl crossed his arms and stepped in front of Eliza, a protection stance for the woman he loved. Didn't he understand that was exactly what Ryder was doing for Violet?

"Watch yourself," Carl warned.

Ryder wasn't about to back down.

Eliza touched Carl's arm and moved up to his side. "Violet is stubborn. It's not me, nor Carl that you have to go to for the answers you seek. It's her." Stubborn wasn't even close to defining Violet.

"Do you think I didn't try? Joel is holding something over her head and if I just knew what it was, I could fix it." Or fix Joel, whichever needed to be fixed.

Eliza's eyes once again landed on the hallway. At first he thought it was the kids she was concerned about, but the look in her eyes told him differently. Violet was here. Which meant Ryder wasn't getting an answer out of either of them. Not now. He wasn't quitting either.

Ryder shrugged out of his jacket and held it toward the woman whose eyes gave her away. "Can you give this to Violet, please." If it was his sweater that had given her the first step to reach out to him, maybe the reminder of his jacket would bring her back to him.

Eliza looked down at it perplexed, but she took it. When her hand reached out, Ryder gently took her arm and brought her ear to his lips, for only her to hear. "I know she's here. I will find out what Joel has done to her and I will give her the happily ever after she thinks that she doesn't deserve. I'm not the bad guy. I love Violet." He let go and turned to leave, but Eliza gripped his arm and he stopped.

Eliza lowered her voice, so only Ryder would hear. "He holds a secret over Violet, but it's not about her. It's about you. He doesn't know about Donald. Check into Donald's finance records the year Joel married Violet and if you can find what he fears you will, then you will have exactly what you are looking for. Give me tonight to find the rest and I will contact you tomorrow."

That was all Ryder needed to know everything was going to be fine. *But tomorrow? Could he wait until tomorrow? What choice did he have?* "Thank you."

Eliza glanced at the jacket with wonder and said, "I will give her this."

"Thank you."

Eliza kissed his cheek. "Let my mistakes make you a hero in Violet's eyes. She needs a hero after all the villains in her life."

Ryder smiled at her. "She needs two."

Ryder left.

He wasn't sure how he was going to spend the night away from Violet, but he supposed that digging that far back into his dad's finances would keep him occupied.

What had Joel done?

As Ryder drove toward home, his chest tight, his stomach sick, he remembered Joel had started a business of some sort back then. It was right before he went bankrupt. Ryder had been dating Courtney at the time and not paid much attention to Joel's business. However, he remembered investing his money and getting a turnover.

Ryder rubbed his hands across his face. He wouldn't know until he got home. He hoped Eliza could come through with enough to put an end to Joel.

Chapter Twenty-Eight

THE NIGHT WAS an endless darkness of sobbing that didn't concluded until the sun rose the next morning and Violet was forced to get the kids ready for Joel's wedding.

She dragged her exhausted body away from the couch to face the day...she couldn't go anywhere near her bed, the sheets or the smell.

It was ironic that Ryder had briefly related her bed to belonging to Joel, but she hadn't ever felt that way about her bed. But now, after two weeks of Ryder being in her life, and in that bed, he'd stolen the comfort it had once given her and replaced it with piercing memories of his touch, his kiss, his low, sexy chuckle that made even her insides smile.

Eliza dropped the kids off early Saturday morning and they raced down the hall to shower.

Violet had prepared a kettle of tea after taking a long shower and soaking her face under a cold washcloth. She'd thought the puffiness under her eyes and the angry words passed between them the night before would pull her mother in for an entire day of reliving their regretful, pathetic, so-called lives. Of course, with the Eliza twist, always able to make a con look like a pro. However, after shutting the door her mother said, "I can't stay long. I have an appointment."

Violet didn't even ask for what. She didn't care.

"I'm sorry about last night," Violet said immediately. "I don't blame you."

"It's alright if you do. I blame myself every day."

"I'm sorry I said those things about Corbin. I know you were protecting him. Momma, we all know you were protecting him and us the best you knew how. I didn't mean those things. I just..."

"Love Ryder."

Violet nodded.

She'd turned and started toward the kitchen. Eliza followed her and slipped onto a stool beside her. "Sweetheart, you should go talk to Ryder."

"I don't want to hurt him anymore than I already have."

"You will hurt him more if you stay away. Violet you've dreamed about finding love your entire life. A love nothing like mine and your father's and I wished it upon you. For years, watching the loveless marriage between you and Joel tore my heart. Your responsibility toward your children was incredible. Your respect, your determination, is stronger than mine ever was. You are stronger than I ever was."

Her mother was misinterpreting the meaning of strength. "I cheated the first day of my marriage. That's anything but strong. It's weak."

"Joel wasn't a peach, Violet. I should have stopped the wedding."

"Momma, it's not your fault."

"It wasn't my resolution either. Anyway, I have to go. I have a meeting," she said like she'd forgotten. Eliza hugged and kissed her daughter, before slipping off the chair. Eliza cupped her face and pulled her forehead to her lips. "My child, you are stubborn," she said. As if Violet had a choice.

Eliza left and Emma entered. Her ready-to-tackle-the-day face fell when Violet looked up at her. "What happened?" Emma set her iPad on the counter. She touched Violet's cheeks and rubbed under her swollen eyes. "Does this have something to do with Joel returning to the pavilion with a couple of black eyes?"

A couple of black eyes? Ryder had found him again. Of course he did. This was the exact reason she had to keep her secret to herself. Her stomach fluttered thinking that Ryder protected her unconditionally, even when he didn't know what he was protecting her against.

"It's a long story," Violet said, not about to get into it with the kids down the hall, her heart dying more every moment, and the smell of Ryder still lingering on her skin from her sleepless night with his suit jacket. *His suit jacket.*

She glanced at the wrinkled material lying on the couch. *Why did he go and give her that reminder of him?*

"I assumed Joel got what he deserved and you and Ryder retired to your suite for the night. I'm sorry Violet, I didn't realize something had happened."

Violet touched her arm. "Life happened. It's fine." It was so far from fine.

"Do you want to talk about it?"

"Do you want to talk about Quinn?"

Emma retracted and sat on a stool, sending her sister an inquisitive blue-eyed look. "Fair enough. I'm not going to even ask how you know about him."

"Fair enough."

They sat in silence until Parker and Sophia were ready to head over to the salon. Violet tagged along, dropping the kids off at the salon with Emma, and then heading up to Joel's room.

With a heavy hand and unsure what Joel's reaction would be, she knocked on the door. There were a lot of mistakes in her life and cheating on Joel was one she needed to resolve before she could move on. *If* she could ever move on. Joel was right about Parker and Sophia looking at him like he'd destroyed their family and Violet hadn't corrected their opinion. She owed him a sincere apology for that night.

Joel opened the door and stared down at her with two black eyes. "You look like shit," he greeted.

She raised an eyebrow at him. "You don't look much better."

He shrugged.

"Can we talk, please. No fighting, I promise."

***

RYDER LOOKED UP as he heard the rumble of tires rolling over the driveway. He hoped it was Violet. He wanted her to trust him and find her way back to him so they could address the current situation together.

Instead, Eliza stepped out of the car with grace and sophistication, just like her daughter would.

Ryder didn't need Eliza to tell him what he'd already discovered: Joel had committed fraud.

His phone call to Eliza that morning had confirmed it. Joel had been pulling an investment scam involving Ryder and Donald. Eliza confirmed the money Joel received to help him pay off the millions he'd stolen was from Robert Caliendo.

Caught. Busted.

Ryder was prepared to race over to Violet's and give her the leverage they needed to put an end to Joel.

But Ryder had demanded an answer to the question he was still in the dark about: Joel's blackmailing information. Eliza insisted they meet in person. So here they were and Ryder had never felt so impatient in his entire life.

"Eliza," he greeted, taking her elbow in his hand and kissing her cheek.

"Ryder."

He didn't continue the formalities. Envisioning Violet's pain and sadness equaling his own was killing him. "What does Joel have over Violet?"

Eliza smiled and chuckled at him.

Ryder wasn't sure what was humorous. Her daughter was being blackmailed by Joel and every second that ticked by was another second of pain she had to endure.

"You are Donald Carlex's son, through and through. That man was no pushover, nor was he a fool. I suspected with the tip I gave you, that you would be able to find what we needed to confront Joel."

"Eliza, with all due respect, I don't want to waste any more valuable time. I want the information that puts Joel away for life."

Her smile fell. "Foolish boy."

Ryder squared his shoulders and crossed his hands over his chest. He was no fool.

Eliza shook her head and her kind and concerned smile returned. "Oh boy, put away the big guns, I'm not here for a show."

Ryder almost laughed at the woman. *Almost.*

"You cannot turn Joel into the authorities, Ryder. He's Parker and Sophia's father and although his choices were bad–"

Ryder cut her off. "Illegal," he corrected.

Eliza drew in a deep breath before continuing. "Yes, illegal but irregardless, this choice isn't yours to make."

"Then tell me what is going on between Violet and Joel, so I can go talk to Violet and we can figure this out together."

"Can we go inside?"

Inside? Inside! His patience was wearing thin, but he invited the calm and collected woman into the house.

They sat on the wicker sofas in the back sun room. A gorgeous glass edition Donald had built for Kathleen to frequent during the winter months and gaze at her gardens, even if they had been completely covered in snow. Ryder poured them some ice water, and downed his in one gulp to quench his dry throat. The suspense was going to be the end of him.

"I'm going to start from the beginning."

As Eliza began the story of Violet and Robert's relationship, Ryder wanted to tell her that Violet had already shared this difficult part in her life with him and that their time was running short sitting here doing it all over again. Within hours, Joel would be married and their window of opportunity to talk with him privately would be gone. But Ryder remained quiet, seeing Eliza's need to tell her side. She was a beautiful older lady, but her past brought out the fine lines across her face and bore sorrow into her usually brilliant eyes.

Hearing Violet's version of her life had been heart breaking, but listening to Eliza open up her perspective of her daughters hard trials, was worse. Ryder found himself lost in her words. Violet had kept so much of her life from him. Ryder found each new fact squeezing his heart more. Robert was a mean son of a bitch, more than people knew, unless you were one of the poor bastards on his bad side.

"Violet is my third oldest child and of all my children, she was the most independent. Since her first steps, she turned away help, determined to take them on her own. But she was there for all her siblings. Her heart is big and when she was young, it was free. She strived for perfection, but she laughed her way there. Her independence is partially responsible for her stubbornness. I had hoped that she wouldn't need proof from a file to stand up to Joel. I had hoped that she could find it in herself to trust you after so many have made it almost impossible for her to do so."

So had he.

"However, this morning I was greeted with a tear-stained daughter who didn't want to talk about it."

Tear-stained? Damn it. Why was he still here?

"That brings us to her wedding and the two of you in the silver ballroom."

Ryder had heard enough. "Violet told me about that night. I'm sorry I was drunk and strayed her away from her wedding. It wasn't my intention."

Eliza's patience evaporated and she rushed the next words out. "Violet wasn't honest with you about her wedding. I wish it was her that would have told you, but it's not. It's me. And to be perfectly honest, I don't want to, but here I am, sitting with you, about to shock the shit out of you and if you could just remain quiet until I'm finished that would be helpful."

Her frustrated tone and fierce words quieted Ryder and she continued.

"I found you and Violet that night, like naive teenagers. You completely drunk out of your wits and her looking at you like you just saved her."

If only she knew what they had done on that window bench only a week ago. "You were wrapped under a tablecloth which I assumed you pulled from a table."

Ryder was pretty sure red rose to his face, as he was envisioning Violet naked and wrapped in the tablecloth.

"You were both naked." Ryder's attention snapped back to the now.

Huh? Both of them naked? Ten years ago? Had he misheard her?

"What?"

"Joel has the two of you on video." *On video? What was this lady talking about?* "You and my daughter have a sex tape that Joel is holding over her head."

A sex tape? Of Violet and Ryder? A sex tape? A sex tape!

Eliza carried on. "Joel is blackmailing Violet. If she continues to see you, he will release the tape, which in turn will result in Parker and Sophia suffering."

A sex tape? If Eliza hadn't sat there confident with her words, Ryder would have been convinced he'd misheard the entire conversation. Only, Eliza's stare told him he'd heard it correctly

A sex tape. Ryder recalled the night he spent with Violet in the silver ballroom, only a week ago, and she'd told him she was trying to refresh his memory. *Violet had been trying to jog their sexual encounter in that silver ballroom ten years ago.* It hadn't worked and they'd ended up creating a new memory. *He didn't remember a single detail of the first time.*

Ryder flushed with embarrassment. First embarrassed that she knew of a past that Ryder didn't even know and second, that he'd taken advantage of her distressed daughter in one of her darkest times. "Eliza, I am so sorry."

Eliza touched his hand. "Don't apologize to me. That night, through Violet's fears and pain, you gave her a light of hope. She didn't see it, but I did. So I want to thank you. When her life was at her lowest point, and broken beyond what I thought could be repaired, when no one was there to stand up for her, not even me..." Guilt formed tears in Eliza's sapphire blue eyes. "...that night, you pushed her back onto her feet. She might have lost her trust in people, but she gained trust in herself and she fought Robert and Joel every inch of their choice to deceive her. And from the hasty, disarranged departure of the two of you, from the lobby bathroom before the Bensen meeting, I believe that was the moment you gave her another push in the right direction of trust."

The lobby washroom? "How do you know about that?"

"A mother's eyes are everywhere." Eliza winked at him. It was no doubt security tapes or maybe she'd even seen them leaving.

"That is kind of creepy, stalkerish behavior," he teased.

Eliza shrugged it off. "I'm a Caliendo. Would you expect any less?" He supposed not. "Do you see what you have to do?"

He had to blackmail Joel.

Ryder nodded.

"Go get that sex tape and leave Joel with the threat of jail time."

Chapter Twenty-Nine

JOEL LOOKED RELUCTANT to let Violet into his room, but finally, after much debate dancing in his tired eyes, he stepped aside.

Expecting to find the room filled with his rowdy groomsmen, she was surprised to find it empty.

"Ryder's not here, if that's who you're looking for. I think it's pretty safe to say we aren't friends anymore and he's not standing by my side today." She heard the gloom of a friend lost and the blame in his voice.

"I'm not here for Ryder." She turned to him. "How did you get that video?"

"I was there."

That's what she thought. Violet looked away from the hurt she saw in his eyes. "I'm sorry," she said. "That was the only time–"

Joel sat on the edge of the bed and cut her off. "I don't need your apology." He rubbed his hands across his face, wincing as they came in contact with his bruises. He looked exhausted.

"You deserve an apology. That was no way to start our life together."

He looked up then, with a strain across his face, pulling at his features. "You're only saying sorry because you want to make peace with me and be with Ryder."

Violet sat beside him. "I would be lying if I said I didn't want to be with Ryder. But, I am sorry if my infidelity hurt you."

"Of course it hurt me. You just said *I do* for the rest of our lives and hours later you were having sex with my friend."

"I didn't know that you knew about me and Ryder. The eve of our wedding, I went into my dad's office and begged him to call off the wedding. I'm sorry if that hurts too, but I didn't want to marry you. I didn't love you. When my dad told me about your ulterior motives–"

"My ulterior motives?" He sounded insulted.

"I'm trying to be honest with you Joel. The least you can do is live up to your part." Violet had to know if he had proposed to her for her money.

"Because you were pregnant with our child?"

She slanted a look at him, feeling as exhausted as he looked and having difficulty mustering up anger. "For my money, Joel. You proposed to me for my money."

"I proposed to you because you were pregnant with Sophia."

"You were bankrupt."

"You were pregnant," he insisted.

Violet sighed loudly and stood up. "Joel, just stop. We are grown adults now, not foolish and hot-headed. I slept with Ryder on our wedding night and you were only interested in me for my money. Just admit it."

Joel stood. "I am *not* admitting to something you and your dad made up. I dated you because you showed interest in me. I proposed to you because you were pregnant with my child. I married you because I thought we could be a family. I didn't divorce you the next day because I was cornered."

Carl had been right. Joel had been a good guy. All these years she'd wasted, hating him for false deceptions. If only they'd talked to each other instead of making their own assumptions and resenting each other.

323

Joel continued. "Your dad blackmailed me after he found out the money I was investing into my business wasn't turning a profit because there was no business."

Violet paused from her own regrets to listen. *No business?*

"After my parents died, I went through their money and yes, I went bankrupt. I didn't tell anyone, not even Ryder, not at first anyway. I was embarrassed and too proud. Then you showed an interest in me and you had connections to money. I may have used my relationship with you to find investors, but I wasn't using you. I liked you."

He had?

"The figures I promised left no room for debate and everyone wanted a piece of the money I promised. Only there was no turnover."

Why was he telling her this? He had committed fraud. *He had committed fraud!*

Her dad would have known and in turn this would have been in her file...or Joel's. Which meant her mother knew. Violet had leverage on Joel. Why had her mother told her to think with her heart, when the evidence had been right there? Because Violet had already shut Ryder out.

"Then you were pregnant and I suddenly had a family again. Me, you and Sophia."

A family?

Violet hadn't known he considered them a family. She hadn't even thought that he liked her. *Thanks Dad.*

"But I was also in trouble. I took a lot of money from a lot of people, including your dad. After you told him about the pregnancy, he used his 'Robert' skills and discovered that I was broke." Joel sighed. "He gave me the money to pay everyone back with interest. It saved my reputation, my life really. He could have called the authorities and I would have ended up in jail, but he didn't."

Violet was quiet. For the first time since she met Joel, they were actually talking and confiding in each other. His tale was sad, their past was sad with so many unnecessary heartbreaks along the way. At the same time, Joel was providing a solution to her current situation with Ryder. He was giving her the leverage to get Ryder back.

After Ryder showed up at her mom's house last night, it was obvious he still wanted her, but that didn't mean Violet was good for Ryder. Listening to Joel, she was discovering she was partially responsible for taking away his happily ever after.

What if she did the same thing with Ryder?

"That's right," Joel said, cutting into her thoughts. "Daddy will have my activities stored somewhere and now you have the upper hand." Violet stared at him in shock. He was letting her go. Joel was letting her have a relationship with Ryder. "I'm not as stupid as you think I am."

Joel sat back down stretching his elbows across his legs and dropping his head in his hands. "I'm so tired of fighting with you. I'm so tired of our kids looking at me like I am the bad guy." He looked at her. "Which I proved to be this week. You know what? I went into our marriage trying. But the first night, our wedding night, you screwed Ryder. And worse, I was there, I saw it."

"And you taped it..."

"I needed something to force your dad's hand. He had me by the balls. I was married to a woman who couldn't stand me. Who slept with my friend on our wedding night. What else was I going to do? If it makes you feel better, it didn't work with your dad either. After he paid off my debt, I was in his debt." The defeat in his voice corresponded with the defeat in her body.

Violet sat beside Joel again and felt connected with him in a way she never had. They were both two pawns in one of her dad's twisted and selfish games.

"It doesn't make me feel better. It makes me sad. I have been mad at you since the day I found out I was pregnant with Sophia. Because I knew my dad would try to force us into a marriage I thought neither of us wanted. I just had no idea the lengths my dad would go to. I shouldn't have believed him, but he was brilliant at making you believe what he wanted. I'm sorry that I ruined your life. That my unstable family ruined your life."

He nudged her side. "Your family didn't ruin my life. I ruined my life, the day I stole money from people. Your family has always been nice to me. Minus Robert, who was never nice to anyone." His sad chuckle was strained. "Even when I wasn't that nice to you, your family still accepted me, treated me with respect and like part of the family. I didn't deserve it."

"I cheated on you the first day of our marriage. Why would you be nice to me?"

"Because I knew you were forced into it too."

Violet laughed her own sadness. "We are a mess."

"I guess we are just like any other family."

Violet shook her head. "I don't think there is another family out there as disastrous as us." And today, in less than an hour, he was beginning his own family and they were sitting here rehashing depressingly down memory lane.

Violet stood up. "Anyway...I should go and let you marry the woman you love."

Joel rose with her. "I do love Missy."

That was good. He deserved to find his love.

"Then I am happy for you. Rumors obviously have made the rounds that you had an affair with Missy. That is why Sophia and Parker are angry with you. I guess we should address that too. After your honeymoon."

He nodded. "I will destroy the video this time. Ryder's not the womanizer I have made him out to be over the years. I only told you those lies to hurt you."

Violet nodded her understanding. If she could stand here and make peace with a man who she had resented, and had resented her for over ten years, couldn't she spend the rest of her, life with a man who loved her? Her heart lightened as Ryder settled himself back inside her heart. She needed to go find him and promise to never run away again, to never hide...or at the very least promise to *try* not to do those things.

"We may not have loved each other, but I cared about you and that night hurt," Joel said.

"I'm sorry."

"I'm sorry about last night, and your office. I doubt Ryder is every going to forgive me."

Ryder was a loyal man. Violet knew they would find peace between them. Maybe not right away, but once he knew about the pain they'd both caused to Joel, regret and guilt would alter his thinking.

"Ryder is your friend. Talk to him. He will understand."

"I wouldn't forgive me if I were him."

"He slept with your wife. So, maybe you two are even."

Joel cracked a smile that lit his darkened eyes. It was refreshing and she was glad he was able to do so. He had a special day today, his happily ever after, and Violet didn't want their past to ruin his day. "That's a warped sense of humor you have there."

She shrugged. "I've been hanging around Ryder too much."

***

RYDER DIDN'T HAVE to knock on the door and wait for Joel to answer it, or give him the opportunity to ignore it and cower away from him like the chicken shit he was. He swiped the key card Eliza had given him and waltzed straight into Joel's room catching him in an embrace with...

"Violet?"

What the hell?

Ryder yanked Joel off Violet, just as he had the night before, only this time he didn't let go. He slammed Joel against the wall and held him there with his arm against his throat.

Ryder turned to Violet waiting for her explanation and it had better be a damn good one.

Violet's beautiful, all natural face was swollen like she'd cried the night away and pink pinched her cheeks and the tip of her nose. Her damp hair fell loose down her shoulders and darkened the sleeves of her blue sundress.

It immediately made him think of her snow–ice–queen outfit and how damn sexy she'd looked in it. They were supposed to sleep the night away in each other's arms, not battle demons of their past. It also reminded him why they were here and that Joel was keeping them apart when he was the criminal.

"Ryder, let him go," Violet ordered, surprising him. Why was he surprised? He'd walked in to them in a more than friendly looking embrace.

Was she really still in love with Joel? Had he been the fool chasing after a woman who was chasing after someone else?

The thought felt like Ryder was the one slammed and pinned against the wall. "What are you doing here?" he demanded, giving Joel a little extra shove against his throat. He made a painful sound and Ryder almost grinned. He deserved it.

Violet folded her arms over her chest, not looking at all like the damsel in distress he had envisioned. Her hard solid stare granted independence.

"What are *you* doing here?" she retorted, like he was one of the bad guys. *The villain.*

"I'm here as your hero. Your Prince Charming. Your happily ever after. Lord, woman, what else do you think I'm doing here?"

"Strangling your best friend by the looks of things."

Ryder glared at Joel. "He is not my best friend."

"Not if you kill him."

"Don't temp me. Are you still in love with him?" Ryder had to know. What other reason would she have to be here? Hugging Joel? Crossing her arms and staring at Ryder like he was the villain?

Violet's eyes narrowed on him. "I'm ensuring that I don't destroy my happily ever after," she said.

"With him?" Ryder's voice hitched up a notch with shock.

Violet's face softened. "No. How can you ask me that after I've already given my heart to you?"

Relief stripped away Ryder's uncertainty, letting the element of her love overflow through his veins.

Violet loved him. Violet loved him!

"Please, let him go."

Joel. Violet's love still didn't change the fact that Ryder was putting an end to Joel harassing Violet. "Give me one good reason."

"You had sex with his wife. On his wedding night. Even if you don't remember, we hurt him, Ryder," she said. The pain in her voice soaked through his anger at Joel.

Ryder hadn't considered it from that point of view...from Joel's point of view. He'd been so consumed with Joel holding this threat over Violet that he hadn't had a moment to consider Joel's feelings about what Ryder had done...with his wife...on their wedding night.

Ryder turned to Joel, a friend, a man who he'd once laughed with, but in recent years had grown apart from. Now, he understood the reasons behind Joel's attitude toward him. *Ryder* had hurt Joel...but Joel had hurt Violet too.

Ryder felt the guilt of his betrayal to Joel. A betrayal he didn't remember, a betrayal that twisted his gut with remorse. But right now, Ryder's loyalty remained with Violet because he had given her his heart too and with that came the urge to protect her, forever.

Ryder lowered his voice. "You left a paper trail. I know all about your illegal activity. The money you took from your friends to invest in a bogus business and Robert stepping in to pay them back, with interest." The blues and purples around Joel's eyes darkened his stare. "I want the tape that belongs to me and Violet and your silence in exchange for my silence. And if you ever think of releasing it, I will have your ass in jail."

"Alright," Joel said.

That came too easy. "Alright?" he questioned skeptically.

"Alright," Joel promised.

"*And* you're not going to hurt Violet again. You're not going to threaten her, make ignorant jabs in her direction, or go behind my back, because from here on in, it's me and Violet as one, as a team. You're in her life, but I'm in her life too and I don't plan on going anywhere. If I ever get wind that you are harassing her, I phone the authorities."

Joel nodded.

Ryder released him and said, "I'm sorry I slept with your wife." Ryder didn't even bother to mention his memory was so hazy, he didn't remember it.

Joel rubbed his throat and nodded his understanding. "I'm sorry about yesterday." Joel glanced between the two. "I will leave you alone."

"It's alright." Ryder crossed the room and grabbed Violet's hand. It fit perfectly into his and he gave her a little squeeze, sending her a wink. "It's your wedding day and your room. We will go."

On their way out the door, Violet called back to Joel, "Go to the salon where the kids are getting their hair done and one of the girls should be able to cover up the darkness around your eyes."

Ryder loved that she was so thoughtful, even after everything she'd been through with that man. He had something special planned for them, but once they were in the hallway, Violet stopped.

"Ryder?"

He turned to her, their arms stretched between them with only their fingers connecting them, and his heart swelled. She painted a face of makeup and wore outfits that defined her outer beauty, but standing before him, with everything stripped away, she was more beautiful in his eyes than ever before, because he knew what was in her heart.

Ryder couldn't wait another moment. He kissed her and then pulled her into his arms and simply held her.

They might have come together under the strangest of circumstances, but he was thankful he'd shown up at Joel's silly wedding planning meeting.

Violet broke the embrace, but she didn't pull away. She leaned back on her flat shoes to look up at him. "I can't promise that I'm not going to get scared when things are hard and sometimes my first instinct is going to be to pull away from you and hide. I've been alone and done it for so many years that I don't even know how to let someone in when things go astray. I'm a hot mess of a thing. I thought I was strong and now I see I cut everyone out because I'm weak and it's easier."

"Violet, you're not weak—"

"My dad has a room of files..." Violet paused as a couple got off the elevator.

"Come on, let's go somewhere private," he said.

"I know just the place."

Chapter Thirty

STANDING IN THE silver ballroom, it didn't matter that this was where Joel and Missy would celebrate their wedding only a few hours from now, Violet and Ryder held hands and shared their own memories of this room. This was their special place and it always would be.

For the Bensen wedding, the room was decorated shabby chic with a touch of country class. Flower-filled chandeliers hung above the tables that held the same cream and purple arrangements spilling over in silver teapots. Lace cream tablecloths matched the chair covers with another splash of purple and teacup favors, wrapped in cellophane around fresh herbs. It was beautiful.

Violet led Ryder to the window seat. Before she had the opportunity to sit, he cupped her face and leaned down to kiss her again. The feel of his lips on hers was like a warm breeze touching her skin and settling her anxiety. How was he able to break through all her barriers and touch the parts of her that she hid? She stretched on her tip-toes in her sandals to get closer to him.

When he pulled away, he spoke first. "Violet Caliendo, I love you. I wanted to confront Joel with you, but you're head strong and independent and I love those two things about you."

"Didn't you call it hiding in the shadows?"

"It's not one or the other. Just because one thing scares you doesn't mean you're weak. There are so many things I love about you. After everything you've endured, I don't blame you for trying to protect yourself. But I promise you, that I will never hurt you. I will never lie to you or make you feel less important than you are. I will spend the rest of our lives together, proving to you that you are perfect even with your quirky flaws. Your mom thinks you need a hero and that I am your Prince Charming. Eliza provided me with the weapons I needed to ensure Joel could never hurt you again."

Her mother. The files.

"But I don't want to be your hero. I want to be your partner, your friend, your lover, and the person you trust enough to bring your problems to."

Violet wanted all those things with Ryder and they sounded magnificent, but she still knew that her life and her emotions were a cluttered disarray.

"Ryder, I'm a mess. My family is a mess. My dad has this room full of files of lives that he's destroyed. Files my mother plans on sorting and then trying to help the people he's hurt."

"That sounds like kindness and love."

Violet sobered. "Last night I knew that I would be able to find something to use as leverage against Joel and his threat and keep us together. I could have confided in you, but I chose not to. I chose to let you go. So here I am, giving you the option to go. I won't blame you. I don't know if I could handle me if I were you. Every time I get scared, I retract so I can figure it out alone."

"I don't want you to let me go."

"Do you really want to be a part of this craziness I call life?"

"Yes."

His quick answer made her smile.

"I never want to be away from you again. I like crazy and dysfunctional, if I get to do it all with you," he said.

He sounded crazy and Violet hated dysfunction, but she loved this man. "I didn't kiss Joel first."

"I know."

"On my wedding night...I kissed you first. I shouldn't have, but even that day with your drunken smile and *really* tacky jokes, I felt a connection with you. I think deep down that's why I approached you in the lobby washroom. If it had been anyone else I guarantee I wouldn't have advanced to them."

Ryder cupped her face with both hands. "I guess it's my turn." Ryder covered her mouth with his. He was delicious and warm. His tongue had a loving touch.

He pulled away. "I am ready to sail off into the sunset with you as we begin the rest of our happily ever after, together."

She moved her arms between them so she could touch the sides of his face. "I gave up on my happily ever after a long time ago. I never thought I would find a man who makes me feel the way you do and that I love as much as I love you. Ryder, yes I want to sail into the sunset with you and start the rest of our lives together. But, it's not only me. Be warned, my children are part of my package and they are not always sweet angels."

He laughed. "Yes. That boy of yours seems to have a lot of you in him. He's stubborn as all hell."

She lightly pinched his chest.

He kissed her again. "Your mother has agreed to keep the kids for a few nights so we can sail the waters. Just the two of us."

That sounded perfect, even if nothing was ever perfect, but with Ryder by her side she was ready to let imperfection challenge them.

"I have to stop by my suite and get some clothes."

"You are not going to need clothes," Ryder said, kissing her cheek, then her throat. Violet felt her body warming with each kiss, lick and nibble. Her head tilted as she enjoyed his touch and her eyes moved across the room, stopping at the head table.

Violet stiffened.

"What?" Ryder asked, pulling away. "What's wrong?"

Ryder's gaze followed Violet's to the four-foot tall ice sculpture sitting at the head table. It was an entangled naked couple making love to each other. *What was it doing here?*

Ryder burst out laughing. "Did you do this on purpose?"

Violet shot him a look. "Of course not. As I recall, it was your fingers that added them."

"I assumed you would have them removed."

"I thought I had."

Ryder let go of Violet and walked around the head table to take in the front view. Violet was afraid to follow.

Ryder's laughter erupted and echoed throughout the ballroom. "This is magnificent. Wow. The detail is incredible," he said, and she could see him moving in to examine the sculpture up close. "Violet, you should check this out."

Violet reluctantly followed and the front of the ice sculpture was extremely meticulous for a naked ice couple.

This was not good.

"This is not funny," she said, even if a smile was forming on her lips. She had to call maintenance and have it removed. ASAP.

"Yes, it is. This ballroom just keeps getting better and better."

"Come on." Violet pulled Ryder out of the silver ballroom and his laughter continued down the hall to her office. She'd left her cell phone in her suite and needed to privately explain the situation to maintenance. Marc met them in the hallway and she quickly gave him the run-down so he could deal with it. The ice sculpture had Marc grinning too.

"Hey, can I talk to you for a minute?" Marc said to Violet, his smile turning into a concerned frown. "It's about Anya."

Violet looked at Ryder with a look that said, *See this is the crazy dysfunction of my family.*

Ryder kissed her cheek. "I'm going to grab my car and meet you at your suite," he said, then whispered in her ear, "You're craziness won't scare me away, so don't even think about backing out."

Violet was never backing away from this man again. She smirked, watching him disappear down the hall. When she looked at Marc, he was grinning at her.

Her face sobered. "What about Anya?" she asked.

Marc got down to business. "Her key card has been activated at her suite in the early hours of the morning for the last few days."

"She's here?" Excitement gripped Violet.

She was okay. Anya was okay.

"She's sneaking in and leaving. Nobody's seen her."

"Why?"

He shrugged. "I don't know, but I asked Quinn Barker to look into it."

Violet frowned.

Quinn Barker had been their father's head of security and although she trusted him, she knew Anya and Quinn hadn't seen eye-to-eye before she left. It only made her wonder, besides security what exactly Quinn had been involved with, in regards to her father's extracurricular activity.

"Are you sure that's a good idea? What's he going to do? Stake out her suite? That sounds creepy."

"We have to make sure it's her."

"Have surveillance rewind the camera system and track her movement in the resort."

"Violet, she's not on any of the cameras. If it's her, she doesn't want to be seen. If it's not her, we need to find out who it is." He was right. "Quinn Barker is the best we have."

Marc always had their best interest at heart, so if he thought Quinn Barker was the man to go with, then Violet had faith he was making the right decision.

But as for right now, Violet had her bag to pack and the man of her dreams waiting for her at her suite.

***

"YOU STILL DON'T have the hang of this."

Violet turned from the snagged line she had...again. How was it that Ryder never snagged his line, yet every time he left her alone she got it stuck? The glare of the sun bounced off Ryder's sunglasses, forcing her to look down, which only heated her desire, as his bare chest tantalized her sights and heightened her senses. He was gorgeous.

"I thought fishing was supposed to be relaxing," she snarled, partially at him, but mostly at the pole in her hands. She yanked on the pole again and the damn thing would not budge.

"Why do you insist on touching the pole every time I leave you alone with it?"

Violet set the pole down where he'd instructed she leave it before he went to get them drinks. "Why do you keep leaving me alone?"

He passed her a bottle of water. "I don't want you dehydrated."

Violet opened the water and took a sip, smirking at him. "A nice cold shower is the perfect solution. I love it when I'm wrapped in your arms under the stream of water, drinking in the liquid from your hot kisses."

He smirked back. "I like this devious and naughty side of you."

She wrapped her arms around his neck and kissed his lips. "Let's go under deck and I will show you exactly how naughty I am."

He laughed a low, before kissing her again. "I have seen how naughty you can be."

Violet paused. "Did you watch the tape?"

He smirked. "Did you?"

"Some of it. My dad watched it."

Ryder frowned. "That's disturbing."

"Possibly my momma and my uncle."

"Are you trying to turn me off?" he growled as a shudder seized his body.

"You're like a light switch." Violet stepped out of his arms. "All I have to do it untie the strings of my bikini..."

She dramatically pulled the knot loose and let the strings hang over her shoulders, still covering her breasts, but teasing him none the less. Desire darkened his blue eyes as he watched.

"Or slip these off." She slid her hands down her side and under the bottoms of her bikini, slowly pushing them down her hips.

"Oh good Lord woman." Ryder reached out and pulled her toward him, filling in the rest of the space with his step. His mouth crashed against hers, hard and rough. He pried her mouth open instantly and slipped his tongue between her lush cushions. She savored in the taste of him, just as she had done for the last three days travelling the waters with him. He softened the kiss, took his time against her lips, then pulled away. "I think you need a cool down," he said.

"What did you have in mind?"

Ryder scooped her into his arms and carried her away from the bow of the boat, through the doors. Violet laughed and kissed his throat. When she thought he was taking her down below to spend the rest of the afternoon in bed, he passed the door and continued toward the back of the boat.

"Ryder?"

He didn't answer, but his smirk said he had something else planned.

He didn't stop at the ladder. *He was going to throw her overboard.* Just like the first day she spent on his boat. "Ryder, no!" she squealed, wiggling to free herself from his grasp.

He laughed and climbed the ladder, stopping at the edge of the swim platform. "You know, that first day when I threw you in the water changed my life," he said.

Violet stopped moving and smiled at him. Her fingers traced his rough jaw line, where he hadn't shaved in three days. She liked this scruffy side of him, the tickle of it on her face and skin.

"It changed my life too," she told him and gave him a quick kiss. "You changed my life."

"I learned you can swim," he said and his grin reappeared.

"Ryder Carlex..." she warned.

The gorgeous grin on his face melted her heart and as he said her full name there was no condescension, only love for her.

THE END

Coming Soon:

Sunset Rivalry

The Caliendo Resort

Book Two, Anya Caliendo

By The Lake Series

Shannyn Leah

SHANNYN LEAH

Collect them all!

By The Lake Series

The McAdams Sisters:

Lakeshore Secrets (Book One)

Lakeshore Legend (Book Two)

Lakeshore Love (Book Three)

Lakeshore Candy (Book Four)

Lakeshore Lyrics (Book Five)

The Caliendo Series:

Sunset Thunder (Book One)

Sunset Rivalry (Book Two)

Sunset Sail (Book Three)

Sunset Slopes (Book Four)

Sunset Shelter (Book Five)

SHANNYN LEAH

Shannyn Leah lives in London, Ontario, Canada. She comes from an entrepreneurial family, who all have a passion for developing new and exciting business ideas. When she's not writing contemporary romance books, into the early hours of the morning, she's antiquing with her two favorite people, her momma and her sister.

Shannyn has published five books in her series, By the Lake, including, Lakeshore Secrets, Lakeshore Legend, Lakeshore Love, Lakeshore Candy and

Lakeshore Lyrics. She is currently working on book one of the Caliendo Resort series, Sunset Thunder, and has a new series ready for 2016.

Join her mailing list to be notified when new books are released, exclusive excerpts and prizes: http://www.shannynleah.com/contact.php

Visit her webpage for extras: www.shannynleah.com

Please join Shannyn Leah on her facebook page if you enjoy her books here: https://www.facebook.com/pages/Shannyn-Leah/418700801622719

If you wish to get in contact with her, please email her at Shannynleah@gmail.com

SHANNYN LEAH

54458425R00190

Made in the USA
Charleston, SC
03 April 2016